## *What the critics are saying...*

ɷ

**Recommended Read!** "...Dramatic, seductive and emotionally gripping, makes A Taste of Control a must read!...Kudos to Ms. Michelle on what I believe is her best story yet!" ~ *Road to Romance*

**5 Hearts!** "...Patrice Michelle has woven an impressive and seductive world of vampires…This book is a complete page turner and impressively abundant with intrigue, sex and charm. I'm looking forward to many more stories from Patrice Michelle, as she is definitely a must-read in my book." ~ *The Romance Studio*

**5 Cups!** "...Ms. Michelle has, yet again, created a fantastic world of vampires and other powerful beings. She then has you watch as these characters come to life with lots of emotions, history, and depth. Adding stimulating dialogue, she then throws in a page-turning plot which you cannot walk away from. Ms. Michelle weaves all this together with breathtaking sexual tension and torrid hot sex scenes, making for one phenomenal read." ~ *Coffee Time Romance*

**5 Stars!** "...*A Taste for Control* is a unique addition to the ever popular Vampire genre! Rich in detail and emotional development there's a tremendous amount going on, from the erotic love story between Rose and Duncan to an ancient curse and mysteries that stem from their ancestors in Ireland…You will want to reread *A Taste for Control* and savor it more each time." ~ *Just Erotic Romance Reviews*

## A TASTE FOR REVENGE

**4 Stars!** "...Lovers of the vampire genre will relish Michelle's sensual tale. A soulful romance, an intricate plot and an intense sexual dance make for an adventure readers will definitely enjoy sinking their teeth into!" ~ *Romantic Times Bookclub Magazine*

**Gold Star!** "...Ms. Michelle has written a masterpiece of love and revenge that is incomparable! It isn't often that the plot, characterization and sexuality of a book come together so completely they result in a truly fantastic work of art. *A Taste_For Revenge* is one of those books…cover to cover. It deserves the Gold Star Award and Ms. Michelle deserves all the accolades I know she will get from this fabulous look into her world of vampires." ~*Just Erotic Romance Reviews*

**5 Ribbons!** "...A TASTE FOR REVENGE is a terrific vampire story filled with action, suspense, heartwarming romance and sensual love scenes. The dynamic characters will captivate you…Patrice Michelle has written an awesome book I would encourage all lovers of vampire romance to read. You will be held captive from beginning to end - there is no lull in this terrific page-turner..." ~ *Romance Junkies*

## A TASTE FOR PASSION

**4 Stars!** "...Michelle creates every woman's vampire fantasy with a hero who is dark, brooding and dangerous, not to mention an exceptional lover. Rana is the perfect foil with her bright outlook on life and sensitive nature. Rana and Lucian must make decisions that alter their lives, all in the name of love. ~ *Romantic Times BookClub Magazine*

**5 Ribbons!** "...Emotional, tender, sensual, sweet, funny, suspenseful, erotic, joyful - these are all words that describe this book. The love scenes are erotic but the emotions behind the actions are tender and very loving as I quickly discovered…" ~ *Romance Junkies*

# Patrice Michelle

# A TASTE for CONTROL

An Ellora's Cave Romantica Publication

www.ellorascave.com

A Taste for Control

ISBN # 1419953524

Edited by: Sue-Ellen Gower
Cover art by: Syneca

Electronic book Publication: July, 2005
Trade paperback Publication: December, 2005

## Warning:

The following material contains graphic sexual content meant for mature readers. *A Taste for Control* has been rated *E-rotic* by a minimum of three independent reviewers.

Ellora's Cave Publishing offers three levels of Romantica™ reading entertainment: S (S-ensuous), E (E-rotic), and X (X-treme).

S-e*nsuous* love scenes are explicit and leave nothing to the imagination.

E-*rotic* love scenes are explicit, leave nothing to the imagination, and are high in volume per the overall word count. In addition, some E-rated titles might contain fantasy material that some readers find objectionable, such as bondage, submission, same sex encounters, forced seductions, etc. E-rated titles are the most graphic titles we carry; it is common, for instance, for an author to use words such as "fucking", "cock", "pussy", etc., within their work of literature.

X-*treme* titles differ from E-rated titles only in plot premise and storyline execution. Unlike E-rated titles, stories designated with the letter X tend to contain controversial subject matter not for the faint of heart.

## *Also by* **Patrice Michelle:**

ꟈ

Kendrians: A Taste for Passion
Kendrians: A Taste for Revenge
Bad in Boots: Harm's Hunger
Bad in Boots: Colt's Choice
Cajun Nights anthology
Dragon's Heart
Ellora's Cavemen: Tales from the Temple II anthology
Hearts Are Wild anthology

# *A Taste for Control*

*Kendrians*

ﻉ

## *Acknowledgements*

*To my critique partners, Cheyenne McCray and Anya Bast, to my editor, Sue-Ellen Gower, and to a wonderful reader, Debbie Smart, thank you for your inputs on A Taste for Control.*

*To the IGTF, thanks so much for all your help.*

*And to Olchobhar Ó Greanáin, thank you for helping me make Rónán as authentically Irish as he could be!*


## *Trademarks Acknowledgement*

The author acknowledges the trademarked status and trademark owners of the following wordmarks mentioned in this work of fiction:

Plexiglas: Rohm and Haas Company

Guinness: Arthur Guinness Son & Company Limited

Vicks: Richardson-Merrell Inc.

NBC: National Broadcasting Company

# *Irish Translations*

*a Chailín* - Girl

*a Chara* - My Friend

*a Chroí* - My Heart

*a Ghrá* - My Love

*a Stór* - My Dear/Darling

*a Thaisce* - My Treasure

*Cosain mé i gcónaí* - Protect me forever

*Oíche Mhaith* - Good Night

*Saoi* - Wise man, sage

*Saoirse* - Freedom

*Shite* - Shit

*Sonuachar* - Soulmate

*Strainséir* - Stranger

*Tá grá agam duit* - I love you

*Tá tú go h-áileann* - You're beautiful

*Tóg go bog é* - Take it easy

# *Kendrian Vampire Terms*

*Vité* - Leader of all the vampires

*Pureblood* - Pure vampire, born a vampire

*Hybrid* - Part pureblood vampire

*Vampri* - Humans made into vampire. Their powers, though vampire-like, are less than the vampire who created them. They must drink blood to survive. Only Hybrids and Purebloods can make vampris. Vampris made by a pureblood vampire will not be able to walk in the sun. Vampris made by a hybrid vampire will have the same tolerance or aversion to the sun the hybrid does.

*Transer* - Human on the brink of becoming a vampri. He's so close to being a vampri, he will do anything for the vampire to take that third bite and make him a vampri.

*Anima* - The mate of a vampire. Once a person is mated to a vampire he/she will have equal physical powers/limitations to his/her vampire mate.

# Prologue



"Sheesh, the crazy things people do for money," Rose Sinclair mumbled as she stared up at the tasteful red and gold Lion's Lair sign.

The regal lion's head insignia reached out and beckoned, tempting her to walk inside the exclusive nightclub. Squaring her tense shoulders, she straightened her black leather miniskirt and smoothed her fitted sweater. Clubbing never had been her thing.

Downtown Chicago was eerily quiet at one o'clock in the morning. She found she missed the sounds of rush-hour traffic and people passing by. Unseasonably warm night air blew against her back as she wrapped her hand around the cool lion's head handle. The music thumped behind the wooden door, begging to be released. As she pulled the heavy door open, the suction caused her hair to blow around her shoulders, temporarily blocking her sight. And that's how she felt…as if she were walking in blind.

"Your invitation, miss?" A burly bouncer stood in her path. He scowled and held out his meaty hand.

*Well, damn, and here I thought turning thirty gave me perks.* So much for plan "A" of just waltzing right into one of Chicago's premier "invitation only" clubs. *Shit. Think of something. Seven grand is riding on this.* She opened the snap on the small purse dangling from her shoulder and riffled through it. "I know I have it here somewhere…"

Someone clasped her elbow in a firm grip and said in a deep voice, "She's with me, Charlie."

Rose jerked her gaze to the man standing next to her. Dressed in an expensive Italian suit, the stranger stood about seven inches taller than her own five-foot-six-inch frame. Skimming past his square jaw, she noted his completely shaved head only accentuated his overall stocky build. She met his serious hazel gaze and guessed him to be in his late forties. When Charlie stepped aside to allow them to pass, she smiled in gratitude at the stranger.

The man escorted Rose inside the posh nightclub, his taller frame shadowing her through the throng of people. The raised dance floor flashed in a kaleidoscope of colors to the thump of the music, while patrons gyrated to the upbeat song. Expensive perfumes and colognes added to the excited atmosphere. Rose was surprised that even at this late hour the club was packed as if the evening had just started. Her eyes adjusted to the dim, murky atmosphere as the stranger led her past the dance floor.

"Have a drink with me."

The deep register of his voice blended in with the music's beat, inviting and alluring, making her want to agree. She nodded and allowed him to direct her to a corner booth in the back of the club.

As they sat down in the plush red velvet cushions, her gaze scanned the patrons. From college-age to people in their forties, they all appeared to be having a blast and…perfectly normal. How did one go about discovering if vampires really existed? Carry a mirror around and maybe a wooden stake, too? The thought made her smile just as much as this wild-goose chase she was on. Vampires…what a crock. If it were Halloween she'd have a much easier time coming up with some kind of proof for her client.

"What amuses you?" her escort asked, an intrigued expression on his face.

Rose jerked her gaze to his. He'd been so quiet she'd almost forgotten about him as she scoped out the clientele.

She extended her hand across the table. "I'm Rose. Thank you for helping me get past Mr. I'm-two-seconds-from-bouncing-your-rear-outta-here."

The man chuckled as he clasped her hand. "James Connor." He surprised her when he rubbed his thumb along her palm and finished, "It was my pleasure."

A strange tingling jolt shot up her arm as his skin brushed hers. Unnerved by the sensation, she quickly pulled her hand away. When James' lips quirked upward in amusement, she resisted the urge to rub her palm on her skirt.

"Your order, sir?"

Rose glanced at the waiter who stood by their table awaiting a response.

"Whiskey straight up and a glass of Pinot Grigio for the lady," James ordered for them.

Both irritated and surprised he'd ordered correctly, Rose waited until the waiter had walked away. "Do I look like the Pinot Gris type?"

He gave her an indulgent smile. "It suited you. I'm very good at reading people."

"Ahh." She nodded her understanding. The ability to read others had always been one of her best talents, so much so her colleagues had teased her about her deadly accurate skill. That talent that had come in handy with every private investigation case she'd worked on. Yet, she couldn't tell what she thought of James. An aura of ambiguity hung around him, literally emanating from him. She neither felt nor sensed his "good guy" status as she'd been able to do with most people she met.

The waiter arrived with their drinks and then hurried off. She picked up her glass and appreciated the faint peach scent before she took a sip. The medium-bodied flavor danced on her tongue, making her smile in appreciation as she swallowed.

Rose looked up to see James staring at her. He'd leaned back in his seat, his expression interested as he held his glass and swirled the amber liquid around.

"What brings you to the Lion's Lair?" His darkened gaze swept her body, lingering at her breasts, before returning to her face.

He was apparently a regular at the club based on the bouncer's deference to him. Maybe he'd be the perfect person to ask about this whole vampire thing. And if he thought she was destined for the loony bin for asking, at least she wouldn't have to worry about ditching him later.

With a smile on her lips, she leaned back in her seat and raised her glass in a salute. "I'm hunting for vampires."

As she took another sip of her wine, she almost choked at the heated look that flashed across his face before he quickly masked it.

James threw back his drink and set the empty glass on the table. With an intense expression, he asked, "And what would you do with a vampire if you caught him?"

The fact he didn't laugh at her statement but instead seemed willing to indulge her surprised her. Why not throw fuel on the flame?

"I'd handcuff myself to him so he couldn't get away." She gave her saucy answer then leaned forward to continue in a conspiratorial tone, "You see, I'd need proof that he was indeed a vampire."

"Would you take him home with you so you could get all your answers?" He raised a dark eyebrow.

She laughed, shaking her head. "I'm a very persuasive woman. I wouldn't have to take him home to get the answers I seek."

A slow grin crossed his face before he spoke in a low, serious tone, "What if I were to tell you that there are at least twenty vampires in this room right now?"

"I'd say you're really working it hard," she said with a laugh while she mentally rolled her eyes. *He's got to be pulling my leg, because this is just too easy to be true.*

An annoyed look crossed his face. "I speak the truth, Rose."

His serious tone gave her pause. Her stomach tensed at the thought vampires might really exist…nah!

Deciding to humor him, she pulled out a pen and small notepad from her purse. "What are their names?"

James flipped his hand in a dismissive manner. "Some are vampri and the rest are young pups. What you need is a pureblood *master*."

At the emphasis he put on the word "master" Rose glanced up at him in surprise, her pen poised over the notepad.

"Pardon me?" Her feminist ire started to rise.

Running his finger around the rim of the glass, James lifted his gaze to hers. "There are five vampire clans that make up the race of vampires called the Kendrians—Kantrés, Rueans, Norridens, Arryns and the Sythens."

Rose wondered at the veracity of his statement for all of two seconds before she began scribbling the names of the clans. Something told her she'd hit pay dirt and there was no way she'd stop now. "Go on," she prodded, her heart racing once she'd written the names down.

"Some clan members have lived for centuries."

"Immortal?" She looked up, shocked at his calm delivery, while her own pulse rushed in anticipation. The man was dead serious.

He shook his head. "Not immortal, but beings who live for a very long time."

She felt as if she'd stepped into another dimension, but hey, may as well go with what she knew…er…or thought she knew—thank God for late-night TV shows. If he was offended by her questions, so be it. But by the details the man was giving her, he was telling her the truth…at least as he saw it. She'd heard of people who believed they were actually vampires, even going so far as living the lifestyle.

"Do they avoid sunlight and drink blood?" she continued.

James nodded. "Each clan has its own special attributes that make the members unique to that clan."

She glanced at her notes. "You mentioned vampri and purebloods. What's the difference?"

"Purebloods are born vampire. Vampri are 'made' vampires by those with pure blood running through their veins."

"Made?" she asked.

"'Made' means that the person was bitten by a vampire three times in as many days," he answered in a patient tone.

*Bitten? Ayeyeyeyye! I just* had *to ask, didn't I?*

Resisting the urge to shiver at the thought, she finished her wine off then jotted down more notes. Her client wanted as much proof as possible. She needed to delve a little deeper. Everything James had told her so far was just his take. Still she had no real proof.

"With the distinctions of purebloods, vampris, and even clan names, you speak as if these Kendrians are a whole community. Where do regular, everyday people fit in among these vampires in your world?"

"We are a whole community, and you fit in tastefully well, my dear," James said in a husky tone as he circled his finger slowly around the glass rim, causing the harmonics to resonate throughout the crystal.

Rose stared at the glass and realized he was making it do that while it was empty. Instead of the glass emanating at the same tone as it should if it held some liquid, the sound changed pitch up and down, almost as if in a chant of some kind. Then the meaning behind his words hit her… "We are a whole community, and *you* fit in tastefully well…"

She jerked her gaze to his, fear spiking. Rose's heart hammered against her chest and her stomach pitched. Great, instead of worrying about others thinking she was nuts to ask about vampires, she'd just picked the one wacko in the whole crowd. Did she have *I'm a freak-magnet* stamped on her forehead?

James' lustful gaze traveled her body before he met her surprised stare. He smiled, displaying two long fangs. The loud music and club-goers' voices faded into the background, leaving only the song's bass thumping in her head. Then his voice entered her mind, adding to the cadence. *You wanted proof. How better than to show you?*

Okaaaaaay, normally she wasn't one to shy from strange things that go bump in the night. She enjoyed a good horror flick just like the rest of the population, but this was just too freaking weird and, holy cow…real! *I'm out of here!*

When the roar of the crowd and music came slamming back, chill bumps spread on her arms at the same time a shiver overtook her. Rose stood and flipped her notebook closed. "Well, that went well. Er, better than expected, actually."

"Sit down, Rose." His voice was low, seductive, almost compelling. He smiled again and she saw his fangs retract back to their normal size. Sheesh, like a light switch!

She paused for a second, feeling the calming pull of his words, but shook off the sensation as she looked at her watch. "Sorry to chat and run, but I've got an early day tomorrow."

James' expression changed from compelling seduction to surprise before a calm look settled. She hesitated, curious. Why had he seemed surprised?

"You'll forget what we spoke of this night." His tone turned serious…almost commanding.

Again with the pulling and tugging sensation. What was that? she wondered. Inexplicable curiosity and fear fought for dominance within her before fear won out. She started to back away. "Uh, as much as I'd like to, it's unlikely I'll be able to forget tonight for a very long time."

"Rose, wait, there's more…" James called out at the same time he flagged the passing waiter.

He sure knew how to dangle a carrot. *Seven thousand dollars…seven thousand dollars,* echoed in her head. She hesitated while he ordered another round.

Once the waiter walked away, James met her gaze with a sincere expression. "Aren't you curious to know the rest?"

# Chapter One

ꙮ

*Duncan Mordoor, wake up, I've been pounding on your door for ten minutes!*

Duncan awoke to the sound of a woman's voice in his head. Her commanding tone pulled him out of the deep sleep he'd fallen into.

Lifting his head, he looked down at his wristwatch, his mind groggy as he frowned at the time. Four-thirty in the morning. *I've been asleep all of two hours, Sabryn,* he responded to her mentally as he got out of bed. *I'm coming.*

Pulling on a pair of black silk lounge pants, Duncan padded down the wide spiral staircase and across his gleaming oak wood floor to open the door.

Sabryn swept her gaze down his body. "You look sexy and well-tumbled. Did I interrupt something?" She raised a perfectly arched dark eyebrow, a curious expression on her face.

With a seductive grin, he reached out and pulled her inside, shutting the door behind her. As she leaned back against the wall, he put his hand on the wall above her and met her gaze. "Are you sure you don't want to be the one who's well-tumbled, love?"

Something akin to desire flashed through her beautiful lavender eyes before she shrouded it behind a wall of indifference. She let her gaze slide over his body while she ran a perfectly manicured nail down his naked chest to the waistband of his pants.

"You tempt me more than most." The promise of her sultry words, and her fingers tugging on the string at his waist, made his cock jump to attention. He started to step closer when she finished, "But that's not why I'm here."

Duncan mentally unbuttoned the top two buttons on her blouse in turn, revealing her generous cleavage. "Are you sure?" he suggested in a husky tone. He glanced at the window. "It'll be light soon and you'll need a place to stay." His voice dropped to a deep rumble as he drew his finger down her chest. "My bed is still warm."

Duncan knew that if he pushed Sabryn, he could have her in his bed in less than five minutes. It had always been this way between them, teasing sexual innuendo, not based so much on intense sexual attraction but more due to mutual appreciation and respect for one another.

Once, years ago, he'd had a glimpse into Sabryn's guarded mind and learned she held a good deal of hurt inside. He knew she'd be a great lay, but he respected her too much to just offer her sexual gratification. He had nothing else to give. The last thing he wanted to do was contribute to whatever emotional issues she carried around. But it never hurt to stroke her ego once in a while, and damn, if she didn't make an awesome sparring partner.

She leaned close to him, her alluring perfume teasing his senses as she whispered in his ear, "As much as I adore this gorgeous body of yours…" She paused and kissed him on his cheek before sidestepping him to walk into the living room. "I'm here on official business," she continued as she buttoned her blouse.

Duncan ran a hand through his hair and followed her into his living room. "What official business?"

She trailed her fingers along the back of his leather couch before she walked around it and settled on the arm, her expression once more composed and businesslike. "It seems you did such a great job helping Ian hunt down Drace, he's asking for your help once more."

Duncan's gut clenched at her news. Why didn't he know Ian needed him? At the same time guilt gnawed at him, his suspicions kicked in. "If Ian needed my help, I'd have sensed it, Sabryn." The truth was, ever since Ian had found his Anima, his vampire mate, in Jax Markson, Duncan had felt the distance grow between him and his twin, as if he were drifting away from his brother.

The realization caused him to take more and more to his music, performing at as many venues as he could book. On a few rare occasions he'd play until the wee hours, hence the two hours of sleep before Sabryn arrived.

"Ah, but your brother is more than a 'rogue' hunter nowadays. Leading the Ruean clan carries with it many responsibilities, including attending the Kendrian leaders' summit."

"What does that have to do with me?" He'd managed not to think about how he and Ian had drifted lately. Sabryn had brought it all slamming back, even if inadvertently.

She gave him a patient look. "It has everything to do with you, Duncan. You know your brother takes hunting rogue vampires very seriously. But with Rana so close to delivering their baby, Lucian needs Ian to be ready to jump in and act as Vìté, to lead the summit if necessary."

"I'm sure Ian appreciates Lucian's vote of confidence in him, but the idea of possibly having to stand in for the leader-of-all-the-vampires during the summit has got to be rubbing my twin the wrong way." Duncan smiled in amusement at the thought. "You know he's never been politically correct."

"Lucian trusts Ian above all others."

Duncan contemplated her comment. Even though Sabryn was a pureblood vampire and one of the highest-ranking members of the Kantré clan, she and her brother, Lucian, had always treated Duncan and his twin with respect. Never once had either of them made him feel his half-human, half-vampire hybrid status made him less than a Ruean pureblood vampire in their eyes.

"There's never a question of trust when it comes to Ian…just whether or not he'll piss someone off."

Sabryn shot him a serious look. "As good as your brother is, he can't be in two places at once."

"What does he need me to do?" he asked, sobering.

"James recently kidnapped a human woman."

"Are you referring to James the 'second-in-command' for the Sythen clan?"

When she nodded, Duncan frowned. "Why?"

Sabryn shrugged. "I'm not certain of the details, just that he kidnapped her and we believe he's holding her at his home."

"Why can't Eamon take care of this?" It irritated Duncan that the Sythen leader wasn't keeping a tighter rein on his own clan members. He didn't want to be drawn into this mess.

She raised her eyebrow at his snappy tone. "As leader of the Sythen clan, you know Eamon will be at the summit, too."

Duncan's suspicious nature roared within him at the knowledge everyone was conveniently unavailable. "Why didn't my brother call me himself to ask for my help?"

"Time is of the essence and Lucian is currently briefing him."

Duncan sighed and ran his hand through his hair once more. He didn't like to get involved. The last time he helped Ian out, Duncan ended up going against his own cardinal rule never to convert a human to a vampri. That day he was left little choice but to convert Ian's friend to a *hybrid* vampri. He should've let Mark die.

"You've grown your hair out," Sabryn commented, drawing him out of his musings. She tilted her head, eyeing him. "I like it a little on the long side, even with your 'bedhead'".

"Flattery, Sabryn?"

"Is it working?" She winked and gave him a hopeful look.

He flashed her a devilish smile. "Like a charm."

"We just want you to save the woman. Let Eamon deal with James."

"I can't take him out myself? Not asking for much, are you?"

She tossed her long black hair over her shoulder with a wicked grin. "I know you can handle it. It's less than an hour before sunrise. The advantage is yours."

He crossed his arms, narrowing his gaze. Something didn't add up—Eamon allowing a Ruean to hunt a Sythen? Ian unable to hunt nor having time to ask for his twin's help himself? The whole scenario reeked of subterfuge but try as he might to scan Sabryn's shielded mind, nothing but sheer honesty projected.

* * * * *

Once Sabryn left, Duncan quickly showered and pulled on a pair of faded jeans, a black T-shirt and his leather jacket. As he slipped on his black boots, he wondered why a human woman would cause James to risk being hunted as a rogue vampire.

Picking up his cell phone and keys, he headed out to the garage. After he'd opened his garage door, he started to get on his bike, but his keen senses picked up a familiar presence. He clenched his jaw, shut the garage door and flipped open a compartment on his motorcycle. After he climbed on his bike, he pushed the button on a second remote, opening another exit to his house.

Duncan left his house the back way and blocked the sound of his motorcycle approaching from Mark Devlin's mind. Parking behind the vamp's truck, Duncan moved so fast, he was standing beside the passenger door before the man could blink. Mark jumped when Duncan tapped on his truck's window.

"Damn, Duncan." Mark hit the button and rolled down the window. "How'd you do that?"

Even though it was still dark out, as a vampri Mark had the ability to see at night. Duncan might have blocked Mark's skills to hear and distracted him from seeing his approach, but Mark should've sensed him coming. Displeased with the surprised expression he saw in the vampri's eyes before the man veiled it, Duncan frowned at him, ignoring his question.

"What are you doing staking out my home?"

Mark raised a blond eyebrow. "I just got off duty. Thought I'd see if you wanted to finally own up to your responsibilities and teach me the 'vampire' tricks of the trade," he finished in an upbeat tone.

Duncan clenched his jaw. Mark was an open book to him, his mind too young in his vampri status to hide his thoughts. He read Mark's mind as easily as he could a human's. Disregarding Mark's attempt to make him feel guilty, he narrowed his gaze. "My brother called you."

Mark gripped his steering wheel and his jaw ticced as he stared straight ahead out the windshield. "I'm here to help, which is more than you've done these past seven months."

Guilt stabbed at Duncan. His chest tightened at the resentment in the man's tone. He pushed the sensation away as he had the past few times Mark had tried to contact him. He may have converted

Mark to vampri to save him from dying, but that was the extent of his involvement. "Don't skirt the issue. I don't want nor do I need a tail. Got it?" he replied in a hard voice.

Mark's eyes flashed, pride apparent. "On this, I *do* have more experience than you."

"Being a cop and a member of a vampire hunter organization can't replace the vast years of being a vampire or thinking like one."

"What the hell, Duncan! If it weren't for Ian training me in the powers I inherited when I became a vampire, I'd be a fucking target for every pureblood who believed I shouldn't exist."

"I knew Ian would take on your training."

"You 'made' me."

"And I can take you out." Duncan scowled and put on his helmet. "Don't make me regret honoring my brother's wishes."

Mark sighed and his tight grip on the steering wheel loosened. "I know you saved my life out of respect for Ian, but you've got to give a little."

"I have nothing to give." Duncan snapped his visor shut and walked away.

* * * * *

Duncan drove his motorcycle straight up to James' front door. He heard the wolves howling inside and didn't bother repressing his grin of satisfaction. Whenever either of the Mordoor brothers came around, vampires were wary, but especially right before they would have to go into hiding from the sun, since neither Ian nor Duncan had the same aversion to light.

He removed his helmet and put it on his bike, taking his time. Duncan wasn't known as the "vampire hunter" among the Kendrians. Ian held that claim to fame, even so far as being dubbed The Enforcer. James should have nothing to fear from him. He pushed the bell and listened to the chimes ring throughout the mansion that had to be at least eight thousand square feet.

The front light came on, bathing the darkened porch in a circle of bright light. He was surprised when James opened the door himself. "Gave the staff a night off?" Duncan asked with a raised eyebrow.

James ignored his question. "What do you want, Mordoor?"

As soon as the vamp pulled open the door, Duncan felt James' mind shut tight, as if a heavy shield locked down, shuttering his mind.

Duncan narrowed his gaze. "I think you know why I'm here, James."

The Sythen vampire visibly stiffened. "I have no idea what you're talking about. State your business and leave. I was about to go to bed."

Duncan grew tired of trying to probe the man's mind. "Where's the woman?"

"What woman?"

*Keep your cool,* Duncan told himself. He disliked playing games, had no time for them.

"The human woman you kidnapped." He found it strange that he couldn't hear a human's heartbeat. But then, he couldn't make out any other sounds either, not even the wolves panting. Nor could he detect their scent. Now *that* spiked his interest.

James' jaw ticced as if he tried hard to suppress his temper before he spoke in an even tone. "I didn't kidnap her. The woman I was with earlier is well and has gone home. Now if you don't mind," he replied then started to close the door.

Sensing the first streams of daylight streaking across the sky behind him, Duncan said, "Glad to hear it," as he pushed his way past James. He walked into the man's elaborately decorated foyer before turning to enter a room that appeared to be a study.

James shut the double doors to the study behind them and followed Duncan into the room. "I said I was going to bed."

Approaching the fireplace, Duncan noted the obvious irritation in the man's tone. When he started to reply, he heard the whirring of the thick shades as they began to cover every window in the house. With the room now doused in total darkness, the men stood facing one another, measuring the other man's worth as their eyes quickly adjusted to the total lack of light.

"Just thought I'd visit for a bit." Duncan leaned his arm on the fireplace mantel and adopted a casual stance.

"Since when do you visit?" James walked farther into the room, a doubtful frown creasing his brow.

"I've been told I should get out and mingle more." Duncan inwardly acknowledged the ironic truth to his words.

"And you chose *my* bedtime to do so?"

"Can you think of a better time?" Duncan knew, the "presumed kidnapping aside", his ability to read minds still threatened the Sythen.

James crossed his arms. "I'm not in the mood, Mordoor."

"You got something better to do?" Before James could reply, Duncan quickly switched gears to throw him off-guard. He adopted an intrigued expression. "Tell me what was it about this woman that so captivated you."

*Must have her*, he heard from James' adamant thoughts before the vamp quickly blocked them once more. He tensed at the possessiveness that emanated from James in relation to this woman. Rage welled inside Duncan, but he tamped it down to focus on riling James further, to glean what information he could.

"There's nothing to tell. I fed, then sent her home."

Duncan sniffed the air, then cocked his head to the side. "Funny. I don't smell any human blood." His voice turned deadly as he narrowed his eyes on James. "Actually, I don't smell or sense anything. Even your wolves, who were howling when I drove up, are silent. You'd think I'd at least hear them pacing somewhere in the house. Why do you suppose that is?"

James shrugged. "Guess you'd better work on honing your skills."

As soon as James finished speaking, a loud thumping sound, followed by a muffled scream, broke the tense, posturing silence that had stretched between the men.

James jerked his gaze upward toward the ceiling. With the vamp's concentration distracted, Duncan heard the very distinctive sound of a rapidly beating human heart. He didn't give James a chance to react as he leapt across the room, grabbed the Sythen by the collar and slammed the vamp against the closed double doors. "You lying bastard. Which room is she in?"

James must've let go of his powerful hold on the house, because Duncan heard every sound now—the wolves panting and wrestling, the woman's blood rushing in her veins. He even smelled her intoxicating scent. As he reached out mentally, he literally felt her fear. The sound of her thudding heart only infuriated him more.

James began to shake and his face changed, shrinking as he shifted to a snake. As the snake formed, Duncan's grip on James' shirt became fruitless. Before he could grab the boa constrictor, it immediately struck out at Duncan then quickly slithered up his arm and wrapped its large muscular snake's body around his neck and upper chest, squeezing hard.

Duncan growled in anger as he dropped James' shirt and pulled at the thick, coiled body wrapped around him. When James' snake fangs sank into his hand, Duncan ground his teeth at the sharp pain. Primal instincts kicked in and Duncan's fingernails extended to claws as he used them to rip at the reptile's coiled body.

James hissed at the damage the claws inflicted. He uncoiled and slid down Duncan's body, quickly shifting to an angry, roaring lion bent on attack as he hit the floor.

Turning to avoid being mauled in the chest, Duncan stumbled forward from the swipe of the huge paw down his back. He yelled in fury at the excruciating, stinging claws that sliced through his clothes as if they were tissue, gouging his skin.

The metallic scent of his own blood filled the room. Fuckin' hell, he had no idea the extent of the Sythens' shape-shifting powers.

A low satisfied laugh reached Duncan's mind as he whirled to face his opponent once more. James lay naked in his human form on the floor, a smug smile on his face. *You've no clue who you're dealing with.*

Fury boiled within Duncan at the man's powers. But more than anything, the vamp's sheer arrogance infuriated him. The Sythen hadn't even bothered to mentally project clothes on himself once he'd shifted back to human form.

Slowly rolling his shoulders to dispel the sharp pain in his back, Duncan met the man's gaze. "How soon you forget, James. I'll always have the advantage." When he finished speaking, he lifted his hands, spreading them toward the covered skylight windows on the slanted ceiling. With a mental push, he sent enough force to knock through the coverings and shatter two of the windows.

James hissed in outrage as the sun streamed into the room on either side of him, closing in on him, caging him where he lay.

Duncan pulled off his black leather coat, feeling nothing but contempt. "Your mist form is prone to scattering so I wouldn't attempt it. Since the sun moves as it rises, I suggest you shift to something small if you wish to live, something suitable…like a rat."

James narrowed his gaze on Duncan, hatred and distrust evident.

Putting his fingers through the rips the lion's claws left in the back of his jacket, Duncan said in a light, satisfied tone, "It seems my jacket will provide very little protection. Something even smaller may be advisable."

Pressing his lips together in anger, James shook his head and spoke mentally, *You'll kill me.*

Duncan cast a deliberate glance up at the lone unbroken covered window then met the man's suspicious gaze. "I could take you out now, but I prefer to let the council determine your punishment." Leaning close, he purposefully let the sun's warm rays touch his face. "And if they don't come to the conclusion I think they should, I'll hunt you down myself." Straightening, he barked in a cold tone, "Shift," at the same time he threw his coat over the man's body.

* * * * *

Duncan followed the sound of the frantic human heartbeat and the constant bumping noise, up the staircase and down a long hall, his shoulders tensing with each step he took. His heart jerked at the muffled scream that pierced the air as he neared the room that held James' captive. When he tried the door and found it locked, his temper snapped. He stepped back and jammed his boot heel next to the door handle, kicking the door in.

As the door splintered on its frame, slamming against the wall, his gaze landed on the woman sitting in the dark as she struggled to free herself from the headboard she'd been handcuffed to. The sight knocked the wind out of him. Holy shit, even from the back she was gorgeous. For one brief second he understood the possessiveness he'd heard in James' thoughts.

The woman sat there in the center of James' king-sized bed on her knees, naked and facing away from him, her long red hair trailing down her back. But it was the sight of the gag in her mouth and her frightened eyes when she jerked her gaze back to look at him that shook him out of his lustful thoughts of her shapely form. When she screamed and began to tug harder against her bonds, he remembered she was human and couldn't see in the dark.

Flipping on the light switch, he forced himself to keep his gaze on her face as he walked right up to the bed and pulled the gag off her mouth. "Are you here of your own free will?"

Her startled aqua gaze narrowed, then flashed in anger. "I've been drugged and kidnapped, only to wake up to find myself stripped, gagged, and handcuffed to a vampire's bed. And you're asking me if I'm here of my own free will?"

"You'd be surprised the sexual games people play," he commented in a dry tone.

She peered around him to the doorway and yanked at the handcuffs with all her might. Urgency replaced the sarcasm in her voice. "Hurry and release me before Count Dracula comes back."

"James has been taken care of," he said as he grasped her chin and tilted her head, looking at her neck. He inhaled to catch James' scent. "Did he take your blood?" he demanded in a harsh tone, harsher than he had intended. But for some reason he had to know.

# Chapter Two

ꞩ

Rose jerked her chin from the man's grasp, reacting to his commanding voice. She let her disgust come across in her tone as she pulled on the handcuffs once more. "God, I hope not. The last thing I remember, I was drinking a second glass of wine. Then I woke up here. I've been knocked out cold for..." she paused, glancing at the covered windows that gave her no indication of the time of day, before she finished, "who knows how long."

The tall, handsome stranger narrowed his lion-like golden eyes as if assessing her. Apprehension rippled through her. Her heart rate picked up when he put his jeans-clad knee on the bed next to her and clasped the back of her neck.

As he pulled her toward him and leaned close, her heart jerked at the thought he might be a vampire too. Did he plan to bite her? She tried to pull away, but his grip was like steel. His overnight beard brushed her cheek while he coaxed in a gentle tone, "*Tóg go bog é.*" He moved to the other side of her neck, treating her to the same strange inspection. What had he said? she wondered. Intuitively she knew he'd told her to be calm since his actions were slower, more attentive than brusque. His hand cupped the back of her head, then shifted to her hair, gently pulling until she turned her head in the other direction to expose her neck.

He smelled so good, like fresh outdoors, leather and all male. When his rough beard brushed her cheek again, she found herself wishing her hands weren't bound so she could touch his light brown hair and run her hands across his black T-shirt, to feel the strength of his broad shoulders and chest.

An unbidden shiver coursed through her when his warm breath caressed her skin. The fact she was totally naked and bound, making her the most vulnerable she could possibly be, only added to her confusion of the strange sensuality of the moment. Her heart rate increased tenfold at the realization that she felt no hesitation with this man, only…complete trust.

His hand tightened in her hair for a brief second before he released her and pulled back to stand beside the bed once more. "Good, he hasn't touched you. One less complication to worry about," he said in a matter-of-fact tone as he reached for the handcuffs that bound her to the wooden headboard.

When he pulled the metal handcuffs off her wrists as easily as if they were made of aluminum foil, Rose blinked at him in surprise. She stepped off the bed beside him and covered her breasts with her arms. "Are you a vampire, too?"

"My name is Duncan Mordoor." He tugged off his black T-shirt and handed it to her. "Here. Cover yourself until we can find your clothes."

Embarrassed heat rode up her cheeks and she grabbed the shirt, pulling it over her head while she mumbled, "Thank you for your help, Duncan."

Shrugging the shirt on in quick, jerky movements caused the material to rub against her wrists. Rose hissed at the pain, then blew cool air on her stinging, raw skin and berated herself for causing such harsh damage to her wrists while trying to get free.

Duncan moved in front of her and took her hand. Raising her wrist to his lips, his golden gaze met hers as the warmth from his mouth grazed her flesh. "I mean you no harm—" he began, then paused. A look of surprise crossed his face before his eyebrows drew together. "What is your name?"

"Rose," she said in a breathless whisper and nodded her assent for him to continue. As he swiped his tongue across her wrist in a gentle stroke, she thought she saw desire flicker in his eyes, darkening the hue to the color of whisky. She gasped at the sensations rolling through her as her gaze landed on the sprinkle of light brown hair across his muscular chest.

Her line of sight dropped to his well-formed abs and she whimpered at the tingling that spread throughout her body from just one swipe of his tongue. Her nipples had immediately hardened and her sex began to throb. Frightened by her instantaneous reaction to this stranger, she tried to pull her hand away, but Duncan laced his fingers with hers and tightened his hold.

"Trust me, Róisín," he said in a husky voice before he turned her wrist and applied the same soothing ministrations on the other side.

Ro-sheen? Why did that name sound familiar and comforting to her? He'd said it with a slight accent. And what he'd said to her earlier sounded foreign too. Was he Irish? "You're a vampire." She panted the statement as he moved to her other wrist.

*Yes, I'm a vampire,* he spoke in her mind.

When he began the process all over again, she lost the ability to string two words together, let alone coherent thoughts. Instead of Rose fearing what he was, this man made her feel cherished, desired and protected.

Why did what he was doing to her feel right and not the least bit bizarre? Instead, the sensation of his tongue running across her skin seemed to be a prelude to what he wanted to do to her in more intimate places. It felt sensual, seductive and incredibly erotic. Every nerve ending tensed in anticipation, waiting for the next brush of his tongue. When it came, a blush spread all over as her body ignited, burning from her head to her toes.

She closed her eyes, fighting the all-consuming sensations. *No. He won't make me feel.* Refusing to acknowledge the tide of emotions rolling through her, she tried to shake them off and swayed, causing her knees to buckle.

Duncan's arm came around her back and he pulled her against his warm, hard chest. An overwhelming sense of security washed over her at the feel of his arm supporting her, pinning her body against his. Her eyes flew open in time to see raw hunger reflected in his gaze before he shuttered it behind a look of indifference.

"Your wounds will heal soon," he said in an aloof voice. He set her away from him then moved across the room to open drawers and closet doors. "James is out of commission for now, but I don't care to linger." Opening a deep drawer in the nightstand next to the bed, he pulled out a stack of folded clothes and tossed them to her. "I presume these are yours."

She captured the clothes, but concern gripped her when he didn't pull anything else out of the drawer. "Is my purse in there? I don't want to leave it behind."

Duncan shook his head then walked back to the closet. He opened the doors, reached up to the shelf and slid his hand across the top. When he pulled down her purse, she breathed a sigh of relief. He frowned as he squeezed the soft, thin, leather material. She held her breath, waiting to see if he was going to ask her about the gun inside.

He didn't say a word about it, but instead of tossing the purse to her, he walked over and put it in her hand.

"Get dressed and we'll get out of here."

Once she'd put on the underwear, sweater, leather miniskirt and her shoes she'd found under the bed, Rose started to hand Duncan his shirt, but held fast to it when she noticed the rips and bloodstains on the back. Deep fear gripped her at the sight. "Ohmigod, what did this?" she asked, then demanded, "Let me see your back."

He tugged the shirt from her hands and shrugged it on. "I'm fine."

At his casual tone, as if his wounds weren't very serious, she glanced down at her wrists and realized her wounds had stopped stinging. Shaking her head in total wonder, she followed Duncan through the dark mansion, then outside. She stayed close to him until he stopped beside a motorcycle on the driveway. Inhaling deep, calming breaths, she welcomed the warm morning sun on her face. She'd never been so glad to see sunlight in her life.

Wait a minute. Duncan had just waltzed outside as if he didn't have a care in the world. "Hey, how can you walk in the sun? I thought vampires and sunlight didn't mix." She squinted against the bright sun and waited for his response.

He gave her a curt nod. "Vampires can go out at dusk or if it's very overcast or stormy out. I'm half-human so I can withstand the full sun." He glanced back to the house with a cocky smirk. "Unlike James."

"You're going to call the police, right?" she asked when he handed her an extra helmet. "I'm not leaving until I know James has been arrested."

"James will be dealt the harshest punishment by our council. If not, I'll take care of him myself."

The dark ruthlessness of his words made goose bumps form on her arms. She didn't doubt for a minute he meant what he said.

Before she could respond, Duncan continued, "After I make this phone call, I'll take you to your car or home, wherever you need me to take you. But before I leave you, we need to talk."

She stiffened then wrapped her arms around the helmet, holding it against her stomach. "Listen, I appreciate you saving me from the 'bad' vampire, but once you take me to my car, you can go your way and I'll go mine. I've got a client waiting on me. I don't have time to waste standing around talking."

His gaze narrowed on her. "We *will* talk, Rose."

"What do you want to talk about?" she challenged him. "You're not going to try and make me forget what I've seen and experienced the past few hours, are you?"

Duncan set his jaw. "You *will* forget everything that happened to you the past few hours. Once I drop you off, you'll also forget my existence as well."

Rose resisted the shiver than zipped down her spine at his commanding tone. At the same time, a strange pressure entered her head, as if a headache was about to start. She winced and held off the pressure in her mind, but she couldn't resist the jolting sensation any longer. She succumbed to the cold tremor that coursed through her but was surprised when it changed to sizzling warmth by the time it reached the ends of her fingertips. Whoa, that was intense.

"When you do that it feels very different than when James tried to make me forget." Her brow furrowed as she rationalized the reason why in her mind. "Maybe it's because you're from another clan. Which clan? The Kantrés, the Rueans, or the Arryns?"

Duncan's expression betrayed very little emotion at her question, but for some reason she knew she'd just thrown him. Big time. He clenched his jaw, turned on his heel and walked away as he pulled a cell phone out of his pocket. With his back to her, she noticed just how broad his shoulders were. She winced at the claw tears and dried blood spatters on the back of his shirt, but she couldn't keep her gaze from straying lower where she noted just how well his jeans fit his nice ass.

As much as she appreciated Duncan's help and his fab body, she didn't like anyone trying to erase her memory or compel her to do his bidding, vampire or not. No one was screwing up this chance to fulfill her dream.

Cell phone in hand, Duncan stood there, contemplating Rose. The fact he couldn't read this woman's mind unnerved him. He'd tried to discover her name and something about her earlier, but she'd totally blocked him. He could sense her, hear her heart beating and he could smell her.

Damn, he could he smell her. Something about her was so intoxicating he couldn't stop from inhaling when he was near her just to catch her spicy rose scent again and again. His discovery she couldn't be compelled *or* have her memory wiped floored him. *My God, no wonder James found her so intriguing.*

How much had the vamp told her about the Kendrians? The woman obviously wanted to keep the information she'd learned about them. To what purpose? Did her appointment have anything to do with the information she'd gathered? And why was she carrying a gun? Shit, he'd never had so many questions in his life and so few answers.

Shaking away the frustrating thoughts concerning Rose, Duncan glanced up when a gust of cool wind blew against him. Clouds had begun to form. He frowned as he dialed Sabryn's number and waited impatiently for her to answer.

"Hey, Duncan," she answered, obviously looking at her caller ID. "How'd it go?"

"James is secured for now. While I take care of the woman, I'll send Mark to keep an eye on James' house until I can come back and retrieve him."

"Mark's a Tracker, Duncan. Vampire hunters aren't my idea of help—"

"He's a vampire, too, and loyal to the Kendrians," he interrupted her in a harsh tone.

Sabryn sighed. "Just in case, I'll send men to help as soon as it's safely possible for them to go outside. Is the woman okay?"

He cast a glance at Rose as she hiked her short skirt to the top of her thighs so she could climb on the back of his bike. The additional show of gorgeous long legs as she settled on his leather seat made his cock jump to attention. His blood boiled at the thought James planned to "take" her without her permission.

"They'd better make James' punishment a harsh one, Sabryn, or I'm going to take care of him myself."

"He hurt her?" she asked, compassion lacing her words.

"The woman is fine."

"Ah, I see." She chuckled at his gruff response. "Bruised your ego, did he?"

"The vamp crossed the line." Annoyed, he punched the button to end the call. As he scanned for Mark's cell phone number in his caller ID history listing, he cast a glance over at Rose once more to see her running her fingers through her hair. Unable to look away, he watched transfixed, his groin throbbing as she shook out her hair, then put on the helmet. She was completely unaware how sexy she looked perched on his bike, her firm thighs hugging the leather seat.

He groaned inwardly at the things she made him think of doing to her, to find out just how far she'd let him go. Not once had he been able to read her, to hear her thoughts. And damn if he didn't want to know what she was thinking when he'd cleansed her wounds.

Earlier, when he'd brushed his tongue against her skin, the look of surprise on her face, followed by the rampant sound of her increasing heart rate, made him want to roar. When he first tasted her blood, it took all his willpower not to clamp down on her wrist and devour.

Her essence was so unique, like an ancient, seductive wine, yet pure and innocent. The intriguing mixture thoroughly intoxicated him. He had to force his lustful thoughts back to a clinical mind-set, focusing on her welfare to keep himself from pulling her hips against his. He'd wanted to find out just how well he'd fit inside her sweet body.

Looking at her now, the memory of her warm, rose-scented body pressed close fresh on his mind, Duncan gritted his teeth and once again had to force his mind back to his task at hand. Staring into the woods to the side of James' house, he hit the redial button for Mark's number. He'd done his duty, saved the damsel in distress. The sooner he got this all over with the better.

"I do believe hell just dropped a few hundred degrees," Mark answered, annoyance accompanying the sarcasm.

"Cut the wiseass comments. I need your help."

"My help? You don't sound like you're on death's door. Did James knock you in the head one too many times?"

"Devlin," Duncan warned.

"What do you need?" Mark's tone instantly changed.

"I've secured James in his home but I have to take care of the woman. I need you to stake out the house and make sure no one goes in or comes out."

"That's a little hard to do on all sides."

"Call your Tracker buddies to help you," Duncan suggested. "If the vamp so much as blinks, take him out."

"He's rogue?"

"In my book, he is."

"Council-sanctioned?" Mark asked for clarification.

Duncan didn't respond.

"Damn it, Duncan, you know if I call in a bunch of human Trackers, they'll want to do what they do naturally."

"If he makes even one move, take him out."

"Got it."

"I'll be back to help as soon as I take the woman—" Duncan cut himself off at the sound of his bike's engine roaring to life.

He turned in surprise to see Rose drive past him as she called out over the loud noise, "See ya, Duncan. I'll leave your bike at the Lion's Lair."

Mark's chuckle in his ear grated on his nerves. "Seems the lady's taking care of herself and you're free to give us a hand."

"She and I have some unfinished business first." Duncan punched the phone off and narrowed his gaze on Rose's retreating back.

He stood there for a few seconds, dumbfounded that she'd had the nerve, let alone the skill, to take off on his bike. He eyed James' bright red, top-of-the-line sports car sitting on the far side of the driveway. Without a second thought, he walked over and tried the driver's side door. Rolling his eyes that James didn't bother locking the vehicle, he slid into the soft leather seat and ran his hand across the ignition.

A spark was all it took and the car's engine purred to life. Before he could let Rose go, he had one more chore to accomplish. Erasing her memory was best for all involved. With his heightened mental capabilities, he should be able to figure a way past her unusually strong defenses.

Duncan waited until Mark showed before he put the pedal to the floor in James' car. He took the car's speed capabilities to the limit as he used back roads and shortcuts to get to the Lion's Lair. When he got to the parking lot and saw his motorcycle sitting alone, his irritation at the woman's gumption spiked.

A rumble of thunder caused him to look up at the steadily darkening sky. He'd noticed the heavy clouds rolling in on his way to the nightclub, but now his irritation turned into concern at the impending storm. He got out of the car, walked over to his bike and was in the process of putting on his helmet when his cell phone rang.

Once he flipped open his cell, Mark called out over the thunder rumbling in the background, "Duncan, this storm's timing sucks."

The fact the sky might be dark enough for James to escape Duncan's makeshift prison of sunlight caused fear for Rose's safety to ripple through him. But he couldn't pit Mark against James. The battle would be an unfair one.

"Tell me the Trackers are there."

"Yep, they just got here."

He could hear the excitement in Mark's voice. Knowing firsthand the extent of James' powers, he warned, "James is a formidable adversary, Mark. His shape-shifting is unlike anything I've ever seen. Do *not* underestimate him or it'll be the last breath you take."

Men's voices, accompanied by the distinct sound of clips being loaded into guns, filtered across the line. "I hear ya," Mark replied before he hung up.

As he closed the cell phone, Duncan couldn't shake the sense of foreboding that washed over him, making his entire body tense. Tracking Rose's scent wouldn't be hard, but tracking her in the rain added a layer of difficulty he didn't need, not with the sky getting darker by the second. Why the hell hadn't he asked her for her last name?

When the first few fat drops of rain began to fall, he opened a waterproof compartment on his bike and put his cell phone in it. Then he quickly put on his helmet and hopped on his bike, kicking the engine to life.

He rode in the rain for half an hour, following her lingering scent. But when the rain began to come down in sheets, the downpour washed away her presence. After fifteen more minutes her scent stopped dead at a T in the road.

He ignored his soaked clothes and the cool spring air on his skin while he sat at the crossroads, his bike's engine rumbling. Left or right? While he debated, the heavy rain slowed until only a fine mist coated his helmet's visor.

The sudden ringing of his cell phone jolted him out of his deliberation. Pulling off his helmet, he opened the compartment on his bike and grabbed the phone, flipping it open.

"Mordoor."

"He's gone," came Mark's terse reply.

"What happened?" Duncan's stomach tensed.

"Several Kantré vamps showed up. If they could be out in this storm, I figured so could James."

"Don't tell me you let the Trackers engage Sabryn's men."

"Hell no! I was able to convince them to hold back, that we were way outnumbered."

"You compelled them."

"Bingo!" Mark sounded pleased with himself. "First 'group' compelling I've ever done. Man, it sucks the energy right the hell out of ya."

Mark's cavalier attitude with his powers was going to get him killed. "If the Trackers find out you're a vamp, you're toast," Duncan reminded him.

"Yeah, living on the edge is just my style."

"Cut to the chase." Duncan didn't like the sense of responsibility he felt for Mark. Why hadn't Ian told the man that as a new vampri, trying to compel so many minds at once would drain his strength considerably?

"The vamps went in and one came out talking on his cell phone," Mark continued. "I heard the Kantré say, 'He's gone, Sabryn'."

Duncan's call-waiting beeped. He quickly glanced at the caller ID display. Returning the phone to his ear, he said, "It's Sabryn. Get out of there, Mark. Whether you know it or not, the Kantrés *know* you're there."

He punched the Talk button. "What the hell happened?"

"The storm happened," she replied, annoyed. "You told me you'd call Mark, not an entire contingent of Trackers, Duncan. My guys sensed them everywhere."

"I did what I could to keep James under guard," he replied in a cold tone, unapologetic for his actions.

Sabryn sighed. "Well, now we're both screwed. James is gone. Just in case, keep the woman safe until we can find him."

Duncan's chest tightened and his body tensed as he gripped the cell phone tighter. He knew exactly where James would go. The man had developed an obsession with Rose. That much he knew for certain.

"I've got to *find* her first," he said before he snapped the phone closed.

*****

Rose drove around on Duncan's bike for the first five minutes, looking for a main road. Once she found one, she made her way back to the Lion's Lair, got in her car and went home, relieved to be back to her normal life. She stood in her bedroom and pulled off her clothes while she thought about the last few hours. They'd provided more strange and unusual excitement in her life than she'd had in her first year as a private investigator.

First she thought she was on a fool's errand that led to a vampire who stripped her naked while she was passed out cold and who obviously planned to take her blood and more. The thought made her sick to her stomach. Then there was the sexy, brooding vampire who made her feel things she'd long ago thought she'd never feel again. And most of all, the eye-opening education…holy crap, vampires existed!

As much as her mind wanted to forget about vampires and linger on Duncan's human attributes, like his gorgeous body and seductive touch, she squared her shoulders and pushed thoughts of him to the back of her consciousness. Glancing at the darkening sky outside her bedroom window, she quickly hopped into a much-needed shower.

After Rose had showered and dried her hair, she pulled it up in a clip, then dressed in a pair of faded jeans and a white cotton button-down shirt. She walked back into her living room and appreciated the light airy feel she'd accomplished by decorating with a mixture of light blue, aqua, navy blue and white accents around her home. Even the gray skies didn't dampen the effect for her. Glancing out her bay window, she noted the strong wind whipping at the trees and heavy rain coming down.

She knew she should be tired with the small amount of sleep she'd had, but her body was going on adrenaline. Once she slipped into a tailored navy blazer to dress the jeans up just a bit, she called to move up her appointment to meet with her client, Mr. Reed, in a few hours.

Mr. Reed was willing to pay seven grand for evidence vampires existed. She had clan names, some Kendrian history and best of all, she had the location of at least one vampire's home. Proof!

Then she'd have enough money to have her procedure done. She prayed it only took one try for success, otherwise she'd be saving for a few more years for another. Her heart swelled when she thought of what it would be like to be pregnant, to hold a child of her own. She brushed away tears that formed in her eyes. Why did artificial insemination have to be so damned expensive?

Thoughts of what it would be like to be a parent caused her mind to wander to her father. She picked up the phone and dialed the number to the Our Home care facility.

"Helen Jenkins please," Rose said to the receptionist.

When the nurse who worked with her father picked up the phone, Rose said, "Hi, Helen, how's my dad?"

"He's having a low day today," the nurse replied. "He asked about your mom again."

Rose closed her eyes, her heart contracting. "Go ahead and have the billing department draft my account for two months in advance this time."

"I'll let Janice know," came the woman's chipper reply.

"And tell my dad I'll stop by today."

"I will, dear. He seems to have grown older this past week. I think your visit will perk him up."

"I hope so," Rose said with a half smile. "See you later." Her heart clenched at the idea her father seemed so down. She was glad she called and would be seeing him today.

When Rose hung up, she jerked her gaze to her front door, frowning at the sound of the doorknob being shaken. Surely the storm's wind hadn't caused that. She walked over to the door and peered through the peephole. Gasping in shock, she jumped back.

James Connor was standing outside her door.

*Oh. My. God.*

He'd found her. How the hell he had, she didn't know—she hadn't even given him her last name. But there he was. In daylight?

Her body tensed all over as she dug in her purse on the entryway table, retrieving her gun. When her driver's license fell out onto the floor, she realized with dread how James had found her. Holding her gun in one hand, she picked up her cordless phone with the other and backed into the living room, intending to dial 911. Maybe if she stayed quiet he'd think she wasn't home and leave.

"I hear your heart beating, Rose. I know you're in there," James' calm tone came through the door.

She called out, her voice quavering, "Get away from me. I'm calling the police."

*Do you really think the police can stop me*? he drawled, his confident voice entering her mind at the same time she saw the deadbolt on her door turn, unlatching itself. Blood drained from her face and her grip on the phone loosened. The dull thud of her phone hitting the carpet caused her to clamp her other hand tight on the gun to keep from dropping it, too.

Rose found herself rooted where she stood in the middle of her living room, transfixed by the extent of his powers. Fear slammed into her in waves as her front door slowly opened on its own. James' stocky build filled the doorway. Rain dripped off his bald head and beaded on his long black trench coat. Thunder boomed, shaking her house. She glanced out her bay window and realized why James could be out during the day—the dark clouds blocked out the sun, protecting him.

Rose's self-preservation kicked in and her heart raced in sheer terror. Raising her gun, she gripped the handle tight. Right when she pulled the trigger, her hand jerked to the left as if directed by someone else.

What the hell? The sight of James' cocky expression and the bullet hole in the doorjamb infuriated her. She moved to grip the gun with both hands in order to steady her shot. But before she could clasp the pistol with both hands, it was jerked from her grasp by an unknown force and flung across the room.

"Invite me in, Rose," he said, his tone seductive and alluring.

The pull of his words felt deep, almost physical. She knew he was trying to compel her to walk forward…to come to him. She even experienced a definite tugging as if he were trying to lift her. She focused on her anger instead of her fear. Relief washed over her when his strong, physical pull lessened considerably.

Why didn't he just walk inside? The morbid thought passed through her mind as she bemoaned the fact he'd so easily disarmed her and had her trapped in her own home. Somewhere in the deep recesses of her consciousness, she knew the answer to her question. He couldn't.

"You can't come in, can you?" Surprised by the calm tone in her voice, she tilted her head to the side and considered what that meant. "Do you really need my permission?" Thankful for all those old vampire movies she'd watched as a kid, she felt oddly empowered by the knowledge.

"Invite me in," he repeated, ignoring her question.

At the look of frustration on his face, she knew she'd guessed right and a little of her fear dissipated. She lifted her chin, rebellion kicking in. "Hell no!"

"I will have you. You are mine!" James slammed his hands against the doorjamb and the entire house shook.

She jumped at the evidence of his strength, her heart hammering even harder at the enraged look on his face. The force of his anger and lust washed over her in waves, sending shivers of revulsion down her entire frame. Taking several steps back, Rose turned to run to her bedroom, to get away from the evil power that emanated from him.

But her bedroom door closed on its own, shutting her out. She turned back to face him. Deep-seated fear squeezed her chest and knotted her stomach.

"Go away, James. You don't have my permission to come in, nor to have me." She tried to keep her voice stern and in control.

A lecherous smile tilted the corners of his lips. "I don't need your permission to have you." He proved the truth of his statement when invisible hands grabbed her waist and began to slide across her breasts and down her stomach.

Rose screamed at his invasion of her body, slapping at the nonexistent hands. "Get your perverted hands off me, you sick bastard!"

"Invite me in and I'll stop," he commanded.

"Go to hell," she panted, her anger overriding her fright as she realized he was getting off on her fear. No man, fiend or otherwise, would ever hold that kind of power over her. She stopped trying to fend him off and stood stock-still, taking his torture as she gritted her teeth and stared him down.

"You might try to psych me with your mental games, but you'll never touch me physically." She drew within herself and swallowed the bile that had risen to the back of her throat while she tried not to focus on his "mental" hands assaulting her body.

"I'll be everywhere you go, inside your head and out until you give in to me." His promise sent a chill of inevitability down her spine, causing nausea to flood her stomach in renewed waves of fear and repulsion.

"You can't have me," she vowed, fighting back the need to vomit.

His touch roughened at her comment and she felt a sharp pain around her nipple as if she'd been bitten. Gasping in outraged fury, she said between clenched teeth, "I'm much stronger than you give me credit for. Fuck off."

"Fuck is a great word, isn't it?" He crossed his arms and narrowed his eyes. "I *want* you to come, to see you fight me as you give in to the fact I will own you—heart, body and soul." As he finished speaking, a determined hand slid down her belly, past the waistline of her jeans and into her underwear.

*Oh, God, no!* Sweat coated her skin and her body began to shake all over as she lost control over her emotions. A loud, hysterical scream reverberated throughout the room. At the same time Rose realized the ear-piercing scream was hers, she saw James' body slam sideways against the doorjamb.

*Duncan!*

He grabbed the vamp by his coat lapels and threw the bastard over the porch. "Get the hell out of here, Rose!" Duncan growled before he vaulted over the railing to land on top of James.

# Chapter Three

ꟹ

Her heart racing, Rose grabbed her keys and dashed out the front door. She ran toward her car as the men rolled around on the grass. The sound of someone's roar of pain entered her consciousness, but she was afraid if she stopped to check on Duncan, James would capture her again.

The rain had slowed to a drizzle, coating her skin and clothes while she unlocked her car and jumped into the driver's seat. Once she slammed her door shut and hit the locks, her hands shook so badly she had to use one hand to hold the other still just to get the key in the ignition.

The force of someone slamming against her door, rocking the entire frame, caused her to scream out in fear. James' furious face loomed outside her car as he yanked the door handle. She bit back a scream when she saw his fist fly toward her window.

At the sound of shattering glass, she turned her head to avoid the flying shards. James' fingers encircled her throat in a vise grip as he bit out, "You're not going anywhere."

Gasping for air, terror rippling through her, Rose blindly groped for the gearshift. When her hand caught the handle, she shifted it to reverse and punched on the gas at the same time.

Excruciating pain sliced through her neck as the car's momentum ripped James' fingers from her throat. Rose sobbed at the fire burning her neck while she quickly put the car in "drive" and gunned the engine. As she sped away, she began to shiver all over with relief at her near escape.

A loud thud slamming on top of her car's roof caused her adrenaline and fear to spike once more. This time she dodged the hand that came through the broken window, blindly trying to grab her. Gripping her steering wheel, Rose jammed her foot on the brake. The car's wheels squealed in protest against the wet pavement at the same time James' body rolled down her windshield and bounced off her hood. His large frame bounced then skidded across the asphalt. The car's engine idled as she waited, watching his still, crumpled body on the road, hoping the impact he'd just taken was the end of her torment.

When James suddenly lifted his head and turned his bloodied face her way, his movement spurred her into action. She lifted her foot off the brake, intending to slam on the gas and run the bastard down when a blur rushed in front of her car. Duncan rammed into James with a roar of rage, knocking him to the side of the road.

Rose didn't wait around. She hit the gas pedal. Her wheels spun on the slick pavement until they finally caught. Burned rubber assailed her senses as she shot forward. While she sped away, she couldn't help glancing in the rearview mirror at the men battling.

"Thank you, Duncan," she said aloud, then whispered, "Please be safe."

With her heart pounding out of control, Rose drove straight to Our Home. She couldn't count on the fact Duncan would beat James. If Duncan didn't succeed, this might be the last time she could see her dad for a long while, or maybe even forever if James caught up with her again. She'd die before she let him touch her.

As she pulled into a parking space, she gave thanks it was a rainy day. Her dad spent a lot of time outside on the main grounds in his wheelchair. He didn't need to see the condition of her car as she drove up.

After she turned off the engine, Rose sat in her car for a long time, taking deep breaths to calm her rioting nerves. Her entire body trembled all over at the near-miss with James. Once her hands no longer shook, she glanced in her rearview mirror to make sure she had a composed expression on her face, then opened her car door.

Pieces of glass fell to the ground as she eased her way out of the car, trying to avoid getting cut. She brushed all the glass out of her seat onto the pavement using a cloth from her glove compartment. Shutting the car door, she made her way to the entrance.

"Hi, Helen. I was able to get here sooner than I expected," she called out in an upbeat tone as she approached the main desk.

"Ohmigod, child, what happened to your neck?" The older woman set down the medical chart she was working on.

"What?" Rose asked as she raised her hand to her neck. Searing pain accompanied her touch. She winced and quickly drew her fingers away to see them coated with blood. The sight made her feel sick to her stomach.

She looked up at Helen with imploring eyes. "I…uh…"

Helen glanced at the receptionist who was staring at Rose with a wide-eyed look and said, "I'll be back in a few minutes. If you need nurse coverage while I'm gone, call Sally." After the receptionist nodded her understanding, Helen moved from behind the desk and put her arm around Rose's shoulders. "Come with me. We'll get your wounds cleaned up and you can tell me what happened."

Feeling weak in the knees, Rose leaned into the woman's soft, cushioned body and inhaled her vanilla scent as Helen walked her down the hall. The nostalgic scent made her miss her mom all over again. She hadn't thought of her mom in a while, but this woman's kindness brought her memory slamming back.

"Thank you for always being so kind to me," she whispered as Helen led her to a small room and shut the door behind them.

Helen directed her to sit in a straight-back chair. The nurse pulled out a first aid kit from the cabinet and rolled a cushioned stool over to sit in front of her.

She opened the kit, withdrew antiseptic and cotton balls, then began to cleanse her wounds. "I've watched you grow up from a scared little girl who'd just lost her mommy to the lovely, strong woman you are today." Helen's brown eyes, full of concern, softened. "Even though I have children and grandchildren of my own, I've always felt like you were mine too in a way."

Rose's heart swelled at the woman's kindness. Her neck burned from Helen's ministrations, but she ignored the pain as she swallowed the lump that had formed in her throat.

Blinking back tears the woman's words caused, she grabbed Helen's wrists to still her movements and said in a quiet voice,

"Thank you for taking such good care of my dad and…for everything." She gave her a smile and released her hold.

Helen returned her smile and began to work on her neck once more. "I think he likes how I spoil him."

Rose looked away, a bit sad. "I think he doesn't want to be a burden to me." Meeting Helen's sympathetic gaze once more, she said with a small smile, "I've even tried to get him to agree to come home with me during his less lucid moments."

Helen threw the bloodied cotton balls in the trash then pursed her lips. "His lucid moments seem to happen less and less often, my dear." A thoughtful look crossed her face, replacing the concerned one. "I still can't get over the fact your dad came out of his year-long coma the same day your mother passed away."

Rose's stomach pitched at the sad memories Helen's innocent comment evoked.

"Thank goodness for Nigel," she said, meeting Helen's sympathetic gaze. "My uncle was my savior during the months after the accident that put my dad in a coma. My mother just wasn't the same. She sat around, staring out the window, listless. I'll never understand life's bitter ironies. I never told you about my mother, did I?"

Helen shook her head as she picked up a tube of antibiotic ointment to apply to her wound. She must've sensed Rose's sadness at the turn in the conversation. Clearing her throat, she dabbed on the ointment and adopted a stern tone. "I see you're stalling in telling me what happened to you."

Rose hesitated. She couldn't tell Helen the truth. If she did, instead of putting a bandage on her neck next, Helen would be measuring her for a little white coat. She decided to tell as close to the truth as she could.

"Let's just say a new boyfriend of mine is no longer a boyfriend of mine."

"Tell me his name," Helen said, anger flaring as she taped a square bandage on Rose's neck. "I'll report him to the police."

Rose clasped the woman's hands in hers and held on. "I'm a tough cookie, remember? As a PI, I know many cops. I doubt he'll be bothering me any longer," she finished with a steely confidence she didn't feel.

Helen stared into her eyes, seeking the truth. "Are you sure?"

Rose tugged on the pair of reading glasses hanging from a beaded chain around the older woman's neck. She gave her an impish smile. "Yes, I'm certain." She stood and squared her shoulders, "Thank you for cleaning me up. I'd like to spend some time with my dad now if he's up to it."

Helen rose from her stool. "He's in the rec room, sitting by the bay window." As Rose moved to leave, Helen said in a sad voice, "He seems to have grown much older in the past few weeks. Wait here. Let me get something for you."

Puzzled, Rose waited while Helen left the room. The older woman returned with a turquoise, white and navy patterned silk scarf. She wrapped it around Rose's neck and tied it in a fashionable bow. "It'd probably be a good idea if your dad doesn't see this."

Thankful for the woman's foresight, Rose leaned over and kissed her wrinkled cheek. "Thank you, Helen. I think of you like a second mom, too."

Spots of pink stained the other woman's cheeks as a pleased grin tilted her lips. Rose hugged her tight then left the room to make her way to the rec room to see her dad.

* * * * *

George Sinclair sat in his wheelchair facing the bay window. Around the room, other members of Our Home were watching TV, playing board and card games or reading. He paid them no heed as he stared out the window. Even from his profile Rose could tell Helen had been right. Her father had aged considerably since she'd last visited him. Instead of his seventy years, he looked more like ninety. Because of the bittersweet nature of her visits, she tried not to inflict herself upon him too much.

Her stomach tensed and she waited for the inevitable when she greeted her dad with a cheerful smile. "Hi, Dad. I've come to visit."

Upon hearing her voice, George turned his face away from the window. When he saw her, his eyes lit up and a look of happy surprise crossed his face. "Anna? Is it really you?"

Clasping his hand, she kneeled beside his chair and looked up at him, her heart breaking. "No, Dad. It's me, Rose."

Sadness gripped her at the look of disappointment on his face before he gave her an indulgent smile. He put his bony hand on her cheek, then ran it over her hair, his gaze following its path. "You look so much like her, little one. I miss her so."

Rose blinked back the tears that always came with the first few minutes of seeing her father. She knew he loved her, but he'd never been the same after the accident…after her mother passed. It wasn't that he didn't want to give. It was more because he couldn't. Each year his lucidity became even more of a rare occurrence. It was as if he preferred to live in a dream world than face his own solitary reality.

Impulsively, she reached up and hugged his neck hard, whispering, "I love you, Daddy." This might be the last time she saw her father. She wanted him to know how much he meant to her.

George hugged her back. A gentle tone entered his voice as he tugged on her arms, pushing her back so he could see her face. "Hey, what's wrong, sweetheart?"

Squatting once more, she said in a calm voice, "Nothing. I just haven't seen you in a while. I've missed you."

George touched her chin and tilted her head so she had to stare him in the eyes. His deep brown gaze searched hers. "You know I love you, don't you, Rose? I'm sorry if I haven't been there for you like Nigel has."

The look in his eyes was the most lucid she'd seen in a long time. Hope swelled. Maybe he would like to come home with her now? Then she remembered her recent troubles with James. Bringing her dad home wasn't an option at the moment.

"I've got some stuff going on right now, but when I get it straightened out, would you like to come home with me?" she asked hopefully.

George looked away and peered out the window. "There are too many memories there. It hurts too much to go back."

Is that why he'd never come home with her? she thought as a hard knot hit her stomach. *My God, all this time, I thought it was me. He's never told me this before.* She started to tell him she'd had to sell their family home and she lived in her own house, hoping to persuade him, but he spoke, meeting her gaze with a steady one of his own. "I don't have much time left."

"No!" she said in a fierce voice, her heart jerking in her chest as she clutched his hand and came up on her knees. "You're doing better. You sound so well—"

"What happened to you, Anna?" Her father interrupted her when he peered down at her neck. His gray brows furrowed as he pulled the scarf away from her throat to stare at the bandage. A worried look passed over his face and he pushed her shirt's collar back, looking for something. "Where's your pendant? You said you didn't need it anymore once we married, but..." He paused, glancing down at the blanket on his legs. "I guess I'm not much help nowadays."

Rose's heart broke at her father's regression back to his dream world...a world when Anna never died. What pendant was he speaking of?

"Dad?" she asked in a soft voice as she clasped his hand.

He looked down at her hand on his and met her gaze once more. "I'm sorry, Rose. I got carried away there, didn't I?"

At her nod, he gave a half smile. "I'm worried for you. What happened to your neck?"

"It's nothing." She tried to brush it aside, but her father had a knowing expression on his face.

"Run to my room and bring me the metal box that's in the far left corner of the bottom drawer in my dresser."

When she hesitated with a quizzical look, he prompted, his voice full of authority, "Hurry, Rose."

Encouraged by his focused mood, a mood seemingly on a mission, she left the rec room, took the stairs to his floor and entered his room. Looking in the exact spot he described, she pulled a long, slender metal box out of his dresser drawer.

Her heart racing from her exertions and at the excitement to see her father so focused, she reentered the rec room and handed him the box.

George set the silver box on his lap. He slowly traced his fingers over the swirled designs as if reliving a memory of ages past. With a sigh, he opened the box and pulled out a long silver chain with what appeared to be a silver locket dangling from it.

Holding the necklace up in the air, he undid the clasp. "Come here, Rose."

Why had she never seen this necklace before? she wondered as she knelt down and lowered her head so he could clasp the necklace around her neck.

Once her father hooked the chain on her, Rose sat back and lifted the locket from her chest to look at it. It was also made entirely of silver and had engraved black tick marks all along the outer edges of the locket. On the inside there was a Celtic trinity knot design that was raised in a three-dimensional fashion. Rubbing her thumb on the locket, she realized a design of some kind was also on the back. Turning it over, she saw the words *Cosain mé i gcónaí*. She met her father's gaze. "This was Mom's?"

He nodded, staring at the piece of jewelry in her hand. "What does it say?" she asked.

George shrugged. "I'm pretty sure it's in Irish considering your mother's heritage, but I don't know what it says. She took it off the day we married and put it away. There was a note in this box from your mother telling me to keep it for you, that it would keep you safe. I'd forgotten about it until today."

Happy to have a piece of her mother to keep with her at all times, Rose hugged her father once more.

He patted her shoulder. "I'm getting tired."

Rose sat back on her heels. "I'll head out then. Take care, Dad. I love you." She stood and kissed him on the cheek.

Her father squeezed her hand. "Take care of yourself, Rose. Keep your mother's pendant on. If she believed in it, then so do I. I don't want anything to happen to my little girl."

She nodded as she turned away. *I hope you're right, Dad. I've got a very bad, very powerful vampire after me. I need all the protection I can get.*

As she headed out into the lobby, Rose called to Helen sitting at the nurse's station, "I'm leaving, Helen." Before she turned to leave, she spoke to the receptionist at the main desk, "Oh, by the way, my window broke and some glass shattered in the parking lot. Think maintenance could clean it up?"

The receptionist nodded and picked up a black maintenance walkie-talkie. "Will do."

As she walked outside, Rose was thankful for the sun that had begun to peek out from behind the clouds. When she opened the door with the shattered window, she made sure no glass remained on the car seat and climbed in her car. She wished she had a way of knowing if Duncan succeeded in taking care of James. The possibility James might have defeated Duncan made her stomach knot, not only for her own safety but for Duncan's. The hybrid vamp had saved her. Twice.

Until she knew for certain that James had been defeated, she planned to make the most of the daylight she had before trying to find a place to hide when dusk approached.

Determined to take care of her responsibilities, she started her engine and drove straight to the bank. Rose wanted to make sure that if something did happen to her, that her uncle wouldn't have any trouble transferring what little money she had to his own account so he could pay for her father's expenses.

Once the paperwork had been taken care of at the bank, she glanced at her watch as she walked to her car. Mr. Reed had agreed to meet with her in an hour.

Opening her car door, she slid in the seat and started the engine. She planned to drive to the Hammond marina to visit her Uncle Nigel. She wanted to let him know about the new arrangements she'd made with the bank before she headed over to meet with her client. Plus, she'd get to catch up with her best friend Michelle, too.

When she neared the marina, Rose realized her gas tank was almost on empty, so she drove to the gas station across the street from her uncle's riverboat casino, the Five Star. She parked next to a gas pump and got out of her car, noting the casino's sign at the top of the boat. She knew the bold sign flashed twenty-four/seven, but set against the sunlit sky, all she saw was the cluster of five navy blue stars in the distance.

She smiled at the sounds of boat horns and river goers in Lake Michigan. When she slammed her car door, even more glass fell on the ground. Rose sighed, swiped the gas pass "card" hanging on her keychain and lifted the nozzle to put it in her gas tank.

"What the hell happened to your car, Rosie?"

She glanced around the gas pump at the sound of Sam's deep voice behind her, to see the big, burly man shrugging out of his leather jacket. He draped it across his motorcycle parked beside the convenience store.

Her stomach tensed as Sam strode over to her with a frown on his face. He'd always been her guardian angel, but today he looked more like a Hell's Angel with his bandana-wrapped head, goatee and row of gold earrings shining in his left ear.

Once she hooked the nozzle's latch so the gas would continue to fill her tank, Rose reached up and hugged Sam while she made up the first excuse that came to mind. "Kids and their baseballs. Hiya, Sam. It's great to see you."

Sam kissed her on the temple and wrapped his arm around her waist as he eyed her window with doubt. "Was someone trying to hit you, little Rose?"

At six-foot-six, Sam did make her feel like a shrimp. She always thought his nickname for her was appropriate. Sam's size and protective nature made her feel so safe, especially growing up in a casino environment. But Rose had a feeling Sam wouldn't be a match against James' vampire strength and supernatural powers—powers she was certain she'd only seen a glimpse of.

"Aw, Sam, you're always so worried," she said in a light tone. She squeezed his waist and inhaled his leather scent. He made her think of a protective big brother.

"I can't help it, munchkin," he said as he tweaked her nose and steered her to the back of her car. "I've known you since you were a knobby-kneed, freckle-nosed, skinny little hellion running around the casino with no supervision whatsoever."

"Watch it with the compliments, bud," she laughed up into his amused face, "or I'll tell everyone that not only did you teach me to ride a motorcycle, but you also taught me how to play chess and appreciate the soothing benefits of classical music."

"You wouldn't dare shatter my tarnished, bad boy image," he shot back with a sheepish grin. His expression sobered and he glanced at the riverboat docked at the marina. "You *are* planning on visiting us, right?"

"Of course I planned to stop by, silly," she said with a grin.

"Good." He stepped away from her to walk back beside her car to stare at her broken window once more. Glancing up at her, his eyebrows drew together. "I don't think you're telling me the truth about your car window."

Her stomach tensed at his comment as he walked back over to stand in front of her. His expression turned serious. "I saw what looks like drops of dried blood on your car door."

Why the hell couldn't the rain have continued for just a little while longer? Damn the man and his astute observation. But then, that's why he was Nigel's head of security. She couldn't let Sam know the truth. He'd insist she stay close so he could protect her. No way was she going to be responsible for drawing anyone else into this mess and take a chance on them getting hurt.

She quickly made up an excuse. "Oh, that was mine. I nicked my wrist trying to get the loose pieces of glass out so they didn't come flying in the car later while I was driving."

Sam put out his hand, his expression concerned. "Let me see your wound. You may need stitches depending on the depth of the cut."

Whew, at least she thought to say it was her wrist. She shrugged her jacket sleeve back and produced a wrist for his inspection.

Grasping her arm, he looked down then narrowed his gaze on her. "Either you're a fast healer or a terrible liar." Concern etched the hard lines on his face. "Tell me what happened. I can help you, sweetheart."

Surprised by his reaction, she glanced down at her wrist to see it was completely healed. Duncan really had healed her wounds. She shook her head in disbelief and raised her other arm to inspect the other wrist while Sam continued, "If this is related to your job…I really don't like you doing PI work alone. I've got a buddy who needs some additional work. I can give you his number."

"No." At the stubborn scowl that formed on his face, she continued in an adamant tone, "Sam, I'm fine. Really."

Sam clasped her shoulders. "Rose, I know you. You're holding out on me. Tell me what's wrong so I can help you."

She opened her mouth to speak when a man's voice interrupted her. "Rose will be fine. You can leave now."

Rose turned at the sound of Duncan's voice. Joy and relief made her heart rate roar in her ears at the sight of the vampire standing a few feet away. He had a gash across his cheek and a cut above his eyebrow, but other than that he looked so damn sexy she couldn't help but stare. His golden gaze drifted to Sam's hands on her shoulders, narrowing.

Sam suddenly released her at the same time he demanded, his blue eyes blazing, "Who the hell are you?"

"Didn't Rose tell you? I'm her bodyguard." Duncan crossed his arms in a nonchalant manner.

Rose felt Sam stiffen beside her. He reached over and pulled the scarf away from her neck, revealing the white bandage underneath. "Apparently you're not doing your job, champ."

"Sam!" Rose responded to Sam's sarcastic tone at the same time she saw Duncan stiffen.

He glanced at her bandage and spoke in her mind, fury in his gaze. *Did James do that?*

If Duncan was alive and well, that meant he had to have defeated James. *Woohoo, thank goodness!* Nodding to answer his question, she said in a curt tone, addressing both men. "I'm fine." Looking pointedly at the two guys staring daggers at each other, she fixed the scarf around her neck. "Despite what both of you may think I don't need a keeper. Period."

A quick glance at her watch told her she didn't have enough time to meet with her uncle before her appointment with her client. "Now, if you'll excuse me, I have an appointment to keep," she said as she walked over and removed the nozzle, then screwed her gas cap back on.

"Like hell," both men said in unison, then glared at each other as if infuriated that the other man dared to use "his" words.

"Listen—" Rose started to say as she approached the men once more.

"Leave us," Duncan commanded in an authoritative voice.

Rose was shocked to see a vacant look cross Sam's face before he turned and walked back toward his bike. She glanced around the gas station lot. No one else was about at the moment. The prospect of being alone with Duncan didn't sit well with her. She tried to call Sam back, but he started his bike and drove out of the parking lot without a backward glance.

Duncan moved to stand in front of her. "Let him go, Rose." He clasped her chin in his hand and turned her face to his. At his touch, her tense stance relaxed and a tingling sensation spread throughout her body, settling in her belly. She reluctantly met his intense golden gaze.

"You never told me your last name," Duncan said.

She eyed him, unsure why he was there. "It's Rose Sinclair."

"You must come with me," he said softly as he ran his thumb along her jawline.

Pulling away from his seductive touch, Rose straightened her spine. She needed to get a grip on herself and her rioting emotions before she addressed him. "I'm glad to see you're okay, but I'm not going anywhere with you. As I said, I have an appointment to keep."

"This isn't up for discussion," Duncan said. When he saw the obstinate look in her eyes, he clenched his jaw and let his hand fall to his side. The woman absolutely infuriated him with her stubbornness. It'd be so much easier if he could compel her to do his bidding. And who the hell was the bozo with the goatee and do-rag wrapped around his head?

"Duncan, you're not my bodyguard."

He'd "read" Sam's protective thoughts over her. When he saw the burly guy put his hands on Rose's shoulders as he approached, as if he were very familiar with her, rage welled up within Duncan. He resisted the urge to knock the man back against the convenience store window for daring to lay his hands on Rose.

Duncan was surprised at how intense his feelings for Rose had become in such a short time. *He* wanted to be the man to touch her, to protect her…to find out how many ways he could make her moan or sigh.

"I don't think you're listening to me," Rose continued while she waved her hand in front of his face. "I have an appointment with a client in a half-hour—"

"James will begin to hunt for you again in a couple hours."

A horrified look crossed her face. "What? You didn't defeat him?"

Duncan shook his head and pressed his lips together in anger. "No. The bastard ran as soon as you were out of sight." *Right before the sun's rays would have fried his sorry ass, too.*

She began to pace behind her car. A frustrated look settled on her face as she bit her thumbnail. Duncan could see the wheels turning in her head. Finally she stopped and faced him. "Okay, you can follow me to my appointment, but you must stay back and out of sight."

He shook his head. "No deal. James will find you again. Your scent is especially easy to track at the moment."

"It is?" A curious expression filtered across her face.

"You're in a breeding state. You may as well lay a breadcrumb path out behind you," Duncan said in a droll tone.

She stepped toward him, her blue-green gaze intrigued. "Are you saying you can tell when I'm ovulating?"

When he gave her a "what the hell did you think I just said" look, she curled her fingers around his forearm and smiled. "Hmmm, maybe I'll just carry you around for a month or two. You're better than my basal thermometer."

Duncan tensed and folded his arms across his chest as extreme jealousy gripped him. Why hadn't he sensed a man in Rose's life? He'd smelled no man's scent on her earlier.

"Hey, it was just a joke. Well, kinda," she amended with a smirk.

The idea she was married and trying to conceive made his chest constrict. He scowled at her. "You're married? I sensed no other in your life," he commented without thinking. The appalled look on her face answered his question faster than he could've ever read her mind—fuckin' hell…why couldn't he read her?

"No, I'm not married, but I do want to have a child."

"Alone?" He looked at her as if she were nuts.

She took a step back, visibly withdrawing. "It's none of your concern. I don't even know why I told you." A look of self-disgust filtered across her face before she adopted a businesslike expression once more. "Like I said, you can shadow me to my appointment."

*There has to be some way to compel her, some way to break through her strong will.* Duncan contemplated his options as he shook his head and stepped forward. Then it hit him. The one time he'd felt a slight drop in her defenses was when he'd cleaned the wounds on her wrists.

"Before we go, let me see your neck," he said in a gruff tone as he stepped close and tilted her chin.

He felt her stiffen while he pulled the scarf away. "I want to make sure you're all right, Róisín."

Rose relaxed a bit at his comment. She began to peel back the tape for him. "Okay, but *no* licking—"

Duncan took her completely off-guard, covering her lips with his.

# Chapter Four

ꩭ

*Duncan's lips moved over hers, dominant yet coaxing. He pulled her close to his heat. His thumb traced the soft skin under her jaw while his other hand clasped her rear tightly, fitting her curves against his erection.*

*Rose's heart hammered in time to the heightened adrenaline pumping throughout her body. She reveled in Duncan's hard chest pressed against hers, his masculine smell and the feel of his stubble scraping her sensitive skin. Clutching his shoulders tight, she enjoyed the play of muscles she felt through his cotton T-shirt, while she returned his kiss, parrying every sensual thrust of his tongue against hers.*

*He slid both hands to her jeans-covered rear, pulling her even closer as he rocked into her. His lips moved to her jaw, then hovered over her wounds, his breath hot against her neck.*

*Rose's entire body tensed in sexual awareness and nerve-clenching anticipation, waiting for him to make the first move, praying he would.*

When I cleanse your wounds, I won't stop, Róisín, *he spoke in her mind, his tone husky, barely controlled.*

*She literally felt the lust that clawed at him, breaking down his good intentions, changing them to pure, unadulterated desire to plunge his fangs into her skin and taste her…take her blood. Her breathing changed to rapid pants when he moved his hips once more, his erection hitting her lower belly. Her hands moved to his hair, threading through the thick silk as she arched her neck, offering herself to him.*

I want to know, *she whispered back mentally.*

*Duncan growled low in his throat. His hand shot through her hair to cup the back of her head in a firm grip, his gaze glittering in satisfaction as he searched her face. When she felt a presence moving inside her head, trying to probe her mind, she instantly stiffened and mentally pulled away.*

*"Stay with me!" he commanded, his tone almost desperate. His hand flexed, tightening in the thick strands. "I need to know…"*

Rose awoke with a jerk, the remnants of her vivid dream shaking her to the core. Her heart still beat at a wild pace and her sex ached in unfulfilled desire. Being kissed and then losing total consciousness left her feeling very much out of control. Intuitively, she knew Duncan wouldn't hurt her, but to wake up in a strange place wigged her out. Rose dug her elbow into the bed underneath her as she sat up and peered into the darkness, trying to see her surroundings.

Rain pounded hard, pelting the ceiling above her head, causing her to jerk her gaze to the angled window and the dark night outside.

When the light came on from the nightstand next to her, she gasped and blinked to let her eyes adjust to the change in light.

*How'd the light come on?* she wondered at the same time she noted her hairclip lay on the nightstand next to the lamp and her jacket was on the end of the bed. She let out a sigh of relief when she looked down and saw she was still fully clothed. She was in a queen-sized bed with a hunter-green comforter partially covering her body. Apprehension gripped her. She scanned the room, taking in the contemporary desk off to her right against the wall and a chest of drawers.

Glancing at the slanted ceiling not more than five feet above her head, she noted the window was a skylight flanked by exposed wooden beams. Her worry quickly turned to anger when she realized nighttime meant she'd missed her appointment with her client.

"I see you're awake." Duncan's low voice came from across the room. His tone sounded almost regretful.

She turned her head in his direction and narrowed her gaze at his casual delivery, as if she'd been an invited guest and not freakin' kidnapped! Again.

She started to speak, ready to blast him for screwing up her meeting. But the look in his eyes froze the words on her lips. Duncan sat in a cushioned brocade chair, his elbow resting on one arm in a casual manner. His gaze was anything but casual. His hungry stare reminded her of her dream and the sexual longing he'd made her feel, the desire to have his teeth sink into her, to know what it felt like. The memory still burned hot in her mind.

When he'd kissed her in the gas station parking lot, taking her by surprise, she couldn't resist his sexual pull. The way his hard chest felt pressed against hers, the heat of his body seeping into her clothes...electricity had jolted straight to her toes when his tongue had touched hers, enticing her to respond.

Duncan's kiss had been one of the most masterful, intimate, seductive kisses she'd ever experienced. It took down all her normal defenses. And that's when he'd zapped her with his vampire mojo. Before blackness overtook her, all she could think of was Duncan, how he tasted, felt and smelled. God, he'd smelled so good—like a mixture of woodsy outdoors, leather and musk.

*So much for* this *vampire not being able to compel me,* she thought in anger. Shaking off the seductive sensations his kiss and her dream had aroused, her temper flared. She sat up on her knees and pushed her hair back from her face, anger rising in waves. "Where the hell am I? I've missed my appointment."

"This is a second home my brother and I co-own. Kind of a 'getaway house'," Duncan responded in a calm tone. He didn't appear the least affected by her tirade. She shoved the covers back at the same time she tried to get out of the bed, ready to let him have it. But her feet got tangled up in the covers and instead of stalking over to him, she ended up flat on her face kissing the carpet. *Oh yeah,* that *was graceful.*

Duncan was there before she could recover, grasping her arm to help her up. She jerked her arm from his hold and stood up on her own, her eyes blazing. "Don't you dare try to be nice to me. I'm so damn mad at you. Thanks to you my client will probably never trust to meet with me again."

Not a single look of regret crossed his face. "Your well-being was more important."

Argh! She wanted to shoot him for his one-dimensional thinking. There *was* a way around it. He *could* have followed her as she'd asked him to, but nooooo, instead he'd ignored her wishes and... Wait...she might still be able to patch things up with her client.

She glanced at her watch then met his gaze. "Where's your phone? Maybe I can reschedule with my client and try to salvage his trust in me."

Duncan's expression turned hard. "There are no phones here other than my cell. You're not calling or meeting with anyone until James has been caught."

Her stomach tensed and her shoulders tightened at his command. She hit his chest in frustration. "Damn you, this is very important to me."

Duncan didn't stop her so she hammered on him some more. But his chest felt like steel and the stoic look on his face told her that her outburst did nothing to sway him. When her pummeling slowed, her anger changed to disappointment. "I've worked hard. I've scrimped and saved and…"

He clasped her wrists, halting her movements. "Enough, Rose." His hard tone had softened yet still held a commanding edge. "You've begun to bleed again."

She pulled a wrist away from his grasp and touched her scarf. "How do you know that?"

Duncan's golden gaze locked on hers. He began to untie her scarf in unhurried movements. *I can smell your blood,* he answered her mentally, his tone gruff. She glanced at his ticcing jaw and the hard planes of his face as she tried to decipher his mood.

Apprehension gripped her. She batted at his hands. "Just get me some more bandages. I'll be fine."

"No!" he barked out as he tossed the scarf to the floor. "I want to see your wound."

The menacing look on his face warned her that she was dealing with a man who wasn't human, but another being entirely, a dark, dangerous, predatory person.

Letting her hands fall, she lifted her chin a notch as he peeled away the tape. "Fine, you can look, but I mean it. *No* licking—"

"Sonofafuckingbitch!" he hissed out as he clasped her chin and lifted it higher so he could fully see her wound.

Rose tensed at the anger that lashed through him. She felt every single wave as it hit him, rolling through his body, tightening his shoulders. Ugly, dark revenge churned in his belly, clawed in his gut.

She gasped at the fact she *felt* his emotions and experienced his ferocity. When his eyes changed from their golden amber to a burnt orange-red, self-preservation kicked in. She tried to take a step back.

But Duncan cupped the back of her neck and held her still as he lowered his forehead to hers. She placed her hand on his hard chest, hoping her touch would calm the beast that seemed to have unleashed inside him.

Duncan's grip tightened. He whispered in her mind, *You're mine to protect and protect you I will.*

When she heard him take several calming breaths, her apprehension lessened. She didn't realize she'd been holding her own breath until she let out a sigh of relief.

He lifted his head, his look tortured and regretful. "I must cleanse and seal your wounds or you'll continue to lose blood and possibly develop an infection."

While he spoke, his hand moved from her head to her hair as his thumb rubbed a sensitive spot behind her ear.

Her blood pumped through her veins at a rampant pace and her breathing turned shallow at the way he made her feel—weak, tense, excited, aroused. Rose shook her head. "No licking."

Duncan raised an eyebrow, amusement reflected in his golden gaze. "Would you rather I kiss you again then?"

His sexy accent laced his words, making her heart thud out of control. Rose quickly tilted her head. "Fine, but don't...don't you enjoy it."

He gave her a feral smile. "I wouldn't think of it."

When his tongue swiped against her wound for the first time, Rose jerked at the initial pain. Another lick and she held back a moan as desire took over, clenching her body. She swayed in his arms and clutched his shoulders. She couldn't help the gasp that escaped her lips when he went back over the same wound another time.

She felt his anger at James rush through her once more, vicious and ruthless as he ran his tongue along another gash. Her body tensed, ready to pull back at the black, violent emotions that emanated from him.

Duncan gathered her closer, refusing to let her go. The next lave of his tongue changed to a slow, deliberate, exploring velvet caress. The assured, erotic pace told her he'd reined in his vengeful thought patterns to more pleasurable considerations. Her lower belly clenched and her core flooded in liquid heat at the sensations swirling through her.

*Your wounds are deep, Róisín. This will take a while.* The gravelly sound of arousal accompanied his words and her stomach clenched in response to his husky tone. She was weakest like this, her mind most vulnerable.

"Think of something to occupy your mind then." She spoke in a matter-of-fact tone as much for herself as for him. She needed to keep her mind distracted from the way he made her feel, the things he made her want.

He clutched her even closer and slid his hand down to her rear. Intentionally pressing his erection against her, his lips grazed her jaw as he rasped, *I can think of much more interesting things I could do to occupy my mind.*

"My wounds," she reminded him even as she moved her hands to his arms. She couldn't stop her fingers from naturally flexing around his hard biceps.

Duncan knew she was right. That he needed a distraction. He was supposed to be healing her, not seducing her. Using his powers, he mentally ran his fingers across the keys on the baby grand piano downstairs. A classical song began to play in the background. Music had always soothed him, allowed him to think, to focus.

Right now he needed all the help he could get. He'd only intended to heal Rose's wounds, to get rid of her discomfort, but he found her scent too inviting, the taste of her dried and fresh blood too alluring. He'd stopped speaking verbally because he didn't want her to see his fangs. They'd erupted at the first taste of her blood. She didn't need to know just how much he ached to plunge his teeth in her throat.

He continued to lave at her wounds, but when she said, "Ohhh, Mozart is one of my faves," as she began to move her hips to the beat of the music, he groaned inwardly. His body instinctively responded to her seductive rhythm. He slid his thigh between hers, his cock throbbing for close contact.

Duncan needed more of a distraction. The music slowly died off and he began to play a jazz song on his sax, accompanying with the piano.

"Hmmm, you've an interesting mix of CDs," she mused aloud. She moved to the music's bluesy change of pace. Subconsciously, she clutched her thighs around his leg, riding him.

Duncan could only grunt in response. He'd thought working two instruments at the same time would be challenging enough to keep his mind on healing her instead of seducing her. Something about Rose told him once he had her, taken her blood, he'd have a hard time not wanting to do so again and again.

He had no clue how long they'd have to hide out here. He hoped to hell it wasn't long because all his good intentions were flying out the proverbial window as her heated body brushed against his erection with her movements.

The song moved to a higher pitch and he found his mind naturally worked the instruments while his body reacted in kind to the faster pace. He began to move with Rose, enjoying the brush of his cock against her lower belly as he took the last lick to close her wounds.

"All done?" she asked in a trusting, panting tone.

Instead of stopping as he should have, Duncan wrapped his arms around her waist and used his powers to raise their bodies off the ground. "Not near enough, *a ghrá*."

When she yelped at the elevation and clung to him, he concentrated hard to retract his fangs. He met her frightened aqua gaze and spoke in calm tone, "*Tóg go bog é.* Have you ever danced on air, Róisín?"

She bit her lip and shook her head, still clutching his shoulders.

He gave her a devilish smile. "Then relax and enjoy the benefits I can offer. I won't let you fall."

Her body began to relax in his arms and he nuzzled her neck, inhaling her intoxicating scent. "You smell just like your name." He swiped his tongue up her neck in a slow, reverent stroke against her skin. She tasted so damn good.

"Mmmm," she responded and this time turned her neck, openly asking for more. Duncan could no more refuse her than stop breathing. While he ran his tongue along her neck once more, he lifted her body higher so his erection touched her mound. As they slowly spun in the air, he rocked against her until he heard her breathing change and her heart hammer against her chest.

He smiled and tilted their position to reclining, laying his body over hers. Duncan moved his lips to her throat. He kissed a searing path down her neck, across her collarbone to the vee in her blouse, wanting so much more.

Rose seemed caught in the moment, too. She'd closed her eyes and arched her back. Moaning, she threaded her fingers in his hair and pulled him closer.

He mentally opened the buttons on her blouse and kissed the curve of her breast. When she gasped at his intimate kiss, he smiled against her skin, then glanced up to see her look down at him, her heavy-lidded gaze lit with desire.

He started to unhook her bra so he could taste her gorgeous nipples but his gaze landed on the locket around her neck. It'd flipped around to the backside and the Irish words inscribed on the back caught his attention. He stilled his movements.

*Cosain mé i gcónaí*, it said. *Protect me, always*, his mind easily translated the words.

Guilt slammed into his consciousness and he immediately straightened their bodies, allowing them to float back to the ground.

"What is it?" Rose asked, grabbing his shoulders. She gave him a dazed, confused, almost hurt look as he buttoned her blouse.

Duncan stepped away and adopted a neutral expression. It was a difficult task. He found it hard to breathe, he wanted her so much.

"Forgive me, Rose," he said, regret lacing his words.

She ran her hand through her hair in an agitated manner. "It's okay. I…um, kind of got lost in the moment myself."

He gave her a half smile as he lifted her locket and rubbed his thumb across the inscription. "I just needed a little reminder of why we're here."

She seemed confused by his comment until she glanced down at her necklace in his hand. Jerking her gaze back to his, she clutched his wrist and said in an excited voice, "You can read it? What does it say?"

"You don't know?" he asked, puzzled.

She shook her head. "It was my mother's. I wanted to learn Irish but she didn't speak it very often when I was a little girl."

He nodded his understanding. "It says *Cosain mé i gcónaí.*"

"Ooh, that sounds beautiful. What does it mean?"

He couldn't help but smile at her exuberance. "It means 'Protect me always'."

Duncan lifted her chin until her beautiful eyes met his. "I'll make sure James doesn't find you. You have my word."

He let go of her chin and glanced down at her pendant in his hand, turning it back over to the front. Running his fingers across the tick marks along the edges, his brow furrowed. "These marks on the outer edge are interesting. Do you know what they represent?"

She shook her head. "No. My mother died a while ago. My father just gave my mother's necklace to me today." She wrapped her fingers around the locket, a wistful expression on her face. "He said my mother told him to give it to me. That it would protect me." She gave him a wry smile. "I guess it was one day too late, huh?"

Duncan shook his head and pulled her close, planting a tender kiss on her temple. "No, *a stór,* it was just in the nick of time."

"I love to hear you speak in my mother's language. How I wish she'd taught me the language of her people." She smiled up at him. "Who taught you Irish?"

He grinned as he clasped her elbow and led her toward the stairs that exited off the loft bedroom. "Let's go downstairs. You can eat while I answer your questions."

* * * * *

Rose had initially felt hurt and rejected by Duncan's abrupt withdrawal, but she found herself thankful for the honor that seemed to run through him. She didn't think she would have stopped him had he pursued their lovemaking. He'd so thoroughly seduced her, had her so completely wrapped up in him and the fact she felt no fear, only desire when he touched her, she would've given him anything he asked.

The music had abruptly stopped right around the same time Duncan called a halt to their foreplay, and she found she missed the beautiful background sounds as they entered his living room. She looked at the sound system and saw it was turned off.

As he directed her to sit at a table covered in tiles of deep burgundy, navy blue and forest green, she glanced up at him, asking, "Is your stereo system on a timer or something?"

Duncan chuckled at her question while he moved into the kitchen to pull out a knife and cutting board. "I guess you could say that." He waved his hand and the stereo turned on.

A traditional Irish instrumental song began to play. The tin whistle, violin and bodhrán drum's uplifting beat filtered from the speakers throughout the house. Rose smiled her appreciation at his choice of music even as she eyed the speakers in the upstairs ceiling in confusion. "I don't remember the music you played earlier coming through the sound system." *Then again, I was a bit distracted.*

"In answer to your earlier question, my mother is Irish."

Duncan's comment drew her attention.

"Up until my brother and I were ten or so, she only spoke Irish to us. Drove my dad nuts when we'd answer him in Irish more often than not. Even now a faint accent still lingers." An amused smile tilted his lips as he began to cut up mushrooms.

"What part of Ireland is your mother from?" She lifted her locket and stared at the design on the front before letting it fall to her chest once more. "I wish I knew what part my mother came from."

Adding olive oil to the skillet on the stove, Duncan scraped the mushrooms into the pan and began to sauté them. A thoughtful expression crossed his face. "She's never said specifically, just commented that she came from the western side of Ireland."

Rose frowned that he didn't know and could so easily have found out just by asking. "I'd want to know everything about my ancestors. Not one tiny detail left out."

He chuckled. "You seem the type."

"What type is that?" she asked, straightening her spine.

He raised an eyebrow at her tone as he set the sautéed mushrooms aside and began to brown a chicken breast in the pan. "Just a very detail-oriented person, Rose. I meant no insult."

He met her gaze as he set a wineglass on the table, an intrigued expression on his face. "Why do you carry a gun?"

Her brow furrowed at the fact she'd had to leave her gun behind at her house. "I'm a PI. Carrying a gun is more for defensive protection due to the nature of my job."

His brows drew together at her statement. "What were you at the Lion's Lair investigating?"

Rose squirmed under his scrutiny. Somehow she felt he'd know if she tried to lie to him. "I was trying to find proof vampires exist for a client."

"What!" He slammed his fist on the table between them, cracking one of the tiles His golden eyes turned a burnt red color in his anger.

Rose jumped to her feet, putting her hands out at the menacing look in his eyes. "Whoa, there, vampire boy. Keep them fangs at bay. I don't know why you're mad."

Coming around the table, Duncan clasped her upper arms. "No way in hell are you meeting with that client, Rose. As a matter of fact, I want his name. Now!"

She tried to shrug out of his grip, but his hands were like steel bands on her arms. "Let me go. I will meet with this client. A lot of money is riding on this."

Seething with anger, Duncan shook her. "Is that what this is about? Money? Is money worth an entire race of people to you, Rose?"

"What are you talking about?" she snapped.

"We are constantly hunted. There are vampire hunter organizations whose entire goal is to wipe out the existence of vampires. The Kendrians are seen as a threat to be eliminated."

She felt blood drain from her face at his comment. "I had no idea," she whispered. Her heart sank at the idea she'd have to give up this client. Still, she fought the idea. "But you could be wrong. He could just be an eccentric man seeking answers."

Duncan's frown remained. "The more humans who learn about us, the higher the risk we take of being exposed on a wide scale. That's why I can't let you give any information to your client. I have no idea what he plans to do with it."

Rose shook her head at the sad realization she wouldn't be able to deliver any information to Mr. Reed. "As much as you think it is, this isn't about the money."

"Then what's it about?" His gaze narrowed.

She didn't want to get too personal again with him, not when he'd looked down at her before.

"It's about fulfilling a dream." She raised her chin a notch to meet his accusing gaze.

"And what dream is that?" His grip loosened as his tone softened.

"It's nothing." She pulled from his grasp and turned her back to him, walking into the living room.

"Rose."

She refused to turn around. When she heard him pulling silverware out of a drawer in the kitchen, tension eased from her body and she relaxed her shoulders.

"Your dinner is served, madam."

She couldn't resist a half smile at Duncan's formal tone as she turned and walked over to the table. Her belly rumbled at the delicious smells and the sight of the chicken breast stuffed with cheese on a bed of tomatoes and mushrooms. "God, it smells wonderful," she said with appreciation as she sat down at the table and picked up her fork.

Once she'd chewed the first mouthwatering bite, she had to compliment him when he sat down at the table across from her.

"This is fabulous!" Embarrassment crept in when she realized she'd been so hungry she started without him. Rose gestured to the empty table in front of him. "Aren't you going to eat?" As soon as the words left her mouth, she realized the man had every right to smack her in the forehead. *Duuuuh…he's a vampire!* She quickly amended, "Er…or do you eat?"

Duncan stood and retrieved a bottle of wine. Pouring himself a glass of merlot, he answered, "Cooking a pleasurable meal is something I do for another, not myself. Kind of a give and take in my mind."

Rose's heart jerked as she cut another piece of chicken. Did that mean what she thought it meant?

Duncan leaned casually back in his chair and gave her a sexy smile as his gaze lowered to her lips, the look in his eyes hungry, dark, desirous.

"And yes, I can eat, for social reasons. Personally, I'm more of a dessert person."

Butterflies fluttered in her stomach at the implication of his words. Was she reading into what he said? When she met his gaze and he smiled, purposefully displaying his fangs, she gasped, not out of fear, but from the knowledge of just how turned on she became at the thought of Duncan biting her. Her heart rate raced out of control and her breathing turned shallow while her breasts suddenly ached for his touch.

She shook her head and set down her fork with a frown, hiding her own desire behind sarcasm. "Great, now don't *I* feel like the fatted calf whose owner wants to make sure she eats well so his meal will be nice and juicy. I'm very appreciative of the tasty meal, Duncan, but I'm not into sharing."

Duncan's fangs retracted back to normal size and his expression turned serious. "I would never take what you aren't willing to give, Rose. If you know nothing else about me, know that to be true." When he finished speaking, he stood and turned his back to her while he re-corked the wine and put it away.

Rose felt like a real jerk. Standing up, she walked into the kitchen and touched his arm. When Duncan tensed at her touch. she dropped her hand. "I'm sorry, Duncan. I didn't mean to offend you."

She held her breath, waiting for him to respond. *How does one go about dealing with a vampire? Were they all this brooding?* Once he finally turned his golden eyes to hers, she began to breathe again. "I sincerely apologize."

Duncan regarded her with a steady gaze. He leaned back against the counter and crossed his arms over his chest. "No offense was taken." Nodding toward her plate, he continued, "Now go eat while your food is hot."

Returning to the table, she sat down to eat. After Rose had eaten every single delicious morsel off her plate, she eyed the glass of white wine Duncan started to pour for her with cautious suspicion. "The last time I drank a glass of wine I ended up naked in a vampire's bed," she quipped in a half amused tone.

Duncan raised his eyebrow as he finished pouring the glass. "If I wanted you naked and in my bed, I wouldn't stoop to deception. I'm bluntly honest when it comes to my desires."

Rose resisted a shiver at the sheer intensity of his comment. As he looked down at her glass, she couldn't tell what he was thinking. But based on his earlier actions where *he* was the one who stopped what they'd started, she honestly believed he had no intention of seducing her.

Now why did that thought bother her? She hadn't imagined the attraction between them. She certainly hadn't imagined that impressive erection he'd pressed against her belly earlier. Then again, he was a *man* even if he was a vampire.

Picking up her wine, she walked over to the contemporary U-shaped sofa. She settled into the center section of the furniture and ran her hand across the soft taupe-colored chenille cushions, appreciating the contemporary yet warm style. When she leaned back against one of the hunter-green throw pillows, she realized for the first time in as long as she could remember, it bothered her that a man seemed determined *not* seduce her.

For many years, she'd fended off unwanted advances and would normally welcome such knowledge. But there was something about Duncan…something she couldn't explain that made him different.

While conflicting thoughts tumbled in her head, Rose took in the room around her. The end tables were a dark polished walnut and the matching entertainment center took up an entire wall. Each section in the entertainment center was filled with the latest in high-tech contemporary audio and video equipment. Her gaze scanned the two packed bookcases that covered both side walls then skimmed past the baby grand piano and saxophone sitting in its upright stand. The instruments took up space in a bay window-style area in the far corner of the room.

Duncan turned off the lights in the kitchen and the entire room went black. Rose waited in anticipation as her fingers tightened around her glass of wine. In the dark, the pouring rain outside seemed to echo throughout the room. She jumped when the gas fireplace on the wall across from the couch roared to life. Its orange and blue flames gave the room a warm, cozy glow.

Duncan stood beside the sofa holding his wineglass. Setting his glass down on the end table, he settled on the cushions. Rose kicked off her shoes and put her feet on the couch, scooting back to give him room. She took a sip of her wine and savored the flavor as she swallowed.

He turned and put his arm on the back of the couch, his knee brushing her toes. Nodding toward her, he asked, "How does your neck feel?"

Subconsciously, she tilted her head, then winced. "It's not stinging anymore, but I'm sore."

His golden gaze held hers as he picked up her right foot and began to pull off her sock.

"Hey," she said and tried to pull her foot back.

But Duncan held firm as he removed her sock and tossed it to the floor. "*Tóg go bog é,*" he said as he stroked his thumb down the middle of her foot. "This should help to relax your muscles."

Rose froze at the arousing sensations that flooded through her at his touch. When his full palm came in contact with the bottom of her foot, her pulse beat a steadily rising staccato rhythm in her ears.

She gripped her glass tighter when he moved closer, set her foot on his thigh and lifted her left foot. Pulling off the other sock, he gave her other foot the same, attentive treatment.

With the fire warming her and his fingers causing all kinds of tingling, sensual sensations to slam through her, hardening her nipples and making her stomach tense in anticipation, Rose had a hard time holding her glass upright. Before she spilled its contents, she set her glass down on the coffee table.

Seeking a distraction from his arousing touch, she asked, "You said you're a hybrid. Which parent is vampire and which is human?"

He met her curious gaze as he massaged her toes. "Both are vampires. My mother was human when she met my father. She was already pregnant before he converted her to a vampire."

His comment piqued her curiosity further. "Vampires can have children?"

"How else do you think we get here? Hatch out of an egg?"

She lifted an eyebrow at his sarcasm, then shrugged. "I know nothing about your race, Duncan." Which was entirely true, but learning vampires could have children with humans definitely had her mind whirling. What if…

"If you had a child with a human, do you think that child would be able to walk in the light like you?"

Duncan frowned at her question. "I have no idea nor will I ever know since I don't plan to have children."

Disappointment coursed through her. "Why?" she asked before she thought better of it.

Duncan didn't answer her. She could tell by the ticcing in his jaw it wasn't something he cared to discuss. Instead, he dug his fingers deep into the ball of her foot, distracting her. She bit back a moan of sheer pleasure. The man certainly knew how to use his hands. Her gaze lowered to his hands on her foot. He had gorgeous hands, long fingers and broad palms. The pads of his fingers were a little rough, which made her wonder what kind of work he did that would cause them to be that way.

Maybe a more neutral question would be best. "So which side of your heritage do you identify with the most?"

When his hands paused, she jerked her gaze to his to see anger flash through his eyes before he spoke in an even tone, "Neither."

She started to ask him what he meant by his comment, but he tugged on her ankle, causing the question to lodge in her throat. Her body slid down the soft fabric until she was flat on her back.

Before she could right herself, he was leaning over her, caging her in, a devilish look on his face. "But I do relish the vampire part of my heritage and all the sensual benefits it can provide." His heated gaze moved to her lips, then her neck before locking with hers once more.

Her breathing sped up at the seductive tone of his words. "Is this some of that 'blunt honesty' you referred to earlier?"

He moved so fast, grasping her behind her neck and pulling her against him, she didn't have a chance to react. His lips hovered over hers as he spoke in her mind, *No, this is my blunt honesty. I want you.* He moved his lips to her jaw. *But I'll want more than sex.* He kissed her neck while his tone dropped to a husky purr. *I'll want everything your body has to offer.*

Rose clung to his shoulders and his hand moved to support her back while he kissed a searing path down to the opening in her blouse. Her body fired all over again, zinging where his lips came into contact with her skin.

"There's something about your touch," she whispered as she threaded her fingers through his hair. "I-I can't explain it, but it's the strangest combination of heated tingling and calming sensation at the same time."

Duncan jerked his head up, his hold tightening on her as his golden gaze searched hers. "You feel it?"

The intensity in his gaze both excited and scared her. She bit her lower lip and nodded.

"Yes—" she started to say, but Duncan cut her off, his mouth covering hers.

A jolt of electricity shot through her at his heated kiss, causing a shiver of sensual awareness to spread throughout her body. Rose moaned against his mouth, accepting the thrust of his tongue as he lifted her off the sofa and held her against his hard body.

As he began to lower her, she wrapped her arms around his neck, unwilling to let go of the kiss, his heat or the amazing sensations he seemed to ignite in her.

Duncan lowered her to the soft carpet in front of the fire and sat back on his heels to stare down at her.

When she felt the buttons of her blouse begin to open on their own, she gasped and started to sit up on her elbows. *Enjoy the vampire benefits,* a ghrá, his voice rasped in her mind as his heated gaze locked with hers.

While he spoke, another button came undone and another. With each button he worked loose from the material, her body heat elevated another degree. Then her shirt fell open and her sex throbbed in aroused anticipation.

Her breath caught in her throat when he reached out and traced the curve of her breast above her bra, his hooded gaze following the path his finger took. With a flick of his wrist, the front snap on her bra came undone, exposing her breasts as the material fell away.

Cool air immediately pebbled her nipples. Rose let a moan escape her lips when he leaned forward to lick one of the hard pink tips. At the same time he pushed her bra straps and shirt down her arms until they lay on the floor.

Facing her, Duncan sat down beside her and cupped the back of her neck to lift her to a leaning position. He lowered his head and captured her nipple, sucking hard on the sensitive bud.

Desire shot straight to her channel, flooding it with liquid heat from the erotic tug of his lips pressing the nipple against the roof of his mouth. The man made her feel things she'd never experienced before. Rose slid her hand under his T-shirt. She wanted to explore his hard muscles, feel his warm skin pressed against hers.

As if he read her mind, Duncan swiftly pulled his T-shirt over his head. Once he'd tossed his shirt on the floor, Rose took in his broad shoulders, sculpted chest and the line of light hair that trailed between his defined abs to disappear into his pants. God, the man was beautiful beyond words.

Reaching out, she slowly traced the sexy line of hair past his hard stomach until her fingers reached the button on his jeans.

When she looked up to meet his gaze while she unbuttoned his pants, she was surprised to see his eyes closed. A muscle jumped in his jaw as if he were concentrating hard.

He moved with lightning speed, grabbing her wrist to stop her movements. His voice entered her mind, swift, hard, unapologetic, yet achingly seductive in its fierceness. *I will take your blood.*

Her pulse jumped at his words, but quickly skyrocketed when he opened his eyes. The burnt yellow color fascinated her.

"This isn't about nourishment, Róisín. This is about deep, sexual satisfaction…for both of us."

Rose took a shuddering breath to calm her rioting nerves and nodded in understanding. She could do this. He made her feel cherished, protected…safe yet strangely possessed by his charisma.

Duncan lifted her hand and kissed her palm, then moved his lips to her wrist, swiping his tongue across the soft skin.

Her channel walls clenched in response, making her want to whimper. Instead she clamped her thighs together to try to assuage the ache that throbbed in heated awareness.

Duncan mentally worked the button and zipper on her jeans as he leaned over and kissed the hollow of her neck.

Unwilling to stop his kisses so she could see, she ran her hand back down his hard stomach until she reached his pants once more. Rose's breathing changed to small, erratic pants as she fumbled with the buttons on his jeans.

She laid down on her back so Duncan could ease her pants and underwear off, her heart pounding at a thundering pace. When she was completely naked, Duncan ran his hand up her thigh, tugging her leg to open her to his searing gaze. Rose tensed as old, buried fears came barreling back to her consciousness.

Duncan paused his movements and his brow creased at the same time she felt a presence in her mind, probing, searching, trying to decipher.

"What's wrong?"

She realized Duncan was the presence in her mind. How could he do that? James hadn't been able to get that close…to walk right inside her head and knock on her consciousness as if demanding to be let in. She held on to her control and shook her head as she put her hand over his. "Nothing. Touch me, Duncan."

He frowned at her comment, but when she moved his hand higher up her thigh and then bent her knee, opening to him, his nostrils flared.

Rose closed her eyes when his fingers trailed through her hair, barely brushing her folds. "*Tá tú go h-áileann*," he whispered.

"What does that mean?" She opened her eyes, breathless at the vibrations he'd elicited with his light touch.

*You're beautiful*, he responded in her mind as his gaze locked on her entrance.

With the fire warming her skin, his seductive words only stoked the desire blazing inside her. A new flood of desire rushed forth, intensifying the aching burning in her sex.

Duncan's gaze jerked to hers as his fingers gathered the moisture and rubbed it against her folds. "I've never been more aroused than I am at this moment," he rasped then slid a finger deep inside her.

Rose forgot all about her apprehension at the erotic sensations echoing through her. She closed her eyes and arched her back, pushing closer to his hand, sighing in pleasure.

When he withdrew his finger, she demanded, "More!" as she clutched his muscular thigh. Rose slid her hand up his leg to clasp his erection through his black silk boxers. Satisfaction rolled through her at the damp spot she felt on the soft material.

Duncan groaned when she wrapped her fingers around him and squeezed. Pulling out of her grasp, he shifted his position. He put one knee between her legs on the floor and leaned over her as he thrust two fingers inside her, withdrew and thrust again. The firelight danced on the shadowed planes of his angular face as he lowered his head to her breast once more.

This time he nipped at her nipple, making her gasp at the pleasure-pain while his fingers stayed buried, rubbing on a sensitive spot deep inside her.

"Ohmigod," she called out. Her body naturally clenched around his hand, desire building inside her to a fever pitch. She bucked, wanting more, needing more.

*Come,* he demanded. He increased his hand's pace and sucked hard on her nipple. *I want to see your arousal spread across your sweet skin, hear the blood rushing in your veins and know just how ready you are to share with me.*

The thought of Duncan biting her made Rose's stomach clench in excitement. She screamed as her orgasm rolled through her in hard, fast waves. Grasping his wrist, she held his hand inside her, wanting to prolong the sensation. Never in her life had she experienced anything so body-rocking.

When her heart rate slowed and the tremors stopped, she met his steady gaze. Duncan's amber eyes locked with hers for a long, heated moment before he withdrew his hand from her body and stood to strip out of his jeans.

Her pulse sped up all over again at the sight of his trim hips and corded thighs. The man had, without a doubt, the most beautiful body she'd ever seen.

He lowered himself to the floor beside her and clasped her chin. "Are you ready to share your body with me, Róisín? In all ways?"

Her heart rammed as she considered the fact his bite could convert her to a vampire. James had said it took three bites in as many days. The risk alone excited her, but she thought it best to ask to be certain.

"I won't become a vampire, will I?"

Duncan shook his head. "Never worry that I would convert you."

Rose nodded as she reached up and slid her fingers in his hair. She smiled. "Personally, I think you're moving too slow."

Duncan's gaze burned with fire as he let go of her chin to grab his jeans. When he pulled condoms out of his pocket and set them on the floor beside her, she immediately tensed.

"No condoms."

His gaze jerked to hers. "What?"

She shook her head, adamant. "No condoms."

"You're ovulating. You could get pregnant."

"I know." The realization that she wanted this surprised even her, but as soon as she said it, she knew her decision was right. She couldn't explain it. A child with Duncan just felt…right.

He clenched his jaw. "I told you I don't want children."

"And I told you I did."

"You want to have a hybrid vampire child? A child who doesn't fit in either race?" Anger flashed in his eyes.

*Is that why he doesn't want children? Because he doesn't like his hybrid status?* "I've learned over the past couple of days, humans aren't the only beings walking around. As a hybrid, my child would be able to better defend himself or herself in life," she replied in an even tone.

Duncan's gaze narrowed and her stomach tensed. The desire that had flared between them quickly died as they squared off.

Turning away, he stood up and pulled on his boxers and jeans. "Your child would be a target. Untrained and unprotected."

"I don't expect you to stick around, Duncan." Rose bit her lip and considered his terse comment as she tugged her underwear and pants back on. Duncan had a point. Without him around, her child would be untrained in the use of his or her powers. She hadn't thought of that.

Forgoing her bra, she picked up her shirt and shrugged into it, buttoning it. Duncan stood beside her, his arms crossed over his chest, a scowl on his face.

"Forget it. It was a bad idea." Rose moved to step around him, heading for the stairs. She needed some time alone.

He wrapped his hand around her arm, stopping her in her tracks. "I still want you."

She met his gaze, her own anger flaring. "You want me on your terms." When his eyes narrowed, she continued, "You asked me to share every part of myself with you. It goes both ways, Duncan."

Duncan leaned close, his voice a deadly purr. "I never claimed to be a fair man. Who knows how long we'll be here together. We both want."

She raised her eyebrow and pulled out of his grasp. "I can control my desires. Can you?" she challenged before she walked away.

She'd only taken two steps when an invisible tongue swiped against the side of her neck. Rose's steps faltered.

*Can you?* his sexy voice, that Irish accent more pronounced, entered her head, taunting her. *You have no idea how persuasive I can be, Róisín.*

"I think you mean ruthless," she countered, angry at the shiver of sexual awareness that had shimmied down her spine at his sheer determination.

"That too."

Fighting back the excitement his swift agreement caused, she called over her shoulder in a tight voice, "Good night."

# Chapter Five

Duncan watched Rose walk up the stairs, her long hair flowing down her back. She held her shoulders up and her back ramrod straight. He might not be able to read her mind, but he could hear her heart kick up and damned if he couldn't feel her desire…literally feel it.

Fuck!

With a flick of his wrist, the fire died in the fireplace dousing the room in total darkness. He stared out the front window into the dark woods as he worked to calm his raging desire for her. Clenching his fists, he took deep breaths then jerked his jeans open to relieve the pressure against his cock. Still his balls ached, needing release.

Opening the front door, he walked outside and closed it as he stood on the porch, staring into the pouring rain. The cool night air did nothing to dampen the heat flaring inside him. He walked to the edge of the porch and raised his hand to place it on the porch post. Leaning his forehead against the back of his hand, he pulled his hard cock from his underwear and squeezed his shaft in sexual frustration. No woman had affected him like this one, had made him want her this much.

While he pumped his hand up and down his shaft, he admitted to himself that part of Rose's allure was the sheer mystery that surrounded her. He'd tried to read her thoughts, but even when she climaxed, she held on to the barrier she'd erected in her mind. How did she maintain such constant control? he wondered.

As the need for release tightened in his groin once more, he relived every curve of her gorgeous body in his mind, her intoxicating rose smell, the soft red curls between her smooth thighs, her sighs of anticipation as her desire built and then her scream of pleasure when she came. The memory of her sweet body contracting around his fingers caused his breathing to increase and his heart rate to speed up. He took a deep breath, trying to regain control, but instead his action caused him to catch the latent scent of her arousal still on his hand.

His incisors exploded from his gums, the sharp points digging into his lower lip. He hissed as he came in explosive spurts into the bushes beside the porch. When his pulse stopped roaring in his ears and the sound of the pouring rain permeated his consciousness, Duncan inhaled and exhaled deeply, trying to relax.

He started to hold his hand out in the rain, to wash away her scent and everything that made him want her to the point of obsession, but his selfish, primal side beckoned him to taste her, to know what he'd missed out on tonight. He slid his fingers into his mouth and fisted his other hand around his shaft again as her delicious flavor slammed into his gut. He wanted more than a taste.

Placing both hands on the railing in front of him, he ground his teeth at the surge of lust that shot through him. Why did she affect him so fiercely? He couldn't lie to himself. Her ability to shield her mind might intrigue him, but the physical attraction went beyond anything he'd ever experienced.

When he'd massaged her feet earlier and she'd mentioned a heated, tingling sensation at his touch, his heart had leapt. He'd experienced the same but had discounted the unique feelings as pent-up sexual anticipation on his part. To learn she'd felt it too only spiked his arousal. All his good intentions, all thoughts of just protecting her and keeping his distance, swiftly disappeared.

But the fact she wanted to get pregnant…that threw him.

Duncan clenched his jaw. He meant what he'd said to Rose. He wanted her and would do what it took to have her, but on his terms. He lived by control and self-discipline. No way in hell was he impregnating her.

But if he didn't, did that mean she'd find someone else who would? The thought of another man touching Rose, let alone making love to her, made his chest contract in painful spasms and anger flash through him.

"Why the hell do I care?" he mumbled as he pivoted on his heel and walked inside.

But the beast inside him wouldn't relent, so Duncan turned to the one thing that had always soothed him. His music.

He walked into the small nook in the corner of the house that was surrounded by huge glass windows on three sides, and sat down at the baby grand piano. Flipping his hand, the spotlight came on over the piano. Since the house had been closed for a while and probably would be after he and Rose left, he didn't bother propping open the piano's top. Duncan closed his eyes and let his fingers fly across the ivory keys, playing a haunting classical song. The music flowed so intricately inside him, he could see the notes in his mind's eye while his heart took to the song.

As he worked his way through the difficult chords, his hunger for Rose dissipated but she still remained in his thoughts.

*****

Rose lay in bed listening to the beautiful song. It sounded so clear, as if…as if it were being played live. Her curiosity piqued, she got up and walked over to the banister, peering down into the living room.

Her gaze locked on Duncan sitting in the spotlight, his head down as his fingers moved across the keys in fluid motion. Her heart pumped faster at the sight he made when he lifted his head. His eyes were closed, the look on his face so involved in the music. The light reflected off his angular face and the natural highlights in his hair. Her gaze dropped to his broad shoulders and the display of muscles in his biceps as he moved his fingers across the keys.

She listened, unable to look away from the emotions she saw filtering across his face. The piece he chose seemed difficult and intense. He played a piece by Beethoven so beautifully she wondered if he could sing as well. She almost walked downstairs and asked him, but her fingers clung to the wooden banister, locking her in place.

*It's for the best to stay away,* she told herself. She should never have insisted on "no condoms", but something inside her, something she couldn't explain, insisted she do so. She had to admit to herself, as soon as the words came out of her mouth, she knew in her heart she wanted someone like Duncan to father her child.

Her conviction intensified as she watched this amazing man play. She had a feeling she was seeing a side to him that she didn't think he often shared, an emotional, sensitive side…a hidden part of him she'd seen just a glimpse of tonight in front of the fire. Duncan appeared to be working through something with his music. After the way she left him, she had a feeling she was part of that "something".

As the song came to an end, she sighed and turned away, unbuttoning her blouse. Fumbling around in the dark, she opened a dresser drawer and pulled out one of Duncan's T-shirts.

Once she put it on, she lifted the soft, worn cotton to her nose and inhaled. His sexy scent smelled comforting. She crawled under the covers as another song started up, this one more poignant than the last.

Rose turned on her side and clasped the locket between her fingers. Rubbing her thumb along the engraved letters on the back, she whispered the saying, *Cosain mé i gcónaí*, relishing the sound of the Irish words on her lips. Duncan's music had slowed and her eyelids closed as the final notes lulled her to sleep.

* * * * *

Rose awoke early the next morning. She glanced up at the skylight to see the sun had barely started to lighten the morning sky. Pulling the covers off, she sought the bathroom, knowing her bladder would thank her immensely. After she'd used the facilities, she smiled at the beautiful décor surrounding her. She loved the warm terracotta floor and the light that came through the tall glass block window that touched from ceiling to floor on a far wall. Cream-colored towels hung from the towel rack near the stand-up shower and more towels lay stacked on a trunk next to a gorgeous claw-footed tub.

Opening one of the small vanity drawers, she smiled when she found an unopened toothbrush and a small tube of toothpaste. Rose brushed her teeth and turned on the taps to the tub as she hummed a tune her mother used to sing to her when she was a child. While the tub filled, she looked under the cabinet for some soap and shampoo. There's more than one way to have a bubble bath, she thought with a smile as she held the bar of rose-scented soap under the running water.

Rose moaned in pleasure as she sank into the bath, enjoying the sweet-smelling warmth that surrounded her. Her hair floated around her, covered in bubbles. When she closed her eyes, she couldn't help but remember the seductive feel of Duncan's warm hands on her body, the way she'd responded to him. She'd never been so uninhibited with another man.

Duncan made her forget the past. He made her want to discover just how passionate she could be with a man who knew how to caress and tease her to a fever pitch of arousal, a man whose kiss alone made her ache for his touch the moment his lips brushed against hers.

She fantasized, reliving the memory of his rough beard on her cheek and then her neck. The sensation of his fingers on her nipples, the rough pads tweaking a response from her. The vivid memory of his teeth grazing the hard pink tips made her sex throb in response. Her breathing increased and she arched her neck as she skimmed her fingers down her belly, intending to relieve the ache between her thighs.

The very real sensation of something brushing against her nipple caused her to gasp. She jerked her eyes open to see Duncan sitting on the trunk next to the tub, his hand in the water below the bubbles.

Dark hunger filtered across his expression. His eyebrow rose as his finger moved around her nipple in a lazy circle. "If you need relief, *a ghrá,* all you need to do is ask."

Dressed in navy blue silk lounge pants that tied at his trim waist, he was naked from the waist up. His biceps flexed as he leaned one arm on the tub and trailed his fingers down the valley between her breasts. When his heated gaze left hers to flick to her breasts, Rose realized that the bubbles had all but dissipated. She wrapped her arms around her breasts and quickly flipped over on her belly in the tub. Leaning on her elbows to hold her face above the water, she turned her head and looked back at him. "What are you doing in here?"

Duncan slid his hand from the back of her neck to her shoulder down her spine and across her bare ass. *You're beautiful, no matter the angle.*

"The door was locked," she said, trying not to let his touch arouse her any further.

His sexy chuckle made her stomach flip-flop. "You're aroused, aching to be filled. Do you really think a door would stop me, Róisín?"

The confident arrogance in his voice made her throb even more. "Ruthless," she reminded him, looking away. She didn't want him to see how right he'd been reflected in her gaze.

"To the core," he agreed. The deep timbre in his voice slid down her spine like a velvet caress at the same time the water inside the tub began to bubble as if he'd turned on Jacuzzi jets.

Rose gasped at the sudden change. There were no jets in this stand-alone tub. As the hard water hit her skin, traveling up the outside of her thighs, massaging her muscles, she glared at Duncan. He leaned forward, both forearms resting casually on his knees. But there was nothing casual about the look in his eyes as he stared at her. His lion-like gaze glittered with desire if he were waiting.

Rose narrowed her gaze on him, ready to let him have it when one of the jets suddenly hit her swollen clitoris. The hard, relentless, pulsating spray of water didn't let up in its intensity.

Instead of speaking, she gasped and found herself arching her back. She panted as she turned on her side and grasped the edge of the tub. Her change in position didn't make a difference. Still the water pounded against her. Her heart thundered in her chest and her body shuddered at the unrelenting onslaught. She wanted to come so bad, needed the release.

*Are you ready to come now?* Duncan asked in a knowing tone.

No way in hell was she giving in. "Fuck...you," she said between rampant breaths.

The jets suddenly stopped and Duncan stood, his hard erection outlined by his silk pants. "Any time you're ready," he growled before he turned and left the bathroom.

Rose worked to control her heavy breathing in the still water. She was so close to giving in, so close to asking him to have sex with her, condoms be damned. If he had gone on another minute she wouldn't have been able to form a single argument.

Climbing out of the tub, she stood on shaky legs and pulled the towel around her wet body. After she towel-dried her hair, she wrapped the towel around her and opened the bathroom door.

Duncan grabbed her shoulders and pressed her against the bedroom wall as his mouth came down hard on hers. Shock rocked through her at the ferocity of his kiss. His rough hands slid up her bare thighs, clasping her ass as he lifted her in the air.

Rose gripped his shoulders, her nails digging into the skin as he plundered her mouth. *Why do you fight this?* he asked as he fit his silk-covered cock against her entrance and rocked her against the wall.

His action brought everything slamming back, all the memories she crammed in that dark place in her mind, hidden so she didn't have to remember, to relive.

Panic set in and she began to fight him. Duncan's entire body stilled and then she felt rage well inside him. Setting her on the ground, he slammed his fist into the sheetrock beside her, shaking the whole wall in his viciousness as he roared, "What the fuck was his name? I'm going to kill him!"

She jerked her gaze to his, her fear disappearing at the look of utter fury on his face. His eyes had turned a fiery red and his fangs were unsheathed to their full length. She had no doubt Duncan would kill without a thought. But more than anything she was surprised he'd gotten past her mental barrier, had walked around inside her head, and found his way into her innermost thoughts. The idea frightened her more than anything.

Shoving him away, she gave a casual wave of her hand and walked toward the bed to retrieve her clothes, "It was a long time ago, Duncan. Leave it alone."

"He raped you, Rose. I won't allow that to go unpunished. I can see his face as clear as day, but I want his name." His tone was lethal.

Rose tensed when Duncan mentioned the past out loud—a past she'd buried away.

Rubbing her temples, she said in a low voice, "I've put it behind me. I don't want to discuss it, Duncan."

She tensed when he pulled her into his arms. He surrounded her with his warmth and kissed her temple. "I'm sorry. I would've been more careful with you if I had known." Regret laced his tone and she instantly wrapped her arms around his waist and laid her cheek on his shoulder.

She buried her nose in his chest, enjoying the soft hair, then spoke in a low voice. "Don't you dare treat me like a delicate flower. If you ever held back with me, that would piss me off more than anything else. I know in my heart you'd never hurt me, Duncan. It's the only reason I allowed you to get close in the first place."

Duncan lifted her chin until she met his gaze. He searched her face for a long moment before he stepped away. "You've got to be hungry. I'll make you breakfast while you get dressed."

What she wouldn't give to know what he was thinking. Rose's heart sank at the detached look she saw in his gaze before he turned and walked down the stairs. One of the reasons she'd never told anyone what happened was because she didn't want sympathy.

Jeff had been an acquaintance in high school. It's not like he was a total stranger. She'd only expected a kiss. But the memory of that night at Cynthia's party had colored her view on relationships in general, no matter how hard she'd tried to let it go. Ever since then, she really focused when she met people, gauging them and measuring their trustworthiness. That's when she discovered she had a knack for "reading" others. Well, except vampires, apparently.

Glancing at the damage Duncan had done to the bedroom wall, her heart jerked as she walked over to the wall to inspect it. Shock slammed through her when she saw that not only had his hand gone through the sheetrock, he'd split the two by four stud as well. No wonder the house had rocked.

How had he read her thoughts and learned of Jeff? Thank God she hadn't thought of his name or she was certain Duncan would hunt him down. The past was the past. She preferred to leave it that way.

She dressed slowly, not wanting to face Duncan. No matter what he'd said, he *would* look at her differently now. The depressing thought made her heart constrict and her stomach clench into a hard knot.

*****

Duncan cooked bacon and eggs for Rose while his mind whirled. He'd wanted to know what she was thinking so badly, he'd pushed her more than he'd pushed another woman, relentless in his need to know if he was the only one seemingly obsessed.

When her mental barrier collapsed as she relived the memory of the night she was raped at a party she'd attended, he'd been surprised by what he learned. While her old fears reared within her, she still held an instinctual trust in Duncan. Trust he didn't deserve.

As for Rose's past…even though she had no memory of the actual rape, awaking aching and sore with no clothes on had been enough to give her a bad taste for all men. She'd learned to control her emotions with an iron fist. He'd solved the mystery of her ability to block him, but the knowledge had come with a cost. A cost he'd carry the responsibility of for a very long time—bringing back a horrible, buried memory.

He'd seen the guy's face as clear as if he were facing him, experienced her confusion when she awoke and the sinking, sick feeling in her stomach at the realization of what had happened to her. She'd been a virgin, too. Fierce, biting fury swept through him all over again. Rage unlike anything he'd ever felt in his life burned like a festering wound in his gut. He replayed the scene in his head several times as he etched the sonofabitch's face in his mind.

The clatter of the spatula falling to the floor, broken in half, brought him out of his vengeful musings. His thoughts shifted back to Rose once more as the bacon sizzled in the pan in front of him.

He'd never felt so violently protective of another. No wonder he'd seen a look of horror on her face when he'd asked if she was married. She wanted a child, but no man in her life. Sex was just sex to her. She had no need for fulfillment, no need to feel or experience the full range of emotions a good round of heart-pounding sex could give her. In that respect, all men were abhorrent to her.

Until him.

She wanted him passionately, ached to be filled. But only to a point. She didn't want to feel anything beyond exploring her sexual urges. Hell, that's what he wanted too, to be able to easily walk away. He should be thrilled, but he wasn't, not at all.

He glanced up as Rose started to descend the stairs. The vulnerable look on her face tugged at his heart—a look she quickly hid when she realized he was watching her. Her mental barrier was back too, stronger than ever.

"Mmmm, bacon and eggs." She gave him a smile as he set the plate of food down on the table in front of her.

After she chewed her first bite, she said with appreciation, "Wow, Duncan, a girl could get used to this."

"Don't," he shot back, angry at the deeper, more primal thought that had wormed its way into his mind at her comment. His gut had clenched in sheer male satisfaction at the idea her comment evoked—the thought of just how much he'd like to provide her the kind of nourishment only a vampire could offer his mate. What would it be like to see her enjoying his blood with such fervor?

A hurt expression crossed her face before she masked it behind an indifferent look and said in an upbeat voice, "So how long am I going to be stuck here with you? I mean, we're going to get tired of each other soon enough." Realization dawned in her expression. "Uh, hey, how often do vampires eat? Aren't you…like…" she stumbled on the word before she finished, "hungry?"

"I'm fine," he said in a gruff tone. He turned away and put the pan into the sink. As he dipped his hands into the hot soapy water, all he could think about was the sound of her blood rushing in her veins, her rapid heartbeat and the knowledge she wanted him.

He'd have to leave the house and feed soon or he wouldn't be able to continue to mask her scent. The rain had helped last night, giving him relief from his constant vigil, but as the day wore on and turned to late afternoon, James would be out hunting. Duncan knew he had to be well-fed in order to protect her.

A stinging sensation slammed into his ass and he turned with a raised eyebrow to see Rose standing behind him with the hand towel at the ready to snap him in the butt once more.

"Good thing you changed into jeans or that would've hurt a lot more." Mischief sparkled in her aqua gaze. She nodded toward the dishes. "I'm drying. It's the least I can do considering you're feeding me."

Duncan suppressed an inward groan at the effect her innocent comment had on him. His cock throbbed and his chest tightened in pent-up sexual frustration. The brief walk he'd had inside her mind only to be so effectively shut out was akin to a cock tease. He wanted to roar out his frustration.

She moved to stand beside him and her intoxicating rose scent seemed to dance seductively around him before it settled deep into his pores. Duncan backed away before he followed his natural instincts. Thoughts swirled in his mind of setting her against the counter and sinking his teeth into her throat while he rocked his raging hard-on against her soft mound preparing her before he plunged his cock into her warm, wet sheath.

When she began to dry the dishes, Duncan walked away. He pulled his acoustic guitar out of the closet and sat down on the couch to pick through a few new chords that had been rambling through his head. Anything to distract him from Rose and the primal desires she elicited in him.

"Quite the multitalented musician, aren't you?" she teased a few minutes later. Tossing her gorgeous auburn hair over her shoulder, she sat down cross-legged on the couch facing him.

At his questioning look, she said, "I saw you playing the piano last night."

Duncan's gaze locked with hers for a second before he glanced down at the guitar strings once more, strumming.

Rose continued, "I've always wanted to learn to play. I still have my mom's guitar she used when she sang songs to me as a little girl."

"It's not so hard to learn," he commented, drawn in by her interest.

She tucked her legs underneath her and scooted closer. Placing her hands on her thighs, she leaned forward to watch him. "As much as I wanted to learn, I didn't know anyone who could teach me."

Duncan's heart rammed in his chest at the thought of sharing his music with Rose. He could show her the basics, put his hands over hers so she learned to hold the instrument right. But he'd have to touch her, wrap his arms around her body. He knew he wouldn't stop there. And right now, she needed space.

Pushing the thoughts away, he set his guitar down against the couch. He glanced at Rose and his gaze landed on her necklace. The locket had come out of her shirt when she leaned toward him to watch him play.

He reached up and clasped the quarter-sized, circular locket, his curiosity piqued. Running his thumb along the unusual tick marks along the edge of the pendant, he said, "These marks make me think of Ogham." His brows drew together in confusion. "But some of them seem cut off."

Rose drew closer. "What's Ogham?"

"It's an ancient Celtic alphabet, said to be used by the Druids. Some people use it as a divination tool today."

"Divination?"

He nodded. "For guidance, a way to live one's life."

She put her hand in his and clasped the locket. A thoughtful expression crossed her face. "From what I remember, my mother was very spiritual so that would make sense."

"When did your mother pass away?" Unable to resist touching her, he wrapped his hand around her much smaller one to keep her from pulling away.

She looked back down at their clasped hands. "My mother died when I was a little girl."

"You were raised by your father then?" He moved closer to her, his body drawn to hers.

When his thigh pressed against her knees, desire flickered in her gaze. She shook her head and said in a breathless voice, "My father had an accident on his way to work one day, leaving him in a coma. My mother died that same year. After he awoke from his coma, my father was never the same. Since he was unable to take care of me, my uncle raised me."

Duncan's heart clenched at her sad family history. "Are you very close to your uncle?"

She nodded. "He's my best friend in a lot of ways."

His gaze touched on the rapidly beating pulse in her neck while the sound of her thudding heart roared in his ears.

She had a beautiful heart-shaped face with high cheekbones and the kind of lips a man only dreamed about, full and pouty. He imagined those full lips swollen from his hard kisses, sliding up and down his cock, sucking him hard. Duncan clenched his jaw as the erotic imagery slammed through him. He traced his fingers down her neck as his lips hovered close to hers. The sight of her pupils dilating and the scent of her arousal fueled his desire. Damn, he ached to slide inside her, to feel her heat surrounding him.

He knew if he kissed her, he wouldn't stop. Rose didn't need a man who wanted to throw her on the floor and have his way with her. The hunger to feed only revved his libido more. He had to assuage his need for blood or he wouldn't be able to control the beast raging inside him.

Releasing her hand, he stood. "I need to eat." He moved with swift strides toward the door and continued in terse tone, "I may be gone for a few hours. Lock the door behind me and stay inside."

"But…James?"

Duncan met her concerned gaze and answered her honestly. "He'll come out as soon as he possibly can. I will protect you, Róisín. I promise."

Rose's heart plummeted when Duncan walked out the door. She'd seen the detached look in his eyes, the way he pulled away from her. The knowledge about her past had changed everything. Disheartened at the thought, she lifted the locket and rubbed her fingers across the tick marks Duncan had seemed so interested in. When the trinity knot design in the middle of the locket moved, she gasped and removed the necklace so she could see it better.

Intrigued by the comment Duncan made about the design along the circular edge reminding him of Ogham, she used her thumb again and ran it across the raised knot design. Again the knot moved. She realized that the center part of the locket was made to move as she took hold of the knot and turned the knot on the locket in earnest. It was almost like a combination lock. She turned it left and then right, noting that the outer etch marks surrounding the locket were actually lining up with the etch marks surrounding the knot if she turned it just so.

She stared at the perfectly aligned marks, her heart racing. They meant something. But what?

Turning the locket over so she could see the back, she whispered the inscription in Irish, "*Cosain mé i gcónaí.*" She jumped when she felt the front of the locket move on its own.

Her pulse racing in her ears, Rose flipped the pendant over in her hand. She gasped to see it was open and a tiny folded piece of paper dropped into her palm.

Her hands trembled as she let the necklace slide through her fingers to land with a light thump on the couch. She held her breath while she slowly unfolded the piece of paper.

*****

He came awake suddenly, surrounded by utter darkness. A heavy weight pushed on his chest, his face, his entire body. The smell of earth permeated his senses, but he couldn't inhale or exhale, turn his head or move at all in order to decipher any other scents.

He lay in his earthbound prison, trapped and waiting to be released. Long ago he'd trained himself not to panic at the suffocating sensation that always overwhelmed him when he awoke. Soon the earth would expel him, the same way it sucked him in, no matter where he stood, no matter how far he ran. When his hour to feed was up, he ceased to exist, to breathe, to live for another year.

He lay there, counting slowly, waiting for the ground to begin to move. When he'd ticked off the allotted time and the dirt still filled his nostrils and ears—unmoving, encroaching, unforgiving—

rage sliced through him. What new torture had The Morrigan decided to inflict on him?

He summoned every bit of power he'd managed to save before the earth came to claim him and he lost consciousness a year before. The force of his anger made the earth shake and the dirt shift, and then he was suddenly expelled from his grave to land hard on his side next to a tree.

He gulped deep, life-giving breaths of air while unforgiving, cold rain lashed down on him. After a few more breaths, the scents all around him grabbed his attention. He pulled his long hair out of his eyes and wiped the caked mud from his face and beard as he jerked his head up to the sky. His gaze gravitated to the leaves on the trees. Then he slowly lowered his head to inhale close to the ground.

Spring.

He wasn't due to come out until the fall.

His eyes narrowed as he deciphered what that knowledge meant. Then a cold, ruthless smile spread across his face.

*****

Rose stared at the paper. One side read *D5431571380F*, and on the other *4NAKBONTANST6*. What did it mean? Intuitively, she knew it was some kind of code, but what?

She put her necklace back on and took the paper over to the desk near the kitchen. Rummaging through the drawers, she tried to find a pen and paper.

Rose found a notepad in the drawer, but she was unsuccessful in locating a pen or pencil. "Does the man never have a need to write anything?" she grumbled as she continued to search. Nothing.

Her gaze scanned the room, looking for a place Duncan might keep a pen. When her line of vision landed on the piano, she strode over to it with purposeful steps.

Disappointment rode through her as she stared at the blank stand. Empty and not a speck of dust either.

She was about to turn away and an idea hit her. Lifting the piano's bench seat, she grinned at the plethora of papers crammed in there. As she rifled through the stacks of music sheets, she noted many of them had been manually filled in, yet no song titles graced the tops. Duncan composed music? Why didn't he name the songs?

Still pondering the puzzle that was Duncan Mordoor, she grabbed the first pencil she came to and shut the bench lid. She'd contemplate Duncan later. Right now she had another puzzle to figure out.

* * * * *

Duncan landed on his feet as he shifted from a raven back to his human form. Covered in sweat, his entire body shook with the need to feed. He'd only made it about a mile from the secluded property before the realization hit him that James could very well use transers to continue to look for Rose during the day while he rested at night. Gritting his teeth, he'd turned back to the property and sat vigil up in a tree near his house.

As he sat there, waiting until nightfall when he'd be forced to remain inside with Rose in order to protect her, he felt every single emotion that rolled through her. He'd felt her disillusionment as he departed and his heart contracted in guilt. But when he returned, he'd been curious to discover her in deep concentration about something, excitement pumping through her.

Jealous at the thoughts of what might have caught and held her rapt attention for hours, he'd stewed and thought up all kinds of scenarios. Damn, he wished he could read her mind. But at least the brief glimpse he'd seen had marked a path to her emotions—a path he could ignore if he chose, but he didn't. He couldn't. It was his only connection to Rose. "Sharing" what Rose experienced felt right to him.

He had to admit to himself that was one of the reasons he couldn't leave to feed. The farther away he got from her, the fainter their connection became. When he could no longer feel her, hear her heart beating, he couldn't leave, not while James still presented a very real threat to her.

So he'd waited and listened to her heart, her breathing, heard her humming as she cooked herself dinner. All the while, her blood rushed through her veins. Sweet-tasting, life-giving blood. Blood he wanted desperately to savor on his tongue. By the time he'd listened to the inviting whoosh-whoosh sound of her blood thrumming through her body for hours on end, he wanted to bite the bark right off the tree he'd perched in.

His hands shook as he swiped up the clothes he'd left at the back of the house before he'd shifted. His cell phone's red message waiting light blinked like a beacon in the night, causing him to pause.

Both relieved and reluctant to check his messages, he dressed first then finally hit the button to call his voice mail.

"Duncan, it's Sabryn. James has been secured. He was caught trying to break into Eamon's estate. The summit will be over day after tomorrow. I've elevated the extent of his actions. His fate will be decided by the council during the summit. Just thought I'd let you know."

Duncan dialed Sabryn's voice mail.

"I want to be informed when he's exterminated," he said in a curt tone, then hit the End button as a sense of frustration washed over him. *I should be relieved,* he told himself. *Now I can move on.* But as he came around the front of the house and caught a whiff of Rose's scent, his groin tightened and his fangs started to lengthen.

Grinding his teeth at his body's reaction and the total loss of control that seemed to sweep over him whenever he came within fifty feet of this woman, Duncan stilled himself after he took the stairs in one leap and unlocked the front door.

Rose looked up from her position on the couch, pencil poised above her paper. "How'd it go?"

*James is secured. Collect your things. After I shower, I'm taking you home,* he spoke in her mind. He didn't want her to see his fangs, nor did he want to acknowledge the hurt look that crossed her face as he started to walk past her with purposeful strides.

"It's late. You can take me home in the morning," came her calm reply as she looked back down at her paper.

He stopped and stared at her, shocked she'd dare defy him in the dangerous mood he was in. His gaze dropped to the notepad in her lap. What had engrossed her so? he wondered. He stared at her face once more, noted the hank of red hair she'd tucked behind her ear as she bit the end of the pencil in obvious concentration.

"I haven't fed," he warned her, hoping to scare her into following his wishes.

"Then go eat." She waved her hand dismissively without looking up. "I'm in no danger now."

The hell if she wasn't. Angered by her disregard for his black mood, he flipped his hand dousing the room in darkness and growled, "When I get out of the shower, it would be best if you stayed upstairs."

He heard her intake of breath and heart rate jump up several notches. A dark, satisfied smile spread across his face before he turned on his heel and leapt to the second level.

*****

Rose shivered at the rough edge lacing Duncan's tone. He sounded dangerous, barely in control. As far as she knew, he hadn't eaten in two days. The hunger had to be gnawing at him mercilessly. Her desire to have him father a child waned compared to her desire for him to look at her the way he had before he'd discovered her past. She wanted to see hunger in his gaze, not just for satiation, but for her.

Setting the notepad aside, she turned on the light and put the folded piece of paper back in her locket, turning the trinity knot to close the clasp. Let him think she heeded his warning, but she owed him for keeping her safe and she'd always paid all debts.

Turning the light back off, she made her way upstairs in the dark. As she pulled open one of the dresser drawers, she heard the water hitting the tile floor in the shower. When her hands landed on something smooth, she paused and drew out the silk shirt. She put the shirt to her nose and inhaled, surprised she didn't smell anything. It was as if the shirt had never been worn.

A little disappointed she wouldn't be sleeping with Duncan's masculine scent surrounding her, she tugged off all her clothes and pulled on the button-down silk shirt.

The smooth material brushed against her nipples, the soft whisper arousing her. What would it feel like for Duncan to put his mouth on her nipple through the expensive material? She bit her lip. Decadent, erotic, sheer blissful torture.

She crawled in the bed and pulled the covers over her, thinking about Duncan's naked body in the shower. She'd love to run her hands down his chest, soaping the hard planes, memorizing every ridge and hollow.

Thoughts of hot water pounding down on them, Duncan's hands clasping her waist while he bent to kiss her jaw. He'd yank her close to press his lips to her neck. His hard chest would press against soft breasts…then the soap would cause their bodies to slide against one another, setting them both on fire…

Rose bit back a moan at the vivid fantasy. Her sex throbbed in keen awareness. She turned on her side, tucked her hand under the pillow, and stared at the closed bathroom door. She'd never fantasized like this.

Her heart jumped at the sound of the shower shutting off. She closed her eyes, pretending to sleep when the door opened and the bathroom light flooded the room.

Duncan's gaze weighed on her, heavy and brooding. Then the light turned off, dousing the room in darkness once more.

She held her breath and waited as his footfalls approached the bed.

"*Oíche mhaith,*" he whispered before she heard him move away.

Rose squeezed her eyes shut to hold back the tears as rejection slammed through her. She'd never felt more alone than she did at this moment.

When the piano's first notes sounded, she jerked her eyes open. Rose sat up and listened to Duncan pour his heart into the song. She felt the loneliness, the desperation, the fierce emotions in each stroke of the piano keys. It wasn't a song she recognized. From the intense up and down play she realized it had to be one of Duncan's own compositions being played in the here and now.

Her heart leapt as her hopes rose. He did feel something. His music told her so. She made her way over to the banister and stared down at him.

Once again, Duncan sat in the spotlight. This time he wore nothing but a pair of black silk lounge pants. She looked down at her shirt and smiled, wondering if she had on the other half of his pajamas. Turning, she quietly made her way down the stairs.

Duncan's eyes were closed as he played with a fierce intensity she hadn't heard the night before. Rose ran her hand across the piano top's smooth surface until she stood in front of him. She saw Duncan's shoulders tense and knew he was aware of her presence.

But he kept his eyes closed and continued to play as if she weren't there.

Pride straightened her spine. She refused to be ignored. Carefully, she hopped up on the piano top. Her silk shirt easily slid across the smooth surface as she moved to the center of the piano. Lying on her belly facing Duncan, Rose propped her chin in her palms and kicked her feet in the air. "I can't sleep. Sing me a lullaby," she said in a voice she hoped sounded seductive.

Duncan opened his eyes and the hunger she saw there before he adopted a neutral look made her stomach flip-flop, taking her breath away.

"I don't sing," he replied in a terse tone as he stopped playing.

The sudden silence in the room hung between them like a heavy curtain blocking each of their emotions from the other.

She tilted her head to the side, hoping to draw him out. "Really? I'll bet you have a beautiful voice."

He clamped his lips together while his gaze slid down the shirt she wore.

She glanced at his silk pants and grinned. "We make a complete set."

Duncan's amber eyes flared and his jaw muscle ticced. His fingers began to move across the keys once more.

She saw him fighting his desire and the knowledge made her smile. The melody Duncan played sounded so familiar, she began to hum the tune at first, trying hard to remember the lyrics. As he neared the end of the song, the words finally came to her and she sang the last verse in Irish. Then she repeated the lyrics in English with a small smile on her lips.

*"Sleep, my sweet darling*

*Knowing your guardian will come*

*Make wise your decision to call him,*

*Above all else, his protection will be done."*

Duncan let the last notes trail off. "I thought you didn't know any Irish?"

She shrugged, surprised that she remembered. It must've been a popular lullaby in Ireland. "Do you know the name of it? I'd forgotten that song until I heard you play the tune. My mother used to sing it to me sometimes at night before bed."

When he shook his head, she rolled over on her back and used her feet to turn her body until she was parallel with the keyboard. She let her head fall to the side and met his intense gaze. "Play something soothing for me."

Rose shut her eyes and waited for a long breathless moment. Once her eyes were closed, her other senses kicked in during the silence that ensued. The masculine scent of his soap teased her senses, enticing a physical reaction all the way to her bones. She had to inhale just so she could take in his scent. Yet the silence still lingered. Her entire body tensed until she felt the first notes start to play underneath her.

Duncan chose a beautiful, poignant song, slow and seductive.

With the sound right below her, she felt as if she'd become his music, not only his inspiration but a true part of him.

When fingers lightly grazed across her silk top, right over her nipple, she jumped at the contact. Goose bumps formed on her skin as the caress slid down the curve of her breast. Her gaze met Duncan's.

The look on his face was one she'd never forget—dark, intense…insatiable—sheer inevitable seduction flickered in those golden depths.

Her heart jerked in excitement when she realized he was touching her mentally, for his fingers still flew across the keys, seducing her with music. It was almost as if he were afraid to physically touch her. The thought made her heart melt.

Rose slowly closed her eyes as his invisible fingers trailed down her belly. She arched her back, unable to keep the moan from escaping her lips at the sensations he elicited within her. Her stomach tensed when a cool breeze hit her breasts. He'd unbuttoned her top and was making his way down the rest of the buttons.

The music continued to play while his touch grew bolder. His hand slid up her rib cage and cupped her breast. When he plucked at her nipple, she bent her knees and put her feet flat on the piano, keening out her pleasure.

At the same time her skin blushed in heated response, her juices flowed south, adding to the frustrating throb within her core. Duncan's presence entered her mind, fierce, dominant, demanding her surrender in body and mind.

*I want to hear what you feel,* a stór, he purred. *Let me in. A mutual sharing is far more pleasurable.*

His seductive words lured her. Her willpower slipped down a few notches when she felt his warm hand palm her inner thigh.

She opened her eyes, locking gazes with him. Though the music still played, the hand on her thigh was very real. The realization he was working the piano mentally—that he couldn't resist touching her—made her libido skyrocket. The predatory look in his eyes stole her breath to the point she thought it might never return. His grip on her leg tightened as he slowly turned her body toward him.

Rose's heart jumped to a full gallop and her breathing came in shallow pants when he clasped her hips and pulled her rear end to the edge of the piano. She barely had time to put her heels on his shoulders before he lowered his head to her body and swiped his tongue across her sex.

His intimate act caused her heart to stutter, intensifying the ache in her body. It felt so right, so incredibly erotic. Her fingers moved to tangle in his damp hair. The scent of his shampoo invaded her senses as she pulled him closer. She welcomed the thrust of his tongue deep into her core, his primal tasting of her body.

Duncan's fingers tightened on her buttocks and she felt him suck her essence. If the tension in his muscular shoulders didn't tell her how much he liked the way she tasted, the sharp pricks of his fangs brushing against her sex certainly did.

Rose stiffened at the sensation while the idea of Duncan taking her blood filled her mind. What would it feel like? Would it hurt?

*I want to know your thoughts.* His husky rasp entered her mind at the same time he ran his tongue along her clitoris. His stubble scraped the insides of her thighs, making her shiver in response.

Rose tightened her fingers in his soft hair, rocking closer to him. "Ohmigod, Duncan."

He circled his tongue around her clit, his movements slow, deliberate, purposeful. Then he placed an openmouthed kiss on her body before he let his lips hover above her clit. He bathed her throbbing nub in moist warmth, close, but not touching. *I want in,* he demanded.

Rose tried to rock against him to release the gnawing tension that had built in her body, but Duncan held firm to her rear, not letting her move.

She felt him in her mind, dangerous, ruthless, waiting.

Tears filled her eyes and her heart raced out of control. She began to shake all over but couldn't get the two words out that ran through her mind—*Please, Duncan.*

She felt his body jerk as if in surprise and then he lowered his mouth and began to suck hard on her clit. At the same time he slid two fingers into her aching core. Her heartbeat echoed in her ears, deafening her, drowning out the music. She welcomed the thrust of his fingers in her channel. His presence remained in her head, hovering, waiting, searching for a crack inside her mind, one he could slide into as easily as he did her body.

If he made her feel so out of control when he didn't know her thoughts... God, what would it be like if he walked inside her head, seducing her mentally as well?

She shivered at the idea right before her body began to spasm around his fingers. Rose cried out his name as she climaxed, rocking against his mouth, accepting the relentless thrust of his fingers deep inside her...wishing for more.

As the waves of her desire dissipated, Duncan withdrew his fingers only to replace them with his tongue. He delved deep inside her, his low groan causing goose bumps to form on her skin.

Butterflies darted in her stomach when she heard him swallow then press closer, seeking more.

Her heart rate began to pick up once more as he continued to lave at her sex. But she didn't get a chance to say a word before Duncan stood and grabbed her around the waist, lifting her off the piano.

He let her slide to the floor, but kept a firm grip on her waist as he walked her backward where he set her shoulders against the cool glass window. Rose slid her hands from his shoulders to his hard chest while Duncan pressed his hands on the glass on either side of her, blocking her in.

The sight of his hard erection jutting against the silk pants combined with the dark, hungry look in his amber eyes, made her legs tremble and a lump form in her throat. His light brown hair was tousled from her fingers running through it and his angular jaw sported the sexiest five o'clock shadow she'd ever seen. He was such a seductive man, he literally stole her breath.

Duncan's silk nightshirt hung from her shoulders leaving her body bare, open to him. He lowered his head and circled her nipple with his tongue, urging the pink tip to an even tighter bud. Blood rushed to her sex once more, flooding it in intense waves of almost painful throbbing.

She whimpered at the sensation, but gasped at the fierce desire that swept through her when he sucked her nipple deep in his mouth and bit down.

Duncan lifted his head, then stepped close, heat emanating off his body. She placed her hands on his hard chest as he pressed his erection against her lower belly and sex. When he took a deep inhaling breath near her neck, she caught the smell of her own scent on him. It was a sexy, lingering reminder of how much he seemed to enjoy pleasuring her. The thought turned her on even more. Duncan made her forget her fears. All she felt when she was with him was sheer, unadulterated desire.

His warm tongue bathed her neck at the same time a low, primal growl sounded in his throat. His chest muscles flexed under her palms as pent-up sexual tension built within him. She ran her hands down his chest to touch his abs, then splayed her fingers on either side of his trim waist. Rose felt Duncan shudder. His entire body tightened as if he fought his need to feed.

When his teeth locked on her throat, Rose gasped in pleasure. She put a hand on the back of his neck and threaded her fingers in his hair. Tilting her head, she offered herself to him.

"I know what you need, Duncan. I won't ask for more than you can give."

Warm air escaped his nostrils, bathing her neck as he inhaled then exhaled. Once. Twice. A third time. Heat and sexual tension arced between them…suspended in the air. Duncan lowered his hand to palm her bare buttock in a firm grip at the same time two pinpricks of pain sliced through her throat.

# Chapter Six

When Rose gasped at the pain, Duncan stiffened and started to pull away. But she clasped his neck, holding him in place.

"I want to know," she whispered as she pressed the tips of her breasts against his bare chest.

The pressure of Rose's hand on the back of his neck, a physical indication she wanted this, was all he needed. Duncan plunged his fangs deeper into her soft skin. He groaned in sheer ecstasy as the taste of her blood rushed forth. Sweet, untainted, intoxicating—the most unique erotic flavor he'd ever experienced.

His hips naturally rocked against her as he swallowed. Rose's moans of pleasure took his desire to new heights. He cupped her sex, wanting to take her against the glass. Fuck protection. He wanted to feel her warm juices flowing down his cock. He wanted to be buried so deep in her she'd have to let him in.

Damn, he wanted in her mind. He wanted…

Her uneven breathing coupled with her hands tugging his pants down made him want to roar. When she wrapped her fingers around his cock, he groaned. His hips began to piston back and forth. Harder. Faster.

Duncan wrapped his fingers around her wrist to stop her from pumping her hand up and down his erection, but when he heard her thoughts, *I want him to let go. I don't think he shares much of himself with others. I want him to share with me,* he let her have free rein.

His heart rammed in his chest as her soft hand gloved his cock, milking him. At the same time he began to climax, he felt her barrier give way in her mind. For a brief second, Duncan experienced all Rose's emotions and thoughts—her excitement and curiosity over his bite, her willingness to share her blood, her fears in opening her mind and how erotic it felt to feel him pulse in her hand as he climaxed against her.

All the emotion he'd never asked from another overloaded his mind as he rocked against her in the most satisfying sexual encounter he'd ever experienced.

"That was incredible," she whispered when he stopped moving. Her voice sounded weak and her grip around his cock loosened as her knees began to buckle.

Duncan swiftly withdrew his fangs and caught her before she slid to the floor. He lifted her sweet, limp body in his arms while emotions rolled through him in overwhelming waves—emotions he didn't want to examine. Before she'd opened her mind, he'd heard her thoughts a couple of times. How was that possible without being inside her mind?

Stepping out of his pants that had fallen to his ankles, Duncan kissed her temple. He knew she needed sleep to recover from her blood loss. He felt stronger, more revitalized than he ever had, while Rose wilted in his arms. As he looked down at her, he realized that in her weakened state, her mind was vulnerable enough that he could erase every memory she had of vampires from the past couple of days. But as he started to carry her upstairs, he selfishly refused to do so. He didn't want her to forget their experience together. Ever.

After he swiped his tongue across the wound in her neck, he kissed her jaw and laid her on the bed. Walking into the bathroom, he retrieved a clean washcloth and ran warm water over the cotton.

Duncan sat down beside Rose on the bed. She laid her hand on his thigh and gave him a tired smile while he bathed her. Once he was finished, Duncan had a hard time moving away. Rose tugged at his heart more than he ever expected. When her eyes began to close in exhaustion, he kissed her gently on the lips and whispered in her mind, *Sleep*, a stór.

* * * * *

Rose awoke, feeling as if she'd been heavily drugged. Her mind spun as she tried to move her limbs, but her muscles were slow to react. She realized she was in her own bed, wearing her sleep T-shirt and her soft comforter was pulled over her.

Daylight streamed through the wooden blind's slats, slanting across her bed in welcoming warmth. Memories of last night came flooding back and for a brief second she wondered if she'd dreamed it all—James hunting her, Duncan and the way he made her feel. Her heart jerked at the thought that everything she'd experienced might have come from her imagination.

She closed her eyes as tears burned and turned her head into her pillow. The action caused an ache to radiate up her neck—right from the spot Duncan had bitten deeply, taking her blood. Sobbing in relief that proof existed, she got out of bed and ran to stand in front of her dresser mirror. Turning her head, she lifted her chin and was disappointed that only a faint bruise remained. Her gaze drifted to her rosy cheeks and the mass of red hair that framed her face, now a total mess. Clasping the ends, she put them to her nose and took a deep breath. Duncan's scent still clung to the disarrayed locks.

His smell brought back arousing memories, causing an ache to spread like wildfire within her. She frowned as she released her hair. Duncan held true to his promise to return her to her home as soon as possible. After experiencing everything else with him, she'd been ready to feel his body against her, to relish his erection sliding inside her. She wanted to experience his width pressing against her walls, stretching her in delicious new ways. Her pulse raced and her heart hammered out of control at the thought.

Annoyed with herself for pining after a man who obviously didn't care enough to spend the night with her, she slammed her fist on her dresser top and spoke in a harsh tone, "Get over it, Rose. You've got better things to do—like solve the mystery your mother left behind."

The phone rang, interrupting her angry thoughts. Relieved by the distraction, she walked to her nightstand. Before she picked up the receiver she noted she had ten messages on her answering machine.

"Hello?"

"Where the hell have you been?"

Rose chuckled at her best friend's annoyed tone. "Mish, you only get this angry when you need me for something."

"I've been trying to reach you for two days," Michelle said. "Sam told me he'd seen you talking to some guy at Gus' Mart day before yesterday. I was pissed you didn't stop by the casino. You're lucky I haven't told your uncle you were so close and not one peep from you."

So much had happened the past couple of days, Rose had completely forgotten about seeing Sam. "Thanks for not telling Nigel. I've just been swamped lately."

"Don't think I didn't tell Nigel to save your sorry butt," Michelle snorted. "I didn't want anything to distract him from his mission."

"Sheesh, and here I thought I was missed."

"Oh, you're definitely wanted and this is how you're going to make it up to me—"

"Here it comes," Rose interrupted.

"I've heard nothing but awesome things about this band called Strainséir," Michelle rambled as if Rose hadn't spoken. "Yet for the life of me I couldn't find out when they were playing around town next. I figured with your investigative skills, you'd be able to help me. But now I've got that part all taken care of, this is where you come in."

Rose couldn't help but grin at her friend's moxie. She'd always loved that about Mish. "If you need me now, it'll have to wait. I'm working a case."

"Nah, I don't need you until tomorrow, early evening. That's when the band's playing at the Pavilion. Yep, you heard me right. They'll be here, at the Five Star. Surely you can take a few hours off."

Rose laughed at her friend's assumption.

"Well, you are your own boss," Michelle said, then immediately switched gears on her. "Now, back to this case you're working...do tell. You know I love all your spy stuff."

Rose snorted at the avid interest in Michelle's voice. "As if you don't have enough excitement going on at the casino, a lot of which *you* cause."

"True," she chuckled. "Are you suuure you don't need a partner in crime? I'm a fast learner."

Michelle was six years her junior and the closest to a sister she'd ever had. Many years ago, when Michelle's mother took over the chef's position in the casino's restaurant, Rose had taken Michelle under her wing. She'd always looked out for her friend, gotten her out of scrapes. At an early age, Michelle had flirted with danger on a constant basis.

If Michelle learned vampires were real… Ha! Her friend would be the first one visiting the Lion's Lair. Michelle had always faced danger with a kind of strange zealousness, hence the reason Rose would never encourage Mish to become a PI. The girl was too reckless.

"This case is personal in nature, Mish."

"Really?" Michelle sobered. "In what way?"

"My mom left me a mystery to unravel."

"How exciting! What kind of mystery?"

"I'm not really sure. She left me a locket and I think it ties to her heritage in Ireland somehow."

"That's it? That's all you're telling me?"

Rose laughed at the Michelle's miffed tone. "That's all I know at the moment. Hopefully I'll know more by the time I come by the casino tomorrow. Er, is this something I'm going to regret?" she thought to ask at the last minute.

"Of coooourse not," Michelle replied with confidence. "Trust me."

"Now *that* scares me." Rose chuckled. "See you tomorrow," she said, then punched the off button on the phone.

*****

Once Rose took a shower, she shrugged into an old sweatshirt and pulled out her mother's guitar from the closet. Sitting on her bed, she placed her fingers over the strings as she'd seen Duncan do and strummed. The acoustic guitar sounded like it needed to be tuned, but she smiled and continued strumming because, even off-key, the sound brought back wonderful memories of her mother singing to her when she was a child.

After a good forty minutes of messing around with the guitar, she returned the instrument to the closet with a mental note to have it tuned. As she stood in front of her mirror combing out her hair, her mind drifted to Duncan. *What is he doing now? He never did tell me what he did for a living. What kind of careers do vampires have? What does a person who lives for a very long time do to occupy his time? For that matter, just how old is Duncan?* She smirked and shook her head. She really didn't want to know.

The smell of shampoo in her damp hair reminded her of their encounter against the window last night. As a rush of desire shot through her at the thought, she met her own aqua gaze in the mirror and was surprised to see the rose color on her fair cheeks. Damn the man. Look what he did to her. She set down her comb with conviction and started to turn away from the mirror and her thoughts of one sexy vampire, when her gaze landed on her sweatshirt.

She tilted her head and stared at the words University of Chicago on her sweatshirt—well, the words ogacihC fo ytisrevinU as reflected by the mirror. Realization dawned and she dashed into her living room for a piece of paper.

The notepad she'd been using at Duncan's house awaited her on the table, her keys beside it. Duncan had written a note on the bottom of the page.

*Word jumbles, Róisín?*

That was it. No "I'll see you later". No "Thanks for the snack and semi-sex". Nothing.

Anger boiled within her but she tamped the emotion down. This is what she wanted. No strings attached. No man in her life. To move on without emotional attachments.

Right?

Shaking herself out of her musings, she sat down at the table and looked over her notes where she'd jotted the message from her mother.

*D5431571380F*

Staring at the sequence of numbers, she rewrote them, reversing the order.

*F0831751345D*

Her heart pounded as she rewrote the last letter. She recognized the first six numbers before her. It was her birth date with four additional numbers tacked on the end.

Rose furrowed her brow. What did the letters at the beginning and the end as well as the four additional numbers represent?

Deciding to set that puzzle aside for a minute, she moved on to the other clue.

*4NAKBONTANST6*

Could it really be that simple? She wondered as she glanced between the two sets she was trying to decode. F was the sixth letter in the alphabet and D was the fourth, just like the number six and the number four on the other un-decoded piece.

*F0831751345D*

*4NAKBONTANST6*

Applying the same decoding method, she reversed the whole jumble in the un-decoded part, then separated the letters into a set of six and a set of four.

*6TSNATNO BKAN4*

Staring at the last set of four letters, her heart thudded as she immediately deciphered the second word. *Bank*. Then she moved to the first set of letters.

TSNATON

Stanton Bank? Yes, Stanton Bank!

The piece of paper held her birth date, the name Stanton Bank…and the mysterious last four numbers. She sat back in the chair, biting her lower lip. The number was too short to be a bank account. Other than bank accounts, what did people have at a bank? An idea struck her and she stood to retrieve her phonebook from the drawer in the kitchen. Flipping to Stanton Bank's listing, her pulse raced as she dialed the number of a nearby branch.

"Stanton Bank, how may we help you?"

"Hi, I'm considering opening an account at your bank. Will I get a free safety deposit box with my account?"

"Yes, if you open both a saving and a checking account," the girl answered cheerfully.

"That's good to know," Rose replied. "I'm the worlds worst with numbers. I'll have my bank account numbers on my checks, but please tell me the safety deposit box number is a short one. I have a tendency to lose paperwork, too," she went on, sounding as scatterbrained as she could.

The woman laughed. "Our boxes are only four digits long, so I think you'll be okay."

Bingo, she thought, then remembered to answer, "Whew, sounds good to me. Oh, one last question. How many branches does your bank have? I'd like to know there'll be a branch close to me no matter where I am in town."

"We have twenty in Chicago and surrounding areas."

"Thank you for your help."

When she hung up, Rose mumbled, "Wonderful. I get to trek to twenty Stanton Bank branches today."

Invigorated that she'd gotten somewhere with her mother's note from her locket, yet even more intrigued by her mother's need for a coded message, she walked into her bedroom to get dressed.

Once she'd pulled on a pair of jeans, a lightweight navy blue sweater and a pair of tennis shoes, Rose headed for the front door. Her cell phone rang, drawing her attention. Trekking back to the kitchen table, she picked up her cell and stared at the caller ID. It was Mr. Reed, her client.

Seven thousand dollars! her mind screamed while her fingers itched to answer the call.

*Is this the only way, Rose? You'll find other clients who won't put Duncan's race at risk.* Shaking her head, she set the phone back down on the table and let it go to voicemail. She really didn't know what she was going to say to Mr. Reed anyway.

"I'll find another way," she said out loud with conviction. Right now, she figured it was best to settle her own past before she could think about her future.

With that encouraging thought, she picked up her keys and headed for her front door. Rose stopped in her tracks when she remembered the last time she saw her car was at the gas station across from the casino. *Damn. It's probably been towed.*

She *could* take her motorcycle, though she didn't relish the idea of driving to several bank branches on her bike. Opening her front door, she held her breath as she peered outside. Relief washed over her to see her car sitting in the driveway, repaired window and all.

"He won't leave me a note, yet he has my car returned in mint condition? That vamp continues to confound me," she grumbled to herself as she locked her house and headed for her car.

* * * * *

Several hours later, Rose pulled into the parking lot of the twentieth Stanton Bank branch, her patience coming to an end. After striking out at the first two banks, she tried her best to get them to give her the range of numbers on the safety deposit boxes by branch, but since she didn't have a key, they refused to give that information out, telling her she had to visit the branches and ask the individual managers for their help. So she'd driven to every single freaking branch, her optimism quickly evaporating with each failure.

As she approached the doors to the last bank, she raised her frustrated gaze to the sky saying, "Mom, this better be the branch."

Rose blew out a breath to release pent-up tension and pulled open the door to the building. She couldn't fail. Her mother left her that message for a reason.

A young girl behind the counter called out, 'Hi, can I help you?"

"Yes, I'd like to speak with your manager please," Rose replied, approaching the counter.

The girl shook her head, her dangle earrings bobbing against her cheeks. "He's not in right now, but the assistant manager is available. Would you like me to get him for you?"

She nodded and waited while the girl went to one of the offices and knocked on the closed door.

She came back to Rose, smiling. "Go on in, he'll see you now."

Rose clutched her purse and approached the short man who'd exited his office with his hand extended. "Hello, I'm Dan. How may I help you today?"

Grasping his hand, Rose gave it a firm shake. "Rose Sinclair. I'm here to discuss safety deposit boxes."

He nodded, asking, "So you have an account with us?"

She released his hand and shook her head. "No, that's what I'm here to discuss with you."

His smile broadened and he turned with a sweep of his arm toward his office. "Then by all means, come in and let's talk."

Preceding him into his office, Rose sat down across from the man's neatly organized desk.

Once he was seated, Dan began. "So what kind of account are you looking to set up at Stanton, Ms. Sinclair?"

Rose shook her head and pulled her driver's license from her purse. "Actually, I'm here about a safety deposit box I believe my mom has at this branch." Handing him a piece of paper with her mother's name and the safety deposit box number on it, she continued, "Here's the information."

Dan looked at the piece of paper and nodded. "Yes, this is one of our box numbers. I'll need you to provide an ID before I can proceed."

Glad to know the bank took their customer's privacy seriously, she handed him her driver's license.

He glanced at the ID and nodded his approval before handing it back to her.

While she put her license away, Rose's heart rate picked up as excitement filled her. It *would* be the very last branch though, she thought with an inward groan. She should've gone in reverse order when she went down the list of branches… Argh!

The assistant manager met her gaze and put out his hand. "I presume you also have the key?"

She bit her lip, then shook her head. "My mother died when I was a little girl. Our house was sold so I have no idea where the key is."

Dan smiled and turned toward his keyboard. Tapping the keys, he said, "Well, let's see if you're listed as a co-owner or beneficiary."

After a few seconds, he frowned and mumbled, "That's strange."

Her heart jerked at his comment. She sat forward in the leather chair, gripping the edge of his desk. "What's strange?"

Dan looked at her and shook his head. "The account is flagged for manager approval only. I'm sorry, but you'll have to wait until Mr. Wainright gets back from his errand."

Disbelief washed over her. To be so close. "Are you serious?"

He nodded. "Yes. You're welcome to wait in the lobby. Mr. Wainright should be back in about twenty minutes or so."

Frustration mounted as Rose walked into the lobby. *Man, I sure could use some of Duncan's vampire powers right about now. What I wouldn't give to be able to compel the man to let me see my mother's safety deposit box.*

Rose couldn't help but wonder about the effort her mother went to in order to hide this safety deposit box. She'd bet her last dollar her father didn't even know of its existence. Settling onto the lobby's cushioned couch, she regretted leaving her cell phone behind. At least while she waited, she could've been catching up on phone calls. One of which needed to be to Mr. Reed to let him know he'd need to find someone else to take his case.

After thirty minutes, Rose glanced at her watch impatiently. The tellers were balancing their drawers and putting their money in the vault, ready to lock up for the evening.

Firm resolution stole over her. No way was she leaving this bank until she had a look at her mother's safety deposit box.

"Ms. Sinclair?" Dan said from behind her.

Rose looked up, her stomach tensing. She was ready to refuse to leave.

"Mr. Wainright will see you now. His office is the first one on the left."

Rose stood and walked over to Mr. Wainright's office.

An older man with snow-white hair came around from behind his desk, an apologetic look on his wrinkled face.

"I'm Frank Wainright. Please come in and have a seat, Ms. Sinclair." Clasping her hand briefly, he apologized. "I'm sorry you had to wait so long. My meeting took longer than anticipated."

"As long as you tell me I can see my mother's safety deposit box, I don't mind," she said with a smile as she shook his hand then sat down across from his desk.

He shut his door behind her, chuckling. "I see you inherited your mother's forthright ways."

"You knew my mother?" She jerked her head in his direction, following him until he sat down behind his desk.

His blue eyes twinkled. "Indeed I did. She was a wonderful woman and very protective of you, I might add," he finished with a smile as he pointed to her.

"Really?" Her stomach knotted at his comment. "In what way?"

Tapping the keys on his keyboard, he said, "She was very particular about her safety deposit box. I tried to get her to put your father's name on it, but she said it was for your eyes only." A sad look crossed his face. "I'm sorry your mother has passed on, but she was insistent no other name be put on the box but yours. So I followed her wishes."

Rose smiled. "Thank you for doing that." Lifting her empty hands in the air, she commented, "I don't have a key. Is that going to be a problem?"

Frank slid a key across the desk toward her. "Here you are."

She glanced up at him in surprise. "You had the key?"

He nodded. "Yes. Your mother said she didn't trust to leave it at home. That it might get lost. She asked that I keep it safe for you."

Rose picked up the key and stared at it, her heart racing.

"Ready to check out that box now, young lady?"

She nodded and followed him out to the empty branch lobby. It was eerily quiet since all the customers and other employees had gone home.

"I'm sorry to make you stay late," she thought to say as she followed him into the vault.

"It's not a problem." Stopping in front of a row of metal boxes he inserted a key in box 1345 and looked at her expectantly. "Your turn."

Rose glanced down at the key in her sweaty palm. Butterflies flitted around in her stomach as she inserted her matching key into its slot and they both turned their keys at the same time.

Frank slid the safety deposit box out and Rose followed him out of the vault to a side room.

Setting the box down on a small round wooden table, he met her gaze. "I've got some paperwork to do, so take all the time you need. Just give me a yell when you're ready to put it back."

Rose nodded and held her breath until he walked out and shut the door behind him.

Her pulse thundered in her ears as she pulled out the wooden chair and sat down in front of the long metal box. What had been so important that her mother went to all this trouble? And why had her mother not told her father?

Rose wiped her damp hands on her jeans and placed them on the box's metal sides to steady them. Taking a deep breath, she lifted the lid.

There were three envelopes in the box. Rose opened the first envelope and pulled out a folded letter. The sight of her mother's handwriting brought tears to her eyes. Swiping away the dampness, she focused on the letter.

*My dearest Róisín,*

Rose's heart jerked at the name Róisín. That had to be her name in Irish, the same name Duncan used whenever he spoke to her.

*Yes, that is your true given name. You always were my "little rose". If you can't read the letter in the second envelope, that's my fault. I thought to protect you by keeping you from learning Irish, but if you've gotten this far, then my guess is you already know a little bit. I wrote the other letter in Irish because I wanted you to seek counsel to better understand the importance of the history I was forbidden to speak of.*

*Don't talk to anyone about this. Instead, go straight to Galway City in county Galway, Ireland. There's a pub there called Lonán's. When you arrive, ask to speak with Siobhán. She'll take care of you while you're there and put you in contact with a man who will explain everything to you. Look for a deeper meaning in his words of advice, Rose. There's a reason we called him Saoi.*

*It's important you embrace your heritage now. Just be as prepared as you can in case you need to protect yourself.*

*Tá grá agam duit—I love you...that's your first lesson in Irish. Learn all you can.*

Rose set the letter aside, pondering at the unspoken things her mother had been forbidden to talk about. She opened the second letter and true to her mother's word, it was a five-page handwritten letter all in Irish. Frustration filled her. She couldn't go to Ireland. It would cost a fortune. How the hell was she going to find out what it said?

Duncan.

The name popped into her mind, almost as if an echo. She instantly shook her head. Her mother was adamant she trust no one but this *Saoi* person to explain the letter to her. Now what was she going to do?

Duncan, her mind repeated.

Well, he did trust her with his own secrets. It wasn't every day one discovered vampires exist. Again, her mother's warning rang in her head and she dismissed asking Duncan for help.

Sighing, she opened the last envelope and smiled at the notepaper clipped to a stack of cash.

*Did you really think I'd make it so hard for you to fly to the land of your forefathers, my darling? There's enough money for tickets, lodging and food while you're in Ireland. Spend it wisely and while you're there, keep your eyes open and trust your instincts until you can meet with the Saoi.*

At least she already had her passport, thanks to a trip to South America a client funded last year. Rose put all the documents and money in one envelope and left the other two empty ones in the safety deposit box. Tucking the stuffed envelope away in her purse, she closed the box and walked out of the room.

Mr. Wainright came out of his office when he saw her in the lobby.

"Are you done now?"

She nodded and handed him the box. "Yes, thank you for your time. Do I need to sign that I took some of my mother's things from the box?" she asked.

He shook his head as he took the box from her. "No, but you'll need to come with me to relock the box."

*****

Duncan pulled on a T-shirt and a pair of black jeans, his thoughts drifting to Rose once again. She'd haunted his mind for the past two days. Never had he relished satiating his hunger as he did with Rose. Yes, he'd needed her blood, but it went deeper than satisfying an empty stomach. While he'd reveled in every swallow he took, his only regret was that he wasn't driving his cock inside her sweet body at the same time.

A shudder of deep desire passed through him each time he played out their mind- blowing encounter in his head. Not only had he tasted her blood and heard her heart racing, but he'd felt every life-giving pound of her heart as if it were his own, experienced her euphoria at being bitten and the sexual power she felt when he came against her.

When it was over, his cock had immediately hardened again. He'd wanted to take her against the glass, hear her panting as he drove into her, experience her thrill when he sank his teeth into her neck again…and again.

The entire scenario was unlike anything he'd ever experienced and it scared the shit out of him. Too much emotion, too much mutual sharing, too much…everything.

After he'd bathed Rose, he'd been overwhelmed with all the emotions running rampant in his mind. Duncan sent her to sleep with his mind racing.

As promised, he took her home. He'd walked away with the hope he'd be able to forget how he felt when he was around her, how much she made him feel off-kilter.

Only, he hadn't been able to forget. Instead, for the last couple of days, he literally ached to know what her warm channel felt like surrounding him, taking him deep, her firm thighs wrapped around his hips.

Shaking himself out of his lustful thoughts, Duncan focused on returning a few phone calls and setting up another gig. But in the end curiosity got the best of him. He called his mother.

"Hey, Mom."

"Well, hello, my long-lost son," she replied.

"I'm not *that* absent," he shot back in a dry tone.

"I'm just shocked to hear from you. I'm usually the one who calls you."

He laughed at the smile he heard in her voice. "Wonders never cease. Actually, I do have a question."

"That's what I thought."

Duncan ignored her assured tone. She always did have a knack of knowing when something was on his mind.

"You remember that lullaby you used to sing Ian and me when we were kids?" He rambled off the last few lyrics that Rose had sung the other night.

"Yes. Why do you ask?"

"Was that a very popular lullaby in Ireland? Last night I did a search for it on the net and I came up with zilch."

"It was regionally known, only in small pockets."

That's kind of vague, he thought, wondering at the hesitation he sensed in his mother's response. "Where did you say you were from?"

"County Galway."

"Do you miss your homeland?"

She sighed. "My life is here and has been for a very long time."

Before he could ask her another question, she said, "Now you've got me curious. What made you think of that lullaby?"

"A human woman sang it the other night."

"Human?" she asked, sounding intrigued.

"She's of Irish descent."

"Interesting. Were both her parents from Ireland?"

"No. I got the impression only her mother came from Ireland."

"Does this woman you talked to have any Irish?" she asked, more than idle curiosity lacing her tone.

"No. Her mother refused to teach her." Duncan picked up on his mother's vibe. She was definitely thinking deeply about something. Unfortunately Tressa Mordoor was the only person who seemed to be able to consistently block his mind-reading ability. Since she was his parent, he'd respected her need for privacy and never tried to break through her mental barriers.

"Ah, someone from my homeland. I would love to speak to this woman's mother. Do you know her name?"

"Rose never said her mother's name other than mentioning she'd passed away."

"That's such a shame. I would've loved to converse with her, since my *boys* aren't around often enough to speak our language. So tell me about this human you have so much interest in," his mother teased.

"There's nothing to tell," he responded in a brisk tone. "She was a case I took on for Ian. I saved her and now we've gone back to our own lives."

"A case? Unless things have changed in the last couple of weeks, I know only Ian hunts down rogue vampires. What does this woman have to do with rogue vampires?"

"Everything. A rogue vampire kidnapped her."

"Who kidnapped her?"

"James Connor, and holy hell did I learn an important lesson about the Sythens' vast shape-shifting ability. I'm going to kick the shit out of Ian for not warning me. My back still aches from the encounter."

"Everyone knows the Sythens can shape-shift to more than a raven," Tressa admonished with a chuckle.

"To creatures many times larger than their own body weight and mass?"

"Uh, no..." His mother paused, sounding tense. "I wasn't aware of that. Are you okay? Did you kill James?"

"I'm fine. James is currently being held until Eamon gets back from the summit. His fate is being decided by the council, but if they don't vote to eliminate him, I'll do it myself."

"Did James hurt the woman?"

"No, but he's obsessed with her and determined to possess her despite her wishes to the contrary."

"I'm sure the council will make the right decision."

"I'll make sure they do," he replied in a steely tone. Just then the call-waiting beeped on his phone. Work called.

"Gotta go."

"Duncan..." his mother called out before he could hang up.

"Yeah?"

"It was nice to hear from you. Let's not make it a year before we talk again, hmmm?"

"Yes, Mother," he replied, then hung up, switching to the other line.

"What do you have for me?"

* * * * *

Rose drove home that night, exhausted after her long day "branch hopping". She made a quick sandwich and went straight to bed. All night she dreamed of Ireland, her necklace and people speaking Irish all around her. Even Duncan appeared in her dream, speaking to her in Irish. She couldn't understand a word he said, but his sexy voice entranced her.

*She walked up to him. "I can't understand what you're saying, Duncan."*

*He pulled her against his chest and ran his hands down her spine to cup her rear in his hands. Jerking her hips flush with his, he whispered in her mind,* Then guess what I'm saying I want to do to you, *a ghrá.*

*Her heart racing, she ran her hands up his shoulders until she clasped his neck. Pulling his mouth close, her gaze locked with his burning golden one. Her lips met his at the same time she answered him mentally,* There are some things that even transcend language barriers.

*Duncan rocked his erection against her and growled low in his throat, thrusting his tongue past her lips. He plundered her mouth, aggressive and dominant, arousing her to a fever pitch of desire.*

*Clasping her buttocks tight, he lifted her up in his arms at the same time he spoke to her in Irish. The seductive tone of his words left no room for misunderstanding what he wanted. She slid her arms around his neck and wrapped her legs around his waist, clutching him tight as his fangs sank into her neck.*

Rose awoke with her heart racing and a throbbing ache between her thighs. She vividly remembered her enjoyment of speaking mentally with Duncan, the excited anticipation of his teeth puncturing her skin and the tugging pull as he sucked, taking her blood. She'd love that kind of sexual power over him. To make him anticipate *her* bite like that. Then again, she'd have to have fangs—something she was definitely lacking.

She gritted her teeth in frustration that the man had not only made her body beg for his, but the vamp now invaded her psyche through her dreams. Rose threw back the covers and stomped off toward the shower, vowing to take a cold one.

While the cold water caused goose bumps to form all over her body, Rose disconnected herself from the emotions that her dream had elicited as well as her thoughts of Duncan in general. Instead, she focused on her need to discover what her mother's letter said.

She'd cleared her calendar for a week in order to fly to Ireland and visit this *Saoi* her mother insisted she see. After she'd fulfilled her commitment to Michelle tonight, she'd visit with her father once more before she took the first flight out to Ireland.

Now that she had a solid plan in her mind, Rose turned the shower off, toweled her body dry, then stood in front of the mirror combing out her wet hair.

Thoughts of Duncan kept creeping into her mind, but she pushed them away, resolving to focus on her upcoming trip and not the seductive vampire who seemed to occupy her thoughts way more than a one-night stand should.

* * * * *

As Rose pulled her motorcycle into a parking spot reserved for Five Star Casino guests, Sam walked out of the riverboat's main door and headed down the walkway. Birds flying overhead squawked as he crossed the dock toward the parking lot.

She got off her bike and removed her helmet, waiting for him as he approached. Minus the do-rag wrapped around his head, his short blond crew cut accented his square jaw well. The navy suit jacket, khaki slacks and dress shoes he now wore transformed him from the rough biker guy she'd seen three days ago, to the imposing-looking head of security he portrayed at the casino.

"Lookin' sharp there, Sambo," she teased as she opened a compartment on her bike and withdrew her purse.

He narrowed his gaze on her before he pulled her into a bear hug. "Why the hell didn't you come visit us the other day? You mentioned stopping by when I saw you getting gas."

*Man, Duncan's mind erasing really does work.* Wrapping her arm around Sam's waist, she walked with him toward the entrance of the casino.

"I'm sorry, Sam. I ran out of time before I had to meet my client." Dang, she hated having to lie to him.

Glancing back at her bike, he returned his gaze to hers. "We need to go riding together. We haven't done that in a long time."

"How about a rain check?" she asked as she walked side by side with Sam across the dock and up the gangway to get to the boat.

He tapped the end of her nose, a smile on his face. "And I'm going to hold you to it, Rosie."

As they entered the boat, several casino workers called out "Rosie!" interrupting their repartee. Rose smiled and waved, enjoying the early morning quiet. A couple of slot machines pinged in the distance and a few diehard gamblers littered the blackjack tables. There was always a general buzz of conversation that accompanied the casino, no matter what the time of day.

But by nightfall, people staying in her uncle's Five Star Hotel across the street or concert attendees from the Five Star Pavilion next to the hotel would be packed on the boat, gambling away. Loud voices and cheers could be heard as people won or lost a round. The bells and pings of all the slot machines going at once always made a cheerful accompaniment. She'd thrived in this vibrant yet unconventional environment.

"Where's Nigel?" she asked, scanning the room for her energetic uncle.

"Rose, my lovely," her uncle called from across the casino as he entered the main room from a side door. He waved to her, while he pressed his cell phone to his ear.

Even if Nigel hadn't called her name, she'd have spotted him in two seconds flat as soon as he entered the room. His bright orange hair was hard to miss.

"Orange, eh?" she said with a fond smile. "That's a new one."

Sam chuckled. "Yeah, he's getting more daring in his old age. And strangely it works for him."

"Tell my uncle I'll be in his office," she said as she turned and headed for the closed door to the left of the cashier's booth.

Closing the heavy wood door, Rose walked behind her uncle's desk and flopped into his expensive, cow print leather chair. Now that the sounds of the casino no longer distracted her, she thought of Duncan again and how easy it would be to ask him for his help translating that letter from her mother. She wished she had some way of getting in touch with him.

Opening the drawer to her uncle's see-through, Plexiglas desk, she chuckled that Nigel had commented he had "nothing to hide" the day it was delivered to his office. Once she pulled out a phonebook, she flipped to the Ms and wasn't surprised she didn't find a Duncan Mordoor listed. He struck her as a loner-type, not one to draw attention to himself or make it easy to find him.

She was in the process of putting the phonebook back when her uncle walked in, still talking on his cell phone.

The strobe light tip of his cell's antenna was pressed against his bright orange hair, making it seem to glow. Rose smiled. Unlike Duncan, her uncle attracted attention like a magnet. He thrived on it.

"Can you hear me better?" he said as he closed the door. "Good. Listen, Jane. I want the band for two nights. I know I already have him for one night. I'll pay his blasted fee for the additional night. He's a hot commodity and my Pavilion could use the headline."

As she listened to her uncle negotiate with the booking agent, she was reminded all over again why he'd been so successful. For all his flamboyant ways, Nigel was a shrewd businessman. He didn't mince words as he went after what he wanted. He constantly amazed her.

When he hung up the phone with a slight frown still on his face, she said with confidence, "You'll get him."

His brilliant blue eyes met hers. "I don't know, sweetie. This is the hardest I've worked to get an act in a long time and for a guy who's never recorded an album, no less," he said in frustration.

"Really?" she asked.

Nodding, he sat down in the guest chair across from his desk and crossed his legs. He gave her a stern look as he smoothed out his black leather pants. "Enough about business. Tell me…what has caused my absentee niece to grace me with her presence?"

She frowned. "I've been around."

Nigel snorted. "The last time you were here, I'd just revamped an entire floor on the boat."

Had it really been that long? Two months? Straightening in her chair she replied truthfully, "Sorry, Nigel. I've been working several cases."

Sitting forward, Nigel put his elbows on his knees. "Is this about the money you need for your procedure?" He frowned. "Damn it, Rose. You're so freakin' stubborn. You know I'll pay for it, just like I've offered to pay for my brother's expenses."

"I wish I'd never told you about that," she mumbled as she sat back in the seat.

"I'm family. Though I think wanting to be a single parent is a bit unorthodox—" he began before she interrupted him.

"Like you can talk, Mr. I-can't-make-up-my-mind."

"Hey, I can't help the fact *everyone* looks beautiful to me," he replied, totally unapologetic about his bisexuality.

"The point is, you made our not-so nuclear family work for us and I turned out just fine."

"A little too stubborn for my tastes."

"You love me just the way I am."

"So true." He sighed and sat back in his seat. "Okay, so what gives? Why the impromptu, early morning visit?"

Rose stilled herself, hoping she worded this just the right way so as not to raise her uncle's suspicions. Handing him the banker's business card with her savings account number handwritten on the back, she said, "I wanted you to know that I've made sure you can get to my savings if, heaven forbid, something should happen to me."

Nigel sat forward again, worry creasing his brow. "What's wrong?"

"Nothing." She shrugged in a nonchalant manner. "I just wanted to make you aware."

"No one 'makes arrangements' unless they think something is going to happen to them. I deserve to know."

"Really, Nigel, it's nothing. I'm just going to take a trip to Ireland to learn a little about my mom's heritage. When I eventually get pregnant, I want to be able to share it with my child. So I wanted my affairs taken care of before I left…just in case."

"Ahhh." He nodded his understanding. "How about someone to go with you to Ireland? Here I am, fifty years old and I've never been outside the US. I'd love to see the beautiful island. I could help you share the memories with my grandchild."

Rose's heart swelled at the love that shone in her uncle's eyes and how easily he called a future child of hers his "grandchild". What kid wouldn't want to grow up surrounded by so much love?

"Awww, now you're making me all teary," she said as she came around his desk.

As he stood and straightened to his full five-foot-ten-inch height, Nigel pulled her into his arms and kissed her cheek. "I love you like my own, Rose. You know I'd do anything for you."

She nodded as she buried her nose in his white cotton shirt, inhaling the sweet, yet commanding cologne he wore. A scent that was so Nigel.

"Yes, I know you would, but I need to take this trip to Ireland by myself. Hey, if you're in the mood for visiting, you *could* go see your brother," she insisted, wishing she could bridge the twenty-year generation gap that had always been a wedge between the brothers.

Nigel sighed. "I know George loves me, but you know we've never really talked on the same level. He'll never accept my bisexuality. It just makes visits with him, well…tense."

She nodded her understanding. "I know, but you can't blame me for trying."

"Keep trying, my sweet. Maybe one day, I'll go and he'll accept me as I am."

She kissed his cheek. "I'm here to hang with Michelle and then catch the act tonight at the Pavilion."

"That band better be worth what I'm paying them," he grumbled, then a hopeful look crossed his face. "You know your room's always available if you decide to stay the night," he suggested.

Rose chuckled. "Always finagling…"

"Why is it so hard for you to consider selling your house and moving into the hotel? I'd like to see you *use* the suite I have reserved for you more than a night or two. You'd have food and everything you need…for free. You have no idea how much I regret that I couldn't help you early on when you had to sell your parents' home to pay for George's medical bills. I wish you would allow me to help you now."

Nigel had never stopped trying to get her to come live in one of the suites. It had always been a longstanding battle of wills between them.

She pinned him with a stern look. "When I have a child, I'd like him or her to grow up in a house on a quiet neighborhood street."

"You did just fine."

Guilt stabbed her in the stomach at his hurt look. "That's not what I meant. You know as well as I do that any child of mine will know this casino and hotel inside and out before he or she is three years old."

"Best you remember that," he said as a pleased smile curved his lips.

She gave him a squeeze and let go. "Well, I'm going to go find Michelle."

Nigel's cell phone started to ring as she opened the door.

"Tell me you have good news," he began, then blew her a kiss before she shut the door behind her.

* * * * *

"Rose!" Michelle called from across the casino's main room as soon as Rose shut Nigel's office door. Michelle darted around people, past rows of blackjack tables, her quick speed belying her height. Rose smiled that Mish's six-foot height always made it easy to find her in a crowd.

When the younger woman finally reached her and pulled her into a tight bear hug, Rose let out a cough. "Hey, ease up there, Mish. You might be as skinny as a twig, but you've got a grip like a lumberjack."

Michelle let her go, grinning. "Sorry, but I can't help myself. I'm just so glad to see you."

Looking up into her friend's face, Rose returned her smile. "It's good to see you, too."

Michelle tilted her head to the side and squinted. "Something about you looks different." She looked Rose up and down. "I can't put my finger on it, but you seem to glow. Ohmigod." Michelle's eyes lit up. She grabbed Rose by the hand and jerked her through the throng of people to the casino's exit.

"Hey, what's up?" Rose laughed at Michelle's strange behavior as her friend dragged her across the street and into the Five Star Hotel, punching the elevator button.

The elevator opened and Mish pulled her inside, pushing the number to take them to her room on the bottom floor.

As the elevator zipped down a couple of floors, Mish's deep blue gaze met hers. "You've met someone."

Rose's chest constricted at her comment. Was it that obvious? Had Duncan left his mark on her so thoroughly?

Avoiding Mish's penetrating gaze, she glanced at the elevator doors that had just opened when they reached the bottom floor and mumbled, "What makes you say that?"

"It's the look in your eyes, Rose." Without another word, Michelle yanked her out of the elevator and down the hall to her room. Picking up the keycard that hung by a string at her neck, Michelle slid it in the lock and opened her door.

Rose allowed Mish to drag her inside, then she moved over to the bed while Michelle shut the door.

Standing beside the door, an expectant look on her face, Michelle took two big steps, then took a flying leap to land on her bed. "You're glowing."

Rose's chest still felt tight at the fact Michelle had read her so easily.

"Do tell!" Michelle continued, facing her as she crossed her long legs Indian-style on the bed, an excited look on her face.

Duncan's vampire status aside, Rose preferred not to talk about him. She didn't even know what she felt for the man other than annoyed frustration.

At her silence, a hurt look replaced Michelle's animated expression.

"You aren't going to tell me, are you?"

Rose shook her head. "It's…complicated."

A horrified expression crossed Michelle's face. She reached out and gripped Rose's hand. "This new man in your life…he didn't hurt you, did he? I'll kill the bastard!"

Rose's stomach clenched at the idea that Michelle could think Duncan would hurt her. No matter what had passed between them, she knew in her heart he'd never intentionally hurt her. Ever.

But she understood where her friend was coming from. Michelle was the only person she'd told about the rape. As painful as it was to talk about it, she'd told Mish when the younger girl had turned sixteen. Rose wanted to protect her devil-may-care friend from herself, to warn her just what could happen if she didn't keep her faculties about her.

"I know what you're thinking." She put her hand over Michelle's and answered as honestly as she could. "I'm just not ready to talk about him yet, maybe…never. But I promise you I'll never allow another man to hurt me, not while I'm still breathing."

Mish gave her an understanding smile. "I just worry about you." Unbending her long legs, she let them dangle over the side of the bed and scooted closer to her. She wrapped her arm across Rose's shoulders. "You're my 'big sister'. I only want what's best for you."

Rose counted her blessings at the number of people who'd shown her love and kindness despite the rocky bumps she'd been dealt in life.

Tugging on a long dark curl hanging over Mish's shoulder, she said, "I love you, too, kid sis. I promise I'll tell you if and when there's something to tell."

At the dejected look on Michelle's face, she continued in an upbeat tone, "But I do have some news about the note my mom left me."

"Lay it on me." Michelle grinned, rubbing her hands together.

Pulling the envelope out of her purse, Rose opened the letter from her mother and relayed the contents to Michelle.

Michelle glanced at Rose's locket. "And you discovered the existence of this because of the locket she left you?"

Rose nodded, smiling at the excited blush that had colored Michelle's cheeks.

"When are you going to Ireland?"

She chuckled that her friend knew her so well. "As soon as I can get a flight, I'm going."

"I want to go with you. I've got savings. I'll talk Nigel into letting me take vacation early. He has plenty of backup dealers."

Rose met her friend's determined gaze. "This is something I need to do by myself, Mish. I have a feeling it won't be my last trip to Ireland. I promise you can go with me next time."

Michelle sighed her understanding. "You'd better keep that promise."

Rose nodded with a grin. "Now that I've spilled about my news, tell me about this event you're dragging me to this evening."

# Chapter Seven

ꕥ

Rose stood, crushed in the crowd of Strainséir fans. Michelle hopped up and down in her excitement for the show to begin. Glancing down at Rose, Michelle yelled over the noise, "Try to look more excited, Rose. From what I've heard of this band, it'll be a show you'll never forget."

"The things I do for my friends," Rose mumbled as she prepared to plug her ears with her fingers. Women surrounded her, ranging in age from young teens to well in their fifties. The disparity in their ages surprised her. But hey, if a mother and her daughters could enjoy this music together, then the band couldn't be that bad, she thought, turning her focus to the stage.

The house lights went down, dousing the room in darkness. The deafening roar of screaming fans grew around her, making the tiny hairs on her arms stand on end. This was fandom at its heightened pitch. A blue light lit up the raised floor, creating a shadowed outline of each band member standing on stage.

The effect elicited the appropriate response. Fans rushed forward, causing her heart rate to increase as they crushed her body between theirs.

"Maybe we should go back to our seats," she called out over the din as she grabbed Michelle's arm.

"No way! I worked my way through this crowd. We'll lose our good spot." Mish's voice sounded just as caught up as the fans around her. She grabbed Rose's hand. "Stay close."

Taking a deep breath, Rose resigned herself to her current position and returned her gaze to the stage, focusing on the lead singer holding his guitar. The crowd began to chant "Stryker! Stryker!"

An electric guitar blared through the speakers, the music sounding familiar to her. Then the rest of the band joined in as the lead singer began to sing. The crowd went wild at the artist's rendition of "Smooth" by Santana and Rob Thomas.

When several lights lit up the front of the stage, Rose's heart jerked and she squeezed Mish's hand.

"See, I told you they were fantastic," her friend called out in reaction to her tight hold.

Rose couldn't believe what she was seeing. Standing up there, wearing buttery-soft black leather pants and a black silk shirt, playing and singing was Duncan. Except, this wasn't a Duncan she'd ever seen before. He smiled at the fans and looked truly comfortable and in his element standing up in front of twelve hundred people, singing his heart out. Singing! And he said he didn't sing.

She wanted to grind her teeth at the outgoing, friendly persona Duncan willingly shared with total strangers, yet he held back from her. Why? she wondered. Yet, as annoyed as she was, she couldn't help but appreciate his musical talent when he set aside his electric guitar, pulled up a stool, took the acoustic guitar his band member handed him, and segued into a slower, angsty ballad called "Hallelujah" in the vein of Jeff Buckley. Damn, the man could belt out a tune…the kind that made goose bumps form on her arms and sent shivers down her spine.

Between songs, Duncan took the time to introduce the rest of his band, acknowledging their talent. As Duncan moved from his version of one famous song after another, he kept the crowd pumped by walking around stage, laughing and commenting at the crazy signs fans held up. His interaction definitely fueled the fans because with each song he performed they grew louder and louder.

At the end of one song, Duncan bent down at the edge of the stage to take some flowers from a fan. He kissed the back of her fingers and thanked her with a sexy smile. Rose couldn't help the jolt of jealousy that shot through her. Shrugging off the strange emotion, she told herself to focus on Duncan as a performer and not as a person.

An hour and a half later, Rose was just as caught up in Duncan's music, but the one thing that struck her was that none of the songs he'd played were his own. When he came back on stage for an encore, the realization hit her as to what had been missing. Duncan might be giving of himself in his music to his fans, but he would only give so far…even on stage, he held a part of himself back. She knew he was talented enough to compose his own songs. She'd heard him playing some of his classical music, seen his notes.

When another woman tried to get his attention from the edge of the stage, Rose's stomach clenched She refused to watch. Turning to say something to Michelle, she realized she was gone. Frantic, Rose glanced through the throng of people, her heart racing. Until her gaze landed on the head of dark curly hair at the front of the stage. The woman's hand Duncan was about to kiss was Michelle's!

Just before his lips connected with her fingers, Duncan's head snapped up and his gaze narrowed on the crowd as if he were looking for something or someone.

When his gaze zeroed in and landed on her, Rose's heartbeat thundered in her ears.

Without missing a beat, Duncan kissed Michelle's hand and stood saying into the mike in a teasing tone, "Are you all ready for a guitar lesson?"

"Yes!" the women screamed in unison, making Rose wince at the high pitch. A hush fell over the group and then women began to call out, "Pick me, pick me, pick me." One woman followed up the incessant yells by saying, "Honey, you can *pick* me anytime and anywhere you want." Duncan laughed heartily at her double entendre, winking at the woman's quick wit.

What the hell was the "guitar lesson"? Rose wondered.

"Hmmm, let me see." Duncan appeared to ponder and then suddenly he pointed to Rose. "How about the lovely redhead?"

"Ohmigod! Go Rose!" Michelle squealed from her position next to the stage.

Rose had no idea what this "guitar lesson" entailed but she was certain she didn't want to find out. Shaking her head, she started to walk backward through the crowd, but Michelle had started a chant, "Rose, Rose, Rose", and the women surrounding

Rose joined in, shoving her up toward the front until she stood beside Michelle.

"I'm going to kill you for this," Rose said to Michelle through gritted teeth.

Michelle's only response was to kiss her on the cheek. "Have fun, Rosie." Then she grabbed Rose's shoulders and turned her to face Duncan as he bent down and took Rose's hand to pull her up on stage.

Once she was up on the stage, Duncan moved to lower the mike to guitar level, then he lifted his acoustic guitar off its stand and called her over to him with a smile.

Despite her efforts to not let the man affect her, Rose's heart rate raced as he unhooked the strap and placed the guitar in front of her. When he moved close, standing directly behind her, the crowd of fans went nuts. As they screamed out "you lucky girl", he whispered in her ear, "Following me, *a ghrá*?"

Her stomach tightened at the seductive timbre in his voice. "This concert was Michelle's idea," she hissed above the roar. "I'm just as surprised as you are, Mr. I-Don't-Sing."

He chuckled, then said loud enough for the crowd to hear, "I think we'll need the strap for this to work standing up, don't you guys?"

His comment brought on even more catcalling and screaming from the fans. Duncan pressed flush against her backside and hooked the strap back on the guitar's neck, locking her body between his heated one and the guitar in front of her.

"That's better," he commented for the crowd's benefit. *Though pressed against your front side is my preferred position,* he suggested in a husky tone in her mind.

Heat rose in her body at Duncan's sexy comment. She inhaled deeply trying to calm her nerves, but her action made her realize just how good he smelled tonight. He'd played hard but had barely broken a sweat, yet the all-male smell mixed with his enticing cologne made her entire body clench in response. He wore cologne for his fans, too? She wanted to choke him. Unsure where to put her hands during this strange exchange, Rose placed one of her hands on the guitar's neck and laid the other one across the guitar's body.

Pressing his body fully against hers, Duncan's warm breath fanned against her neck as he placed his fingers around hers. He manipulated her fingers until she'd formed the note for G, then he strummed the guitar. While she held the instrument's strings down so Duncan could continue to strum, the pads of Rose's fingers began to go numb.

She couldn't help the smile that crossed her lips when she realized why the pads of Duncan's fingers were so rough. The piano might help him relax, but this was the instrument he played his heart out on.

As the music resonated throughout the room, Duncan's fans screamed, "More, more."

Unconcerned, Duncan switched her fingers to another note, then continued to play. He pressed his erection against her buttocks and echoed the fans' sentiments in a seductive tone in her head. *My thoughts exactly, Róisín All I want…is more.*

With the hot spotlight shining down on her and Duncan's comments turning her body into a molten furnace, Rose used sarcasm to call her libido back into order.

"I'll bet you use your vampire powers to play the guitar with the speed you do."

Duncan stiffened behind her as if insulted by her comment. "There's only one way I use my powers when it comes to performing."

Apprehension gripped her when several of the fans, in their fanatic rush to get close to Duncan, were trying to get past the Pavilion's security guards to climb up on stage.

When he finished speaking, Duncan waved his hand from one side of the stage to the other and a sudden calmness seemed to wash over the crowd. Women climbed down and backed away. They still smiled but the obsessed looks on their faces were gone.

"My God, that worked," she whispered. *How cool would that be to be able to command a room like that?* she wondered in awe.

Duncan chuckled. "It helps keep the band's life sane."

Once he'd unhooked the strap on the guitar and stepped away from her, Duncan lifted the mike back up to the correct height and addressed the crowd. "Thank you being such a fantastic audience tonight." Then he turned to her and Rose realized twelve hundred pairs of eyes were on her, waiting.

Unsure what to say, she put out her hand, saying, "Thank you for the lesson."

Holding his guitar by the neck, Duncan took her hand. "It was my pleasure."

Expecting him to kiss her fingers as he'd done with all his other fans, Rose held back a gasp of surprise when he gave her a sexy smirk and turned her hand over, planting a kiss on the tender flesh of her palm.

A collective "Awwwww" came from the crowd at his intimate kiss. His public display of intimacy caused heat to rise up her neck and spread across her cheeks. Unable to form a coherent response, Rose pulled her hand away and walked down the side steps of the stage.

As the stage lights went black and the house lights turned on, Michelle met her at the bottom of the steps. Jerking Rose into her arms, she hugged her tight, saying, "Stryker kissed your palm and pressed his body against yours! You can't take a shower for at least a week."

Wheezing from Michelle's tight hold, Rose pulled out of her arms. "Uh, I think I'll keep my normal bathing routine, thanks."

"How can you be so blasé?" Michelle fairly screamed in her ear as they made their way out of the concert.

"Because he's just as human as the rest of us." Rose stopped walking when she realized what she'd just said. She'd called Duncan human. In her mind, his vampire powers aside, he was human to her…in all the ways that counted.

Rose resumed walking. "You were right. It was a great concert. Thanks for insisting I go with you."

"See, I'm good for you, Rose." Michelle preened, flipping her long hair over her shoulder. "You spend too much time working and not enough time playing. Even though I'm jealous as sin you got the 'guitar lesson', I wouldn't have wanted it to happen to a better person…well, other than me, of course."

Rose looked at her watch. "Well, I guess I'd better be going home."

Michelle shook her head. "Oh, no you don't. I've got plans for the evening."

"It's nine o'clock. What do you want to do now?"

"I want to meet the band," Michelle said with a wide grin.

"I'm sure my uncle can arrange it." Rose laughed.

"Nah, even better. I heard they planned to check out Rosco's after the show."

"They'll be mobbed…" Rose started to say, thinking of the bar right next to the Five Star Hotel. Then she remembered Duncan's display of power over the crowd and his comment about keeping the band's life sane.

Michelle's brow furrowed. "You would think so, but for some reason I've heard the fans respect the band so much, they keep their distance. And I will…unless they talk to me first, which I'm bound and determined they will," she finished with a cheeky grin.

* * * * *

Duncan leaned past someone sitting on a barstool to retrieve the longneck the bartender handed him.

When he reached in his jeans pocket to pay, the man grinned and shook his head. "Tab's on the house, sir. Thanks for the business."

Duncan eyed the crowd of people waiting in line at the bar and his band mates having a blast with the fans on the dance floor. He recognized many faces from the concert. "I'd say you're swamped tonight."

The dark-haired man nodded as he rang up an order. "Yeah, I'll be tired, but hey, the bills will get paid."

Duncan raised his beer in salute to the man. As he put the bottle to his lips, his body began to tingle all over. His vampire senses had kicked in.

Ian had arrived. Glancing at the bar's entrance, Duncan nodded to his brother and moved to wait at a nearby standup café table for Ian to approach.

Ian weaved and shouldered his way through the crowd until he reached the table. "Someone having a party? This place is packed," he commented.

"I heard some concert just let out at the Pavilion next door," Duncan replied in a bland tone before he took a swing of his beer.

"About the case," Duncan started to say, then paused. His gaze narrowed on his twin's broad smile. Ian didn't try to hide his thoughts and Duncan immediately jumped in his mind. He pressed his lips together in anger when he learned Ian had been aware of Rose's strong mind-blocking ability from the beginning. That he sent Duncan on purpose, thinking the woman might intrigue him. Intrigue him? What the fuck? He was like a man obsessed.

Shaking off his irritation, Duncan refused to be baited. "How'd the summit go?"

The expectant look on Ian's face changed to annoyance. "They're winding down. I cut out early when I got your call to meet you here."

Duncan's grip on the beer bottle tightened. "And James' fate?"

"Is being decided now."

"There shouldn't be anything to debate," Duncan snarled.

"The debate wasn't if he should be eliminated, but by whom. You know my choice."

Staring into his brother's intense golden gaze, Duncan knew Ian's wishes. He'd eliminate the vamp in a heartbeat.

"Eamon is insisting he be the one to take James out. I argued he was too close to James, that he'd known him too long." Ian looked at Duncan with steady regard. "Did you learn anything from James' thoughts as to what's going on?"

Duncan set the beer bottle down on the table with a thud. "One thing I know, I ought to kick your ass for sending me to battle with a vampire whose shape-shifting ability is unlike anything I've ever seen. A little 'hey, he's capable of kicking your ass across town, so watch your back' would've been helpful."

Ian's brows drew together in a deep frown and his shoulders tensed. "What the hell are you talking about? You knew the Sythens were shifters."

"I didn't know they have the ability to shift beyond their weigh and mass," Duncan countered.

At Ian's surprised expression, Duncan cocked his head to the side. "You really didn't know?" He picked up his beer and took another swig, contemplating that bit of news. "Neither did Mom."

Ian clenched his fists, his expression as hard as granite. "What the hell is going on? Sythens with hidden shape-shifting powers? Eamon and I are going to have a talk. I never would've sent you if I had known."

"Gee, thanks for the confidence 'dere, bro." Duncan rolled his eyes.

"You know what I meant," Ian snapped. "I'm just fucking pissed at the games Eamon seems to be playing with people's lives, since he was the one who called me and told me about James kidnapping the human woman. Granted, he wasn't happy when he found out I'd sent you in my place..."

Duncan stiffened. "He was annoyed, was he? Fuck Eamon. I'll take James out myself."

Ian shook his head, a thoughtful look on his face as he rubbed his jaw. "No, I don't think it was your physical ability he was worried about. Now that I think about it...I'll bet it was your mental ability. He was worried you'd discover something."

Glancing at his brother, Ian asked, "You don't have a clue as to why James kidnapped that woman?"

"You mean, other than the fact he's a lunatic who's absolutely obsessed with Rose?" He shook his head. "His mind is very strong. I couldn't breach it."

Frustration crossed Ian's face. "I know Eamon's hiding something." Pulling out his cell phone, he dialed a number. "Lucian, I want to interrogate James. Stall on Eamon's request to destroy the vamp. I've discovered some hidden powers the Sythen possesses. I have a hunch Eamon knows, too."

Duncan's stomach tensed. He didn't wait for Ian to relay the information. Instead, he used his powers to listen to Lucian's response.

The Vité chuckled. "Right now *everything* is stalled. Your mother just showed up, insisting she speak with Eamon immediately. He's in the library talking to her. I admit a certain curiosity myself."

"My mother's speaking to Eamon?"

"That's what I said."

"I'll be there in half an hour." Ian snapped the phone closed. He glanced at Duncan. "I know you heard that."

Duncan nodded, his brow furrowing. "Mom seemed tense when I called her earlier today."

Ian's eyes widened in surprise. "You called Mom?"

"She's my mother, too," Duncan replied in a dry tone. "I called to ask her a question about a song she used to sing to us when we were kids."

"Which one?"

Duncan shrugged at his brother's curious look. "The Irish lullaby she sang to us before bed."

Ian laughed and leaned across the table to put his hand on Duncan's forehead. "You feeling okay? All this sentimentality ..."

"Bite me," Duncan snapped, knocking away Ian's hand. "Rose sang the same song and hearing it again made me curious as to its origins in Ireland. That's all."

Ian sat back in his chair, a knowing smile on his face. "Ah, Rose, is it? She's singing lullabies to you? Did she put you to bed, too?" he teased with raised eyebrows.

"She's— " Duncan started to speak but cut himself off when he saw the object of their conversation enter the bar alongside the tall brunette from the concert. Rose wore one of the sexiest outfits he'd ever seen on a woman. Her top was a black corset with a drawstring tie that barely held in her creamy breasts. But it was the skintight black leather pants that laced all the way up the side of her legs, giving a glimpse of skin along her thighs that made his stomach clench in swift sexual response.

Noting several men approach Rose, jealousy sliced through him, making his shoulders stiffen. He clenched his fist and heard the empty beer bottle crack, then crumble in his hand. Ignoring the wounds on his palm, all he could think was, *Why the hell is she wearing an 'I want to be fucked' outfit?*

Ian had followed his line of sight. At the sound of Duncan's bottle shattering, he turned his gaze back to his brother and gave a low whistle. "I take it that's Rose. A redhead, hmmm? Talk about all fire. Ready to share now?" He threw back the comment his twin had made to him when Duncan first met Jax.

"Like hell," Duncan growled, then stood up.

"Aw, come on…it's only fair. You got to kiss Jax," Ian continued to tease.

Duncan's gaze narrowed on his twin. "Keep it up and I'll tell Jax."

Ian immediately sobered. "Watch it. My Anima knows how to wield weapons, remember?"

"Indeed I do." As Duncan walked off, he spoke in his brother's mind. *I want to know why Mom's involved in this. Call me once you've spoken with her.*

*****

Rose smiled at the two men who'd immediately claimed her and Michelle's attention, pulling them onto the dance floor. She recognized the taller one dancing with Michelle as the drummer from Duncan's band and the shorter one who danced in front of her as the keyboard player. As she gyrated to the upbeat music, she sensed Duncan's presence somewhere in the room. She wasn't sure why she could feel him, but she did. Maybe it was because she'd been so aware of him up on stage earlier. It was also why she'd insisted on going shopping at the casino's clothing store for an outfit that would knock his socks off.

The music ended and a slow song started up. She smiled and turned to walk off the dance floor when John, the man dancing with her, cajoled, "Awww, come one, just one more dance."

He looked so sincere. She laughed and started to put her hand in his when a large hand clasped hers.

"Sorry, John, she promised me this dance," Duncan said.

Michelle grabbed John's hand before he could walk off the dance floor, purring, "I've never slow danced with two men before. How about it, handsome?"

The drummer grinned and moved behind her so John could dance in front. They looked like one big happy dancing sandwich, but Rose couldn't help the protective streak that welled up in her.

Duncan must've sensed her unease based on her tense stance. He turned her to face to him. "She'll be fine."

"But, she's a bit impulsive..." she began, worry in her tone as she looked back at her friend.

Duncan hooked a finger under her chin and forced her to meet his gaze. "I guarantee that nothing she doesn't want to happen will happen to her."

She clutched his wrist, her gaze searching his. "You've compelled the two men?"

Duncan flicked his gaze to his colleagues then back to her. "If they decide to remain in Michelle's company, they will feel a strong urge to keep her safe. Even alcohol and sexual desires won't overcome my wishes. I guarantee they won't hurt her, Róisín."

Relief washed over her and she relaxed as Duncan pulled her in his arms.

Locking his arm around her waist, he slid his thigh between hers and moved their bodies to the beat of the music.

Duncan's cologne smelled so good, she laid one hand on his hard chest and hooked the fingers of her other hand in his jeans belt loop so she could lean close and inhale. God, she wanted to drown in this man. Her stomach tensed and her heart rate revved quickly at the way he made her feel.

Weak.

Needy.

Aroused.

The realization he had her emotions by a string hit her like a bucket of cold water. Rose stiffened in his arms and mumbled an excuse to get a drink as she tried to pull away.

"No!" His hand grasped her upper back, holding her in place, while his stormy golden gaze locked with hers.

Her heart knocked hard on her chest as he held her gaze for a long, tense moment. They stood there, stock-still among the people slow dancing on the dance floor.

Duncan lifted the hand she'd placed on his chest and kissed her palm. His gaze followed his thumb as he rubbed the pad across her fingers. "This is the sweetest hand I've ever felt wrapped around my cock. I've thought of nothing else since." He met her gaze once more and started dancing again. "I want to know what *you* feel like wrapped around me."

As her pulse jumped, he leaned next to her ear and said in a husky voice, "I want to move inside you, to feel your legs wrapped around me…to hear you scream out when you come."

Rose's lower stomach muscles clenched at his sexy words. Her nipples jutted against the corset she wore, aching for his touch. Her sex began to throb in time to the slow-moving, sexual thump of the music. Stilling herself, she refused to let him hear her breathing change.

As if he sensed her tensing up, Duncan pulled her hips forward and rubbed his erection against her mound. She gasped when he kissed her throat and whispered in her mind. *I hear your heart racing, feel every pump of your blood thundering through your veins and damn it, I smell your arousal. You want this just as much as I do.*

Rose had moved her hands to his shoulders when he pulled her body forward. Fear raced through her at the reality of his words. She did want him. Desperately.

Digging her fingers in his shoulders, she gritted out, "Fine. A good fuck is something we both need," before she let go and turned to walk off the dance floor.

Duncan's arm snaked out and grabbed her around the waist. Yanking her back against his warm, hard frame, he warned, "Don't think for one minute you'll hold back your emotions from me. You'll feel every heart-pounding, body-rocking one down to your lovely toes. That, I promise you."

Anger washed over her and she gripped his hand, trying to pull it off her. "Arrogant ass," she hissed, furious with herself for still wanting him.

His hand clutched her waist like a steel band, unmoving. "That I am, but before we leave I'll warn you now..." He paused and pushed her hair over her shoulder, then brushed his lips down her neck. As he slowly made his way back up, Rose felt his sharp incisors scrape across her skin. Goose bumps formed on her arms, but she held back her gasp of excitement.

"I *will* take your blood again, *a ghrá*. Guaranteed," he finished in a dark, hungry tone before he let her go.

She glanced at him over her shoulder and gave him a haughty look. "You'll have to beg for it."

His fangs retracted back to normal size and Duncan gave her a steely smile. "We'll see who does the begging." His expression was way too confident.

Flipping her hair back over her shoulder in a kiss-my-ass manner, she walked over to Michelle and told her she was leaving for the night.

Michelle glanced at Duncan waiting behind Rose and met her friend's gaze. "I hate you," she said with a friendly smile.

"Love you, too, Mish." Rose reached up and kissed her friend's cheek before she walked off the dance floor.

Rose strode past Duncan and headed toward the door without looking back. She didn't have to—she sensed his presence close behind her. As she reached for the door, a tall man stepped in front of her, blocking her path.

"Leaving without introducing this gorgeous woman, Duncan?"

Rose's body tensed at the slightly accented voice. It sounded just like...Duncan's. She jerked her gaze to the man's face and stumbled back in surprise.

Duncan caught her and spoke to the man who looked exactly like him. "Ian, meet Rose Sinclair. Rose, meet my brother."

Regaining her balance, Rose glanced from one brother to the other while she collected her composure at the shock of discovering Duncan had a twin. She held out her hand to shake Ian's. "It's amazing. Except for your hair length, you two look truly identical."

Ian shook her hand and winked at her. "I'm the better half of the egg."

At Rose's laughter, Duncan said to Ian, "Weapon-wielding Anima, bro, remember?"

The brothers stared at each other for a second. When Duncan's expression turned resolute, she realized they were communicating mentally. Damn, she wished she had the ability to read minds.

"Hey, down here, fang boys." She crossed her arms when the brothers looked at her. "It's rude to speak…er…or in your case, not speak, about someone in her presence."

Ian raised his eyebrow. "Perceptive little one, isn't she?"

"That she is," Duncan agreed in a wry tone.

"I give up," Rose said, irritated that she seemed to be the brunt of some silent joke. She started to walk around Ian, but Duncan clasped her elbow at the same time Ian placed a hand on her shoulder, stopping her exit.

Ian's warm golden gaze met hers and he gave her a genuine smile. "It was nice to meet you…" he paused and glanced at Duncan in surprise, "Róisín."

Taken aback that he knew the name Duncan called her, Rose looked up to see an equally surprised look pass Duncan's face before he masked it behind an impassive one.

"Keep in touch with me about that other matter," Duncan spoke to his brother.

Ian let go of her shoulder and gave him a curt nod.

Once they'd walked outside, Rose started to ask, "How'd your brother know--"

But she didn't get to finish her sentence. Duncan's warm hand clasped her neck. He pulled her around to face him as his mouth claimed hers in a dominant kiss.

Surprised by the possessive nature of his kiss, Rose hooked her fingers in his jeans belt loops and opened her lips, accepting the sensual thrust of his tongue against hers.

His hard body felt so good aligned with hers. The rough brush of his whiskers chafed her lips, but she didn't care. She wanted everything he offered, wanted the passion she saw him give to his music and his fans. She wanted to see that side to Duncan…the side that was open and not so tightly controlled.

*I refuse to let you hold back from me tonight,* he spoke in her mind, his tone adamant, almost angry.

Fear swelled within her. He pushed too far, prodded too much. She felt his presence lurking in her mind, fierce and persistent.

Rose shoved at his chest and panted out in anger, "Take what you can get, Duncan, that's all I'll offer."

Duncan grasped her chin and tilted her head so her gaze met his in the dim light outside the bar. "Make no mistake, Róisín, you *will* open to me tonight…" He paused and raked his gaze down her body. His angry tone dropped to a seductive rumble. "In every way."

Despite herself, Rose's pulse spiked at his provocative words. She brushed past him, scared by the depth of emotions this man evoked in her. "Don't count on it, vamp."

She walked up to her bike and lifted her leg over the leather seat. Meeting Duncan's penetrating gaze, she placed her helmet on her head. Amusement shot through her at the heated look on his face when she kicked the bike to life.

A sexy smile tilted the corners of his lips as he approached.

The man planned to hitch a ride. Nonononono! He'd run his hands all over her body the entire trip home. Determination to remain aloof filled her. She revved the engine.

"Find your own ride, Mordoor," she said before she flipped her visor shut and backed the bike out of its parking spot.

Rose hadn't driven more than a block when the sound of another motorcycle came rumbling up behind her.

Her heart raced to see Duncan pull his bike up beside hers. She saw his arrogant expression through his visor. He saluted her, then popped his bike's front wheel before he took off ahead of her.

Not to be outdone, Rose gunned her engine. The wind felt cool on her skin, but Duncan caused a heat to spread through her that kept her entire body warm.

Seeing an incline on the side of the road ahead of her, Rose turned her wheel and grinned. Her bike easily took the ramp and remained airborne until she landed next to Duncan.

She couldn't explain it, but she literally felt his anger at her. Her entire body tensed at the sensation that rippled down her spine. Probably jealous, she thought as she revved her engine and did a wheelie of her own. When her front wheel landed back on the ground, she took off like a shot ahead of him.

Rose and Duncan arrived at her house at the same time. Her adrenaline pumped at the exhilarating ride as she took off her helmet and hopped off her bike. She flicked her gaze back at Duncan parking his bike, then started to walk up the pathway to her house. His heavy footfalls stalked behind her, making her subconsciously pick up her pace until she reached her door.

As she started to insert the key in the lock, Duncan's hands landed on her shoulders and he jerked her around to face him, slamming her against her door. A dark scowl creased his brow and his golden gaze seemed to glow, it was so intense.

"Have a care for yourself, Rose. I heal very quickly. You don't."

Her heart raced at the anger he displayed. Why did he care if she risked her life?

She lifted her chin a notch. "That's what makes it a risk." Tilting her head, she gave him a devilish smile. "Imagine how crazy I'd be on a bike if I were a vampire?" As soon as she said it, excitement filled her. What would it be like to be a vampire? To face Duncan as an equal?

Duncan's jaw ticced and his grip on her shoulders tightened. The tortured look in his eyes made her stomach clench.

"What is it—" she started to ask, but he jerked her toward him, pressing his mouth against hers.

Rose gasped at the savage ferocity in his kiss. She was surprised she wasn't afraid of this barely controlled beast Duncan seemed to be hiding inside him. Instead, the dominant slant of his lips gliding over hers and the possessive way he grabbed her rear and jerked her hips to his only turned her on more.

Wrapping her arms around his neck, she clutched him close and moaned against his mouth. Their tongues dueled, thrust and parried until her breathing increased.

Duncan pulled his mouth away, his own breathing harsher than she'd ever heard it before. "Inside now, or I swear I'll take you up against the damned door for any passerby to see," he grated out, gripping her waist tight.

Rose didn't need someone driving by to experience her love life firsthand, even if Duncan's threat sounded awfully tempting to see if he'd really follow though on his promise. Seeing the volatile look in his eyes, she turned in his arms and unlocked the door. Duncan grabbed the knob and opened the door at the same time he placed a hand at her waist and ushered her inside.

Sexual power surged within her when he shut the door. She turned and walked backward into her living room, kicking off her boots in the process. Her heart hammered as she switched on a lamp and waited for his next move.

Duncan pulled off his black shirt and tossed it to the floor. His gaze shifted to molten amber when it traveled up her skin-tight leather-clad legs, past her exposed belly to linger at the swell of her breasts above the leather corset she wore.

Rose let her own gaze roam his sculpted abs and chest. Her breasts tingled while her gaze followed the line of fine hair that narrowed into a vee past his jeans. When he started to walk toward her, her entire body tensed in sensual awareness.

But Duncan didn't touch her other than to untie the leather string at the bottom of each pants leg. After that, he walked in a slow circle around her, reminding her of a lion circling its quarry, sizing up her worthiness to be his prey.

The anticipation was killing her. Rose took a deep breath, but she refused to let her gaze follow him as he circled behind her.

She let out an involuntary gasp of surprise when he pressed his hard bare chest to her back at the same time his hands landed on her thighs. Duncan planted a kiss on her shoulder and the heat from his hands radiated to the bare flesh peeking through the leather lacing.

"This is a 'fuck me' outfit if I've ever seen one," he stated, then kissed her neck. "I swear, baby, this better have been worn just for me or I'd have killed any man who dared to touch you tonight."

Even though he was right, Rose started to laugh at his arrogance. But her laugh came out as a choking gasp when he gripped the leather strings on either pants leg near her hips and yanked upward.

"Owwww," she yelped as the leather zipped through the grommets on the tight pants, rubbing and burning the skin on her thighs along the way. *That hurt like hell,* she thought. Not to mention the fact she stood there in only a sexy black thong and her top, since her pants were now a heap of leather on the floor.

Before she could examine the damage he'd done to her legs, Duncan dropped to his knees beside her. "Stand still," he commanded. His warm hand clasped the inside of one naked leg at the same time his other hand caressed her bare buttock. With a heated look in his golden gaze, he ran his tongue up the outside of her thigh, tracing the red welts that had begun to form.

Rose closed her eyes at the erotic sensations that rocked through her. Nothing could've prepared her for the attentive, protective act of Duncan healing her skin with his tongue from her lower thigh to her hip. She'd prepared for a battle of the sexes. Not this almost reverent loving of her body. Unconsciously, her fingers wove through his hair, tangling in the thick, silky mass.

Desire swirled in her belly when he planted a kiss on her hip before moving to the other thigh and giving it the same sexy ministrations. But this time, his grip on her inner thigh felt more intimate. While he set about healing her skin, his hand moved higher and the tips of his fingers brushed the juncture where her thigh met her body.

After he laved her wounds, he kissed his way back up her thigh, his fingers gripping her leg in a firmer hold.

Rose opened her eyes when she felt his heated breath through her silky underwear. Michelle had insisted she shave almost all her hair down there if she were going to wear a thong, which left her shaven skin around her sex ultra-responsive.

*I'll bet all this newly exposed skin is very sensitive,* he spoke in her mind right before his tongue traced down the front of her thong. Rose groaned and intuitively rocked closer as he moved lower. Staring down at his broad, muscular shoulders, she tightened her fingers in his hair, holding her breath in anticipation.

When he clasped her buttocks and slid his tongue along her lower lips, tracing an erotic path, the heightened sensations he created along her newly exposed skin were almost her undoing. She had to work hard to keep her legs from collapsing at the tingling heat running from her sex up to her breasts.

Duncan slid a hand across her buttocks and grabbed the back of her underwear. Fisting his hand in the soft material, he pulled it taut between her legs. Groaning, he sucked harder on her sex now that he had better access to her. *You taste so damn good. I can't decide which I like more, your blood or your sweet flavor.*

"You'll be the one begging for it," she reminded him with conviction, despite the fact she had to pant out the challenge.

*Don't bet on it, a thaisce.* He ran his tongue along the thong's path between her lower lips before he flicked it inside her.

Rose's eyelids fluttered closed at the sensual sensations rocking through her. The thong now pressed down hard on her throbbing clitoris. She felt a sudden tug and her underwear tore, falling into Duncan's hand. He had to move his mouth to remove the cloth and before he could return his mouth to her body, Rose tapped him on the shoulder. She had to regain the upper hand with him or she'd be a pile of weak muscles and bones lying on the floor, begging him to take her before he was done.

Duncan glanced up at her, his look full of dark hunger.

"You plan on going at it right here in the living room?" she asked with a raised eyebrow, trying to lighten his intensity and her own churning emotions.

He grinned as he placed his hands on the back of her thighs, then slid his fingers down to the back of her knees. "For starters," he answered right before he jerked her knees toward him.

Rose yelped and tried to catch herself as she fell backward toward the floor. Duncan caught her hands, then lowered her to the soft carpet. Before she could move, he'd pinned her body with his and pulled her arms over her head.

Her body instantly reacted, flooding in renewed wet heat at the rough sensation of his jeans-covered erection pressing against her damp, aroused core.

Duncan rocked his hips against hers and smiled. "You're so hot and wet, I feel you through my jeans."

"Too bad you'll have to let me go to remove them," she quipped with a knowing smile.

Duncan glanced down at the laces on her corset, then looked back at her, a wicked grin on his face. As the laces on her corset began to come untied on their own, causing her heart to race out of control, she challenged him even more.

"You and your vampire powers. You might be able to mentally unbutton and unzip your own pants, you'll still have to release me to take them off."

"Who says I'll take them all the way off?" he shot back. When he finished speaking, he mentally undid the last of the lacing and the material fell open on either side of her body. Rose's heart rate soared.

Her bare breasts jutted upward toward him as if they had a mind of their own. Traitors, she wanted to yell at her puckered nipples. Instead, she taunted, "You're a bit overdressed, don't you think? You'll have to let me go now."

Duncan lowered his head and nipped at her nipple. Glancing up at her, he teased, "These are just too hard and aroused not to give them a moment of attention."

Unable to help herself, Rose arched her back, pressing her breast closer to his warm mouth, but he backed away with a devilish smile.

"About those pants," she reminded him, tugging to release his hold on her arms.

He pressed her wrists to the floor and commanded, "Stay."

Wondering what he was planning, Rose left her arms where he placed them as he moved to crouch between her legs. He encircled her ankles with his warm fingers.

*Bend your knees just a bit,* he said mentally. Intrigued, she complied, bending her knees slightly and placing her feet flat on the carpet.

Duncan nodded in satisfaction and stood up, staring down at her. Desire flickered through his gaze as it swept down her body. "You're very beautiful. I've thought of nothing else but seeing you just like this."

Rose wasn't prepared for the emotions his words evoked within her. She wanted, needed his touch, his heat. Yet she didn't know if she could handle even one night with this man, he made her so desperate for his touch. She started to get up, but her arms wouldn't budge. Surprised, she tried to move her feet. Nothing. She truly felt as if she were bound to the floor. Somehow he'd figured out a way to compel her. That had to be the only explanation. Her angry gaze flew to his as he slowly unbuttoned and unzipped his jeans.

"Release me," she hissed out.

Duncan didn't say a word. He just stared at her with that ravenous look in his eyes.

Tugging harder on her invisible bonds, she tried to remain calm. "Very funny. You've proven that you can take your jeans off while still holding me. Now let me go."

A knowing smile tilted his lips as he stepped out of his jeans, retrieved a condom from his jeans pocket and began to roll it on. Heaven help her, but Rose's sex began to throb in aching awareness of his size as she watched his fingers push the condom all the way down his shaft.

She knew from firsthand experience—literally—just how thick he was. She'd barely been able to get her hand around him the other night. Duncan was easily eight inches in length and nature hadn't skimped in the width category either.

He lowered himself to the floor and crawled over her body until he was above her. His golden gaze locked with hers, his own serious and resolute. "I won't let you hide from me tonight. You'll allow yourself to experience every emotion you've ever held back from a lover. Do you understand, Róisín?"

Panic seized her at his statement. "How dare you!" she gritted out, trying to get up once more.

Duncan swiftly lowered his mouth to her throat and locked his teeth on her jugular, making her freeze in her movements.

He spoke in her mind, his tone intense. *I dare, because I can. I know your mind. I know you trust I'd never hurt you. Ever. Tonight is about trust and…* he paused and released her neck to plant a kiss on her throat before he finished in a husky whisper in her ear, "it's about letting go."

# Chapter Eight

ꟹ

Rose didn't know what to say. She lay there, aroused and panicked, unable to form a coherent response as Duncan slid the corset out from underneath her.

Kneeling between her thighs, he leaned on his elbows and planted a gentle kiss on the curve of her breast.

Rose sighed at his tender touch. This she could handle.

But when he moved his mouth to her nipple and laved at the hard tip, then sucked it inside his warm mouth at the same time she felt his presence in her head, demanding to be let in, Rose couldn't give in. If she let him in her mind, he'd know just how much he'd been on her mind and in her dreams the past couple of days. He'd know how much it bothered her to wake up in her own bed when she'd hoped to wake up in his the other day. He'd have too much power over her.

Duncan moved to her other breast, giving it equal tantalizing attention as she felt even more pressure in her head.

Rose blinked through the forceful sensation tapping on her outer consciousness, demanding entrance. Her body was responding in kind to Duncan's seduction. Her sex pulsed in a desperate need to feel him inside her while her heart rate thundered in her ears.

"I can't," she responded in a heavy pant to his mental presence waiting to be let in.

Duncan's lips moved down her belly and his hands cupped her buttocks, elevating her hips.

Rose met his glowing golden gaze. "I'm not capable of sharing the emotions you seek from me, Duncan."

Duncan's gaze turned stormy. "It's not a matter of *can't*, it's a matter of *won't*," he insisted before he lowered his mouth to her sex and ran his tongue along her slit all the way to her clitoris. Without hesitation, he latched on and began to suck hard.

Shuddering sensations slammed through her at his relentless attention to her swollen bud. Again, she felt his presence in her mind, angry, resentful, dominant…waiting.

When Duncan slid two fingers inside her channel and began to rub on her hot spot, Rose arched her back and rocked her hips to the rhythm of pleasurable sensations rolling through her.

"Duuuuncan," she breathed out.

*Open to me,* he insisted in her mind.

Her head thrashed back and forth as she fought the tide of emotions ricocheting through her. *No, I can't let this feel so good. I won't let him make me.* In truth, Duncan made her *feel* so much, even she couldn't sort through the jumbled emotions slamming into her.

He withdrew his hand from her body and she kept her eyes closed, breathing a sigh of agonized relief from the onslaught of emotions. She wanted to come so bad, but this orgasm came with a price she was unwilling to pay.

The heat of his body moving over hers and the nudge of his cock pressing against her entrance caused Rose's eyes to snap open.

She thought she saw deep hurt in his gaze before his mouth covered hers. She tugged on her invisible bonds, but Duncan hadn't released her. His tongue swept against hers, angry, possessive. As she kissed him back and lifted her hips, waiting to accept his thrust, Duncan's pace slowed. He seemed to want to explore her mouth, to let her know just how much he enjoyed the act of kissing. The feel of his cock pressing against her core, but not penetrating sent her libido into overdrive.

She bucked to let him know what she wanted, but Duncan only stayed just outside her reach, taunting her with a gentle nudge and "almosts".

*Let me in, Róisín,* he spoke in her mind once more as he moved his lips to her neck and pressed them against her pulse.

This time, he slid partially inside her. The sensuous stretching of skin felt so good. Rose whimpered when he withdrew once more.

"No," she whispered.

Duncan slowly guided himself a little farther inside her. "Release me," she panted. She wanted desperately to wrap her arms around his shoulders, to keep him close, to make him forget this ridiculous game and take her body. Make her forget why she didn't want to feel.

"You've had the ability to release yourself anytime you wanted," he replied and kissed her jaw. Rose lifted her arms, realizing they weren't held down as Duncan had led her to believe. Had she subconsciously wanted to give herself to him? To give him total physical control if she couldn't give it to him mentally?

When he began to speak in Irish to her, mumbling sexy words in her ear she didn't understand, she ran her hands up his muscular back and clasped him to her. Wrapping her legs around his waist, she said, "I can't understand you, but I know you want to be right where you are."

Duncan thrust inside her to the hilt with a guttural groan then captured her gasp of initial pain in another bone-melting kiss, turning the sensation into sheer pleasure.

When he began to shaft her, slow and sure, he spoke mentally. *Your body tells me that it wants to be right where it is, too,* a ghrá – *accepting me. But I want to hear your thoughts.*

As her lower muscles absorbed each thrilling plunge he made inside her, Rose dug her nails into Duncan's back. "I can't."

"Then *tell* me what you feel," he ground out at the same time he picked up his pace, rocking into her body with forceful thrusts.

Her entire frame shook with her impending climax, but Duncan's lesson of speaking to her in Irish was a good one. She'd desperately wanted to know what he had said to her, what sexy words he'd spoken.

Tingling sensations rippled through her all the way to her core. "I love how you make me feel," she panted out, lifting her hips to absorb every bone-melting jolt he gave her. "Sexy, wanted and so desperate to have you inside me I can't see straight," she finished with a wail as her walls began to contract around him. "God,

Duncan!" she gripped his shoulders tight, holding him close as her body clenched in a deeply satisfying orgasm. At the same time, she felt his shoulders and back tense.

"You feel so good," Duncan said in a hoarse voice. He rammed into her again and again as if he couldn't get deep enough. His chest felt heavy and hard, pressing against her breasts while the force of his aggressive pistoning caused another orgasm to hit her. When he climaxed, Rose rode the wave of desire swirling between them until they both collapsed in each other's arms.

Rose's heart raced while Duncan's body settled over her. She welcomed his warmth and his blanket of weight. Tangling her legs with his, she ran her hands down his back, surprised by the light sheen of sweat she encountered. Smug satisfaction filled her. She'd gotten to him more than he showed. The realization made her frown. Wait a minute. He'd demanded she share when he continued to hold back. Why did he constantly hide himself from her?

Tapping him on the shoulder she said, "Er…um…I've got to go to the bathroom."

Duncan lifted his head, then kissed her jaw before withdrawing from her body. Rose felt a piercing loss in the pit of her stomach the moment he separated himself from her. The sensation was so strong, so gripping she actually stumbled on the way to her bedroom.

"You okay?" she heard him ask from the floor.

Grasping the back of her couch for support, she waved her hand behind her. "Yeah, I'm fine," before she continued to the bathroom.

Duncan watched her leave the room and wondered what she was thinking. Damn, it rankled she wouldn't let him in. Rose had the strongest will of any being he'd ever encountered. Her mind was like a steel trap, reinforced with an impenetrable wall. He knew she had emotions clamoring to be shared and he wanted to *hear* those emotions. He wanted to share in her climax, experience what she felt. But she blocked his every move.

Propping himself up on his elbow, he contemplated the complex woman. When Ian shook her hand, he'd experienced a connection with Rose that had surprised Duncan. It was as if Rose were some kind of conduit to the special twin connection Ian and Duncan shared. Somehow, Ian instantly knew the name Róisín that Duncan called her.

*She's special, Dunc,* Ian had said mentally.

*She's a very strong-willed woman,* Duncan had replied in the same manner, his tone neutral.

*No, whatever it is, it's deeper…more…fundamental,* Ian had countered, sounding intrigued.

Rolling over on his back, Duncan was forced to acknowledge Ian's words. The fact Ian picked up on it disturbed him more than he cared to admit. Duncan couldn't explain the automatic trust Rose had in him from the first moment they met, especially considering her past. Nor could he explain his need to know her thoughts, to push her to share her emotions.

The more intimate he became with Rose, the deeper he felt her every physical reaction. He'd experienced her wooziness when she'd gotten up to go the bathroom, felt her force herself to stand up straight…and damn it, he'd never experienced such simple things with another. But when it came to her sexual reactions to him, he ran into a well-guarded fortress.

His inability to overcome her strong mental block pissed him off, because what just occurred was the best damn sexually satisfying and physically draining experience he'd ever had with a woman, even without taking her blood. For the first time in his long life he'd wanted to share the experience, to share with her what he felt, every single shudder.

When she'd climaxed, he wanted to take her blood…his body demanded it. He'd had to lock his jaw and clamp his mouth shut. It hurt like a sonofabitch since he'd been unable to control his fangs extending. The sharp points dug into his lips as the need to mate hammered within him. He'd come so close to just letting go and taking her blood, the primal urge was that strong. She said he'd beg for it…she was damn near right!

Never had he been forced to hold back the beast within him as much as he did with this woman. Then again, he'd never met anyone like Rose before. No one made him this insatiable, this desperate, this mother-fucking confused.

Grinding his teeth at the conflicting thoughts rambling through his mind, Duncan stood and resolved to keep his emotions under control when it came to Rose. Control came first.

Always.

Rose walked out of her bathroom, rubbing the pads of her fingers on her left hand. While she'd washed her hands and dried them on the towel, she'd noticed the tingling numbness, yet she couldn't figure out what she'd done to cause it.

"What's wrong?" Duncan asked.

She glanced up and her gaze landed on his naked form. Her fingers momentarily forgotten, she let her gaze slide over his gorgeous, naked body. He'd disposed of the condom and when her line of vision strayed to his impressive cock, it hardened instantly.

"Nice to see you, too." She glanced up with a grin only to see a frown on his face.

He stepped closer and gripped her hand, repeating in a forceful tone, "What's wrong with your hand, Róisín?"

"I don't know. My fingertips are numb and I'm not sure why."

Rubbing his thumb across her fingers, he glanced at her. "Is it only the fingers on this hand?"

She nodded, only to see a knowing grin spread across his face before he used his hold on her hand to jerk her forward.

"Hey, it feels weird," she commented, then let out a yelp of surprise when he threw her body over his shoulder and headed for her bed.

"I know, love," he commented with a chuckle before he tossed her body on the soft bed and landed on top of her.

"What's so amusing?" she asked when Duncan rolled to his side and pulled her close.

He lifted her left hand and stuck her first finger in his mouth, swirling his tongue around the sensitive tip.

Her stomach tightened in response to the tingling sensation his seductive act caused.

"It's from playing the guitar. Though it usually takes extended play time to cause the numbness for someone new to learning."

Rose remembered the time she'd spent on her mother's guitar and nodded her agreement. "I…um…practiced on my mom's guitar for a while yesterday, too."

"Ah." He raised a knowing eyebrow as he moved to the next finger and the next, giving them the same treatment. Her heart rate rose with each finger he caressed with his tongue. When he had her pinky in his mouth, instead of a gentle swipe of his tongue, he sucked on the small tip. Her nipples hardened, aching to be sucked…just like that.

Duncan's grip on her hand tightened as if he sensed her thoughts. The rough sensation of his fingers moving across the back of her hand made her realize what he was doing. Pulling her pinky from his mouth, she grabbed his hand and sat up on her elbow.

"You were healing my fingers, weren't you?"

Running her thumb across his callused fingertips, she met his languid gaze with a curious look.

"Why don't you heal your own?"

Duncan's relaxed gaze sharpened at her question. Glancing at her hand he planted a kiss on her palm. "It's a part of me," he simply stated, then moved his lips to her wrist.

Butterflies fluttered in her stomach as he trailed his kisses down her arm, but she refused to be sidetracked. "Like your music?"

He flicked his gaze to hers before lowering it to her shoulder to follow the trail his fingers made across her naked skin. "Like my music."

Goose bumps formed at the heated path his fingers traced down her collarbone and across the curve of her breast. "Why did you lie to me about your ability to sing?"

He didn't look at her when he responded in a low tone, "It's a part of my life I keep separate."

"You mean you hide behind."

When he jerked his gaze her way, anger flaring in the golden depths, she barreled on. "Why don't you allow others to see this entertaining, personable side of you?"

Duncan let his gaze fall to her breasts. He tweaked her nipple, but didn't respond to her question. She bit back the moan that threatened to escape. The fact he refused to discuss this other persona with her angered her, making her want to push him out of his comfort zone. "Even with your fans, you hold back."

That got his attention. Duncan's gaze met hers once more, a shocked look on his face. "Hold back?"

"I've heard you play your own music. Saw notes for songs you've composed. Why don't you sing a song you've written?" When he didn't answer, she continued in a lower voice, "You give without really giving just like you do when we're together."

Duncan's gaze darkened. "You're the pot calling the kettle black if I've ever seen one."

She sat up, more furious than she'd ever been in her life. "Bullshit, Duncan. You expect me to open my mind to you, but you hold your real self in constant check as if..." she paused, thinking through the reasoning why, then continued, guessing, "as if you're afraid of rejection."

Duncan sat up, his eyes glowing in his fury. "I've never wanted a woman as much as I want you, Rose. I'd fuck you into next week if I could."

Rose trembled in sexual awareness at his lurid words, his adamant tone and tense, squared shoulders.

"Yet you still held back from me. You didn't take everything I offered you," she countered.

He gripped her arms. "What did you offer me that I didn't take?" he said in a low tone, his voice on a dangerous edge.

"My blood."

Duncan slammed her back on the bed, pinning her to the mattress. Thrusting his hard thigh between hers, he gave her a feral smile and replied mentally in a volatile tone, *Are you offering, a ghrá?*

The sight of his fully extended fangs made her heart ram against her chest and her stomach clench in an inexplicable primal response. She arched her back and turned her head so he'd have better access to her neck.

Duncan growled at her silent offer and lowered his mouth to her neck, clamping his teeth on the soft skin.

"Are you asking?" Rose taunted him in a husky tone. Threading her fingers in his hair, she slid them down to his neck to pull him closer.

She gasped when tiny sharp pinpricks grazed her throat, holding her still but not piercing her skin. Duncan slid his hand between her thighs, cupping her sex. Running his finger through the bit of hair left between her legs, he found her plump nub and rubbed it in a small circle.

The rough pad on his finger caused exquisite friction. Rose couldn't help herself. She groaned and rocked her hips in response to his seductive play of her body.

*Are you asking?* he challenged in a seductive tone, applying pressure.

In response, Rose slid her hand down his tight stomach muscles and wrapped her fingers around his erection.

Duncan shuddered when she stroked him, then growled low in his throat.

His threatening response made her wet with need.

"Yes, damn you. I'm asking," she panted out.

Duncan bit her at the same time he thrust two fingers deep inside her body.

His groan vibrating on her neck lessened the swift pain, turning it into a jolt of extreme pleasure shooting down her body straight to her sex. Her walls instantly clenched around his fingers and Rose screamed out at the dual erotic sensations. She bucked against his hand as he sucked hard on her neck, taking her blood.

*I can't read you.* She heard the frustration in his voice as he spoke in her mind. *Tell me,* he demanded.

"It feels indescribably good…don't stop," she whispered between pants, digging her fingers into his neck and arching her back to get as close as she could. "Tell…tell me what I taste like," she whispered, her pulse racing. Knife-piercing desire curled in her lower belly and her body ached for release.

Duncan grunted when she clenched her hand tighter around his cock. He twisted his fingers around and began stroking her G-spot, his movements relentless, assured.

*You taste like…mine!* he responded in a fierce, resolute tone.

The intensity in his voice, the sheer need sent her right over the edge. Rose keened in bliss at the all-encompassing sensations and myriad emotions flooding through her. Wave after wave of ecstasy started in her channel and roared through her body.

For a brief second, she let down her mental barrier and was surprised at the breath of renewed strength that slammed into her. The sensation was unlike anything she'd ever experienced, strange and rejuvenating, but scary enough to cause her to lock her mind once more.

Duncan let go of her neck and laved at her wound. Withdrawing his fingers from her body, he rolled over and pulled her in his arms, kissing her forehead.

Rose's hand had fallen away from his erection during her climax. She placed her hand back on the ridge of hard flesh and stared at him. "You didn't come." Gripping his cock, she leaned over and placed a kiss on the soft skin.

His erection jumped in her hand but Duncan pulled her back in his arms saying in a gruff tone, "Another time. I've taken your blood. You need to rest now."

"But I want to know what you taste like—"

Duncan kissed her mouth, cutting off her words. When she began to respond, tangling her tongue with his, he pulled away and pushed her head down on his shoulder.

"Rest."

The truth was, she did feel tired, but she didn't like being ordered around either or feeling as if he'd withdrawn from her. He was doing it again. She'd be damned if she'd let him hold it all back.

"Sing me a song and I'll rest," she said against his chest.

Duncan's body tensed at her request. Rose trailed her fingers back down his stomach toward his erection.

He grasped her hand and planted a kiss on her palm before he began to sing the Irish lullaby "Sleep, My Darling" to her.

Rose closed her eyes and listened to the familiar Irish words fill the room. Duncan's deep voice radiated from his chest. His perfect pitch and intonation reached out and grabbed her in the gut, causing goose bumps to form on her arms. She laced her fingers with his and snuggled close. Sliding her leg between his, she closed her eyes and let his beautiful voice lull her.

Something about Duncan felt so right, she couldn't put it to words. When he trailed off, she said in a sleepy voice, "Promise you'll sing to me again. I love your voice."

He kissed the top of her head. "Go to sleep, Róisín."

Duncan's body ached as he held himself still, waiting for Rose to fall asleep. Damn, the woman knocked the snot out of him. His entire body roared for release, especially when she said she'd wanted to taste him. For the brief second her mental barrier was down, he'd read her curiosity over what *his* blood would taste like. The knowledge had shocked the shit out of him, ramming straight to his groin.

Blowing out a sexually frustrated breath, he tried to understand why he was so freaking tired. Of course, holding off from climaxing while he took her blood did take superhuman strength he didn't really have. He wanted nothing more than to fall asleep with Rose, but he knew if he woke up with her in his arms, he'd take her blood again.

And by doing so, he'd seal her fate.

He knew it took three bites in as many days and while there was a day between that they hadn't seen each other, he knew he wouldn't be able to keep his distance if he hung around another day or two. He didn't want to chance the risk. There was no fucking way he'd convert her to a hybrid vampire. Stroking her soft hair, he closed his eyes.

One thing he knew for certain, he wanted her, cherished this woman like no other. He'd just have to make sure he only saw her every few days so he wouldn't turn her. Hell, for his own sanity, he'd *have* to keep his distance. The more he took her blood, the more addicting she became. He knew the next time he was in Rose's presence he wouldn't ask permission to take her blood.

The next time, after spending at least three days away, even if he'd fed well before he came to Rose, he'd be so revved up to have her, he'd take what he wanted without question, probably more than once. Rose's blood wasn't sustenance in his mind, but a deeper, more primal and satisfying fix every time he tasted her.

And yet, *she'd* knocked him for a wallop, too. This last time with her was so intense, so different. He thought only of pleasing her, making her want what he could offer her. And she took it all. He'd never felt so zonked after a sexual encounter in his life. If he felt this out of it now, he could only imagine what he'd feel like if she sank her fangs into him in a…full vampire mating.

No! His gut clenched as the subconscious thought entered his mind, grabbing hold of his chest and squeezing. Hard.

Duncan slid out from underneath Rose's soft, warm body and walked out of the room. Quickly dressing, he refused to acknowledge the possibility. He never planned to mate. Ever. Mating required more than he could ever give.

Once he was dressed, he glanced back to her bedroom, his stomach knotting. He'd never ached so much for another, never felt so torn.

One thing he knew for certain, he'd be counting every one of those seventy-two hours. When the danger of converting her was over, he'd be back—insatiable for more. Turning on his heel, he left her house and mentally locked the door behind him.

* * * * *

*Swift pain stabbed him in the gut, like someone shoved a knife deep and maliciously twisted to make the blade tear sinew and flesh…to drag out the torture. Duncan clenched his abdominal muscles and grunted, turning away. Groans of pain sliced the air, but they weren't his. At least he didn't think they were. Duncan crouched in the pitch dark, wondering why he couldn't see anything.*

*Another sharp pain slammed his spine this time, knocking him to his knees in its intensity. He roared in anger. His fangs exploded in his gums and his nails extended into claws as he pivoted on the balls of his feet and lashed out at his unknown assailant.*

*"Show yourself, you fucking bastard!"*

*A bolt of bright light flashed before his eyes, blinding him. Excruciating pain splintered through his skull. Duncan fell to the ground holding his head and groaning at the unbelievable pressure pounding inside his mind.*

"*Duncan*!" Rose's heartrending scream shot through the darkness, jerking him out of his nightmare.

Duncan awoke panting. His lower stomach muscles tensed and flexed in response to the nightmare's remnants still inside his mind. He sat up and tore the sheets off his sweat-soaked body as he threw his legs over the side of his bed. Glancing at his hands he was surprised to see them shaking. Duncan ground his teeth and ran his hands through his hair to steady them. What a helluva nightmare!

When his phone rang, Duncan grabbed it off his nightstand with relief. Anything to wash away the dream's surrealistic grip.

"Hello?"

"Whoa! You didn't know it was me?" Ian said, sounding surprised.

Duncan snorted. It was true, even without caller ID, he usually knew when his twin was calling him. "I just woke from the worst nightmare."

"Yeah, I sensed something wasn't right with you. Glad to know it was just a vivid dream. Man, you must be projecting like hell, Dunc."

Duncan rubbed his forehead, unable to shake the weakness that seemed to overtake him.

"You have any news about Mom?"

"That's why I was calling. I went back to the Summit House. All the leaders had left except Lucian. Mom was still in the library talking to Eamon. I asked Lucian if he knew anything but he was as in the dark as we are. Then Mom and Eamon walked into the boardroom and asked to meet with Lucian alone. Alone!"

"Bet you were pissed."

"I expected Lucian to back me up, but he asked me to wait in the library."

Duncan sensed his brother's frustration. "This just gets stranger and stranger, eh bro?"

"When Lucian, Mom and Eamon came back into the library, Lucian told me that he'd decided to let Eamon eliminate James."

"What the fuck! Lucian has to know Eamon's too close."

Ian sighed. "The thing of it is, I think Mom was the one who convinced Luc, swayed his decision."

"Tell me Mom talked to you, told you what the hell was going on." Duncan's shoulders tensed at the turn of events.

"That's the hell of it. She didn't. When I insisted she tell me how she was involved in this, she strode past me saying, 'I've got to talk to your father first'".

"That was hours ago, right?" Duncan ran his hand through his hair, irritated. "Why hasn't she told you yet?"

"Dad was out of town, purchasing another one of his 'antiques'." Ian blew out a breath. Duncan could just picture his brother rubbing his jaw in his frustration. "If Mom doesn't call me in the next half hour, I'm going over there."

The lack of news didn't help Duncan's sense of unease. "I would go with you, but I have something I need to take care of."

"Does it have anything to do with a certain redhead?" Ian asked. "How'd it go last night?"

Duncan ignored his brother's smug tone. "Something's not right, Ian."

"I told you there was something about her."

"No, that's not what I mean. I *feel* that something's not right."

"Then why the fuck are you still talking to me? Get the hell over to her place and find out."

Duncan closed his eyes and fought the constriction in his chest. "I can't. If I go there, I know I'll take her blood again. I'll convert her."

"And that's a bad thing? You obviously have a connection with this woman."

Sometimes having a twin who seemed to know you better than yourself really bit the big one. Duncan clenched his jaw and remained quiet.

"Why do you think you *feel* her? Have you heard her thoughts? I'm talking about *hearing* her without consciously listening in her mind? Rose is the one person I've seen you show a deep interest in, the one person even *I* have a connection with through you… This woman is your Anima, Dunc."

Hearing his brother voice the words that'd been rumbling around in his subconscious hit Duncan hard. His chest felt as if it were going to explode. "I won't convert her, Ian. I refuse to mate," he said through gritted teeth.

"Get the fuck over it! If you can't trust yourself to be alone with her, take Mark with you, but if you feel in your gut something just isn't right, get over there."

"It was just a dream," Duncan insisted, trying to convince himself.

"Are you willing to take that chance?" Ian countered. "Call Mark. I'm going to get some answers from Mom. Keep your cell with you."

Duncan hung up the phone, then glanced at the clock. Four in the morning. His stomach churned in hunger, stronger than it had in a very long time. Why was he so hungry? He'd just fed a few hours ago. A wave of queasiness hit his stomach, the kind of ache that came with sheer emptiness. Inexplicable concern for Rose roared through him.

His mind made up, he picked up the phone and dialed Mark's cell.

"Twice in one week! Will wonders never cease?"

"Can the sarcasm, Devlin. This is important."

"What's up?"

"The benefits of being my vampri," Duncan replied in a derisive tone. "I need your help."

"Do I need to call in the trackers again?"

"No. I just need you to do me a favor. To check on someone for me. You're closer to her house than I am. I'll meet you there."

Duncan heard Mark's car starting. "Sure thing. What's the name and address?"

He gave Mark the address. "Her name is Rose Sinclair."

"Ice Queen Sinclair?" Mark hooted. "How do you know her? Did she freeze your balls off?"

"What the hell are you talking about?" Rose was the furthest he'd ever seen from an Ice Queen.

"Whoa, calm down. That's just the name the boys down at the precinct call her. They've all tried to get her to go out with them, but she turned them down cold."

Duncan couldn't help the smile that spread across his face at the knowledge Rose acted anything but the "Ice Queen" with him.

"So you know Rose?"

"Yep, she comes in from time to time when she's working on a case."

Relieved that Rose wouldn't freak out if Mark got to her house before he did, Duncan said, "I need you to go by her house and check on her. I'll meet you there."

"Will do. By the way, how do you know Rose?"

"She's the woman James kidnapped."

"The one who drove off on your motorcycle?" Mark laughed out loud.

"I'll see you there." He ignored Mark's jibe and hung up the phone.

* * * * *

He shifted from his raven form to his human form outside her home. Without money or a passport, he'd used his powers to compel his way through the airport's international gates. He'd had a grueling flight from Ireland. Using his shifting ability, he was able to dodge the sunlight, but the effort left him so exhausted by the time he arrived in the States during the day, he'd stayed hidden in an airport closet until hunger forced him to seek food. After he'd gorged himself on the blood from three women and two men passing the closet he'd taken up residence in, he'd left the airport at three in the morning.

Revenge rose up in him as he immediately followed her scent across town. Yet, the need to protect battled within him, tamping down his own desires as the Goddess had promised.

How many times had he cursed this pitiful excuse of a life The Morrigan had condemned him to? Hatred pumped in his veins, swift, dark…unforgiving.

His cold eyes swept the perimeter of her home, looking for enemies. Anger welled that she wasn't there. That he'd have to track her down.

While walking among the human race, he'd projected black clothing on himself…a fitting color for his mood. He smirked at how real his black trench coat swirling around his boots would look to anyone who saw him. As he approached her front door, he hoped that in the long years since he'd last seen her, she'd learned more defensive moves. She'd need them. The Morrigan might've given him an edict he couldn't disobey—to protect his priestess at all costs—but the Goddess didn't remove his desire to have her powers…or what she thought were his desires.

Instead the truth festered within him, twisting the man he once was into the beast he'd become today. He couldn't wait to toy with her, to take her to the brink. Then he'd exact his revenge. He didn't fear death. He'd gotten what The Morrigan thought he'd wanted. Immortality. But as the Goddess would soon discover, even she wasn't infallible.

He narrowed his eyes and relished kicking the front door open. The wood splintered and the panel gave way. Scanning the room, his shrewd gaze took in the surroundings. Her scent clung to his nostrils like the sweetest nectar, but his entire frame stiffened when he smelled another vamp's scent permeating the house.

"No!" he growled, rushing forward to the area in her home the scent radiated from the strongest.

When he walked into her bedroom, his gaze landed on the bed with its torn sheets. Noting the drops of blood on a pillowcase, he picked up one of the pillows and licked the red liquid that had soaked the soft white cotton.

Confirmation snapped him to attention. This wasn't Anna, but her descendant. He tasted no other vamp's blood, but he'd definitely scented another vamp. Did this mean what he thought it meant? She wasn't yet mated to this vampire? Was this male vamp the threat he'd been called forth to protect her from? This mysterious vampire smelled like him, but different. He hadn't known there were others in the United States. The knowledge surprised him.

Would this vampire's powers rival his? Excitement made his stomach tighten. He looked forward to finding out. Cataloging the other vamp's scent in his mind, he dropped the pillow and glanced outside.

He had less than an hour before sunrise. With a derisive twist of his lips, he wondered what would become of him if Anna's descendent mated, rendering his protection unnecessary. Would this strange land's earth swallow him where he stood? Would he be doomed to reside his days stuck in this foreign land's earth and away from his homeland's soil?

His gaze landed on the surface of the dresser against the far wall. Noting the deep, claw-mark gouges in the wood, he approached. He frowned and laid his hands over the marred wood, drawing his fingers through the long burrows. It was as if someone had clung hard to the surface, then pulled back or fell. The marks were too close together to be a male's. These were smaller…definitely female. Putting his fingers to his nose, he inhaled and rage filled him.

The male vamp's scent didn't just cling to hers, it commingled with hers. Anna's descendant was converted. Fury swept over him at the new information. He met his own gaze in the mirror above the dresser and the cold steel-colored eyes that stared back at him surprised him. Where had the deep blue color gone? He ran his fingers over his clean-shaven face, noting the harsh lines that surrounded his mouth. He might not have aged but his face had taken on a hard, merciless look.

The phone rang, distracting him. He turned his gaze to the offending sound, and moved to pound the machine to oblivion.

"Rose, it's Helen. I got to the phone too late to answer your call, but I got your message. I don't mind going in early to have your father ready to meet you. Honey, I'm worried about you. You sounded stressed. Well…I guess you're on your way, so I'll see you in half an hour—"

He picked up the phone and spoke to the woman, compelling her. "Give me directions to this place."

The woman gave him directions and agreed to meet him there immediately.

Satisfaction filled him as he hung up the phone. Her name was Rose. He could've tracked her scent down, but he had very little time left before sunrise. Being one step ahead of her gave him an advantage.

Glancing in the mirror once more, he surveyed the ruthless, icy smile that tilted the corners of his lips.

The male vamp's scent might be intertwined with hers, but no male vampire's blood was mixed with Rose's. That meant she wasn't mated yet, and there was no way he'd let her feck up his chance to remain above ground. As long as she was unmated, her need for protection kept him out of the earth, kept him breathing, moving and feasting. The curse might compel him to find her, to keep her safe…but he had his own agenda to fulfill.

Now that he was free of his prison of dirt, he'd take his body to the full extent of his pain tolerance to exact the revenge that had kept him sane for over two hundred years.

# Chapter Nine

ꝏ

Rose drove into the Five Star Hotel's parking lot and lowered her forehead to her car's steering wheel. She took deep breaths to calm her shattered nerves. Pulling the keys from the ignition, she slid her shaking hands between her thighs to steady them. Her heart thundered in her ears, loud and clear, but slower than she thought it should be for the panicky way she felt.

Her gut clenched as she glanced at her wide-eyed, troubled expression in the rearview mirror. She had no idea what was happening to her. She just remembered waking up to excruciating pain in her belly and back. Sharp, shooting, unforgiving pain made her scream out and double over in a defensive posture. She'd tried to get out of bed, to call someone, but the horrific shards of pain slicing through her were too much. She clung to the bed, panting through the unrelenting waves.

Her head had pounded in agony. She truly felt as if someone was trying to unscrew it right off her body. It felt so real, so painfully palpable, she'd crawled over to the mirror to see for herself that her head was still attached. With supreme effort, she stood to see her reflection, but when she finally made it upright and confirmed she looked normal despite the pain, a bright light had splintered through her skull, taking her to her knees. She'd gripped the dresser, trying to hold on, but she couldn't. Her fingers pulled away from the wood as she fell over onto her side crying out for Duncan to help her.

And just where had the jerk gone? Then again, if he'd tried to comfort or help her while all that pain had gripped her, he would've been the one with the gouges on his body instead of her dresser. At the very least, Duncan would've thought she was possessed.

What was going on?

Taking a deep breath, she opened the car door and was surprised by the strong smells that assailed her senses. Freshly laid asphalt from the construction work being done across the street, the woman's cologne clinging to the man stumbling out of the casino twenty feet away. She even smelled the alcohol on his breath. Ugh. Her stomach churned.

When she started to stand, her knees buckled and she fell back in her car's seat once more. She felt so damn weak…as if she needed to eat an eight-course meal to give her the strength to get out of her car.

Gritting her teeth in frustration, she forced herself up once more and shut the door. She'd driven to the hotel early on purpose. This way she wouldn't run into anyone she knew while she retrieved her mother's paperwork as well as her passport she'd stuck in the same envelope. She didn't know what was going on with her, but somehow she intuitively knew…it had to do with her mother and she didn't want to have idle chitchat with anyone at the moment.

As soon as she retrieved the paperwork from her room in the hotel, she planned to go see her father. To ask him if he remembered anything about her mother's past. Then she'd book her flight to Ireland. She felt desperate for answers.

When the drunk exiting the hotel started to pass her, he stumbled. Without a thought, she reached out and grabbed him, catching him on the way down. She held him by his shirt, hanging in the air a couple of inches above the hard asphalt. Surprised that this two-hundred-pound man felt as if he weighed nothing more than a napkin, she pulled him to his feet.

"Thanks," he mumbled at the same time she heard him say, *Damn, she's fuckable.*

Angry at what she realized she'd just heard—his thoughts—she dropped his sleeve.

"Go home to your wife and kids, Dan."

The man's eyes widened and he took several steps back. "How'd you know my name? And that I was married?" Then his gaze narrowed and he snarled, "Are you following me? Did she hire you?"

Rose's stomach growled, rumbling in emptiness. She heard his heart rate increase in fear and anger. Why did she hear his thoughts, know his name or his marital status? And why the hell was the sound of his blood pumping through his veins akin to hearing yummy popcorn popping in one of those machines at the movie theater?

Her stomach rumbled again and she turned to walk away, but the man grabbed her arm.

"Hey, lady, I'm talking to you."

Anger rose within her. Rose grabbed his hand and pulled it off her arm.

The man yelped and fell to his knees, cradling his hand. "You've crushed my hand."

Surprised by his total weenieness, she replied, "I said, go home," then walked up the stairs and entered the hotel.

*Okaaaaaaay, that had to be the most bizarre interchange I've ever had.* Her stomach growled again, the hollowness sending a wave of nausea through her.

*I wish I'd eaten,* she thought as she walked through the main hotel lobby. But the smell of the early morning breakfast being prepared in one of the hotel's restaurants almost made her lose what little contents her stomach held.

*Ugh, I must've passed the "I'm really hungry" stage and moved into the "If I eat right now, I'll hurl" stage.*

Rose had just punched the elevator button to go downstairs to her room, when she heard Michelle's hyper voice call out, "Rose!"

*Oh shit.* She turned to see Mish running across the lobby's gleaming tile floor to come a sliding halt beside her. "Ohmigod, I just had the best night of my life," she gushed.

Rose met her friend's excited gaze. She couldn't believe it…the scent of sex clung to Mish. And Rose caught two distinct male scents as well. Why could she smell them? Did someone rub Vicks under her nose and activate some dormant heightened sense of smell she never knew she had? Damn, maybe she could apply to be a bomb or cocaine sniffer for the police. What a cakewalk job that'd be.

Shrugging away her rambling thoughts, Rose narrowed her gaze. "Tell me you didn't sleep with both of them."

Mish's cheeks turned red and she glanced around the quiet lobby. *Uh-oh, should I lie to her? I never took Rose for a prude.*

Rose stiffened at the thoughts that spilled forth from Michelle.

Tossing the ends of her hair over her shoulder, Rose said in a calm, even tone. "I'd prefer the truth..." *Even though I wish like hell I couldn't hear your thoughts.*

Michelle gave her a mischievous look. "Okay, okay...yes, I slept with both men. I've always wondered," she started to say, then put her hand on Rose's arm and rushed to finish, "But I did make them both wear condoms."

Rose sighed and shook her head, saying in a dry tone, "There's always that. You seem none the worse for wear."

"I'm on top of the world," Mish said, twirling around. Then she faced Rose once more and raised her eyebrows. "You look way too serious for someone who's just sneaking in at four a.m. How'd your evening with Stryker go?"

"Duncan," Rose supplied.

"Oooh, Duncan. What a sexy name. Now spill."

She stepped into the elevator and Michelle followed her in. Rose pushed the button to her floor and replied in a miffed tone, "He didn't stay all night." Shrugging off her annoyance, she continued, "I've got to get my paperwork and head over to see my dad."

"At this hour?" Michelle asked, glancing at her watch.

Rose nodded, stepping off the elevator when it arrived at her floor. "Helen's going to open the doors for me. Dad was always an early riser. He should be awake. I'm hoping to catch a flight to Ireland today if I can."

As she turned to head down the hall to her room, Michelle called after her, "Something about you seems different."

*Tell me about it,* Rose thought. "I'm fine. I've just got a lot on my mind at the moment."

*****

Duncan's cell phone rang when he was almost to Rose's house. Mark's caller ID displayed on the readout.

Flipping open the phone, Duncan answered, "What is it?"

"Rose's door has been kicked open and I smell a latent scent of another vampire who was recently here."

Duncan's stomach pitched. "Be there in one minute." He closed the cell phone and gunned his car's engine.

Duncan's wheels squealed when he slammed on the brakes and halted behind Mark's truck.

Mark poked his head outside Rose's front door as Duncan approached with purposeful strides. "She's not here. The cop in me made me walk in—"

"For Rose's safety we'll ignore the rule," Duncan interrupted him in a curt tone.

"Well," Mark started to speak, then hesitated.

When he paused, Duncan automatically jumped into his mind, seeking answers the younger vamp held back.

*God, what he must've done to her.*

Rage and fear radiated through Duncan, squeezing his heart. He growled low in his throat and shoved past Mark. Inhaling deeply, he followed his senses, tracking the path the other vamp had taken. It led him right to Rose's bedroom. With each step he took, dread filled him.

Stepping inside Rose's bedroom, he took in the sight of her ripped sheets and gouged dresser top. Visions of his dream came slamming back. She'd been in severe, excruciating pain.

Duncan's hands fisted at his sides. With supreme effort, he stayed rooted where he stood when all he wanted to do was tear into anyone near him. He heard Mark fall into step behind him and closed his eyes to calm the beast roaring within him. Taking deep breaths, he concentrated on the mixture of scents in her room.

Separating out his own scent and Mark's, the intruder's scent slammed into him full force. Duncan was surprised at the power behind this vampire, power he'd never encountered when mixing with the other clans. The man's apathy literally hung in the air around Duncan as if taunting him. Clenching his jaw, Duncan opened his eyes.

"What do you smell?" Mark asked quietly.

Duncan turned and narrowed his gaze on his vampri. "I smell a Sythen."

"But James has been captured."

Duncan shook his head. "It's not James."

Duncan walked over and started to touch the deep furrows in the dresser top. Made by small hands. A woman's, not a man's. His hand shook so bad, he had to curl his fingers into a fist to calm his rioting emotions.

When he stared at his own golden gaze in the mirror, knowledge he'd been holding back slammed into his consciousness.

What he'd dreamed, all the pain he'd experienced…it was Rose converting to a vampire—a Sythen. The bastard let her go through the conversion in a conscious state. He'd let her suffer. The sick fuck.

"Did you see this? Your senses are far superior to mine. Might be a place to start," Mark said.

Duncan turned to see Mark holding a pillow from Rose's bed. Hope and dread fought a raging battle within him as he approached.

Grasping the pillow, he stood there, holding it, staring at the drops of blood. His heart had never beat so hard.

"Aren't you going to check it out?" Mark prodded.

Duncan met his anxious gaze then lifted the pillow to taste the drops of blood.

The vamp's flavor, strong and ancient coated his tongue, making him want to puke. But he was too relieved to discover no other blood mixed with Rose's. She might be converted, but she wasn't mated to the vamp. Not yet at least.

The small taste also helped him focus on Rose, seek her out on a subconscious level. She was alive and currently not fearful.

Throwing the pillow down, he turned on his heel, striding from the room.

"Hey, you going to share your thoughts?" Mark asked, following him out of the room. "I can sense the change in your mood."

"She's alive. I've got to find her," Duncan simply stated as he made his way out of Rose's house.

Mark followed him out, shutting the splintered door behind him. "If you want my help, you need to clue me in."

Duncan stopped mid-stride on his way to his car. He turned back to Mark. "Thanks for your help."

Mark stopped walking and a shocked expression crossed his face before he composed himself. "You're welcome. Now tell me what the hell is going on so I can help you find Rose."

Duncan sighed. "I do need your help since I need all my wits about me to track her."

"Lay it on me."

"Call Ian and inform him we've got another rogue Sythen on our hands, a very powerful one. Tell him to talk to Eamon and find out who this vamp is."

Mark frowned. "Hey, if this vamp has Rose and he's as powerful as you think he is, you'll need backup. You shouldn't go after him alone."

Duncan narrowed his gaze. "I believe the Sythen converted Rose but for whatever reason didn't mate with her. At least not yet." Hope filled him. "Maybe she somehow fought him off. I don't know. Finding her is my first priority."

"What is it about this one human woman that is making all the Sythens go bonkers?" Mark asked, shaking his head as he opened his car door.

Without a second thought, Duncan replied, "There's something special about her."

Mark jerked his gaze to his. "That sounded personal and not just an objective observation."

"It's very personal. Call Ian, fill him in and find out what you can," he said before he got in his car.

* * * * *

Rose arrived at the retirement home feeling so sick if she'd had any food in her belly she'd have lost it as soon as she parked her car. As it was, her stomach rolled in hunger, clenching and cramping to be filled. As soon as she met with her father, she'd find something to eat...if the strong smells didn't make her throw up first.

She got out of her car and made her way to the entrance. Helen met her at the glass door, a worried look on her face.

Opening the door for her, Helen said, "Are you all right? You look as if you're in pain."

She met Helen's concerned gaze. "I'm just feeling a bit worn out. Is my dad up?"

Helen nodded as she wrapped an arm around her shoulder and guided her to the front desk. "Yes, he's the only resident awake at this early hour, so he was excited to learn he'd have two visitors today.

"Two?"

"He's talking with the nice gentleman who came by for a visit. Ooh, his Irish accent sent tremors down my spine." A dreamy expression crossed Helen's face. "I've never seen such arresting eyes on someone before. They reminded me of molten steel."

Rose jerked her gaze to Helen's once more, her heart rate picking up. "Where are they?"

"They're in the rec room, dear."

Rose took off down the hall, her stomach tightening even more. Who was this Irish man visiting her father?

A shiver coursed though her as she hurried down the hall. It was eerily empty. She usually passed a nurse or resident or two on her way to the rec room. Today, only the whooshing heartbeats of sleeping residents behind closed doors greeted her. She paused for a second. How strange that she could hear their heartbeats. Shaking her head, she began walking at a brisk pace once more. She had to get to her dad.

Rose arrived at the entrance to the rec room to see the stranger, his long black hair hiding his face as he leaned over her father. His hands gripped the older man's upper arms, while her father's bony hands clutched his broad shoulders as if here were hanging on for dear life.

From across the room, she heard her father's rapid breathing, sensed his heart thudding in his chest as he pleaded in a desperate whisper, "Please..."

Her father took a deep breath and then his heartbeat stopped as if instantly cut off. When the man let him go and his body slumped back in this wheelchair, Rose's heart jerked, disbelief rocking through her.

"No!" she screamed and took two steps.

She didn't have time to ponder how she landed beside her father all the way across the room. Crouched next to his wheelchair, rage engulfed her, shutting out all rational thoughts. "What have you done?" She launched her body toward the stranger, ready to claw his eyes out.

His hand shot out, encircling her throat as his dark eyebrows drew together over cold-as-steel eyes. Her gaze strayed to the inch-wide streak of white that slashed through his pitch-black hair before locking with his penetrating stare. His hold on her neck tightened in a viselike grip. The smell of rich earth and outdoors rushed over her as he forced her to her knees, a satisfied smirk crossing his angular face.

"Ye're a fine bit of stuff." A heavy Irish accent laced his words as his hard gaze scanned her face. Lifting her mother's necklace with his other hand, he glanced down at it, read the inscription on the back, then gave her a lethal smile. "Now that ye've summoned me, yer protection is me duty to fulfill. Let's get started."

Even more outraged by his odd, emotionless comment, Rose clawed at the tight hold he had on her neck. She wanted to scream at him, to rip his heart out, but taking a breath was difficult at this point. She was unprepared when he lifted her off the ground and flung her across the room.

When her body slammed hard into a far wall, swift pain radiated through her on impact. As she slid to the floor, she thought for sure every bone in her body was broken. Rose fell to her side in agony, unable to catch her breath. Her vision began to blur, but the only thought that entered her sluggish mind was the fact her father was gone forever. Killed by a powerful, evil bastard.

* * * * *

*Wake up.*

Rose heard the deep growl in her mind but she didn't want to come out of the blissful darkness she'd fallen into. She rolled over onto her side, moaning at the hunger raging through her. The need to eat, to survive overrode her fear of the man who'd killed her father. He was somewhere close. She could feel him, feel the impatience radiating from him.

Grass tickled her cheek and the smell of earth permeated her senses. Her gaze started to come into focus and it landed on a pair of black boots standing beside her. She realized she was outside but she couldn't have been passed out long because it was still dark. How could she see him so clearly as if it were daylight?

The man squatted a couple feet away from her. His black shirt clung to his muscular chest and arms. Eerie smoky eyes narrowed on her. If she'd had the energy, she'd gouge those cold eyes out.

"My father," she hissed at him.

"I hear yer stomach rumbling," he said, ignoring her. "Ye need to eat."

"You killed him, you bastard," she shouted with everything she had. The loss caused a deep pain to fill her heart. She tried to move, to crawl away from him, but damn it, she felt so weak and helpless when all she wanted to do was torture the bastard, make him pay.

"Yer aul fella's dead," he said in a matter-of-fact tone. He met her gaze for a long moment, an impassive look on his face. "The nurse is taking care of him as ye'd instructed her to do if he passed."

"I didn't give Helen official permission…I-I mean, I know we talked about it—" she started to say, then shrieked, "You had no right to initiate my father's burial preparations." Fury and sorrow engulfed her, making her sick to her stomach. Her empty belly pitched and rumbled, rebelling at the waves of conflicting emotions running through her. Rage, sadness and helplessness slammed into her…all laced with healthy dose of fear. He was a cold-blooded killer.

The man's expression darkened. He stood and turned to address someone. "Come."

With great effort, Rose was finally able to sit up. She saw Scott, a male nurse who worked at the retirement home, step forward.

"Are you okay?" he asked, concern in his gaze as he squinted in the darkness. A lock of blond hair fell over his eyes as he started to lower himself to the ground to check on her.

The stranger put a hand on Scott's chest, stopping his descent. His steely eyes turned toward her again.

"Ye need to eat."

"You'd better pick out a cemetery plot," she gritted out through clenched teeth, rage overcoming her grief and fear. If she gave in to the fear, it would consume her. Better to die fighting.

"Ye have to feed," he ordered, ignoring her threat.

Why the hell would he care if she ate? He just planned to kill her anyway. She glanced around the wide field he'd taken her to. It had to be the field behind the rest home. Rose met his gaze once more. His choice of word—feed—was just like something Duncan would've said. Ohmigod, was it possible the man was a vampire? He felt familiar to her somehow. She remembered she'd tingled when he'd touched her…just like with Duncan and James. Her heart pounded and her head ached at the realization he had to be a vampire. She had no chance in hell of killing him…at least not easily.

But…that meant if he expected her to "feed", he thought she was one, too. The thought of drinking someone's blood made bile rise in her throat. She clamped her lips shut to keep from throwing up and shook her head. When she regained control over her roiling stomach, she panted out, "You're insane. I'm not a vampire."

"Vampire?" Scott asked, shock and disbelief on his face as he glanced at the vamp. "Are you some kind of nutcase?"

"Whisht!" the vamp said in a low, commanding tone. Scott shut his mouth as if an invisible hand had been clamped over it. He just stood there, staring at them.

"I'll kill the vamp who converted ye," the vamp bit out. "He's obviously the reason ye've called me."

Rose gritted her teeth, fury building to a frenzy within her. "You seem to have an easy time killing. And for the last time, I'm not a fucking vampire."

The stranger got down on one knee and grasped her chin. Anger made his cold eyes seem to dance like liquid mercury.

"I don't have time for this shite. I know ye hear the blood rushin' in his veins, smell the sweet scent callin' to ye." His deep voice lowered to a menacing purr. "Embrace yer new life, Rose. Eat."

She jumped at the last word. As soon as he'd spoken it she felt her incisors lengthen inside her mouth, brushing against her lips.

Hunger clenched her stomach and she clamped her lips shut, her chest tightening. *No! This can't be happening. I'm not a vampire.* But the truth didn't lie. Her entire morning started to make sense—her heightened senses, her strength with the drunk man in the parking lot, her ability to jump across the room…and her pulse, thumping at the sound of blood pumping in Scott's veins.

A satisfied look crossed the vamp's face. He used his thumb to raise her upper lip, exposing one of her incisors. Sliding his gaze back to Scott, he said, "Dinner is ready."

Rose jerked her head away from his touch, hunger clawing within her. But her old human self wouldn't let go. "I won't take his blood."

The stranger snarled and stood. Grasping Scott's arm, he jerked him closer and said in a cold tone, "He won't feel a thing." The vamp's fingernail extended and he sliced a two-inch cut on Scott's wrist.

"Ow!" Scott yelped, grasping his arm. Panic crept in his voice as he stared at his wrist. "God, I'm bleeding."

"Except that," came the vamp's curt comment. Turning his icy gaze to Rose, he continued in a droll tone, "Better seal his wound. They say wrist cuts can be lethal."

Rose had gasped at the vamp's disregard for Scott's well-being when he sliced his wrist. She quickly crawled over to put her hand over Scott's wound, hoping to stop the flow of bright red blood.

"Help me!" Scott wailed, falling to his knees.

"Help him, you bastard!" she screamed up at the man.

He crossed his arms, a stoic look on his face. "Only *you* can help him."

Her heart racing in fear for Scott, Rose grasped his arm and pulled him close. When she ran her tongue across his cut to seal the wound, her stomach cramped in response to his sweet flavor. Instead of wanting to vomit at the taste of his blood, she savored it. His blood didn't taste metallic at all, but more like a fine dinner wine. *I want more,* she thought as she fought the need to take the man's blood.

Scott's appreciative moan didn't help. He swayed toward her. "That feels so good. Does it feel even better if you suck on it? Do it," he begged.

*I know ye want to kill me,* the vamp spoke in her mind. *If ye want a go at me, ye haven't a prayer if ye don't eat.*

The instinct to survive reared its ugly head and Rose gave Scott what he wanted. She sucked on his wound, taking the blood he offered. With each swallow, her hunger abated, but she found she couldn't get enough. She sucked harder, leaning closer. Scott's eyes were closed and he groaned as if he were having an orgasmic experience.

"Enough," the stranger commanded. "Ye'll take too much."

His harsh words jerked her out of the euphoric state she'd fallen into. Rose carefully laved Scott's wound closed. She hated the vampire even more for making her take an innocent man's blood.

Scott fell back on the ground panting and staring up at the early morning sky. "Damn, I'm tired, but that was amazing."

The stranger pulled Scott to his feet. Turning him toward the facility, he said in a dry tone, "Good lad. We're always open for a donation twenty-four/seven."

Feeling renewed and stronger than she ever had, Rose glared at the loathsome vamp.

"He can't go to work after donating blood."

He rolled his eyes, then took a deep breath as if to give him patience. "Ye've got the rest of the day off. Go home and sleep," he called after the nurse.

The vamp turned his penetrating gaze back to Rose and started to say, "Now back to—"

Rose didn't give him a chance to finish, she launched herself toward the vamp, intending to choke his pathetic life out of him. "You bastard!"

The momentum knocked them to the ground. Rose landed on top of him, clocking him hard in the jaw with her fist.

His head snapped back at the impact. He grunted but swiftly grabbed her wrists and rolled her over on her back, pinning her to the ground. His silver eyes blazed in anger. "I've had enough of explaining meself. Ye might be newly converted, but ye've proven ye're worthy of yer heritage. The lesson begins now."

She felt him enveloping her, surrounding her mind, not like Duncan, but different…almost as if he were trying to suck the energy right of her.

If he wanted to play mental games, she'd come out the winner. With a concentrated effort, she blocked his invasion. "Fuck you!" she said as she mentally shoved him away. The vamp went flying backward until he rammed into a tree twenty feet away.

Rose quickly stood and the act made blood rush to her head. She leaned forward, putting her hands on her knees as she took deep breaths to keep from losing consciousness.

The vamp got up, brushed the dirt and debris off him and leered at her. Taking two long strides, he launched himself in the air, coming at her like a bullet.

Shocked by the show of his powers, Rose stood there rooted to the ground.

*Defend yourself,* he growled in her head, jerking her out of the trance she'd fallen into.

At the last second, survival instincts prevailed and Rose jumped straight up in the air, avoiding his hit by mere inches.

The vamp landed on the ground, rolling to his feet. He pivoted on his heel, facing her once more. "Ye're a quick learner." His voice was almost appreciative.

The thought made her want to puke. Rose growled and leapt at the man. Grasping his neck, she pulled him to the ground. Jamming her knee into his chest, she encircled his neck and squeezed with all her might. The bloodlust railing within her surprised her, but at the moment she didn't give a damn.

"You killed my father and turned me into a vampire. How did you bite me without me knowing it?"

Before she knew what had happened, he'd grasped her wrists and rolled her over on her back once more. This time he held her arms above her head. "I didn't bite ye. Another converted ye."

"Liar!" she spat, trying to pull free of his tight grasp. "You erased my memory."

He laughed at her comment. "Shite, I can't. Yer will is the strongest I've ever seen. Even stronger than yer mother's."

Rose stopped struggling, shocked by his comment. Blood rushed in her ears. "You knew my mother? Who are you?"

A surprised look crossed his face as if he didn't expect her not to know who he was. "Me name is Rónán Keegan and yer mother is the reason I'm cursed," he bit out. Leaning close, he inhaled next to her throat. "In spite of me anger…I bet ye'd be a good ride, Rose. Goddess knows I want to take yer blood. The need rages within me."

Fear welled within her and Rose prepared to fend him off, to keep those fangs out of her body. But she didn't get a chance, because he swiftly rolled over and gritted out, "Defend yerself."

Pain slammed into her as he jerked her arm, sending her flying across the field to land in a heap a good fifteen feet away.

Aching all over, Rose raised herself up on her arms. Why was he toying with her? Why didn't he just kill her? Get it over with?

Breathing heavily, she brushed her hair out of her face in time to see Rónán running toward her. Panic set in when she saw the vamp convert to a black jaguar mid-stride. Thick muscles rippled in his shoulders as the animal thundered toward her, roaring his jaguar's cry, his white teeth bared.

"I don't want to die," she whispered out loud.

*Shift and defend,* she heard him hiss in her mind.

Rose crouched low on the balls of her feet. She clutched the grass and earth with her hands, feeling strange. She was preparing to jump out of his path again when he repeated, *Shift and defend, for fuck's sake.*

A growling scream came from deep within her at the same time her muscles began to twitch. Her shoulders and legs felt as if they were breaking in two, no longer a part of her.

She ignored the biting pain, concentrating on the animal leaping toward her. Rose jumped and turned in the air, ready to grasp the fur on the jaguar's back and take him down that way.

Instead of her arms and hands, she saw red furry legs and long, sharp claws. Blood welled as her claws raked down the jaguar's back.

*Raaaaaagh,* he growled, turning his head and snapping at her claws as he landed.

Rose released her hold and leapt off his back, landing on all fours. Shocked by the knowledge she'd converted to a jaguar, she could only stare at Rónán.

Blood seeped from his wounds and he took a slow, tight circle until he faced her once more, his long tail twitching just above the ground.

*Tell me why ye summoned me? Did ye call me 'cause of the one who converted ye?*

*Summoned you?* She gave a mental snort of anger. *I didn't summon you.* Rose was shocked at how easily she fell into talking mentally, but as a jaguar, she probably didn't have the physical ability to vocalize anyway.

He lowered his massive jaguar head and pawed the ground, his eyes narrowing. The rising sun reflected in his metallic gaze, making it appear even colder and devoid of emotion. Dangerous and lethal were the only two words that came to mind when she met his icy stare. Why wasn't he burning to a crisp? And if she was a vampire, too, then why wasn't she?

*Ye did summon me. Through the necklace ye have on.*

Rose remembered the chill that went down her spine when she'd opened the locket at the same time she's spoken the words "Protect me, forever" in Irish. Then the English translation of the lyrics to the "Sleep, my Darling" lullaby her mother used to sing to her came flashing into her mind.

*Sleep, my sweet darling*

*Knowing your guardian will come*

*Make wise your decision to call him,*

*Above all else, his protection will be done.*

Realization dawned and she asked, *Was my mother a vampire like you?*

He shook his jaguar head. *Yer mother was special.*

The rising sun reflected off his shiny black fur, highlighting the blue-black color and magnifying the stark contrast of the white stripe down his side.

*I don't understand*, she whispered.

He lowered his head and pawed at the ground once more, impatience reflecting in his stiffened stance. *Tell me where to find this vampire who converted ye.*

Rose's mind whirled. If he spoke the truth and he hadn't bitten her, then Duncan had to have converted her. She felt the sun warming her bare skin and realized that while she was thinking, she'd let go of her jaguar shape and had converted back her human form—her naked human form.

When she lifted her gaze to Rónán's, the heated look in his jaguar eyes didn't bode well for her. Spying her torn clothes on the ground a few feet away, her heart rammed in her chest. She shakily stood on her feet, her hands extended. "Don't even think about it."

The jaguar's nostrils flared and his ears flicked back and forth as he slowly advanced on her, a low purring sound punctuating each step he took.

Rose took a deep breath to let out a "bloody murder" scream. Instead, she gulped in surprise when someone slammed into the jaguar's side. As the man and cat rolled in the grass, another person lifted her body in his arms.

This time she did scream as she began to fight her captor. Then she heard Duncan's voice in her head. *Go with Mark. Now!*

Fear and relief rushed through her when she saw through the blur of fists and claws flying back and forth. The man fighting Rónán was Duncan. Rose struggled once more, turning to speak to the blond man holding her, "He'll kill Duncan."

Mark's grip on her tightened. "Duncan can't concentrate on fighting if he's worried for your safety."

Understanding filtered into her mind and Rose stopped struggling. "Put me down. I can run faster on my own."

Mark nodded, setting her down. As they ran, Rose took one last look back. When she saw the jaguar bite Duncan's shoulder and heard his roar of pain, she stopped and started to turn around, but Mark gripped her arm. "He's a male vampire, Rose, a stronger fighter than you. Let him fight."

"Then why doesn't he shift so he's on equal footing?" she argued.

Mark tugged on her arm. "Because he's limited in his shifting abilities."

"He is?" Rose asked, worry for Duncan's safety ramping up once again. She started to pull away from Mark's grasp. "I can help."

Mark tightened his grip and nodded toward the early morning sun. "The vamp's affected by it. I can sense his power weakening."

Rose concentrated on Mark's comment. She turned to see Duncan land a blow to the jaguar that sent the big cat flying. Apparently Mark was right.

Nodding to him, she started running again. Once they reached the parking lot. Mark fished out his keys and unlocked his passenger door. "Get in."

Rose slid into the passenger seat. Now that the imminent danger had lessened, the cool leather reminded her of her naked status. When Mark climbed in and started the engine, she said, "Please keep your gaze on the road."

Mark didn't look her way as he pulled out of the parking lot. "Duncan and I saw you shift. So I'm assuming that Sythen converted you. But no matter what clan we're from, we all have the ability to project clothes on our forms if we wish."

She glanced at his profile in surprise. "We do?"

He nodded. "Concentrate on clothing yourself. Imagine being dressed."

Rose closed her eyes and took deep, calming breaths. When she opened her eyes, she saw jeans, boots and a black sweat jacket clothing her body. Wow! Now that was cool!

"Try to keep the image in your mind until we arrive at Ian's house," Mark said, glancing her way. "Jax is about your size. She should have something for you to wear."

Worry for Duncan still gripped her. "Can't we just wait a safe distance away?"

Mark shook his head. "He insisted I take you to Ian's."

She grabbed his arm. "And I insist we don't leave him completely."

Mark started to speak, then he paused for a second and met her gaze. "Duncan just communicated with me. The vamp got away. He shifted to mist. Duncan says he'll meet us at Ian's."

Relief washed over her that Duncan survived. "I'm so glad he's okay." Even though she was thankful Duncan was unhurt, Rose had to admit to herself she wasn't all that unhappy the vamp got away. She wanted to kill Rónán herself. Something told her the battle wasn't over between Rónán and her. She'd get her opportunity. The vamp had to pay for murdering her father.

Rose closed her eyes against the overwhelming sorrow that swept through her. Her father was gone. Clenching her jaw, she squeezed her eyes tight to hold back the tears that had surfaced. She needed to stay focused. Not fall to pieces.

Forcing herself to focus on something else, her curiosity got the best of her. She glanced at Mark once more. "You said Duncan communicated with you. How did he speak to you mentally without standing in front of you?"

"Vampires can communicate mentally over short distances. Since I wasn't very far away, Duncan was able to speak in my mind." Mark paused and smiled. "On the other hand, Ian and Duncan seem to be able to speak mentally over much greater distances. I guess their twin bond allows them greater flexibility."

"Ah, that makes sense. Is Jax Ian's vampire mate?"

Mark nodded as he glanced her way. "Have you met Ian and Jax?"

She shook her head. "Just Ian. Even though I know they're twins, I'm still amazed at how much they looked alike."

"They couldn't be more different," Mark chuckled.

Silence filled the car. As the adrenaline running through her system continued to lower to normal levels, Rose glanced down at her hands for the first time. Traces of blood caked between her fingers and under her nails…a physical reminder of who or, better yet, *what* she'd become. The knowledge almost overwhelmed her. "I'm a vampire," she whispered. Closing her eyes again, she swallowed hard and told herself that if she hadn't been converted, she wouldn't have stood a chance with Rónán.

"Hey, it's not so bad…being a vampire." The empathy in Mark's voice made her open her eyes.

"What would the boys at the precinct say if they knew about your darker side?" she asked with a half smile.

Mark flashed a wide grin her way. "They wouldn't believe it."

She nodded her agreement with him. "You haven't always been a vampire?"

Mark shook his head. "No. Seven months ago I was human."

Rose inhaled, taking in his scent. He smelled familiar to her but she couldn't pinpoint why. "Were you converted against your will?"

Mark met her gaze for a brief moment, then looked back at the road, gripping the steering wheel tight. "A rogue vampire put me on the edge of conversion, hoping to use me against Ian. But I was too far gone and too wounded. I wouldn't have lived if Duncan hadn't converted me."

Rose's eyes widened. No wonder he smelled familiar to her. "Duncan converted you?"

"Not that he doesn't regret it every time he looks at me."

Mark's comment surprised her. "Why do you say that? You appear to be loyal to him and a good person."

"Duncan's got this thing against converting humans."

Rose's heart ached at his words. Duncan didn't want to convert her? Then why did he? She remembered Duncan making a similar comment to her when she first met him, but after all they'd been through, somewhere deep in her heart, she'd hoped he'd changed his mind. Her stomach roiled at the knowledge nothing had changed…but her.

She rubbed her temples, trying to make sense of the jumbled mess her life had become. One thing she knew for certain, Rónán's comments made her more determined than ever to go to Ireland.

Thirty minutes later they turned off a main road onto a dirt road that led deep into the woods. Rose knew they were heading to the North Shore area, somewhere between Highland Park and Lake Forest. She kept her gaze straight ahead, curiosity getting the best of her to see how Duncan's twin lived. They emerged into a cleared field and drove up the gravel driveway until they reached a two-story house. With huge picture windows gracing the second level above the front door, a steep pitched roof and a wide front porch, this house was the perfect place to get away from the city.

Mark parked the car and Rose got out, inhaling the scents all around her. Off in the distance she smelled murky leaves and dirt, heard the rush of water moving at a fast pace. Lake Michigan.

The front door opened and a beautiful woman dressed in a white long-sleeved T-shirt and jeans stepped out. She crouched down and rubbed her black cat's back as it weaved in and out of her legs before she stood and quickly wound her long dark hair up behind her head. Retrieving the set of chopsticks she had clamped between her teeth, she secured her hair with the sticks.

"You must be Rose," she commented with a smile.

Rose nodded and approached the porch, extending her hand. "And you're Jax. It's nice to meet you." She tried to hold her hand steady but the cool spring air brushing across her naked skin made goose bumps form.

Before Jax's hand connected with hers, Rose remembered her bloodstained hands. She jerked her hand back, saying in embarrassment, "Would you mind terribly if I washed up?"

Jax gave her an understanding look. "Sure you can." She then addressed Mark. "Duncan coming soon?"

Mark nodded. "Right behind me. Rose will need to borrow some of your clothes. She's newly converted and projecting clothes at the moment."

Heat suffused Rose's cheeks at Mark's inadvertent reminder she was stark naked.

Jax laughed, throwing her arm around Rose's shoulders. "It's okay, Rose. I kinda went through the same thing the first day of my conversion. Hey, you're shivering. If you concentrate you can regulate your body temperature too," she said while she steered Rose up the porch steps and into her home. "Why don't we go upstairs and I'll find you something to wear. Then you can take a shower."

"Where's Ian?" Mark asked, following them inside and shutting the door.

As Jax led Rose up the stairs, she turned and called down to Mark, "Ian's at his mother's right now. I expect him back soon."

Something about Jax felt very comforting to Rose. She appeared confident and happy with her lot in life. Rose let Jax lead her down a hall and into a bedroom that took up half of the second floor. It too had large picture windows and a deck with a gorgeous wooded view. With its masculine colors of browns and navy blues, the room had a warm, lived-in feel. It had to be Jax and Ian's bedroom.

Letting go of Rose, Jax moved over to her dresser and pulled out a teal-colored T-shirt similar in style to her own. Glancing over her shoulder at Rose, she eyed her up and down, then withdrew a pair of jeans from the drawer. "You look to be close enough to my height though slightly slimmer in the hips. My jeans should fit you well enough." She raised an eyebrow. "Do you need underwear, too?"

Rose bit her lip and nodded, trying hard not to break down in front of this woman.

Grabbing a bra and underwear from another drawer, Jax said, "These are brand new. Ian has a tendency to…er…shred mine so I keep plenty on hand."

Rose took the clothes and responded in a shaky voice, "Thank you for your kindness, Jax."

Jax grasped her chin and raised it until their eyes met. "I don't know what happened to you, but I'll do anything I can for my Anima's twin. If he's asked us to help you, then you mean a lot to him. Duncan is a complicated man, one who doesn't show his emotions." Her lips quirked in amusement. "I knew a woman like that once."

Rose smiled. "Thank you for understanding, Jax."

"Come." Jax led her out of her room and back down the hall. Entering a door on the left, Jax pulled her inside another bedroom decorated in earth tones and deep burgundy.

"You can stay here, use the shower, take a bath…do whatever you need to do to relax." Heading toward the door, Jax grasped the handle and turned back to her. "You may be newly converted, but I sense an unusual depth in you…" She paused and a thoughtful look crossed her face. "I'm here if you need to talk."

Rose stared at the closed door and whispered to the empty room, "I wish to hell I knew what that depth was."

Depositing the clothes on a cushioned chair, Rose started for the bathroom when she saw the telephone sitting on the nightstand next to the bed.

Glancing at the bedroom door, she walked over and picked up the phone. Rose dialed Our Home's number and held the phone to her ear, her hands shaking. While she waited for Helen to answer, she forced herself to take deep, calming breaths. Helen didn't need to hear a bawling Rose on the other end of the phone, but she was determined to find out what Rónán had ordered Helen to do with her father.

"Our Home," Helen answered.

"Helen, it's Rose."

"Rose, dear…" the other woman's voice broke and she sniffled. "I'm so sorry about your dad, but I've honored your request and started the paperwork on him."

"My request?" she asked, her voice hitching as her heart clenched in her chest.

"Yes, you mentioned cremation to me a long time ago."

Rose blew out a sharp breath to keep from breaking down altogether. She was relieved that Helen had remembered their discussion about her father's wishes even if it wasn't official. "Thank you, Helen."

"If you're up to it, come by either today or tomorrow to sign all the official paperwork. I've arranged for your father's remains to be sent here so you can pick up the urn."

Rose closed her eyes at the inadvertent pain Helen's words caused. It was all happening so fast. "I'll be there. Thank you for all your kindness, Helen."

"You're welcome. Take care, sweetie, and I'll see you soon."

Rose hung up the phone, took a deep, calming breath, then punched zero for the operator.

"How may I help you?" the lady asked.

"Please connect me to International Aire's reservations line." She waited until a clerk picked up the line.

"International Aire, would you like to book a flight?"

"Yes. Out of O'Hare airport flying to Ireland tomorrow morning."

"Which airport do you want to fly into?"

"Whichever is closest to the western side of Ireland."

"That would be Shannon. Will that be one passenger?" she asked.

"Yes."

"I have one flight going tomorrow at two-thirty in the afternoon. Would you like to book it?"

"Yes, I would. One passenger."

"Okay, I've got your seat reserved. And how would you like to pay for that?"

As Rose rattled off her credit card number and expiration date, she felt a sense of rightness settle over her.

"You're all set. Thank you for choosing International Aire."

Rose hung up and felt a little better for having done something to try and figure out what was going on. How did her mother have a past with someone who looked Rose's age? All the questions, fears and worries rumbling around in her head were enough to send her over the deep end.

With a deep sigh she headed into the bathroom and turned on the shower full blast.

Stepping under the scalding spray, she let go of the mental projection of clothes around her. She was surprised at how natural it had felt to keep herself mentally clothed. Once she'd created the illusion, she maintained it without conscious thought.

As the warmth seeped into her skin, relaxing her, so did the emotional hold she'd held tightly around herself.

Fear and anger battled within her. She didn't know exactly what she'd become. Duncan was involved, but she had some weird connection to Rónán, too. God, she wished she had all the answers instead of nothing but questions.

As far as she remembered, Duncan had only bitten her twice. Didn't James say it took three bites within as many days to convert someone to a vampri? Had he bitten her another time without her knowledge? Even though she couldn't explain it, in her heart, she knew Duncan had converted her.

So why had he left her to suffer through the conversion alone? The shit! Was he afraid she'd rip him a new one while she was converting? she thought with a sob. The memory of the pain was still fresh in her mind. She was going to choke Duncan when she laid eyes on him, even if being a vampire was probably the only thing that saved her life when she'd battled Rónán.

Rose realized she could wallow in self-pity that her life had been inalterably changed, that she was no longer human, or she could embrace who and what she'd become. A powerful vampire had killed her father. She was going to need all the superhuman strength she could muster to defeat Rónán. She'd deal with the whole "blood drinking" issue later. She was still amazed at how good that nurse's blood had tasted going down. Shaking away the thought, Rose lathered her body with soap and her mind drifted to her father once more.

Unbidden sobs slowly started until they racked her body, making her shake all over. She'd never see her father again. Never give him a hug or hear his voice…never hear him ask for her mother again.

She closed her eyes and wrapped her arms around herself as she leaned against the tile wall. At least he was with her mother now. Even though sorrow weighed heavy on her heart, she couldn't help the rage that tore through her at the thought of her father's murder.

Straightening, she moved back under the spray and let her rage overshadow the pain and sorrow tightening her chest. She'd have her closure when she signed the paperwork for her father's remains. Maybe getting that done today would be best. She had to remain strong. She couldn't focus on hunting down Rónán and killing the murdering bastard if she was a basket case.

Rose watched the water sluice over her, rinsing away the suds. As the bubbles slid down her body, circling her legs and across her feet, she let every worry and fear she brought into the shower wash down the drain with the suds. With a flick of her wrist, she turned off the water and once again, her emotions. Only fierce resolution remained.

She sensed Duncan's presence in the bedroom, felt his fierce impatience as she toweled her body and hair dry. Wrapping the towel around herself, she tucked the edge between her breasts, taking her time. Let him wait.

When she opened the door, she didn't expect to be slammed against the bathroom door, nor did she anticipate the anger she saw in Duncan's eyes.

# Chapter Ten

ꟾ

"Why?" he snarled, caging her in with his hands on the door.

Rose had never seen Duncan so angry. He'd always had an icy calmness about him. Nor had she ever felt so furious with another. Her temper flared at his unwarranted behavior. She was the one who should be railing at him.

"Back off!" Without a second thought, she slammed her hand against his chest. The impact sent him flying across the room and bouncing off the far wall.

Duncan grunted but landed on the floor on his feet. He'd changed clothes into a black v-neck sweater and faded blue jeans. She noted from his clean smell and damp hair, that he'd showered, too. But he hadn't left that battle with Rónán unscathed. There were four red furrows on his left cheek.

"Looks like Rónán gave you a love pat," she taunted him in her anger.

Duncan let out a roar and before she could take one step he'd leapt across the room and had her backed against the door once more. Fisting the towel between her breasts, he raged, "Do you know how hard it was not to take your blood while I fucked you on the floor last night? How I fought the urge? I didn't sense a bit of fear from you when you spoke with that Sythen. You work fast, Rose. Why did you let him take your blood? Did he give you the baby you wanted?"

Duncan's head snapped to the side when her fist connected with his jaw. Only his hold on her towel kept him rooted where he stood. He slowly turned his furious gaze back to her as she bit out, "How dare you!"

Duncan jerked her forward, clamping his teeth on her throat. *You're mine!* he spoke in her mind at the same time his incisors pierced her skin.

Rose gasped at the erotic sensation and the brief pain his action caused. The emotions she felt emanating from Duncan were the most he'd ever shown. Underlying his anger was a fierce, connected possessiveness that shocked her down to her toes.

As soon as he bit her, Duncan stiffened against her. He spoke in her mind, confusion lacing his words. *Why don't I taste another? I saw you shift to a jaguar. He smelled like a Sythen, yet I don't taste him on you.*

"Why did you leave me to suffer through converting alone?" she asked, holding back the tears that threatened at the memory of her pain.

Duncan withdrew his fangs and laved her wound. Clasping her arms, he met her gaze with a puzzled one. "You think *I* did this to you? It takes three bites from a vampire within as many days for a human to be converted. I made sure I only bit you twice."

Rose tensed and pulled away, her gaze narrowing on him. "You mean you never had any intention of converting me?"

"No, I didn't." The resolute expression on his face punctuated his answer.

She turned her back to him, hurt more than she thought she'd ever be by that knowledge. "I want you to leave."

Duncan grasped her shoulders, turning her to face him. "I want to know what the hell is going on."

"You are the only vampire who's bitten me, Duncan. The only man I've allowed to touch me."

Duncan's hands fell away, then anger flared anew. "It's not possible."

When she just stared at him, not saying a word, he tried to pull her in his arms, but she sidestepped his touch. He dropped his hands to his sides. "I never would've left you to suffer converting, Rose. If I had converted you, I would've found a way to compel you to sleep through it," he whispered as if in physical pain. "I'm so sorry you went through what you did, but I was not the man responsible." He ran a hand through his hair, clearly agitated.

"Go figure. You'd have to think another vampire converted me before you showed some emotion," Rose responded, folding her arms over her chest in annoyance.

Duncan's expression hardened. "It goes both ways, *a ghrá*." He raised his eyebrow, jealousy reflected in his gaze. "I heard some of what that Sythen said to you. How do you know him? He seemed to know you, know what you were capable of."

Beyond the comments he made, Rose heard Duncan's voice enter her head, *I wish I could shift like that.*

"He said his name is Rónán Keegan," she answered, then asked, "Why can't you?"

"Why can't I what?"

"Why can't you shift like Rónán?

Duncan's eyes widened. "Did you just read my thoughts?"

"Uh, no. You spoke in my mind."

"Like hell I did." Duncan narrowed his gaze. *This is insane. I don't want anyone in my head.*

"Too bad. You're broadcasting as clear as NBC."

"I don't feel you," he insisted, then frowned. "I want you the hell out of my head, Rose. Cut it out."

Rose shrugged. "I can't. It's not a conscious effort on my part. Maybe you should work on blocking like I do," she mocked, crossing her arms over her chest.

"This is insanity." Duncan ran both hands through his hair and began to pace.

*He tried his best to kill me. Said he'd never let me have her. Why is Rose so damn important to these Sythens? He's more powerful than James, fighting through an hour of sunlight and clearly blocking the pain of his festering flesh. What could stop this madness? A full mating with Rose?*

Duncan stopped pacing and looked up at her, his expression resolute. As he started to walk toward her, Rose backed up, her hands raised. "Don't even think about it, bud. I'm sure as hell not mating with you."

"You *will* mate with me. We're already connected mentally. This makes sense."

"Mating is not what you want, Duncan. You didn't even want to convert me. I won't be anybody's pity case."

Duncan crossed the distance between them in two long strides. Clasping the back of her neck, his expression as hard as granite, he said, "I will keep you safe." His gaze dropped to her lips then met hers once more. "If you challenge me, you'll lose. We will mate."

As if to punctuate his vow, he pulled her forward and bit the other side of her neck, sliding his fangs deep.

Rose froze and fought the sensual emotions raging within her. "Quit biting me," she managed to hiss out.

Duncan withdrew his fangs and slowly ran his tongue up her neck to close the wound. He lifted his head and met her gaze, saying in a dark, husky tone, his Irish accent heavy, "You can always bite me back, *a thaisce.* You asked me what you taste like…you taste like a fine honeyed wine, more potent and aged than any other I've ever tasted."

Her stomach fluttered at his words, the way he made her sound…almost intoxicating.

He pulled her chest against his and used his thumb to elevate her jaw as he lowered his head and slowly slid his fangs into her neck once more. *Do you hear my blood pumping in my veins? Aren't you curious to know what* I *taste like?*

Rose's lips hovered next to the vein in Duncan's neck and her fangs automatically lengthened at his mention of tasting his blood. She wanted to know. Desperately.

Her heart hammered in her chest. She cupped his rear and ran her tongue along his neck, tasting his skin. Duncan let go of his hold on her throat and laved her wound closed.

When she licked his neck once more, Duncan groaned and wrapped his hand around her waist, clasping her close.

"Taste me," he encouraged at the same time he slid his other hand up her inner thigh.

Rose's body ached for his touch and anticipation bubbled within her. She scraped her incisors along his neck, her breathing turning shallow while her sex throbbed and her breasts tingled underneath the soft towel.

Duncan's hand rose higher at the same time he rasped, "Open your legs."

Unable to resist his touch, Rose took a step, her stomach tensing as pent-up desire curled within her.

*Just one taste,* she thought.

When Duncan's fingers rubbed her clit, she moaned against his neck.

"Taste me," he insisted at the same time she heard his mental thoughts—*Mate with me*—in her mind.

Rose jerked back, anger rushing through her. "That's it, isn't it? If I take your blood, I'll be mated to you."

Duncan met her gaze, an unapologetic, determined look on his face. "I can't explain how you were converted by being bitten twice. You claim I converted you...regardless of the how of it, I'll do whatever it takes to keep you safe."

"Including seducing me into unknowingly mating with you?" she railed, backing out of his hold.

Pointing her finger toward the door, she locked her jaw and hissed through her clenched teeth, "Out!"

"Rose," he began.

"I said 'out'."

Duncan stared at her for a long moment then started for the door. Opening it, he turned to her once more, a dark expression on his face. "You'll need blood soon."

The unspoken "and I'm going to damn well make sure it's mine" hung in the air between them.

Rose lifted her chin a notch. "I have a will made of steel."

He raised his eyebrow at her bravado. "We'll see just how much I can test that steel will of yours."

Duncan walked downstairs fuming. The woman drove him insane. He knew she held back from him. Refused to share with him how she was connected to Rónán, but there was some strange, twisted link between them. The thought made him tense in furious, unbridled jealousy.

He'd been able to read some of Rónán's thoughts while they battled. The vamp wanted to rip his heart out. If it weren't for some swift, evading moves on Duncan's part, the Sythen would have succeeded. One thing he heard loud and clear, Rónán wanted him out of the way, the threat Duncan represented eliminated.

The vamp's lust for Rose permeated Duncan senses, inciting a vicious, bloodthirsty side to him he never knew existed. He fought like a man possessed and quite literally he was, because there was no way he should've been able to fend off the jaguar's powerful jaws any other way.

And then there was Rose…the sight of her shifting back from a red jaguar to her human form made his heart lurch. She looked so beautiful and vulnerable…he knew the Sythen had converted her. Anger at Rose, anger at himself and sheer rage at the Sythen who dared take his woman warred within him.

His foot hit the bottom stair as the thought echoed in his mind.

His woman.

His mate.

When Rose's warm breath caressed his neck, he wanted to feel her fangs pierce his skin. He wanted to be the one to give her the blood she needed to survive.

Always.

The realization hit him hard. He craved Rose's touch and everything she had to offer him. He wanted her for a mate. His *Sonuachar*…his vampire Anima. He didn't give a shit about fitting in any longer. There was only one person he cared about and she was stubbornly refusing his advances. Ruthless determination rippled through him. No other would dare touch her while he breathed. He clenched his fists as he walked into the living room.

Mark stood by the window, staring outside, his hands shoved in his jeans pockets. Jax sat in a leather chair looking up at Ian who sat on the chair's arm, talking to her.

They all looked at him when he walked in the room.

"How's Rose doing?" Jax asked.

Duncan ran a hand through his hair, gritting out, "She's in my head."

"That's great news." She smiled. "She's using her powers to talk to you mentally."

Duncan frowned at her. "No, I meant she's in my freaking mind, reading my thoughts."

They stared at him and then all three of them burst into laughter.

"What's so damn funny?" Duncan growled at them.

Ian sobered and stood. Approaching him, he clapped his hand on Duncan's shoulder, an amused expression tilting his lips. "Welcome to our world, Dunc."

"I'm not that bad."

"Yes, you are," all three vamps said in unison.

Jax stood and approached Duncan with a knowing grin. "But we've just learned to block you—"

"Speak for yourself," Mark jumped in with a disgruntled look.

Jax cast a glance Mark's way, chuckling. "Well, some of us are more proficient at it than others." Winking at Mark, she turned back to Duncan. "It takes time and conscious effort, but you can block her, too."

"This is different," Duncan insisted. "I don't feel her in my mind like you guys have said you've *felt* my presence. She's just there, hearing my thoughts like…"

"Like an Anima would?" Ian asked while he wrapped his arms around Jax's waist and pulled her against him, kissing her on the neck.

"We're not mated," Duncan said, frustration rising within him.

"Don't tell me you don't think she's your Anima." Jax gave him a surprised look.

Duncan ground his teeth. "She refuses to mate with me."

Ian chuckled. "Sound familiar, *a ghrá*?" he asked Jax.

Jax glanced up at her Anima with an innocent look on her face. "What are you talking about? I was *such* a pushover."

"If you count kicking my ass on several occasions, pushing *me* over, then I'll agree," Ian said. He met his brother's gaze. "You've just got to figure out a way to convince her she can't live without you."

Duncan gave him a dangerous smile. "She has to eat…eventually."

"Wait a minute, Mark told me that the Sythen converted Rose. Had you bitten her at all?" Jax asked.

Guilt swept through him at Jax's question even though he knew she was referring to Rose's conversion in general, not the battle of wills that just occurred upstairs.

"She claims I converted her."

"Whoa! Talk about dropping a bomb." Mark pushed off the wall. "But we saw her shift to a red jaguar. Only Sythens can shift into various forms, right?"

"Not into something as large as a jaguar," Ian answered in a clipped tone.

"I can't explain it." Duncan blew out a breath in frustration. "I only bit her twice prior to her conversion. Yet just now, I didn't taste the Sythen on her. If, by some strange miracle, I inadvertently converted her that might explain her ability to read my mind."

He narrowed his gaze on Ian. "Someone has to know more about these Sythens. What did Mom tell you?"

Ian's jaw ticced as he crossed his arms over his chest. "She refused to talk to me about Eamon and James. She said she wanted you present as well."

Duncan turned on his heel, headed for the door. "Let's go. I want answers."

He mentally spoke to Mark as he reached the front door. *Mark, help Jax block Rose's scent. We may be a while.*

*Will do*, came Mark's swift reply.

"What about Rose?" Jax stood in the foyer.

Duncan let Ian precede him out the door before he turned to answer Jax. "She's not speaking to me at the moment, so some time away is probably best. Mark will help you keep her safe." His voice softened as he spoke in her mind. *She's my Anima, Jax, in all the ways that matter.*

Jax nodded. *It's about damn time you showed some emotion.*

When he smiled, glad to have won her over to his cause, she finished as only Jax would. "But don't think I won't remind her that taking your blood will mate her to you, regardless of her wishes. She needs to walk into this with her eyes wide open."

Duncan snorted and replied in a dry tone, "She's well aware," before he walked out the door.

* * * * *

Duncan and Ian entered their parents' home and immediately walked down to the basement. Tressa Mordoor looked up from the book she was reading when they walked into the expansive library. Floor to ceiling bookshelves lined the walls so tall a rolling ladder had been installed.

Marcus Mordoor levitated in midair next to the books, a thick tome open in his hands. He floated to the ground, closing the book when his feet hit the floor. Dark brows drew together over cobalt eyes.

"Why does it take your mother requesting you both here for me to see my sons together?" He moved to stand next to his mate who sat in a velvet-covered reading chair.

"New addition to the library?" Ian nodded toward the book in his father's hand.

Marcus smiled. "Took me two years to acquire this one, but watch." His father handed his mother the book and held his hands apart. Sparks flew between his fingers, arcing until they connected with the sparks from the other hand. He lifted his hands above his head and the arcs grew, surrounding him.

"Come toward me," he said to Ian.

As Ian walked toward his dad, Duncan said, "I swear sometimes I think you have more in common with the Kantrés than the Rueans."

When Ian got within a foot of his father, Marcus said, "Try to touch me."

Ian eyed the sparks. "Is my hair going to stand up on its own after this?"

"Just try, son."

Ian moved his hand and it seemed as if he was touching an invisible wall.

Marcus grinned, a proud look on his face. "What do you think? It's like my own personal force field."

Ian rubbed his jaw, smiling back. "I can see something like that coming in handy."

His father lowered his hands and addressed Duncan, "In answer to your comment, I *do* have Kantré blood in my family."

"You do?" Tressa looked surprised by his statement as she stood. "You never told me that."

Marcus cut his gaze back to his Anima. "The connection is distant, decades old, so it never occurred to me to tell you."

Her face brightened. "See, so you understand why I didn't…"

Her mate's face darkened. "Don't even try it, Tressa." Nodding to Ian and Duncan, he continued, "They have a right to know their heritage."

Ian and Duncan exchanged a "what the hell?" look before they met their mother's gaze.

Tressa eyed her sons as she played with a long strand of strawberry-blonde hair that had fallen from her French twist.

Sweeping her arm toward the couch, she took a breath. "Sit, boys."

Duncan crossed his arms over his chest and scowled. "I prefer to stand. I don't plan to stay long."

"Your mother told you to sit, Duncan," Marcus said in an authoritative voice.

Duncan looked at his dad in surprise. His father spent so much of his time in his books, seeking magical knowledge, Duncan often forgot the man was a vampire to be reckoned with in his own right.

While Ian and he sat down on the couch, his mother smoothed her hands over her royal blue silk lounge pants and then tugged her belt tighter around the matching crossover top.

"I told Ian I would only talk to both of you at once because I thought it best if you found out at the same time." She took a deep breath and met their curious gazes. "You're not half human."

"You're shitting us," Ian said with a laugh at the same time a sinking feeling hit Duncan hard in the stomach. He stood, fisting his hands by his sides. "Then what the hell are we?"

Tressa narrowed her gaze on Ian and Duncan. "Watch how you address your mother." She turned to Duncan. "You can get back to your woman when I've told you the rest."

Duncan's eyes widened and he glanced at Ian. "She just read my mind."

"As a priestess of the Atruans, I've always had the ability to read others' minds." Tressa's comment drew his attention back to her. "I've just never told anyone."

"Why?" Duncan growled. "Because you were too busy pretending to be human?"

"You're out of line, son," Marcus intervened. "I might've just learned of your mother's heritage, but I now appreciate and understand her reason for secrecy."

"What are the Atruans?" Ian asked in a quiet tone. He too had risen from the couch and stood beside his brother, his shoulders tense.

Tressa's gaze shifted from one son's face to the other. "The Atruans are known in the United States as the Sythens."

Rage welled within Duncan. All this time he thought he was half human.

"Why did you hide this from everyone?" Ian prodded.

"Over two centuries ago, I was born in Ireland, a member of the Atruan clan, but I wasn't like the rest of the vampires. I could walk in daylight. I didn't have fangs. I could read minds, I had broader shape-shifting abilities…my powers varied from the others. I also discovered I aged slower than the Atruan vampires of my blood. When I was seven, I went to live with the priestesses, as the Elders called us."

"Us?" Ian asked.

She nodded. "Apparently every few decades another 'special' female vampire was born, with similar differences from the Atruan clan. The clan Elders saw the potential for problems with aggressive male vampires who might want to mate with a female of such unique powers, so they declared an edict we were to be treated as priestesses and not allowed to mate.

"We were assigned a Guardian, a male vampire who had been handpicked by the Elders because of his unique ability to shape-shift to creatures much larger and heavier than his human form. Their special powers gave them an advantage over typical male Atruan vampires with limited shape-shifting abilities. The Guardians' entire existence was to keep us safe, not only from the males in the clan, but from another supernatural race known as Harvesters who preyed on the Atruan vampires."

"Were they a type of vampire hunter?" Ian asked.

His mother shook her head. "Not really. The Harvesters were like parasites, using us for a power source. They had the ability to harvest some of the vampire's powers as their own. But fortunately for us, the Harvesters only worked alone, preying on loner vampires who'd been separated from their clan. Because their narcissistic nature didn't allow them to be discriminatory, Harvesters also drained each other's powers if given a chance."

"They sound like a formidable foe," Ian said, concern etching his face.

"They could've been. But they never killed their quarry. In their minds, we were their 'power' supply and the fountain of youth all wrapped up in a 'life source' cocktail. If a Harvester came in physical contact with a vampire, given enough time, the Harvester would not only accumulate some of the vampire's powers, but the act would also shave years off the vampire's life while extending the Harvester's life span. Each 'hit' the Harvester took from a vampire usually supplied him with vampire-like abilities for a number of years."

Ian and Duncan glanced at each other, frowning.

"Don't concern yourselves with the Harvesters. They aren't a threat here." A satisfied smile crossed Tressa's face. "You see, when the Harvesters absorb some of the Atruans' capabilities, they also acquire their weakness—they can't walk in the daylight. So even if they could figure out a way to avoid sunlight while coming to the US, the extreme use of their powers to do so would drain them considerably. They would have no way to 'recharge' their powers without a vampire handy."

"How did you end up in the United States?"

A sad look crossed his mother's face at Duncan's question. "The Elders' system failed. Several of the Guardians who already felt powerful because of their Guardian status became even more arrogant. They wanted more power, coveting the longer lives the priestesses had. One night they attacked and kidnapped several of the women, intending to mate with them. If their plan worked, the Guardians' hope was that their mates' bite would extend their lives."

"Were you taken?"

Duncan sensed the anger in his brother's question. The same rage that filled him at his mother's story.

She shook her head. "I was just twelve at the time and thankfully my Guardian was one of those who refused to go along with the attack."

Her eyes softened as she continued, "We lived a peaceful, secluded existence, interacting with humans on a very limited basis. The Gods knew about us, but never intervened…until that day. Angered by the Guardians' treachery and the discovery the male vampires basically sought immortality, The Morrigan struck them down, freeing the women. But instead of killing the men, The Morrigan cursed the Guardians with a driving need to always protect their priestesses. In the end, the Guardians who betrayed their priestesses got the very thing they sought…immortality, but it came with a price.

"The Goddess told the traitorous Guardians they would reside their years living in the soil, only to be allowed to leave the earth once a year for an hour to feed. Once their time was up, they would return underground to await their priestesses' call for protection, which may never come." She sighed then forged on with her story.

"That's why we left Ireland. The Morrigan told the priestesses to leave the island, that staying there would only encourage the

Guardians to seek us out when they arose once a year. You see, the Goddess didn't erase their need to take our powers. She saw it as the perfect punishment—leaving the desire to mate with us burning in their heads forever while they were cursed with the need to protect us above all else. It was a conflicting driving force the Guardian vampires were condemned to suffer…for eternity."

"James is a Guardian," Ian simply stated.

Tressa gave him a solemn nod.

"And so is Rónán Keegan," Duncan followed up.

Tressa's eyes widened. She put her hand over her heart and took a step back. "Rónán? You've seen him?"

Duncan gave her a solemn nod. "Yes. He attacked Rose. She's the human James kidnapped."

Tressa grabbed Duncan's arm, her green eyes searching his face. "Rose's mother's name? Did you learn it?"

He shook his head. "No. All I know is she left her a locket that read 'Protect me forever' in Irish on the back."

"Oh no!" Tressa's face drained of color.

Duncan caught his mother as she swayed on her feet. Lifting her in his arms, his chest tight with fear for her and for Rose, he tried to remain calm as he walked Tressa to the couch and laid her on it.

"What's wrong? I know Rónán's after Rose, but not why. Do you know?"

Tressa gripped Duncan's hand as Marcus sat down and put her feet on his lap, a worried look on his face.

"She must be Anna's daughter. Rónán was one of Anna's Guardians. The other's name was Séamus Flannery. There were always two Guardians in case something happened to one of the Guardians during an attack. When I spoke with Eamon, he told me James Connor was Séamus Flannery. He said all the Atruans changed their names when they came to the US via ships all those years ago. Becoming the Sythen clan, changing their names and even eliminating their Irish accents must've been their way of making a fresh start."

"Rose is Sythen?" Duncan asked in a quiet tone while shock slammed through him in relentless waves.

"If her mother was Anna Brennan, then yes, she's at least part Sythen."

Duncan felt the blood drain from his face. He'd disregarded Rose's assurances he was the vampire who converted her. But maybe her hybrid status was what made converting her with just two bites possible. Rose had told him the truth. Ian's hand landed on his shoulder. His brother squeezed.

"Remain calm, Duncan. Rose will forgive you. We need to learn the rest."

While Duncan fumed, his mind swirling over the knowledge Rose truly was his, had been converted by his bite, his mother continued where she left off.

"After the attack and the Guardians' curse, the Atruan clan fell apart. Many left. Not only did The Morrigan encourage the priestesses to leave Ireland, but she also told us that in return for her help we must never speak of our past to anyone. Before the priestesses moved away from Ireland to blend in with human society as best we could, each priestess took a vow to protect herself and her future children from any other Sythen male who might try to repeat history.

"We all decided on a different vessel to call forth our Guardians, even the ones who hadn't gone rogue. When the Guardians were originally appointed by the Elders, they each took a vow to protect us for life. The priestesses agreed that the Guardians were only to be summoned if we faced an enemy stronger than we ourselves could fight.

"We thought that the summoning vessel was the best way we could protect ourselves and loved ones by using something we could pass on. We also created the lullaby, 'Sleep, My Darling'. The lullaby was our way to let our children know they had a protector without directly revealing our past and breaking our vow to The Morrigan. The locket you mentioned must be how Rónán was summoned, even if it wasn't intentional."

Duncan's mind was still coming to terms with the fact—however innocent—he'd converted Rose. The guilt almost overwhelmed him.

Tressa turned his chin until he met her serious green gaze. "I hear your thoughts. My guess is you're correct. Your Ruean-Sythen status mixed with her hybrid Sythen heritage is why she was converted with two bites. You couldn't have known."

Worry for Rose paramount, Duncan shook his head. "I'm confused. That Guardian, Rónán, wasn't bald like all the other Sythens."

"Did he have a white stripe in his hair somewhere?" his mother asked.

"Yes, in his jaguar and his human form."

She nodded. "As a warning to all the Atruan male vampires, The Morrigan cursed every Atruan male with a white stripe in his hair so he'd be easily identifiable by a priestess if she ran across one again in the future. I guess that's why all Sythens are bald. They didn't want to draw attention to their past or their own shame, so they shaved their heads. But when they are in shifted form, the stripe will appear no matter what form they take."

Ian rubbed his jaw, a curious look on his face. "How is it that Eamon and James didn't recognize you or vice versa for that matter?"

His mother glanced his way. "I was just seven when I left my clan members so I didn't know many of the male vampires. I admit the Sythens' scent did pique my curiosity, but it had been a very long time since I'd smelled another Atruan, so I passed my thoughts off as nostalgia for my homeland.

"As for Rónán and James not knowing me... I took your father's name when I mated with him, and because Marcus converted me, as you well know, the process of being 'made' is a physiological change. Even though I retained my unique priestess mental abilities, all my Atruan physical abilities disappeared to be replaced with Ruean ones. I grew fangs, I needed blood to survive, I could no longer walk in the sunlight or shape-shift like I once could. I'm sure your father's Ruean blood running through my veins also masked my Sythen scent. Considering I was very young when I was separated from the male vampires, neither Eamon nor James would recognize me as a grown woman."

"A much older woman than her mate," Marcus interrupted with a mischievous glint in his eyes as he moved to stand by her side. "And all this time I thought that tingling I felt when we first met was heightened sexual awareness between us."

"It was." She gave him a sheepish grin, then sobered. "And to your 'older woman' comment..." She narrowed her gaze on her Anima. "I'll probably still outlive you."

He pulled her fingers to his lips and said in a sincere tone, "I hope that's the case, my love, because I wouldn't want to live a single day without you."

The love reflected in his mother's eyes as she looked at Marcus made Duncan's stomach tense. He realized just how much he wanted Rose to look at him like that.

Tressa met Duncan's gaze. "It wasn't until you mentioned James shifting to a shape larger than his human form that I began to wonder. Like I said, I'd always felt the Sythens seemed familiar to me. I confronted Eamon and he admitted he was indeed an Atruan. He also confirmed my suspicions that James was one of the Guardians who didn't revolt all those years ago. Eamon was very surprised to see James acting so out of character over a human woman."

Duncan stood and paced, his mind whirling as he absorbed all his mother had revealed. He couldn't believe all the years he thought he was something he wasn't. He stopped pacing and met his mother's steady gaze.

"Can I shape-shift beyond a raven?"

She nodded. "My guess is, yes, you should be able to if you concentrate. Even though you're half Ruean, I was still full Atruan when I became pregnant. You inherited my mind-reading abilities, so you probably have the ability to shape-shift as well since it takes some mental effort to accomplish the task. She glanced at Ian. "You and Duncan can both withstand the sunlight, so you'll only know for sure if *you* can shape-shift to other forms if you try."

While Ian nodded his understanding, Duncan began pacing again thinking about the Guardians and the situation he and Rose were right in the middle of. Coming to a halt, he asked, "If Rónán is cursed with immortality, can he be killed?"

Tressa shrugged. "I'm not sure. We weren't given all the details."

Duncan's brow furrowed. "I saw Rónán with Rose before I got to them. I didn't imagine what I saw. He was attacking her and I know he definitely had it in for me. He was also able to withstand the sun for at least an hour. He suffered but he stayed as long as he could, fighting me. He wanted me dead and out of the way."

A worried expression crossed Tressa's face. "The Guardians didn't have the power to withstand the sun before. Rónán's driving force must be stronger than I expected."

"The sudden appearance of Rónán makes some kind of weird sense if he was called forth by accident, but what about James?" Ian asked. "If he didn't revolt all those years ago, why now?"

She shook her head. "Only James can answer that question."

"Has Eamon eliminated him yet?" Duncan asked his mother.

"He said he'd take care of James today."

Duncan glanced at his brother and spoke in his mind. *Let's get over there and make sure it's done after we get the answers we seek.*

Tressa grasped Duncan's arm and forced him to meet her gaze. "Eamon knows James better than anyone."

First Rose and now his mother. "Reading my mind again?" He raised an eyebrow in annoyance.

A resolute expression crossed her face. "I'll do whatever it takes to protect my sons."

They stared at each other, tempers flaring…locking horns.

The phone rang, breaking the tense silence. Marcus picked up the handset from the end table.

"Hello?"

When his body tensed and he beckoned to Tressa, Duncan immediately tuned into the phone conversation.

"I-I need to speak with Tressa," Eamon's pained voice came across the line.

Marcus handed his mate the phone and pulled her close to his side as she put the earpiece up to her ear.

"What's wrong, Eamon?"

He took a ragged breath. "Bring Lucian and Duncan to my home. James has escaped and I have to set this right."

Tressa jerked her gaze to her youngest son. Duncan's chest tightened in enraged fury that James was once again free. His heart jerked in worry for Rose and he met his brother's gaze. An unspoken agreement passed between them. Ian nodded his consent to help hunt the bastard down. Duncan was glad she was safe with Jax and Mark.

Duncan met his mother's questioning look and shook his head. "We have a rogue vampire to hunt down first. Two in fact."

Tressa spoke to Eamon. "I'll bring Lucian right away, but Duncan and Ian are going after James."

"It's daylight," Eamon argued, his breathing sounding labored. "I chose to eliminate James with the daylight almost upon us so that in the event I failed, he'd be vulnerable and Ian could hunt him down. I-I don't think I'll make it, Tressa. Please."

Duncan pulled his cell phone from his pocket and walked away from the group, dialing Ian's home phone. Jax answered.

"Hello?"

"Jax, it's Duncan."

"Duncan, I was just—" she started to say but he interrupted.

"We've just discovered James has escaped. Ian and I are going to try to find him, but I wanted to warn you to keep an eye on Rose."

"I was just about to call you. Rose is gone."

"What!" he roared. "How?"

"She'd asked us to take her to town, but I told her that you'd take her when you got back. I…uh…guess she didn't like that answer. Apparently she snuck out her bedroom window. Mark's truck is gone. We were just getting ready to go after her when you called."

As fear raced through him, Duncan clung to his anger to keep him focused. "I know her scent better than anyone," he said in a controlled voice. "Take your cell phone with you and we'll keep in touch."

Closing his cell phone, he met his mother's gaze as she hung up the telephone. "Do you trust Eamon?"

When she nodded, he said, "Rose is out there. Alone. You know you can't go to Eamon's until the sun goes down. As soon as you can, go. We'll call you later."

Marcus put his hands on his Anima's shoulders and turned her to face him. With a steely expression in his eyes, he said, "No more secrets."

She hugged him close and laid her head on his broad chest, whispering, "No more secrets. I'm glad the weight is off my shoulders."

Marcus kissed the top of her head. "About that force field…I believe I can work it to protect us against the sun…at least temporarily."

Tressa lifted her head, her eyes alight with wonder. "You constantly amaze me."

Marcus gave her a cocky smile, then sobered. "It'll wear me out to protect us both, so I'll have to depend on your powers to defend us if necessary once we're at Eamon's."

She squeezed his waist and winked at him. "I like this teamwork thing."

"I'll follow you there," Ian insisted. "I know Mom trusts Eamon but I want to know it's not some kind of trap. Once you're safe, Jax and I will start hunting for James."

His father met Ian's gaze and nodded. "I'm concerned Eamon won't make it to wait until Lucian can come in the evening. Protecting two is going to be dicey enough. You can call Lucian and fill him in on the situation on the way over there."

Duncan nodded to Ian and his parents and turned on his heel. The sooner he found Rose, the better. He owed her one helluva an apology. He hoped she'd forgive him…eventually. One thing he knew for certain…he had a mate to find and protect.

# Chapter Eleven

ꟙ

Rose felt like a real heel stealing Mark's truck, but she had two things to take care of before she left the country tomorrow afternoon and she preferred to do them alone. Duncan's refusal to believe he converted her stung more than she cared to admit. *You don't want a permanent man in your life, remember?* she told herself, but the ache in her heart remained nonetheless.

Duncan was everything she hadn't known she wanted in a man. Yet he hadn't planned to convert her, had never planned to mate. Ever. The shit! Somehow she'd find a way to convince him he was the culprit who'd converted her, not Rónán…even if she had to kick his ass to finally convince him. But for now, she needed to focus on her tasks ahead.

Her heart pounded and her chest tightened as she turned into the Our Home parking lot and cut off the engine.

Pulling the keys from the ignition, she walked over to her car and looked around the empty lot before she reached under the fender for her hidden spare key. Once she'd unlocked the car, she grabbed her purse with her mother's paperwork and her passport inside and slung the strap over her shoulder.

Locking the car, she slid the key in her pocket and headed for the entrance of Our Home.

Helen enveloped her in a bear hug as soon as she walked in. "Honey, I'm so sorry."

Rose held back her tears with great effort as she returned Helen's hug. "Thank you for taking care of my dad, Helen." She stepped back and wiped away a tear that slid down her cheek. Taking a deep breath to calm herself, she said, "I'm here to sign the paperwork."

Helen nodded then walked back to the desk. She opened a drawer and withdrew a folder, setting it open on the desk.

"I've marked the places you need to sign to make it easier for you, and I transferred the excess funds back to your account."

As Rose signed the paperwork, Helen continued, "If it's any consolation to you, your father looked so peaceful when I found him." A sad smile tilted her lips. "He even had a smile on his face."

Rose's heart ached at her words. She knew the circumstances of her father's death, knew the bastard who'd taken his life…taken her father away from her. He would pay.

But Helen didn't need to know the ugly details. She finished signing and closed the folder, pushing it back toward the older woman. "Thank you for your thoughtfulness."

Rose stifled a new wave of tears, fought the need to scream her anger over his murder, then straightened her spine, collecting herself. "I'm going out of town for a few days on a business trip anyway. Some time away will help me come to terms with my dad's death. When I come back, I'll take care of my father's wishes for his remains."

Helen patted her hand. "I'm so sorry, Rose, but I honestly believe your father is in a happier place now."

Rose nodded, acknowledging the truth of Helen's words. "I know you're right. It's just hard to let go. Now I get to tell my uncle his brother is gone."

Helen gave her a sad smile and waved goodbye.

* * * * *

"Hey, Rosie my girl," Nigel called out in a jovial voice. He dashed across the main casino floor on the riverboat. She watched him weaving in and out of the patrons. As he approached and saw her expression, his own turned serious. He pulled her into his arms, hugging her close. "What's wrong, sweetheart? Whatever it is, I promise I'll do everything in my power to fix it."

Rose hugged his waist and rubbed her cheek against his cashmere sweater. "I'm afraid this is one thing you can't fix, Nigel."

He put his hands on her shoulders and leaned away a little so he could stare into her eyes. "What's wrong?"

Rose wrapped her arm around her uncle's trim waist and steered him toward his office. "Come on, let's talk in private."

Nigel shut his office door and grabbed her hands. Guiding her to one of the chairs across from his desk, he sat down in a chair opposite her and waited for her to speak.

Rose met his concerned gaze and spoke as calmly as she could. "Dad passed away this morning."

Her uncle's hands tightened on hers for a brief second and a regretful, sad look crossed his face.

He swiped the tears away that had started to form in his eyes and straightened his spine. Turning his head to the side for a second, he sniffed to pretend he hadn't allowed the tears to surface.

Then he met her gaze once more. "Did he suffer? Please tell me he went peacefully."

Rage welled within Rose once more, so sharp and hard her chest felt as if would burst with the need to tell her uncle the truth. But she couldn't. As silent tears fell down her cheeks, she kept her face as composed as possible. "He didn't appear to have suffered. He died in his sleep."

Nigel nodded. "I'm so sorry, honey. Even though George and I were never really very close, I'll miss him, too." He squeezed her hands. "But at least he's no longer sad all the time. He's with Anna…where he always wanted to be."

With supreme effort, Rose tamped down the wave of fury that swept through her and nodded her agreement that her father was in a better place. Her chest constricted that she'd had to lie to her uncle about the circumstances of her father's death. Rónán would pay.

"I've taken care of the arrangements and when I get back from Ireland I'll fulfill Dad's wishes with his cremated remains. There won't be an official funeral."

"Would you like me to be there with you?"

She shook her head. "Dad asked me to do this alone. He knows your strong beliefs against cremation."

Nigel nodded his understanding, then his brow creased in concern. "I don't know if you should travel so far away by yourself so soon after losing George."

"Now more than ever it's very important to me to learn what I can about my heritage," she said in an adamant tone.

"Then I'm going with you."

Rose tensed. Even though Nigel, with his bisexual background, was accepting of people from all walks of life, and he'd even dabbled in some clairvoyant and other paranormal groups in his past, she wasn't prepared to tell her uncle about her vampire heritage. Not yet.

She shook her head. "I've already booked my flight to Shannon for tomorrow morning. You and I both know you can't just leave the casino at the last minute."

Nigel stood and paced, thinking out loud. "I could have Sam watch over the place. He knows it like the back of his hand."

"Nigel."

"Yeah, that would work. Then Michelle and her mom could help fill in if the need arose."

She could almost *see* the wheels turning in her uncle's mind. "Nigel."

This time he stopped pacing and met her gaze.

"I know you only have my best interests at heart, but I'm fine to do this on my own. As a matter of fact, I'm looking forward to it." Her voice dropped and she finished in a whisper, "I need the time away."

Her uncle frowned. "I don't like it, Rose. I'm your only parent now. I worry."

Rose stood and hugged him tight around the neck. "You're the best! I promise I'll call you from Ireland."

Nigel wrapped his arms around her waist and gave her a bear hug and a kiss on the cheek. "You'd better check in often."

She managed a smile. "I promise."

Glancing at the clock on his desk, Rose pulled away. She didn't realize how much time had passed. It was already one in the afternoon. More than likely Jax and Mark had discovered she'd taken off in his truck by now. Which meant Duncan would soon know. She knew the stubborn vamp would come after her...probably pissed.

Let him come.

She kissed her uncle on the cheek and turned to open his office door. "I've got to go. I still have to get a few things for the trip."

"Don't forget to keep in touch," Nigel called after her as Rose left his office and headed for the casino's entrance.

Rose thought about going home, but she decided against it. That'd be the first place Duncan would look for her. Instead, she headed to the mall to buy a few sets of clothes to mix and match while she was in Ireland. She didn't plan on making a fashion statement and her credit card would thank her for her frugality.

An hour later, Rose packed her purchases into an inexpensive roll-on bag she'd picked up at a baggage store. She stowed the suitcase on the floorboard of Mark's truck, then started the engine.

She had one more errand to run and she damned well planned to make it there before she headed back to Ian's house. She wasn't a fool. Ian, Jax, Duncan and Mark could provide the best protection against Rónán until she learned to use her own powers—whatever the hell those powers were.

Rose couldn't help the sense of sadness that gripped her as she approached Saint John's memorial cemetery. After she parked Mark's vehicle, she locked the door and headed up the long center sidewalk toward the cemetery gates.

Her grip on the flowers she'd purchased tightened and her heart felt as if a heavy weight had been placed over her chest as she wound her way through the plots. When she reached her mother's gravesite, Rose's heart constricted even tighter at the sight of the tiny white flowers that grew on her mother's grave. She'd thrown the seeds there every year, hoping they'd take root The cemetery people forbade wildflowers, only allowing cut flowers to be placed on the graves.

Laying the bouquet of white roses against her mother's tombstone, Rose let the tears fall as she squatted and traced the etched inscription in the cool marble with her fingers.

*Here lies the woman of my dreams,*
*a wonderful mother to her child and my life partner.*
*She will always be missed.*
*Anna Brennan Sinclair*

Rose frowned when she realized the only date on the tombstone was the date of her mother's death and not the date of her mother's birth. Why hadn't she noticed that before?

"You were born on August 12th, 1937, right?" she said aloud, then sighed. "I guess that's one thing I won't know for sure about you."

Placing her hand flat on the tombstone, Rose whispered, "Why did you keep so many secrets?"

"To protect you."

Rose jerked her gaze to Duncan who stood behind her, staring at her mother's gravestone with an inscrutable look on his face.

"You shouldn't have gone off on your own." His expression turned stony when he met her gaze.

Rose glanced at her mother's grave once more and spoke in a low tone, finishing her conversation with her mother, "Now Dad is with you."

"I thought your father was still alive," Duncan said in a puzzled tone.

Fresh tears fell and she abruptly swiped them away. "My father…di—" Her voice broke over the words, but she finished as she glanced back at Duncan, "died this morning."

A shocked expression crossed his face and he swiftly pulled her to her feet. "I'm so sorry, Rose. I didn't know."

"You were too busy accusing me of letting another vampire convert me," she sniffed, then sighed. "I'm too upset to fight you right now. I'll kick your ass when I'm feeling more like my old self."

Duncan lifted her in his arms and buried his nose against her neck. "I have so much to apologize for, but for now we need to get you back to Ian's where you'll be protected. You're vulnerable out here in the open."

"I'm done with my errands for now anyway." Rose handed him Mark's car keys as well as her own. "My car's at the retirement home." She snuggled closer to his warmth, feeling safe despite her anger at his stubborn pride.

Duncan glanced at Rose's mother's grave one last time. His gut clenched as he read the name. Her maiden name was Anna Brennan. His mother was right. Rose was indeed a descendant of an Atruan priestess.

And he'd been the vampire who'd converted her to a Ruean…or at least part Ruean.

He felt sick to his stomach with guilt.

Rose tucked her head under his chin. The sign of ultimate trust on her part made his heart ache. He kissed the top of her head and headed for Mark's truck. Nodding to Jax and Mark across the parking lot, he threw Jax his keys and mentally told her to follow him. He glanced at Mark and threw Rose's keys to him.

*Retrieve Rose's car from the retirement home and meet us back at Ian's.*

While Duncan drove Mark's truck back to Ian's house, he noted the suitcase under Rose's legs. Why the suitcase? he wondered. He glanced her way several times. Swift, biting possessiveness, unlike anything he'd ever experienced in his life, swept through him each time his gaze landed on her face. *She's mine. Made by me.*

Despite his guilt, he couldn't help the pride that filled his heart. *All mine.* The need to protect Rose, to complete their mating at all costs was the only thing that mattered to him right now.

That and the hope she'd forgive him enough to trust her heart to him.

Rose glanced at him and for a second he tensed, wondering if she'd read his determined thoughts. The tired look on her face told him she hadn't bothered. He didn't know if he should be relieved or worried. He tried to step inside her mind, to discover her feelings, but Rose's narrowed gaze warned him to keep his distance.

Duncan gave her a sheepish look and returned his attention to the road.

* * * * *

When they arrived at Ian's home, Duncan insisted on carrying Rose inside. It worried him she didn't try to fight him, but instead laid her head on his shoulder. Rose had been through so much in such a short time. He couldn't begin to understand how she was feeling deep inside. As he carried her past Jax and Mark who stood in the hall, Duncan spoke to Jax mentally, *Tell Ian I'll be down later.*

She nodded her understanding as she watched him walk upstairs.

Duncan laid Rose on their bed and pulled off her shoes. Once he'd kicked off his own, he crawled in beside her and pulled her body close to his, spoon-style as he whispered in her ear, "I know you're tired so I'll save the major talking until tomorrow, but I do want to apologize for doubting you."

His grip tightened around her waist. "Things worked beyond my understanding." He paused and took a breath. "One of the reasons I was so angry was because I thought someone had taken away what I had come to think of as my 'right'."

"Your right?" She turned in his arms to lie on her back and look up at him.

Duncan slid his hand across her breast and down her belly, letting his gaze follow its path. "You and I have a connection, a spark whenever we touch." *That goes beyond our being vampires,* he thought with conviction. "If any man converted you, I wanted to be that man."

Her serious gaze locked with his. "You didn't want to convert me."

He clenched his jaw that she seemed to want to hold on to that thought, regardless what he said. "You know damn well why I didn't want to convert you, Róisín."

"If I'd been special, meant something to you, it shouldn't have mattered."

Duncan gripped her waist. "Don't you see? I didn't want you to experience life the way I did, never really belonging to either race."

Rose put her hand on his face, her eyes full of tears. "I know my conversion was an accident on your part, a fluke. I'm coming to terms with it. We can't change what has happened. You've apologized for acting like an ass about it. Let's not bring it up again."

Duncan traced his finger down her jaw. "I'll give you fair warning now. I'll do everything in my power to mate with you."

"I'm not taking your blood," she said in an adamant tone. Then she placed her hand on his neck and pulled his head close to hers as she finished in a seductive tone, "But I'll take anything else you're willing to offer. Doing something that makes me feel alive is exactly what I need at the moment."

His lips brushed hers. "You'll have to eat eventually, *a ghrá*."

Rose wrapped her arms around his neck and ran her tongue along his lower lip. *You're such a stubborn man. I'm only hungry for one thing right now.*

She bathed his neck with her warm breath as she finished, "And that's sexual gratification. Take off your clothes."

Duncan's cock ached to be deep inside her. They'd work out the rest later, but like Rose, he needed their connection, needed to remind her why he was the only man she'd revealed her emotions to while they'd had sex. He sat up and shrugged out of his shirt, then helped Rose out of her clothes before he removed his pants and boxers.

Lying back down beside Rose, he quickly pulled her underneath him at the same time he slid his thigh between her legs, nudging his erection against her sex.

Rose didn't object. Instead, her gorgeous eyes glittered with desire. She placed her hands on his shoulders and arched her back. "I want to feel you deep inside me. Now."

Duncan entered her in one powerful thrust. Rose cried out, then moaned, griping his shoulders.

When he realized this was the first time he'd entered a woman's body without protection between them, Duncan groaned at the ultimate feeling of closeness. Damn, she felt so hot and wet and so fucking good. No more condoms. Ever! He withdrew and slammed into her once more, gritting his teeth at the sensations rocking through his groin. He was on fire.

Rose keened and dug her fingers in her shoulders. "God, you feel so good," she panted, rolling her hips underneath him.

Duncan fought hard to keep from losing it. The woman rocked his world on many levels. He'd caught a glimpse of her fangs as she spoke and the sight revved his libido to full throttle. He felt every single thump of his heart beating inside his head, experienced every pulse right down to his cock. He held back his release and forced himself to remain elevated above her on his elbows. He refused to get too close to her neck. The way he felt right now, he might lose his tightly held control and take her blood without her consent.

Rocking her hips against him, Rose cupped her hand behind his neck and tried to pull him closer.

Duncan held his position, gritting out, "No."

Her strength surprised him when she yanked his mouth close to her neck. "Bite me, Duncan. I want to feel the pain and the pleasure. I need to feel alive…to experience you taking me. Again."

Her desire fueled his own. Duncan's nostrils flared as he inhaled, catching her intoxicating scent. She was going to kill him. His heart felt as if it were going to burst from his chest if he didn't sink his teeth into her sweet flesh. But as ruthless as he was in his desire to mate, her well-being would always come first.

He stopped thrusting and remained deep inside her as he gritted out, "If I take your blood, your hunger and the need to take mine will overwhelm you."

"I'm stronger than you give me credit for. Now, bite me, damn it. I want you."

Duncan saw the brief flash of her fangs once more. That erotic sight caused a jolt of sheer sexual adrenaline to shoot through him. He grasped her hair and slowly bent her head back. He laved at her thudding pulse once, twice and a third time before he bit her harder than he ever had.

Rose's gasp followed by her moan of sheer pleasure echoed throughout his body as he moved his hips. Never had he pounded inside another as he did Rose, thrusting in rapid, heart-pounding jerks. The woman made him feel so out of fucking control.

She screamed and raked her nails down his back, taking each of his thrusts with counterthrusts of her own, encouraging his rough joining.

When her body began to shudder around his, Duncan felt a shock run through him as if a bolt of electricity moved from his head to his cock, splintering throughout his body. He groaned at the intensity peaking inside him.

True to her word, Rose didn't bite him, but damn if that strange sensation wasn't the most unique, erotic encounter he'd ever experienced. He exploded inside her, his hips moving quickly at first, then slowing. He relished the fact his fluids bathed her insides and the knowledge he'd just taken their lovemaking to a more intimate level.

When he stilled inside her and withdrew his fangs, Rose ran her fingers down his back, panting, "That was beyond incredible, but why didn't you take my blood?"

Duncan leaned up on his elbows, reluctant to withdraw from her body. He reveled in their connection and wasn't ready to give it up. Not yet.

He frowned down at her when he saw the rosy color in her cheeks. The woman looked absolutely radiant. Why wasn't she clawing at him to take his blood? *He* sure as hell wanted to feel her fangs sink deep in his neck.

"You've been through a lot. I wasn't going to take advantage of you by taking what little blood you need."

When she nodded her understanding, he continued, his tone turning intense. "But don't think I'm going to give up on our mating. I've never been more determined than I am about this."

Rose traced her finger along his jaw, a devilish smile on her face. "I'm more stubborn than you, but you just keep right on trying, Duncan Mordoor. Nothing makes me dig my heels in more than a challenge."

Duncan wanted to grind his teeth at her stubborn stance. Somehow she'd managed to turn the tables on him and wear him out. Again.

He needed to gain the upper hand. Rolling over, he took her with him and pressed her head against his shoulder. "There was no protection between us, *a ghrá*."

He felt her tense and then relax with a shrug. "I'm no longer ovulating, so it doesn't matter."

Duncan's jaw clenched. Damn the woman.

"Sleep. I know you're tired."

Her head popped up and she gave him an impish smile. "Actually, I'm feeling rather refreshed." She started to push away from him as if she was going to get up, but Duncan clamped his arms around her body, locking her to his side.

"No way. You're resting."

"If you're feeling wiped, feel free to rest," she insisted, trying once again to get up.

He held fast, growling out as he stared her down, "You might think you're more stubborn, but you haven't begun to see my stubborn side."

Rose sighed and laid her head back down. "Fine. If you need my warmth to sleep, it's the least I can do."

"Thanks for your generosity," Duncan replied in a dry tone.

"No problem." She ran hand across his glistening chest "Plus, I like the way you smell after we've had sex."

Duncan chuckled. No matter how much she infuriated him, she still got to him, right in the gut. He kissed the top of her head. "I do what I can to please, *a thaisce*. Now rest. We'll talk later."

* * * * *

As worn out as he felt, Duncan forced himself to stay awake until after Rose had fallen asleep. Then he'd dragged his tired butt out of bed and went downstairs to see Ian.

"Did Rose kick your ass?" Ian teased. "I've never seen you looking like someone beat the piss out of you before."

"Bite me," Duncan snapped as he flopped onto the couch. He ran a hand through his hair, frustrated. "What's the status on James?"

Ian shook his head, a grim look on his face. "I haven't had any luck finding him yet, but I do have some news."

Duncan perked up. "What news?"

"Eamon died from the wounds James inflicted."

Duncan tensed. "Did Mom find out what he wanted to tell her before he died?"

Ian nodded, a solemn look on his face. "You're not going to like it."

"What else is new lately?"

"Mom and Dad put Lucian on the speakerphone while Eamon told them some disturbing news." Ian wrapped his arm around Jax's shoulders as she entered the room from the hall. "You should hear this too, *a ghrá*. Where'd Mark go?"

"He went to eat, then to call in to work to take a few days off so he can help us track down James."

Ian's gaze narrowed on Duncan. "You really owe Mark, Dunc. He'd gone above and beyond for you on this."

Duncan nodded. "I know. Over the past few days, I've come to appreciate what it means to have friends you can depend on."

Ian gave him a curt nod, letting the subject drop.

"Tell us your news," Jax encouraged Ian.

"Remember when Mom said there were two Guardians for each priestess and that James and Rónán were Anna's Guardians?"

Duncan nodded at his brother, his stomach tensing.

"Before James left Eamon to die in his own pool of blood, he told Eamon that *he* was the Guardian who'd attacked Anna, not Rónán. He laughed at the irony that the Goddess had cursed and condemned the wrong man."

Duncan's gut clenched at the news. While his mind raced over what Ian had just revealed, his twin continued, "Mom said the Guardians were the most familiar with their priestess' scent. My guess is…James ran into Rose, caught Anna's latent scent, and his desire for more power, to succeed where he'd failed in the past, caused him to disregard the Kendrians' rules for dealing with humans."

Duncan clenched his fists then finished Ian's thought process. "He plans to take over where he left off."

"Are you absolutely certain Rose is Anna's descendant?" Ian asked.

"Yes. I found her at the cemetery, visiting her mother's grave. The name on the headstone read Anna Brennan Sinclair." Duncan contemplated what Ian had told him, then narrowed his gaze. "Rónán may have been innocent in the past but the vamp attacked Rose. He'll die for his actions."

Ian gave a heavy sigh. "Then you're not going to like the rest of what I'm about to tell you. Eamon insisted Lucian appoint you the new leader of the Sythens."

"I'm a Ruean, not a Sythen," Duncan countered in a terse tone.

"You're half Sythen, Duncan," Jax reminded him.

"That wasn't the part I thought you'd have a hard time with."

"There's more?" Duncan addressed Ian, his voice turning harsh in his anger.

Ian nodded. "Not only did Eamon ask that you be appointed leader of the Sythens, he asked that Rónán be appointed as your second-in-command."

"Is he insane?" Duncan jumped up from the couch to pace the floor.

Ian shook his head. "He was quite lucid and rational in his request. He regretted the injustice that had happened to Rónán. Apparently, James also revealed to Eamon that he was the one who told the Goddess he'd tried to stop Rónán from taking Anna when she'd found the two men locked in battle over the priestess.

"According to what James told Eamon, he attacked Anna from behind. While Anna still lay there unconscious, Rónán attacked James, trying to protect Anna. They fought and James had just landed a powerful blow to Rónán, knocking him out, when The Morrigan arrived. James convinced the Goddess he was the one trying to protect Anna from Rónán. I guess since Anna never 'saw' her attacker that's why she didn't refute The Morrigan's decision."

"Rónán has not shown himself to be protective over Rose," Duncan said. "Quite the opposite."

"Eamon's rationale is that Rónán needs to know he's been given another chance. And as a second to you, you can keep a close eye on him to make sure he's toeing the line, so to speak."

"Lucian believes this load of shit?" Duncan stopped pacing and faced his brother.

"Lucian trusted in Eamon's integrity."

"What integrity? He'd hidden some of the Sythens' powers as well as their true origin from the entire council."

"He did it to protect his Sythen clan as a whole from prejudice for the past sins of a few. The Kendrians have benefited from the Sythens, not suffered, Duncan," Ian reminded him.

"You buy into this bullshit, too?" He couldn't believe his own brother agreed with this nonsense.

"Rónán's status remains to be seen, but yes, I agree you should lead the Sythens. You're the perfect person to do so. With your mixed Ruean-Sythen status, you could help bridge the gap and mediate the fallout from the other clan members that will surely come when the Sythens' past is revealed. You know it'll have to come out."

Duncan shook his head at his brother. "Seven months into your new role as Ruean leader and you're as brainwashed as the rest of the clan leaders. I prefer not to get involved in Kendrian politics."

Ian's face darkened and he took a step forward. "Watch what you say, little brother."

Jax placed a hand on her Anima's chest. "Calm down you two." She met Duncan's gaze with a steady one. "You're not thinking clearly because you haven't fed in a while. I hear your stomach rumbling. Go eat. I promise we'll keep an eye on Rose. She won't slip out without our knowledge again."

Ian and Duncan stared each other down. The battle of wills between the two brothers continued at a subconscious level.

After a full minute of tense silence, Duncan nodded his agreement with Jax's suggestion and turned to leave. Glancing back at his brother, he said, "Tell Lucian I refuse to lead the Sythens."

Anger swept through Duncan as he pulled off his clothes and dropped them on the porch. Shifting to a raven, he flew to the nearest park to eat. Once there, he had to feed from three humans before he felt back to his normal self. What the hell was wrong with him? He'd never felt so hungry and drained in his life.

Once his stomach no longer rumbled, Duncan erased the humans' memories of his presence, then took off running as hard and as fast as he could through the woods that lined the park. He needed to expend his anger.

All these years he'd thought he was someone else. All this time he'd felt like an outsider, never getting involved. Now he was expected to direct and lead a clan? Sheer anger and frustration raged within him.

As his emotions spiked, Duncan pushed his body harder, running until he felt sweat trickle down his temples.

When exhaustion finally made his legs give out, Duncan collapsed in the dense woods and rolled onto his back to lie staring up into the canopy of trees above him. For a while his labored breathing was the only sound he heard until his heart rate slowed. Then the sounds of the birds chirping and water racing down a creek bed entered his consciousness.

He turned and lifted himself up on his hands and knees as he thought about his mother's comment about his shifting ability.

Duncan closed his eyes and concentrated on the form of a lion, just like he did when he shifted to a raven. Nothing happened. Not a twinge or a shudder of change.

Frustration mounted and he pounded the ground with his fist. A rustle of underbrush drew his attention and Duncan opened his eyes to see a cougar staring at him from atop a fallen tree.

The cat's ears twitched and he sat down on his haunches, clearly curious of the naked human in his domain. The cougar's long tail flipped back and forth against the log as if he were evaluating Duncan. Duncan let his gaze travel the animal's tawny coat. He listened to the cougar's heart beating at a rapid pace in his chest. Closing his eyes, Duncan let the cat's form reappear in his mind, concentrating on every nuance he could absorb.

When his body began to shake and shift, Duncan heard the cat let out a cougar cry and run off. Duncan smiled when he glanced down at his tawny-colored paws. He looked back and flipped his long tail. He trotted in a full circle and leapt upon the fallen tree where the cougar had been, elation sweeping through him. He'd done it. He'd shifted to a cougar.

Duncan's euphoria died a quick death. Since he couldn't shift to a lion, he considered the fact his shape-shifting must be bound to animals of less than or equal to his similar weight and body mass. There was no way he could compete with Rónán and James with their vast shape-shifting. All he knew for a fact was that a lion or a jaguar would certainly have an advantage over any animal he could convert due to his weight limitations.

The lone cougar poked his head out from behind a nearby tree, a deer's leg dangling from his mouth. Then he bolted back into the woods, dragging the leg behind him. Duncan ducked when a much larger cougar jumped over him to take off after the cougar. His heart raced at the near-miss, but the sight of the two animals made him chuckle mentally. It was as if the cougar was telling him, "It's not the size that matters, but who ends up with the spoils."

Duncan stared into the woods where the larger cougar had chased after the smaller one and a sudden revelation occurred to him. He didn't have to be bigger to defeat James and Rónán. He just had to be smarter and use his skills to his advantage against the two Guardians. Duncan was nothing if not devious.

Feeling more confident in his capabilities, Duncan shifted to a raven's form and took flight to return back to Ian's. When Rose awoke, they needed to talk.

* * * * *

Hot, moist decadence lapped at her body. Rose moaned in her sleep and intuitively rocked her hips closer to the source of pleasure.

She came wide awake with a gasp when she felt something swipe against her slit, then plunge inside her channel.

*Afternoon,* a ghrá, Duncan spoke in her mind as he palmed her buttocks and gave her sex a wet, openmouthed kiss.

Rose's toes dug into the sheets and she arched her back when he sucked at her sensitive clit.

*How hungry are you?* He seduced her with his sexy voice as well as his talented mouth and tongue.

Her fangs scraped against the insides of her lips, not so much for food, but for a deeper sexual bond. She shook off the thought that entered her head and breathed out, "I'm good. Not hungry at all."

Duncan raised his head, a frustrated look on his face. "How can you not be starving? You haven't fed."

"There was that male nurse Rónán compelled…" she began before she thought better of it.

Duncan moved over her quickly, caging her in, his eyes glowing red in his anger. "You take blood from no one but me, Róisín," he growled.

"Get over it. I'll take blood from whomever I damn well please."

"Try it and I'll kill him before you get your first swallow."

The look of jealous fury on his face made her hold back the flippant remark she almost made. The man was dead serious.

"You can't mean to starve me into mating with you."

His golden gaze narrowed on her. "That isn't my intent, but Kendrians are very possessive of their Animas. The thought of you taking blood from another goes beyond anything I can accept."

"Again, I'm-not-your-Anima." She spoke slowly as if she were talking to a child.

Duncan's gaze searched her face as he speared his fingers through her hair and cupped the back of her head. "You admitted the connection we had. How can you deny it, Rose? How can you deny us? Do you not feel we are the same?"

His last sentence caught her attention. She frowned. "What do you mean 'the same'?"

He rubbed his thumb along her jaw, letting his gaze turn tender. "Every time I touched you, there was a spark, a familiarity I couldn't deny. Rose, you're a descendant of the Sythen clan. Your mother was known as an Atruan priestess, a member of the Irish Atruan vampire clan."

Rose's heart jerked at his comment. Pulling away from his touch, she crawled backward until her back pressed against the tall headboard. She clutched the pillow against her chest, her eyes wide and full of disbelief.

"How do you know all this? Did you read my paperwork?"

Duncan frowned at her accusing tone and the sound of her heart rate picking up. "What are you talking about? What paperwork?"

Rose looked away, mumbling, "Never mind."

He moved closer and touched her chin, turning her face back to his. Regarding her with a steady, intense gaze, he repeated in a determined tone, "What paperwork, Róisín?"

Her back stiffened and she narrowed her gaze on him. "What makes you think I'm a member of this Atruan clan and what does that clan have to do with the Sythens?"

He literally felt the distrust emanating from her. "My mother told me."

"Your mother?" A confused expression crossed her face.

Duncan nodded and shared the entire Atruan-Sythen history his mother told him yesterday. Rose sat there quietly while he talked. When he finished and she didn't say a word, he finally asked, "Are you okay?"

Tears welled in her eyes and a lost expression filtered across her features. "My poor mother. Why didn't she warn me?"

Duncan wiped away a tear as it fell down her cheek. His heart lurched for the way Rose had to discover her true heritage, for all that she'd lost in such a short time. "From what my mother said, I can only assume your mother was following her oath to The Morrigan. It was just a fluke you happened to run into James."

She shuddered at his comment. "To think James was one of my mother's Guardians."

"Your mother knew him as Séamus Flannery," Duncan said before he told her the story about the Atruans changing their names when they came to the States.

"James, Séamus. It doesn't really matter what he called himself." Her voice turned hard and her shoulders tensed. "And Rónán...the bastard tried to kidnap her. I should've killed him while I had the chance."

Duncan almost told her the truth about Rónán, the one Ian just conveyed about Rónán's innocence, but he didn't. He didn't buy into it. No matter the past, in his mind, Rónán was just as dangerous as James. Rónán might be a condemned man for a crime he didn't commit, but he'd seemed just as deadly as James. If Rose kept Rónán clearly in the "bad guy" category in her head, she'd be very wary of the vampire whose supposed job it was to protect her at all costs.

"Maybe we'll get lucky and he and James will kill each other," Duncan snorted.

Surprise reflected in Rose's gaze. "James hasn't been eliminated?"

He shook his head. "He mortally wounded the Sythen leader and is running around free at the moment—hunting for you, I'm certain."

"If he was the Guardian who didn't rebel all those years ago, why would he be hunting for me now? It just doesn't make sense."

"You're a desirable woman. Need I say more?" he gave her a neutral answer.

Rose glanced at the clock on the nightstand as she shook her head. He heard her heart rate stutter, then rapidly speed up before she threw her pillow at him.

"Ohmigod, I can't believe I slept 'til noon. I've got to go!" She jumped off the bed, landing on her feet.

Duncan caught the pillow and watched her gather her clothes, her movements rushed. "You can't go anywhere. You need to stay here so we can protect you."

Rose walked into the bathroom, calling over her shoulder, "No can do. I've got to make a flight in a couple hours."

Duncan followed her into the bathroom. His chest tightened at the thought she planned to leave. "Where are you going?" he asked in a casual tone as she turned on the shower.

Rose stepped under the spray and pulled the sliding glass door shut, calling out over the water pounding against the tile floor, "I'm going to Ireland to find out all I can about my mother's past."

Duncan's stomach clenched and he tried to remain calm as he crossed his arms over his chest and leaned against the doorjamb. "I've told you everything you need to know. There's no reason for you to leave now."

"Open my purse and pull out the paperwork. There's a letter written in Irish from my mother. I believe it will confirm what you've told me. All I know for certain is that I need to call a woman named Siobhán and arrange a meeting with the Saoi."

Duncan walked back into their room, opened her purse and scanned the paperwork she asked him to read over.

He returned the paperwork where he found it and walked back to the bathroom doorway.

"You're correct. Your mother's letter pretty much sums up what I've told you."

"That's what I thought."

There was no way she was going anywhere without him. While his gaze traveled her gorgeous body through the frosted glass, his cock hardened instantly at the idea of taking her against the wall in the shower. He stepped forward and slid the glass door back.

Rose had suds in her hair. Her eyes were closed against the water as she spoke. "After hearing what you've told me, I'm even more determined to go now. I've got to find out how to defeat a cursed Guardian. Hopefully, I'll learn even more about my Atruan heritage while I'm there."

Good point on learning everything they could about eliminating Rónán, he thought. He wasn't sure how Rónán managed traveling from Ireland to the US without being exposed to some daylight, but he'd seen the Atruan's willpower firsthand. The vamp's extreme actions put him in a category all by himself—of the unstable variety.

With two maniacs on her trail, leaving the country for a while might be the best thing for Rose. Their absence would give Ian, Jax and Mark more time to find the rogue vamps.

Duncan stepped into the shower, desire flowing through him as his body craved closer contact with Rose. Grasping her waist, he pulled her against his chest. "Then we'll go together, *a thaisce*."

Rose gasped when his hard body pressed against hers. Soapsuds caked her hair as she clasped his shoulders and stared into his eyes.

Her lips set in a determined line. "I'm doing this on my own, Duncan."

He threaded his fingers in her hair and tilted her head back until the water ran through it. Running his fingers through her long strands to loosen all the suds, he replied in a determined tone, "This isn't up for debate. As your mate, I go where you go. Always."

* * * * *

Rose stood near the airline's ticket counter, waiting for Duncan. Her gaze landed on his perfect ass encased in a pair of faded jeans. She scanned the fine-gauge burgundy sweater that stretched across his broad back before letting her gaze move to his light brown locks and overnight beard. Her heart rate kicked up at the shadow on his jaw. If she didn't know better, she'd think he purposefully left it like that just to entice her more. Infuriating man.

Rose sighed. She really didn't like the idea of Duncan going to Ireland with her, but the stubborn man refused to take no for an answer. Plus, as he pointed out, "In your quest, you might run across other documents in Irish and need my translation expertise."

The idea he was worming his way into her life, making her need him more than she'd ever needed anyone made her stomach tense. *And rumble a bit, too,* she thought, walking farther away so Duncan wouldn't hear the telltale gurgling sound. He didn't need any more fuel for the "we will mate" fire.

Looking away, she gripped the handle on her travel suitcase and let her gaze scan the airport. At this hour, the terminal buzzed with activity. The smell of fresh roasted coffee at a nearby coffee stand wafted her way and she smiled. For a brief second, she considered getting a cup of the rich brew, but the thought of drinking it, the way it would taste to her now with her belly completely empty, made her stomach churn.

Rose jumped when Duncan's arm came around her waist from behind. He pulled her back against his hard chest and the faint smell of his cologne surrounded her. Trailing his lips down her neck, he whispered in her ear, his voice a velvet purr, "You and me and a few days on a beautiful island. Alone. Sounds perfect."

A shiver coursed through her at his seductive tone. Rose closed her eyes and clamped her lips shut when she felt her incisors begin to lengthen. Clenching her jaw, she worked hard to regain control, to not be drawn in by Duncan's charisma. She would *not* take his blood.

When her fangs shortened back to their normal size, she pulled out of his grip and stared up at him. "This is a business trip, Duncan. Nothing more."

Duncan's gaze narrowed at her comment. His jaw ticced and his shoulders tensed.

"Rose..." he began when the PA system announced their flight was beginning to board.

Rose let out a breath of relief at the interruption. Excitement coursed through her as she turned and walked through the gate and down the gangway toward the plane. She was doing it...going to Ireland. She had so much more at stake with this trip. Even now, everything Duncan had told her still whirled in her mind.

She wondered how Duncan was taking the fact he wasn't half human like he'd thought he was. She realized he'd had a few surprises of his own these past couple of days. She glanced down at him as she reached the top step to enter the plane. He winked at her.

*He's doing just fine,* she thought with a smirk as she stepped into the plane.

Duncan's seat was closest to the window and Rose's was beside him. *How the hell did he accomplish the feat of sitting next to me?* she wondered as Duncan took her suitcase and stowed it away in the compartment above their heads before doing the same with his.

Duncan flashed her a sexy smile as if he'd read her thoughts. Rose narrowed her gaze, then waited for him to seat himself before she could sit down. Ever since she discovered she could read Duncan's thoughts, she'd purposefully stayed out of his mind. She didn't need the extra sexual stimulation of knowing his determination to mate with her or the motivation behind it. It hurt enough to know he'd never planned to convert her, let alone mate with her. She didn't want to discover any more surprises. Her mind was already on overload.

As people continued to file onto the plane, Duncan leaned close. "This trip is what we make of it. It's a long flight, *a ghrá*. I love a captive audience. I'll get to whisper all kinds of suggestive comments in your ear."

Rose groaned inwardly, her heart hammering at his comment. She dug her nails in her palms, hoping she'd find an Irishman willing to donate a pint, of the bloody kind, on her way to the bathroom in one of the pubs…which would be their first stop in Ireland if Duncan kept this up.

Just then, Nigel's face popped up from the seat in front of them. "Hiya, Rosie. Surprise!"

"Uncle Nigel!" Rose said. She was so relieved at the distraction her uncle provided there was no way she could be mad at him for ignoring her request to go alone on this trip. "What are you doing here?"

Nigel's gaze darted from her face to Duncan's suddenly stoic one. "Well, I know you said you wanted to go alone, but I just couldn't let my little girl go by herself. Like I said, I've always wanted to go to Ireland. So here I am." When he finished speaking, he put out his hand to Duncan. "It's good to see you again, Stryker. Small world, eh?"

Duncan took his hand, his Irish accent heavier than she'd ever heard it. "It's Duncan Mordoor, Nigel, and I'm here with your niece."

Her uncle's raised eyebrow and Duncan's disgruntled expression and gruff tone caused an amused smile to spread across Rose's face. She could tell Duncan sure as hell didn't expect a chaperone on this trip. "Duncan's a friend of mine, Nigel. His mother is from Ireland."

*Why didn't you tell me your uncle was Nigel Sinclair?* Duncan asked.

*You never asked.*

Nigel ran his hand through his brown hair and said with a laugh, "Well, it looks like you'll have two escorts, my dear."

Fully amused by the wrench Nigel seemed to be putting in Duncan's plans of seduction, Rose glanced at her uncle's hair. "I see you've gone back to your natural color, Unc."

Nigel grinned, ran his hand through his hair once more and winked at her. "Yeah, I figured blending in would be best on this trip."

Another passenger tapped Nigel on the shoulder so she could get to her seat next to the window. Nigel waved to them. "Gotta sit down for now. I'll pop back up later."

"Great," Duncan muttered.

This time Rose didn't hold back her laughter.

When a blonde woman said, "Excuse me," Rose quickly sobered and met her gaze. "Yes?"

"Do you mind if my oldest son sits next to you? I'll be across the aisle with my younger two."

Rose smiled at the dark-haired little boy staring at her with wide inquisitive blue eyes. He appeared to be around seven or eight.

"Not at all," she replied at the same time she heard Duncan's low groan in the background. Ignoring the annoyed vamp, she asked the little boy his name as he pulled off his backpack and seated himself beside her.

"I'm Todd," he said in a voice that sounded mature beyond his years.

"I'm Rose." Looking back at Duncan, she said, "And this is Duncan."

Duncan just nodded, then turned to stare out the window.

Todd buckled himself in and said in an excited voice, "This is my first time going to Ireland. I can't wait to visit my cousins."

"What are their names?" Rose asked.

He nodded, lifting his backpack to pull out a mini-photo album. Pointing to two boys with light brown hair and mischievous grins, he said, "These are my cousins, Sean and Danny. They're a year older than me. I'm going to visit them in Sligo then travel around with my mom sightseeing for a few days."

Todd's mother leaned over and smiled. "He'll talk your ears off if you let him."

Rose laughed, enjoying the boy's enthusiasm. "He's fine."

Duncan couldn't believe his rotten luck. Not only would Rose's uncle make it difficult to seduce her into mating with him, but having a kid sitting next to them put a damper on his plans to entice her with sexy talk the entire trip. He consoled himself this was the first connection. He and Rose had a much longer flight on the second leg of the trip to Ireland.

Nigel turned around, speaking to Duncan through the crack in the seats. "The good news is I was able to get a seat beside Rose on the next flight so I guess we'll all be together then."

"That's great." Duncan forced a smile. Just great. He glanced at Rose as her uncle turned back around. She hadn't heard Nigel, she'd been so busy talking to Todd.

Duncan's annoyance faded, turning to appreciation as he watched Rose with the little boy. She was patient and encouraging when he showed her pictures he'd drawn for his cousins. She'd make a good mother. The thought made him smile. He'd never thought about having children. Had never pondered what it would be like to hold a miniature version of himself in his arms, to train his child in his powers. His chest swelled at the idea and Duncan couldn't hold back the smile that spread across his face. Their child.

The wheels began to move as the plane taxied down the runway. He watched Rose pull a piece of gum out of her purse and wondered if she were chewing it to keep her ears from popping. He almost told her she didn't need it anymore now that she was fully converted, but stayed quiet. Maybe keeping a routine was good for the soul.

"Can Todd have a piece of gum?" Rose asked the boy's mother. When the woman nodded, Rose handed a piece to Todd.

Once the plane was airborne, Rose blew a bubble.

"Will you show me how to do that?" Todd asked in awe.

"Sure. First you have to chew your gum really good, then start to flatten the gum with your tongue like this. Then, you push your tongue through the gum and blow, like this." A bubble formed, then popped.

Todd grinned. His expression changed to one of concentration as he chewed. His brow furrowed while he tried to mimic what she'd shown him. Rose turned to face Todd to show him again how to blow a bubble, this time in slow motion.

As he listened to them discuss bubble-blowing techniques, Duncan's gaze traveled to Rose's gorgeous hair. She'd worn it down. He wanted to touch it, to run his fingers through the long red locks and inhale her sweet scent.

"I think I got it," Todd said in a determined voice.

Duncan heard a *pffthunk* and then Todd's worried voice. "Uh-oh."

"Um, maybe don't use so much force when you try to blow." Rose's tone sounded calm as she slowly turned to face Duncan. She held a hank of her hair out toward him, while a plea for help reflected on her face.

Duncan chuckled at the wad of gum that was now embedded in her long strands.

He raised an eyebrow. "Bubble-blowing lessons are over, I take it?"

She gave him wry grin. "He's just excited to learn." Her look turned hopeful as she spoke in his mind. *Got any vampire tricks up your sleeve to help me out?*

Duncan stared at her sparkling aqua eyes. The woman took his breath away. He lifted the lock of hair with the bubble gum in it and noted Todd's curious stare.

*You need to go to the bathroom,* he compelled the boy.

Todd unbuckled his seat belt and said to his mom, "I gotta go," before he headed to the back of the plane.

Once the child left, Duncan leaned over and blew a breath of cool air on the gum.

Rose watched him with a look of surprise on her face as he blew once more, chilling the gum to a hard lump. When he peeled the gum off her hair and dropped it in the scrap of paper she held out, Rose started to thank him, but he took advantage of their close proximity and the boy's absence.

His lips covered hers in a slow, seductive kiss.

Satisfaction rippled through him to hear her heart rate gallop to attention. Rose put her hand on his jaw as her tongue brushed against his, a feather light caress.

Duncan swiped his tongue inside her mouth once more, taking her gum.

She sat back in her seat with an intrigued look on her face. "Thank you, Duncan."

Duncan had never wanted her more. He winked at her and settled in his seat, chewing the stolen gum, enjoying her taste. His hopes for their full mating while in Ireland lifted once more.

# Chapter Twelve

ꕤ

He heard the vampire walking outside, then the front door slowly opened.

"Come in," Rónán called out. "Rose isn't here at the moment, but I'll be sure to let her know ye stopped by."

His lips curled into a smirk when he heard Séamus' heart skip a beat, felt the tiny sliver of fear that coursed through the vamp.

He knew Séamus well. They'd been like brothers long ago. Before the fecker betrayed him.

The front door slammed into the wall, the look on Séamus' face livid. He stepped inside, his eyes boring holes into Rónán. "What have you done with her? She's mine!"

Rónán stood up from the couch in unhurried movements, stretching like a languorous cat just up from his nap.

"You entered her home without her permission," Séamus roared, his fists clenched tight by his sides.

Rónán gave the living room a casual, sweeping gaze, then met Seamus' furious stare. "I no longer follow the rules. Following the rules got me a lifetime sentence." He paused, his gaze narrowing. "But then ye already knew that," he finished in a lethal tone.

Séamus seethed where he stood, the veins in his thick neck bulging in his anger. "You should've stayed in Ireland, buried away."

Rónán's knuckles popped as he curled his hands into bunched fists by his side. "Even if ye weren't the threat Rose called me forth to protect her from, I'd relish taking ye out on me own, Séamus. I've waited a long time to stand in front of ye, contemplated the many ways I'm going to make *you* suffer, *a chara*."

"My name is James now," he said as he lunged toward him, roaring his rage, his claws extended.

Rónán sidestepped Séamus' hands and shoved the vamp against a side wall with a mental push.

"I've had a long time to perfect me mental skills, a couple centuries to be exact, but then, who's counting. I'll relish every moment in taking me revenge."

Séamus pushed off the wall and jumped over Rónán's head as he approached. Landing on his feet, Séamus turned around to face Rónán at the same time he shifted to a lion, roaring his anger.

*Your curse will be your downfall. Your first priority is Rose. Everything else comes second,* Séamus hissed in Rónán's mind.

Rónán spread his arms wide, glancing around the room. "Do you see Rose anywhere?" He let his hard gaze land on the lion's eyes. Like the ring of a sword being drawn from its sheath, he laid down his deadly vow. "There's just the two of us here, *James*. I'll call ye by yer Americanized name since this foreign soil is where ye'll take yer last breath. I plan to kill ye with me bare hands, to rip out that heart that beats in fear in yer chest. Before it's all said and done, only one of us will live."

His threat hung heavy in the air, a blanket of assured death drifting between them. The undercurrents in the room took on a life all their own. Rónán felt the vengeful energy building between them as they circled each other. Their measured breathing punctuated their steps as they each waited for a chance to strike.

James roared and took a swipe at Rónán with his huge lion's paw.

Rónán moved at the last second, avoiding his claws. "What's the matter? Afraid to face me as a man?" he sneered, goading James further.

"The better man stands before you," James bit out as he shifted back to his human form.

Rónán took advantage of James' arrogant pride and rammed his shoulder in the other man's gut, knocking him across the table to land on the kitchen floor. Before James could recover, Rónán leapt over the table and landed on the vamp's chest. Hard.

James' grunt of pain accompanied the whoosh of air that escaped the vamp's lungs. James shoved at Rónán's feet digging into his chest. His swift action sent Rónán flying back into the living room.

Rónán curled his body in the air, landing on the floor in crouched position. Hunched over, squatting on the balls of his feet, he jerked his enraged face back to James He started to stand when a sharp piercing pain slammed into his chest, spreading in agonizing splinters through his body.

Rónán looked down to see a knife buried in his chest. It had missed his heart by a mere inch. He ground his teeth at the pain as he pulled the knife from his body. Blood gushed from the hole the knife left behind. He laid his hand over his wound, concentrating on heat. While he worked to repair his body, he glanced up in time to see another blade hurling his way. James' evil laughter followed in its wake.

"You said to fight you as a man. The human form is the most devious and deadly of all."

Rónán caught the blade between his palms, then swiftly flipped the knife in his hand, grasping the handle. "I know this truth better than anyone," he grated out at the same time he gathered his mental powers.

All five knives from the butcher block on the kitchen counter flew out and turned. The blades slammed into James' back, tearing into muscle, bone and sinew, one right after the other.

The man shrieked in pain, then twisted to try and remove the knives manually since Rónán's mental powers negated his own. While he used his stronger mental powers to shove the knives deeper into James' flesh, Rónán flipped the blade in his hand once more, preparing to aim right for James' stomach. Dying of a stomach injury was one of the most painful ways to go. He'd make sure the vamp couldn't heal himself.

Holding the knife aloft, he paused for a second. Defeating James was going a lot faster than he'd anticipated. He wanted the bastard to suffer, to pay.

But James was right about one thing. Rónán's duty was to Rose first. James was a very real threat to her. Alive.

Rónán lowered the weapon, conflicting desires swirling in his mind. He wanted to *live* a little longer, to breathe air, to wallow in a good hard fuck with a willing woman. He didn't know what forces determined when Rose was no longer threatened and would therefore send him back to the earth, but with her absent at the moment, James could live.

For now.

While he debated, a sharp pain sliced through Rónán's hand, causing him to drop the knife and hiss in pain.

Rónán looked down to see a short metal bolt embedded in his palm. He jerked his gaze to a beautiful dark-haired woman lowering her crossbow pistol at the same time she raised an automatic gun toward him.

"I think Duncan would prefer to take James out himself," she said with a smirk.

Rónán disregarded the pain radiating from his hand as he pulled the bolt all the way through his hand. He started to leap toward her, ready to battle when he heard a distinct click of two more weapons behind him.

"Try it and you're a dead vamp." A man's voice came from behind him.

Rónán glanced toward the voice. The man looked like the one he'd fought…the vamp who'd converted Rose.

Rage welled within him. His entire body tensed as muscles flexed. He prepared to pounce, ready to kill.

The man stood in the bedroom doorway, his gun trained on Rónán's back. An older woman walked out from behind the vamp holding a gun on him and said, "Hello, Rónán."

Rónán stared at the woman, unsure why she seemed so familiar.

"It's Tressa Shannon." She provided the answer to his unspoken question.

At the same time James repeated her name in a surprised, yet pained voice, Rónán felt Tressa's presence in his mind, peeling away the layers he'd built, working her way past his defenses.

Self-preservation kicked in. Without a thought, he turned, using his mental powers to knock the dark-haired woman who'd shot him back against the door, opening an exit for himself.

The male vamp roared his fury and gunshots sounded, preceded by white-hot pain riddling his back. Rónán stumbled at the onslaught, falling to his knees. James took advantage of the distraction, converting to a raven. The knives buried in his back clattered to the floor as he flew out the open door.

Rónán started to shift too when he heard Tressa's commanding voice in his head.

*Sleep, Rónán.*

Blackness consumed him, but he fought it hard. He'd sleep when he took his last breath.

*Sleep*, her voice softened, sounding so peaceful and benevolent. He lost the battle, succumbing to her mental powers.

*****

*Awaken, Rónán.*

Rónán smelled her violet scent permeating his senses even before he opened his eyes. He lay on his back on a sofa or bed, somewhere soft, while she leaned over him. He could feel the heat of her breath on his cheek. His back ached like a motherfucker, but he refused to moan at the pain.

Instead, with lightning speed he grasped her neck and opened his eyes to narrow his gaze on Tressa.

Cold metal pressed against his temple at the same time someone grabbed his neck in a death grip. Two men growled at once, "Release her. Now!"

Tressa laid her hand over Rónán's on her neck. Her gaze danced between the older vamp and the younger one who stood on either side of the couch. Each one held a menacing expression on his face.

"Ian, put your gun away," she said to the one he'd fought before. "Let go, Marcus," she addressed the older, dark-haired man. "He won't hurt me."

When the metal withdrew and the hand around his neck moved away, Rónán ground out, "Don't count on it."

Tressa's calm gaze met his once more. "Do you want a chance at a life, Rónán?"

Her comment captured his attention. He let go of her neck and sat up. Glancing down at the blanket covering his naked form, he curled his lip in amusement. "Ye vamps ashamed of the body ye're born with?"

"We prefer not to see yours," the man named Ian snapped.

Rónán glanced at him, narrowing his gaze. The man's hair was shorter than the man Rónán had fought. He sniffed the air, taking in his scent now that he was closer. He smelled different, too. This man's reaction to Rónán's attack on the dark-haired woman spoke volumes. Rónán smelled their commingled scents.

"Ye're his twin," he stated in a matter-of-fact tone.

"Duncan and Ian are my sons." Tressa glanced back at the dark-haired woman who'd shot Rónán in the hand. She stood behind Tressa, her gun still trained on him. "And this is Jax, Ian's mate."

Tressa met the older man's gaze who stood behind the couch. His arms were crossed over his chest and protective anger emanated from him as Rónán flicked his gaze to the man. "The man behind you is Marcus, my Anima."

"Ye mean yer *Sonuachar*?" He provided the Irish word for soulmate.

At her nod, Rónán sniffed the air around Tressa's mate and gave a derisive snort. "He's from another vampire race. I can't place his scent."

"Indeed he is," Tressa said. "But this conversation is about you, not us."

Rónán stared at her, waiting to hear what she had to say.

"We're aware of James' treachery and how you were betrayed."

Rónán shrugged as if her comment didn't matter one way or the other to him.

"We want to offer you a chance to redeem yourself in The Morrigan's eyes. Join with Ian and Duncan to defeat James. Maybe then the Goddess will forgive you and lift the curse."

He gritted his teeth, rage rushing through him at her suggestion. "She owes *me* an apology. I refuse to ask forgiveness."

Rónán stood, heedless of the blanket that fell to the floor. He noted the muscle that ticced in Ian's jaw at his refusal to mentally clothe himself. Rónán gave him a ruthless smile.

"I answer to no one but meself."

"Let's put him out of his misery." Ian cocked his gun and aimed it at him once more.

"Can't you see he's intentionally goading you?" Tressa said to Ian.

"James will die," Rónán promised. He eyed the guns trained on him while he gauged his speed of converting with Ian's trigger finger.

A rush of adrenaline shot through him as he bent his knees and bolted straight up to the ceiling. The three bullets that were embedded in his body fell to the carpet with soft thuds as he converted to a fine mist and floated straight into the venting system.

"Shit," Ian hissed. "How'd he shift to mist as wounded as he was?"

Rónán wanted to laugh at the anger radiating through the vamp. Instead he mentally spoke to all in the room, finishing his vow. *Duncan will die, too. Rose is mine to protect.*

"Screw the benefit of the doubt. He's a dead vamp."

Tressa met her son's furious gaze. "There's a darkness within him that's raging a battle with the good side. I think the dark side is what helped him overcome his Atruan vampire limitations." She sighed.

"He's unstable. We can't trust him."

"He's been horribly wronged and cursed. That had to have twisted him somewhat. Rónán's been given an offer. Let's hope his good side overcomes his bad one and he decides to join us instead of fight us."

"You're more forgiving than me."

Tressa met Ian's gaze. "I've been inside his head."

* * * * *

Once they arrived in Shannon, Rose called and got directions to Lonán's Pub in Galway City. While Duncan took care of renting a car, Nigel asked the questions she knew were burning in his head.

"Now I know why you wanted to go *alone* on your trip. If I had known you knew the popular singer, I'd have asked you to negotiate a second night at the Pavilion on my behalf with him."

Rose chuckled, knowing the utter chaos going on in Duncan's life. "I just met Duncan a few days ago, Nigel. I don't think I'd have had much pull with him."

Nigel's brows furrowed. "You just met him and he's going to Ireland with you?"

"He invited himself." Rose watched Duncan signing the paperwork. The man had nice hands, short clipped fingernails and broad palms. Those sexy callused fingers sent shivers down her spine.

"You could've uninvited him." Nigel gave her a knowing smile.

As Duncan approached them, Rose answered in a whisper, "True, but he can speak and read Irish so at least while we're touring he could read the Irish on the historical placards to me."

"Uh-huh." Nigel snorted as Duncan tossed the keys in the air and said, "Let's go."

Rose climbed in the passenger seat of the rental car while Nigel got in the back. Duncan stowed their luggage in the trunk and slid into the driver's seat.

"This is just so weird sitting on the opposite side of the car," Rose commented, staring out the windshield from the left side of the car.

"Tell me about it," Duncan agreed, starting the engine.

"Well, you could've made it easier on yourself and rented an automatic."

Duncan put his left hand on the gearshift and gave her a sexy grin. "I love a challenge, *a ghrá*. I thought you knew that about me."

Rose didn't mistake his double meaning. She just shook her head as she gave him directions to Lonán's pub.

*****

Rose loved the scenic view Galway County offered, the moss-covered rocks and crags, glimpses of waves crashing against the shore as they made the hour-long trip to Galway city. The misty morning only made the lush green countryside seem to glitter like a well-polished emerald. Hence the nickname for Ireland—the Emerald Isle, she thought with a smile. Her excitement at being there was bittersweet though. Her father would've loved Ireland. His death weighed heavily on her heart.

She rolled down her window a bit to catch all the scents and to clear the sad thoughts from her mind. Cool air rushed through the crack, making her feel a little better.

When she began to shiver at the crisp air, Rose came out of her sad reverie and shoved thoughts of her dad to the back of her mind. She was glad she remembered to bring a lightweight jacket, but couldn't believe she didn't think to at least buy a disposable camera.

Taking in as much of the scenery as she could as they drove past, she said, "It's gorgeous. How I wish I had my 35mm with me."

Duncan picked up her hand and kissed her palm. "We'll come back again, Róisín. Ireland is our homeland. We both have a lot to learn about it."

Rose met Duncan's gaze and thought of the promise he made…as if they'd always be together. He sounded so sincere. She stilled herself, refusing to be drawn into his web of seduction. *He didn't plan to convert you, remember?* she reminded herself.

"What do you think, Nigel?" Rose asked, pulling her hand away from Duncan's grasp to turn and look at her uncle.

Nigel's head was leaning against the backseat. His mouth gaped open as he quietly snored in his sleep.

Duncan chuckled. "Looks like the excitement and long flights finally got to him."

Rose glanced at her watch. "I guess all our internal clocks will be messed up a bit during this trip due to the time differences."

"It's best to tough it out when we get there. Staying awake will make adjusting to Ireland's time easier."

Rose nodded her head in agreement. She was too keyed up to sleep anyway.

Duncan parked their car behind the pub and cut the engine. Nigel awoke saying, "Are we here already?"

Rose laughed at her uncle and got out of the car. The trio made their way to the front of the pub and knocked on the door.

The door unlatched and a woman with short, spiky, dark hair opened the door. Squinting, then stepping out of the sun's path, she said with a genuine smile, "Ye must be Rose. I'm Siobhán Lonán." She beckoned them inside. Once they'd all filed in, she shut the door, saying in her heavy Irish accent, "We don't open the pub until three in the afternoon."

Turning to Rose, Siobhán grasped her chin and turned her to face the dim light filtering from outside. Her chocolate-brown gaze scanned her face, scrutinizing. "Ye look just like yer mother. I miss Anna's sweet smile."

"Were you a little girl when you knew Anna?" Nigel asked, clearly puzzled that this forty-something-year-old woman would know his sister-in-law who'd been close to fifty when she died over two decades ago.

Siobhán laughed, her brown eyes twinkling. "Oh, I like this one," she said and started to answer his question when Rose spoke in her mind. *I know you're an Atruan, Siobhán, but my uncle has no idea I've been converted to a vampire. Please, I'm not ready to tell him yet.*

*But ye were already half vampire,* Siobhán answered, sounding puzzled.

"It's nice to meet you, Siobhán." Glancing at the men, Rose said, "This is Duncan Mordoor and my uncle Nigel Sinclair."

When Duncan shook Siobhán's hand, the Atruan said to Rose, *What manner of vampire is he? I smell Atruan on him, but the other…*

*He's part Ruean, a vampire clan in the United States.*

*I smell him on ye, part of yer essence. Did he convert ye?*

Rose nodded, answering Siobhán, then she smiled at her uncle. "Nigel, in answer to your question, yes, Siobhán knew Mom many years ago."

Nigel took Siobhán's hand and bent over her fingers. His eyes twinkled as he kissed the tips. "It's truly a pleasure to meet you, Siobhán."

She gave him a wide grin, cutting her gaze to Rose. "Oooh, he's a charmer, too."

Nigel winked at her, then straightened and let go of her hand. "I told Rose, I wanted to come to Ireland to sightsee. So far I love the scenery in Galway City."

Siobhán chuckled at his comment and released his hand to walk behind the bar. Lifting a ledger from underneath the counter, she opened her scheduling book and looked at Rose. "Well, I just had two people book for the week, so I only have two rooms available."

"Perfect, Nigel and Duncan can bunk together," Rose said.

Duncan cut his gaze to Rose. "What?"

Siobhán raised her eyebrow. "Um, it's a queen-sized bed."

"Rose and I—"

"That'll be fine," Rose interrupted Duncan. "We're only here for a few days."

*Like hell I'm not sleeping in your bed,* Duncan spoke in her mind. To which she responded, *That should keep your attempts to seduce me at bay.*

"Okay, it's settled then." Siobhán scribbled a note in the scheduling book and brought out some keys from behind the counter. By the amused tilt of her lips, Rose guessed the woman could sense the undercurrents going on between Rose and Duncan.

"Whatever works. I'm just happy to be here." Nigel beamed at Siobhán.

"Come on, I'll show ye the rooms and then ye can get settled."

Nigel immediately followed Siobhán as she walked through a door that led down a long hall. Rose fell in line behind him. Duncan was close on her heels. She literally felt his anger like a dark cloud hovering around her, ready to let loose the storm churning inside it.

*I'm your mate. I will sleep where you sleep.*

*You aren't my mate,* she countered as she turned down another hall that was lined with doors to the left and right.

They reached the first room on the left and Siobhán opened the door, handing the key to Nigel. "Here's yer room. I'm sure ye're hungry. I'll whip up some biscuits and we'll have a bit of tea together once you're settled."

Rose looked up at Duncan and held back a laugh at the muscle ticcing in his jaw. "Why don't you guys go get our luggage while Siobhán shows me to my room?"

Duncan didn't say a word. He just pivoted on his heel and started down the hall. Turning to watch him walk away, Rose couldn't help but dig at him a little more.

*Oh, by the way, I did tell you my uncle is bisexual, right?*

Duncan stopped mid-stride, his shoulders tensing. *Rose!* His tone warned he was about to lose his temper, big time.

Chuckling, she beat a fast retreat down the hall, following in Siobhán's footsteps.

Siobhán opened her door and flipped on the light switch, then followed Rose inside the room. Rose eyed the cast-iron double bed with its floral down comforter and white eyelet bed skirt. She itched to walk over to the window, pull back the eyelet curtains and lift the room-darkening shade. But out of deference to Siobhán's aversion to the sun she'd seen earlier, she held back.

Siobhán shut the door and grasped her hand, pulling her over to the bed. "Sit, child," she said in a mother-like voice.

When Rose sat beside Siobhán, the older woman turned curious eyes her way. "You're the first Atruan priestess to come back home. Tell me how I can help you."

"I'm not a priestess, but Anna's descendant," Rose corrected.

Siobhán nodded her understanding. "But as her descendant, you carry her special powers, Rose. You are a priestess in your own right." Siobhán bowed her head in a sign of respect.

Rose lifted her chin, searching the older woman's gaze. "I don't need servitude, I need guidance, Siobhán." She took a deep breath and told Siobhán everything that occurred the last few days, minus the mating issue between her and Duncan. She felt that was too personal and something she and Duncan needed to work through on their own.

When she finished, feeling drained from having to recount the events, Siobhán hugged her, saying, "Before yer mother moved over to be with the other priestesses, she was me best friend. I cried when I heard she was kidnapped by her Guardian." She ran her hand down Rose's hair. "Me poor child. I'm so sorry for yer loss. So much has happened in such a short time."

Rose returned her hug, then pulled back. "Now you see why I need answers." Lifting her brow, Rose let amusement reflect in her gaze. "Starting with how you can look so young. If you knew my mother, then you're well over two hundred years old."

Siobhán laughed. "Ye're a tough one, just like yer mother. Because I choose to serve as a liaison for the priestesses should they ever come back, the Saoi used his powers to slow my aging."

Rose perked up at her mention of the man her mother insisted she speak with. "Can you get me an audience with the Saoi?"

Siobhán nodded. "Indeed, that's why I'm here. But a meeting place will need to be set, so it might not be until tomorrow."

Grabbing Rose's hands, the woman's eyes sparkled. "In the meantime, tell me about yer uncle. I find him intriguing."

"From the way my *single* uncle's acting, I definitely think the feeling's mutual." Rose winked.

Siobhán's smile widened. "Ye know he'll need someone to keep him occupied while ye visit with the Saoi…"

Rose laughed. "I was hoping you'd be able to help me out."

"I'm yer humble servant." Siobhán bowed her head, though her lips curved in amusement. She stood and a wide smile spread across her face. "I'm going to get started on your uncle's biscuits."

The mention of food reminded Rose how long it'd been since she'd fed. And the pub seemed empty at the moment. She'd have to find a way to slip out and eat soon.

"Um, I need to eat, too. Got any suggestions where I could go to find a willing donor?"

Siobhán's brow furrowed in confusion. She started to speak when a knock at Rose's door interrupted her. Her eyes brightened and she gave Rose a mischievous look. "Problem solved. See you in the dining area in a few."

Rose sighed and stood as Siobhán opened the door, greeted Duncan and then walked off down the hall.

Duncan entered Rose's room and shut the door behind him.

"We need to talk," he said in a controlled tone as he set her suitcase down next to the door.

"There's nothing to talk about. I have my room and you have yours." Rose lifted her chin and crossed her arms under her breasts. The act drew his attention to her chest. Her teal green ribbed turtleneck only showed off her curves more, making his cock jump to attention. Duncan narrowed his gaze as he stalked toward her.

When he stood in front of her, he mentally lifted her body in the air so that they were eye level. "You are my mate. Your body craves mine as much as mine does yours." He wrapped his hands around her waist and yanked her against his chest.

His trailed his lips across her jaw. "All I could think about on the trip was having some time alone so we could make love until we were both spent. I miss your warmth and seductive scent surrounding me."

He felt her shudder in his arms and Duncan smiled, pressing a kiss behind her ear. "But more than anything I hunger after your sweet taste, Róisín, I miss the way it feels going down as I suck and swallow," he finished, setting her on the ground.

Rose's breathing turned shallow and he saw her work hard to maintain control, to force her rapid heart rate down to an even beat. After several seconds, she lifted her gaze to his and stepped out of his embrace, shaking her head.

"I have to stay focused while I'm here."

Duncan curled his fists by his side. "You must eat. I've never seen a vampire go without sustenance as long as you. It's not normal."

She lifted her chin a notch, her blue-green eyes full of challenge. "I told you I have a strong will."

"I hear your stomach growling, feel your hunger like an animal clawing in your gut..." Running his hand through his hair, he mumbled, "This is ridiculous."

"I can run out for a bit and grab a bite," Rose said in an amused tone.

Duncan set his jaw and anger flashed in his eyes as he crossed his arms over his chest. "Try it and I'll cut his balls off."

"It could just as easily be a woman," Rose countered.

Duncan paused, intrigued by the idea of watching Rose feed on another woman's neck, but every fiber in his body roared in protest.

"I made you. I'm your mate and it's my responsibility to feed you—mine alone."

Rose sighed, spreading her hands. "Then we're at an impasse. I'm no one's responsibility."

Frustration filled Duncan that she constantly chose to twist his words. "That's not what I meant," he started to say, but she walked past him, opening the door to her room.

"Come on, I'm sure Nigel's waiting for us at a table."

Duncan blew out a breath of sheer impatience. He followed Rose down the hall and back into the pub.

The smell of pastries cooking and tea steeping made Rose's stomach turn. A sudden, painful cramp in her stomach caused her to pause mid-stride on her way to the table.

Duncan wrapped his arm around her waist, grumbling in her head, *Stubborn woman.*

"You okay, Rosie?" her uncle called out as Duncan led her to the table.

Rose slid in the booth across from her uncle, eyeing the pot of tea.

*Remember what I said before, vampires* can *eat for recreational purposes,* Duncan reminded her.

*I'll throw up if I even touch a crumb.*

"I'm fine, Unc, just a little jet-lagged," she answered with a smile.

Nigel buttered a piece of brown bread. "You'll feel better if you eat something, sweetie."

*When are you planning to tell your uncle about us?* Duncan asked.

Picking up the pot of tea, Rose poured herself a cup. "I think I'll just have some tea for now."

*Obviously, he knows there's "something" going on,* she replied to Duncan in a sarcastic tone.

*I meant that you're a vampire. You can't keep it from him forever.*

*I'll tell him when I'm ready.* She refused to look Duncan's way as she added cream and sugar to her tea.

"So where do you want to go this morning?" Nigel asked, oblivious to the mental battle going on between Rose and Duncan.

*You'd better tell him soon, or I will. He has a right to know I'm his nephew-in-law.*

"Oh, I thought maybe we'd take in the shops we passed on the way in. Nothing too strenuous on our first day here. I'm kind of beat," she told her uncle.

*Would you stop with this mate nonsense,* she hissed in Duncan's mind.

*It is not nonsense. I'm taking this very seriously as should you. I'm your mate, Rose. Fucking deal with it.*

She narrowed her gaze on Duncan. *You are not my—*

Siobhán came out of the kitchen carrying a tray. "Here we are." She set down a plate complete with eggs, sausage, potatoes and a grilled tomato in front of Nigel. "Per your request, a traditional Irish breakfast. Eat up, love."

Glancing at Rose and Duncan, she asked with a smirk, "What shall I get you two?"

"Just strong coffee," Duncan said.

Rose's stomach pitched and careened at the smells wafting across the table. As she watched her uncle dig into his meal with gusto, she thought, *God, I'm going to be sick.*

"Rose, I need your help in the kitchen, please," she heard Siobhán's voice as if from far away.

Rose jerked her gaze to Siobhán's questioning one, then looked at Duncan. "Excuse me, Duncan."

Duncan got up from the booth and let her out. He eyed her all the way to the kitchen.

Once they'd entered the kitchen, Rose spoke in Siobhán's mind. *If you have something to say to me, say it mentally. Duncan's listening, I'm sure,* she said, rolling her eyes.

Siobhán grabbed her hands and pulled her to a stool. Once Rose sat down, she said, *I had hoped ye would feed while ye were alone with Duncan. I hear yer belly rumbling, Rose. Why are ye torturing yourself?*

Reluctantly, Rose explained the "mating" battle of wills between her and Duncan. When she finished, Siobhán chuckled in her head. *Ye mean ye don't know?* At Rose's confused look, she tsked. *Well, of course ye wouldn't if yer mother never told ye about her powers.*

Clasping Rose by the shoulders, she met her gaze. *Ye're a psychic vampire, well, at least partially since Duncan converted ye and now ye're part Ruean.*

*What does that mean?* Rose asked.

*It means, love, that ye can feed via a psychic connection with another. It's why ye've been able to go as long as ye have without needing blood. The reason yer mother didn't have fangs was because she fed another way…psychically.*

At Rose's look of disbelief, she continued, *Think about it, from what ye told me, once yer father had the accident, yer mother turned listless, slowly fading to nothing until she died.*

Rose closed her eyes at the sad memory then opened them nodding.

*Me guess is yer mother refused to "feed" from yer father because he was in a coma and she knew he didn't have a way to regain his strength if she "fed" from him.*

Rose tucked her chin into her chest, stifling a sob at the sad situation her mother had found herself in.

Siobhán cupped Rose's chin and raised her head until her warm gaze locked with Rose's. *It went both ways. Yer father needed yer mother, too. When he awoke and she was gone, he'd lost something he'd always had…his psychic partner.*

Siobhán's hand on her chin fell away as Rose shook her head, willing the tears away. *My father didn't know. I'm sure of it.*

Siobhán's gaze softened. *It doesn't matter if he knew or not. His need for yer mother, on a much deeper level, always remained. From what ye've told me of yer father's condition when he awoke as well as his downhill progression near the end…he had to have suffered a lot without Anna.*

Rose's chest constricted. She wanted to scream at the heart-wrenching truth Siobhán spoke. Instead, she bit her lip, holding back.

The kitchen door opened and Duncan entered, a worried look on his face.

"Rose?" he called out, until his gaze landed on her. "Are you okay, *a ghrá*?"

Siobhán put her hand on Rose's head and smiled at Duncan. "She's fine. We're just talking about her mother."

Duncan's gaze locked with Rose's. *Is this true? Are you really okay?*

When Siobhán's hand lifted from her head, Rose nodded, then sniffled. "I'm just a little sad right now."

"She'll be out in a minute," Siobhán said in a calm voice.

Duncan waited for Rose to nod in agreement before he walked out of the kitchen, the door swinging closed behind him.

*He's connected to ye already, Rose. He felt yer sadness and responded as only a mate would…seeking to protect ye.* Siobhán grasped Rose's hands and squeezed. *Don't you see…Duncan has been "feeding" ye. The stronger the connection, the deeper the emotion, the more he provides ye. As connected as ye are to Duncan, ye'll receive the most "food" from a sexual encounter with him…a time when yer emotions are the most involved.*

Rose's spirits lifted at the news. She clamped her hand over her mouth to stifle her surprised laughter. *No way! Ohmigod, he'd have a cow if he knew this.*

*Are ye sure he doesn't?* Siobhán asked. *After all, ye told me his mother is a priestess and that she told him about her past.*

Rose was surprised by the fact Duncan's mother didn't tell him either. *There's no way he knows. He's been trying too hard to get me to take his blood, using seduction as his weapon of choice.* She shook her head, even more convinced.

She jumped off the stool and hugged Siobhán. *Thank you for telling me. It makes sense now. Every time we've made love, I've felt fulfilled, satiated, and now I know why.*

Siobhán set her away, a concerned look on her face. *But ye're also part Ruean…a clan of traditional vampires like the Atruans. They need blood to survive. There may come a time when a psychic feeding won't be enough, Rose. There's a reason ye now have fangs. There are far worse things than being mated to a sexy man like Duncan.*

*He doesn't love me,* Rose said in a sad tone, her heart heavy. It was the first time she'd admitted out loud and to herself why she held back from Duncan. *He feels a responsibility for me. That's all. I have to have more.*

Siobhán shook her head, pursing her lips. *Ye're very stubborn. Just remember, Duncan has grown to need yer connection, too. Ye have a responsibility to him, to "feed" him psychically as well.*

The realization Duncan might have come to depend on her shocked Rose. She had no idea. What a freakin' mess. She sighed, unsure what to do.

As if she read her thoughts, Siobhán smiled. "The answer will come to ye in time. Don't fight it so." Tilting her head, she asked in an upbeat tone, "So, ye're here in Ireland…the home of yer ancestors, what sights are ye going to see today?"

* * * * *

After visiting several sites in Galway, Rose chuckled that she, Duncan and Nigel spent the last bit of daylight touring the Eyre Square shops in Galway City—like the Americans they were.

Duncan had walked off on his own while Nigel accompanied her into a small store so she could pick out a pair of earrings for Mish.

"What do you think?" she asked, holding the silver earrings with Connemara marble and a Celtic knot design.

Nigel shrugged. "Looks good to me."

"Some help you are," she said, handing the earrings to the clerk to ring up.

"You think Siobhán likes me?" He shoved his hands in his corduroy pants pockets and cast a hopeful look her way.

Rose grinned. "Ready to get back, are you?"

He gave her a sheepish smile. "Is it that obvious?"

"Maybe you can offer to help her out tonight, behind the bar or something," she said with a wink as the clerk handed her the gift in a bag.

"That's a great idea." His brow furrowed as he followed Rose out of the shop. "Where's Duncan?"

"I'm here." Duncan pushed off the post he'd been leaning on and faced them.

He looked so sexy, standing there in his navy sweater and faded blue jeans. His amber gaze seemed to drill into her as if wanted to devour her. Rose fought the shiver of awareness that skidded down her spine.

Duncan's hand came around her back as he escorted her down the street. "Ready to go back? You look tired, Róisín."

Rose did feel tired. Even though she'd slept late that morning, all the travel time and sightseeing had finally taken its toll. She nodded and walked beside Duncan and Nigel the rest of the way to the pub.

When they arrived at the pub, Rose saw the tables as well as the bar were packed with patrons.

Siobhán waved to them from behind the bar as they walked in. "Have a good time?" she called out over the din.

Nigel handed Duncan his purchases. "Hey, Dunc, put these bags in my room for me. Don't wait up, kids, I plan to be out late."

Rose chuckled at the beeline he made straight for the bar as he called to Siobhán over the crowd. "This place is packed. Need a hand behind the bar tonight?"

As he followed her down the hall, Duncan asked, "Will Siobhán be able to help you meet with the Saoi your mother talked about in her letter?"

"Yes. She said it'll probably be tomorrow before I can meet with him."

Even though Siobhán's words about Duncan needing her still rattled around in her head, Rose couldn't reconcile the idea of Duncan depending on anyone but himself. He was so contained, so in control. She stopped in front of Duncan and Nigel's door and turned to him. "Good night, Duncan."

Duncan's gaze searched her face in the dimly lit hall. He lowered his head and brushed his lips across hers before straightening once more.

"*Oíche mhaith, a ghrá.*"

"What does that mean?" she asked in a breathless voice, finding it hard to walk away from him.

"It means, 'Good night, my love'." He turned and unlocked his door, going inside.

Rose stared at his closed door, conflicting emotions raging within her. He'd said, "my love", yet he'd walked away. Just like that. No fighting. No arguing. Had he finally given up on them?

She turned away, tears stinging her eyes as she made her way to her room. Fumbling with the key, she finally managed to unlock her door.

Once inside, she shut her door and leaned against it, letting her package drop to the floor.

She resisted the urge to jump inside Duncan's head, to listen to his thoughts, but the desire to know overrode her steel will.

When she reached out with her mind seeking Duncan, she encountered a solid wall. She felt his presence but heard nothing but her own rampant breathing and thudding heartbeat. He'd finally figured out a way to block her.

Rose sighed and took off her clothes. Crawling into bed naked, she pulled the covers over herself. After listening to her stomach's growling noises for a while, she finally fell into a deep, exhausted sleep.

* * * * *

Rose awoke to the sound of a bodhrán drum and flute playing downstairs in the pub area. She lay in the dark listening to the traditional Irish music. The Celtic song made her smile as she glanced at the clock on the nightstand. Ten o'clock. She'd been out for a while. Without conscious thought, she intuitively used her mind to reach out for Duncan. When she didn't feel his presence, she jerked upright in her bed, concern racing through her.

Rose threw back the covers and quickly opened her suitcase for a new set of clothes. Stepping into a clean pair of underwear and jeans, she opted to forego her bra as she pulled on a button-down citrine cardigan then slid on her ankle boots.

After she ran a brush through her hair, she quickly brushed her teeth and tried to think where Duncan might have gone. It wasn't like he knew anyone in Ireland. Then again, he'd spoken Irish on every occasion he could to anyone who'd respond since they'd arrived in Ireland, so who knew where he was.

As she shouldered her way through the crowd of people gathered around the six musicians playing their instruments in an impromptu music session in the center of the pub area, Rose caught sight of Nigel working behind the bar with Siobhán. She started to wave to them but the two were so engrossed in each other, she didn't think they'd notice her anyway.

Chuckling, she left the pub and rubbed her arms as soon as she walked out into the night air. She smelled the briny ocean breeze blowing in from the Galway bay and assumed the close body of water added to the cool May air buffeting her body. Rose regretted not bringing her jacket but didn't want to brave the crowd to go back in and get it.

Instead, she lifted her nose and inhaled deeply once more, hoping to catch Duncan's scent. Faint traces of his masculine smell mixed with cologne wafted her way. She turned and started walking down the rows of stores, following her nose. The first prickling of jealousy splintered its way through her. Who was he wearing cologne for?

The thought of him feeding from another woman's neck made her chest ache. She stopped mid-stride as the whole concept struck her. *God, I hadn't considered the details of Duncan having to feed. And damn it, considering I'm refusing to mate with him, it wouldn't be fair of me to ask him to only take men's blood.*

With a frustrated sigh, she began to walk again. When she stopped in front of a place called "No Boundaries", the sound of contemporary American music drifting outside and the sight of twenty-something men and women brushing past her to open the door and walk inside made her pause. She walked a little farther but couldn't catch Duncan's scent.

Glancing back at the "No Boundaries" place, swift jealousy swept through her. What the hell was he doing there? she thought as she opened the door and walked inside.

When she entered the bar-dance area, her temper boiled. He was in a freakin' nightclub?

Music blared as locals and tourists gyrated to the latest American hit. Body sweat mixed with perfumes and cologne wafted her way. The intensity of the smell made her rub her nose. *Ayeyeyeye, I've really got to get a handle on how to turn down this keen sense of smell thing.* She couldn't help but shake her head at the irony that she was at a nightclub that catered to American music *in* Ireland. *Wait 'til I tell Mish about this. I'll bet good money she'll want to come here.*

She scanned the crowd on the dance floor but she didn't see Duncan. Annoyed, Rose let her gaze pan the entire place once again. She felt his presence. She knew he was here, damn it. When her gaze landed on Duncan sitting at the bar drinking a Guinness, she straightened her spine, turned away, and took the three steps down into the sunken dance floor.

Rose's spirits lifted when she saw Duncan immediately set down his drink and make his way to the dance floor with purposeful strides. Dressed casually in a black v-neck sweater and black cargo pants, the man never looked sexier in her eyes.

The song "Yeah!" by Usher was playing and Rose smiled as her body began to naturally move to the fast-paced music. When Duncan approached, she raised her arms and began to rock her hips to the upbeat song, all the while she kept her gaze locked with his intense golden one.

She moved deeper into the crowd and Duncan followed, his gaze never leaving hers. Rose swiveled her hips, rocking suggestively. She couldn't seduce Duncan with words right now, nor did she want their own stubbornness to intervene with what they each needed from the other, so she let her body speak for her.

Someone grabbed her hips from behind and began to dance with her. Rose paused, her heart jerking as she glanced back to the man in his mid-twenties.

Before she had a chance to say anything, a fearful look crossed his face and he immediately lifted his hands, stepping away from her. When she returned her gaze to Duncan, the deadly look on his face, the sheer possession, made her stomach clench in excitement.

Rose began to dance once more, gliding her hands down her breasts to her waist and hips as she gave Duncan a sexy come-hither smile.

When Duncan reached her, he slid his hand across her hip as he turned and moved behind her. Rose let him pull her hips back against his. She welcomed his hard-bodied warmth, her heart rate elevating.

Lowering her arms around his neck, she pulled him close. Duncan kissed the side of her throat at the same time his hips matched her grinding, seductive movements, beat for beat.

When the music segued into the slower, body-rocking seduction of "Candy Shop" by 50 Cent, Duncan turned her in his arms and pulled her flush against his body.

Rose reveled in the sensation of Duncan's hard thigh sliding between hers. He cupped her rear, molding her to him like they were two halves of a perfect puzzle. She wrapped her arms around his neck and her heart rate increased even more when she felt his erection rub against her hip.

As if he knew the song's suggestive lyrics affected her, Duncan whispered them in her ear at the same time he took one of her hands and cupped it over his erection.

Rose left her hand where Duncan placed it while he slid his hand under her hair, rubbing the back of her neck. He traced his thumb along her jaw, turning her head until she met his intense gaze.

*Don't torture me tonight, Róisín.*

# Chapter Thirteen

ꙮ

She whispered back, *My room's unoccupied at the moment.*

Duncan immediately stopped dancing and grasped her hand. Dragging Rose through the crowd and up the steps from the dance floor, he didn't slow his determined stride as he made his way to the entrance. They left the club to the sound of an alternative song starting up.

Rose couldn't help but laugh at Duncan's stoic demeanor. He didn't speak at all as his fingers threaded with hers, locking hard on her hand before he took off down the street.

Her heart felt both light and full at the same time while she walked beside him at a brisk pace. When they reached Lonán's Pub, the music session was still going on. Rose jerked on Duncan's hand as he started to walk through the crowd. "Don't you want to stay and listen for a bit?"

*Another time,* he spoke in her mind without breaking his stride. He wove through the crowd toward the back of the pub, his determined pace never wavering.

Rose followed—or was tugged along, rather. She waved to Nigel who was handing two pints of Guinness to customers standing at the bar. The smile on his face thrilled her. She'd never seen her uncle look so happy. *How will he feel when he finds out Siobhán is a much older woman with fangs to boot?* she thought while Duncan made his way down the hall.

Rose didn't have time to ponder on the subject because Duncan had reached her room and held out his hand.

Handing him her key, her heart raced in anticipation.

Duncan unlocked her room and tugged her inside, shutting the door behind her.

Tossing the key on a side table, he lifted her locket and rubbed his finger across the Celtic trinity knot. Then he let the charm go and met her gaze, his shoulders tense. "No matter what happens tomorrow, no matter what new things you learn from the Saoi, nothing will change what's between us, Róisín. Understand?"

Rose realized Duncan was truly concerned.

Lifting the bottom edges of his sweater, she nodded to let him know she understood.

Duncan pulled his sweater off and dropped it on the floor. His gaze, full of dark hunger, landed on her nipples jutting against her cardigan. Then she felt her buttons begin to give way.

Rose's breathing increased as the material slowly opened. Now that she was aware of her psychic powers, she recognized the energy zinging between them for what it was…a natural give and take.

When the buttons were all undone and the material separated but still covered her breasts, Duncan reached up and touched her shoulders. His warm fingers slid the soft cotton sweater down her arms until it fell to the floor at her feet.

His burning gaze dropped to her nipples as he brushed his fingers across a hard tip. The gentle caress of skin against skin made her stomach tighten. Then he slowly lowered his hand to the button on her jeans. Gripping the material in a tight fist, Duncan yanked her body close.

Rose's heart rate skyrocketed. She was surprised and so incredibly turned on by Duncan's mercurial, scarcely controlled mood.

"I've never ached this fucking much for another," he rasped as his lips trailed down her neck. He planted a kiss on her shoulder. "You grab me in the gut, shake me up and spit me out, leaving me feeling like I've wrestled with a five-hundred-pound gorilla."

Before she could speak, Duncan's mouth claimed hers, his tongue thrusting deep. He tasted of salt and beer and his own masculine flavor. When Rose kissed him back, he pulled away, his expression serious, intense.

"You're going to need my blood to sustain you tonight. I'm not holding back and I'll expect the same from you."

Rose ran her hand down his stubbled cheek and gave him a seductive smile. "I promise I'll give you a night to remember." When he leaned close and inhaled next to her neck, she finished, "But I won't take your blood."

As soon as the words were out of her mouth, Duncan let out a low growl and shoved her against the door. He clamped his fangs hard on her throat, thrusting past the thin skin.

Rose's knees almost gave way at the pain followed by sheer pleasure his act elicited. An unbidden gasp escaped her lips as he spoke in her mind.

*I hear your heart racing, smell your arousal. See how this affects you?* I *want to feel that erotic pleasure from you, experience your fangs sinking deep while your body clenches around my cock.*

She could feel the pent-up frustration emanating from him. Rose moved her hands between them, yanking at his pants buttons until she could grasp his cock through his boxers.

Rubbing the silk material up and down his shaft, she smiled when he groaned against her neck and clutched her tight. Her eyes closed as she concentrated on building energy inside herself.

She pushed his underwear down and out of the way, wrapping her fingers around his hard shaft once more. Intuitively, she sensed that skin to skin contact helped her forge a stronger connection between them. The sound of his uneven breathing, his blood rushing through his veins and his heart pounding, caused her fangs to unsheathe. But she forced herself to concentrate on Duncan's needs, not her own.

When she felt as if she would explode from the desire-filled heat raging inside her, Rose blew a soft breath against his neck at the same time she let her energized emotions funnel through her fingers.

Duncan grunted and released his hold on her neck to set his forehand against the door behind her. He rocked his hips while her mental white-hot heat bathed his groin. She felt the tingling sensation between them and pressed her lips against the rapid pulse beating in his throat.

*Take what I offer,* she whispered.

He jerked away from her hold, breathing heavily. Clenching his fists by his side, he hissed out, "Why must you always fight us?"

"I'm giving you what I can." She tried to keep her breathing on an even keel as she kicked off her boots and stepped out of her underwear and jeans. Her heart raced and her sex ached to be filled, throbbing to her pulse's rapid pace.

Duncan stepped out of his shoes and took off his jeans and boxers in jerky, angry movements. His eyes glowed red as he tossed his clothes to the side. Facing her, his fangs fully extended, he roared, *I want more! I want your fangs sinking in me. I want to hear you sucking my blood in greedy need, to feel your pulls all the way down to my balls.*

Rose's body heat jumped several degrees at the barely leashed control emanating from Duncan and primal picture he painted of them together. His impressive erection jutted against his belly, reminding her how good it felt when he filled her to the hilt. Her stomach flip-flopped and her body fought her mind, telling her to screw her convictions and give in.

But somewhere deep inside she regained her control once more. She straightened her spine, along with her resolve. "Taking your blood comes with a price I'm not willing to pay."

His jaw tense, Duncan stepped close to her and ran his finger along the wounds he'd left on her neck. Stepping back, he lifted his blood-coated finger to his mouth, then slowly sucked the red liquid.

Desire filled his gaze. "I want to taste you again, but I won't take what you haven't replaced."

Disappointment washed over her as she realized Duncan refused take her blood while they made love. She wanted…no…needed him to. The connection between them was strongest when he was locked on her neck, swallowing her blood. Only then could she give him what he needed in return.

Her gaze melded with his as she raised her hand to her neck. Running her fingers across the wound he'd just touched, she slowly slid her blood-covered fingers down her throat, past her collarbone, then feathered them across the curve of her left breast, leaving a life-giving, tempting trail behind.

Duncan's gaze followed the visible, scarlet path her fingers created. His expression darkened and his nostrils flared. She could feel the hunger raging within him.

"Don't tempt me like this!" His arm and shoulder muscles flexed and his chest rose and fell as if he were exerting extreme effort to hold back.

Dark, conflicting emotions whirled within him. She felt them deep in her belly. He seemed so tortured. She had to remind herself she was doing this for him, even if he wasn't aware.

Touching her wound once more, she moved her fingers past the curve of her breast to circle around her nipple.

Raising her gaze to his, she lowered her hand to her side and said in a husky voice, "Take what you want."

A primal growl erupted from Duncan as he cleared the space between them in one long determined stride. Grasping her hips, he lifted her in the air. Rose clasped his shoulders, anticipation making her sex ache.

He pulled her close and nudged his erection against her entrance at the same time she wrapped her legs around his waist. When Duncan lowered his head and bit just above her areola, Rose arched her back, keening in sheer sexual bliss.

She moaned as he wrapped his mouth around her nipple and began to suck in long, hard drags, taking her blood and giving her sheer pleasure in return.

Duncan's hands clasped her hips in a tight grip. His hips rocked into her as he allowed gravity to pull her down over his shaft.

Sheer sexual excitement shot through Rose while his erection sank inside her body. Duncan released her nipple and laved his way up her collarbone to her neck, cleaning her skin as if he didn't want to miss a single drop. As he ran his tongue up her neck, he lifted her up and down his erection in slow, methodical thrusts, building her desire to a fever pitch.

Rose's stomach clenched as her impending climax spiraled through her. She dug her nails in Duncan's shoulders and moaned when his fangs sank deep in her throat once more. The erotic sensation slammed into her, initiating a multilayered climax that flowed through her in wave upon wave, to the point she wondered if her heart would beat right out of her chest.

Rose let the passion build between them, then instinctively used a mental push to give Duncan back what he needed.

She felt the spark slide down his body and back up, then back down before he withdrew his fangs as his knees gave way. Rose closed her eyes and focused on catching him before they hit the floor. Concentrating, she mentally lifted their bodies and laid them on her bed.

Duncan gave a primitive grunt as he clamped his teeth on her neck once more. His grip on her buttocks tightened as he pistoned into her, his rough thrusts bringing her to climax all over again.

When his orgasm slammed into him, he released her neck to roar out his pleasure. At the same time she heard *Damn, Róisín!* inside her head.

Rose reveled in the give and take between them. She kissed his neck and hugged him close until his body slowed within her.

Duncan looked down at Rose, his body humming. He'd never felt so good, almost energized from their lovemaking. Her cheeks were flushed from their exertions, but she appeared tired.

Worry filled him. He'd bitten her several times. Had he taken too much of her blood? He'd tried to take very little, just enough to heighten their joining, but Rose's blood was more than addictive. Her essence had become a necessity for him. He didn't know if he'd be so generous the next time they made love. He hoped to hell she agreed to become his mate soon.

Kissing her jaw, he chuckled when her languorous gaze widened as his erection instantly hardened inside her.

"Again?"

Duncan nuzzled her neck and ground his hips against hers. "It's your fault. You feel too damn good."

She kept her arms wrapped around his neck and whispered, "I think I overdid it."

"What?" Duncan asked, raising his head to stare at her.

"Um, what I meant was…I think I need more rest. I'm exhausted."

Duncan teasingly nipped at her neck. "What you need, *a ghrá*, is my blood. I promise it'll be the best pick-me-up you'd ever had. Satisfaction guaranteed," he finished with a wink.

Rose shook her head and turned in his arms, facing away from him as she snuggled close. "I just need some sleep. That's all."

She sounded so tired. Duncan felt pangs of worry twinge once more in his gut. He pulled the covers over them and slid his hand down to her belly. Splaying his fingers across the soft skin, he kissed her temple. "You must eventually eat. You won't be feeding for one forever."

Rose put her hand over his and mumbled, "I know," before he heard her breathing turn even in her exhausted sleep.

Duncan's heart swelled that she at least acknowledged they would eventually have a child together, even if she was half asleep when she said it. Her stomach grumbled, sounding like a herd of elephants. The physical sound punctuated his point that she needed to feed. Fear and guilt gripped him.

Technically Rose could've fed, like he had, on her way to the club tonight. It's not like he was around to stop her. And in truth, he had to ask himself, would he? Human blood was a source of nourishment. Nothing more, nothing less. But the idea of Rose's fangs sinking into a man's neck, her swallowing another's blood…sheer rage rippled through him at the mere thought.

Rose did mention taking blood from a female, he rationalized in his mind. Would he be able to accept that? If she were pregnant, he damn well would. Hell, he'd find the women and bring them to her. Yet the thought of someone else's blood nourishing his child in her womb would eat at him, drive him insane with territorial jealousy. He wouldn't be a fit man to be around.

Duncan kissed Rose's cheek. His hand on her belly flexed. "My Anima…"

Rose truly was the woman for him. From the top of her stubborn red head to the tips of her gorgeous toes, she made him ache when he looked at her, shudder when he touched her and reach a plateau of euphoria he never thought possible when he made love to her.

Tonight was beyond spectacular. Rose took well to her vampire powers, lifting them when she'd literally brought him to his knees. While she slept, he flicked his tongue across her neck, closing the wounds he'd caused. His incisors lengthened once more at the small taste of blood. Duncan lifted Rose's hand and placed it across his throat. Her warmth comforted him, while his groin tightened at the thought of Rose digging her fangs into his flesh.

He groaned and kissed her palm before lowering her hand under the covers once more. Forcing his lurid imagination to relax, Duncan closed his eyes and counted his blessings Rose was his. He would protect her at all costs. It was only a matter of time before they mated.

* * * * *

The next morning Rose sat across from Nigel in a booth trying her best to choke down a cup of tea without puking her guts up. If she didn't eat something, her uncle would begin to wonder about her. Duncan sat beside her, drinking his cup of coffee. Several other B&B patrons were eating their breakfast. Conversation buzzed in the room while the smell of sausage and biscuits wafted from the kitchen.

Nigel took a long drink of his coffee and rubbed his stomach. "I'm starving. Those smells are killing me. I can't wait to have more of Siobhán's wonderful cooking."

"Uh," Rose managed to grunt out. The smells were making her nauseous. She took another sip of her tea, hoping to alleviate the empty stomach feeling.

Nigel set down his coffee cup and glanced surreptitiously left and right. Leaning forward, he said in a low voice, "You're not going to believe this but…" he paused, glanced around again then continued, "Siobhán's a vampire."

Rose promptly choked on her tea, spewing it all over the table.

"I know it sounds unbelievable, and at first it wigged me out, but you know how into that paranormal group I was a couple years ago. They don't have anything on Siobhán..." Nigel said as he grabbed napkins to mop up the mess she made.

Duncan's low chuckle entered her head. *Now would be a good time to tell Nigel, Róisín Just a guess but I think he might be open to the idea.*

Rose cut her narrowed gaze over at the sarcasm in Duncan's tone. *You just find this hilarious, don't you?*

*A real knee-slapper,* he replied in a droll tone even though obvious amusement danced in his amber gaze.

Nigel was still rambling on. His cheeks had turned red. "Last night we...uh...well, let's just say there's chemistry there."

Rose held up her hand and croaked out, "That's way more information than I need to know. I get it."

Nigel shook his head. "No, you don't. She doesn't just like to bite, she took my..."

"I got it—" Rose started to say when Duncan cut in.

"She believes you, Nigel."

Nigel jerked his gaze to Duncan. "She does? How do you know?"

"Because she and I have been speaking mentally about it."

"Duncan!" Rose jerked her gaze to stare him down.

Duncan casually picked up his coffee, took a sip then set it down. His gaze narrowed on her. "If you don't tell him, I will."

Rose's heart contracted in apprehension as she glanced at her uncle. Nigel's gaze darted between them, clear confusion and interest reflected in his expression.

"What's going on, Rosie? What did Duncan mean you two are speaking mentally? I didn't know you had clairvoyant powers."

Rose glanced down at her drink. Her fingers gripped the cup so hard her knuckles turned white.

Duncan's hand covered hers. *He loves you, Rose. He deserves the truth.*

Rose met her uncle's blue gaze and breathed out, "Duncan and I can speak mentally because we're also vampires."

At the look of disbelief on her uncle's face, she spoke in Nigel's mind, giving him the proof he needed for him to accept what she said. *I speak the truth.*

Her stomach tensed as she watched myriad emotions flicker across Nigel's face from shock to hurt to firm acceptance.

Leaning back in his seat, his expression turned serious. "Start from the beginning and tell me everything, Rose." It was the most father-like Nigel had ever sounded. Rose couldn't help the sense of relief that washed over her.

Duncan clasped her hand and rubbed his thumb along the inside of her palm. "Go ahead, Róisín," he encouraged in a soft tone.

Taking a deep breath, Rose told Nigel about James and how she and Duncan met. When she got to the part where Duncan accidentally converted her, Nigel's body tensed and he narrowed his gaze on Duncan.

Rose gripped Duncan's hand and rushed on to tell Nigel about her mother's past and the rest of the story, minus Rónán's part in her father's death. She didn't want to totally throw her uncle off the deep end with that kind of information.

She'd just finished her story when Siobhán walked up with a plate of food for Nigel. As Siobhán set the dish down on the table, Nigel said, "So you really did know Anna all those years ago?"

Siobhán's gaze met Rose's, her eyes wide in surprise. "Ye told him everything?"

Rose bit her lip and nodded. Sighing, Siobhán shooed Nigel with her hand, silently telling him to scoot over so she could sit beside him in the booth.

Nigel slid over and Siobhán sat down. "I'm so glad you know everything, Nigel. I didn't feel it was my place to tell you about Rose."

Nigel picked up Siobhán's hand and kissed it, love reflected in his gaze. "So you're into younger men, are you? Here I am, a fifty-year-old man, just an infant in comparison."

Siobhán chuckled. "You've lived the life of two men, *a stór*."

Worry crept back in Nigel's gaze when he addressed Rose. "When is your meeting with the Saoi?"

"This evening," Siobhán supplied the answer.

"I'm going too," Nigel said with conviction.

Before Rose could object, fear for her uncle's safety paramount, Siobhán cut in. "Duncan will keep Rose safe, Nigel. No offense, but the Saoi only meets with vampires, not humans."

"We can always change that," Nigel replied.

Siobhán turned her surprised gaze to Nigel at the same time Rose said, "No!"

Deep hurt twisted in Duncan's gut at Rose's swift response…as if her uncle becoming a vampire was horrifying to her.

His grip on her hand tightened when she tried to pull away. *I won't let you regret us. Ever,* he said in a determined voice in her mind.

Nigel stared at Siobhán. He kissed her hand. "I never thought I'd meet someone who would accept me as I am, past and all."

Siobhán gave a low laugh. "I've lived long enough to see everything, Nigel. Nothing shocks or surprises me."

"That sounds like a challenge to me," Nigel said.

"Now I know where she gets her stubbornness from." Duncan chuckled.

Ignoring the tense resistance emanating from Rose, Duncan lifted her hand and kissed the back. "Where are we going today?"

"How about the Aran Islands?" Siobhán piped in.

* * * * *

Siobhán recommended Inis Mór, the largest of the three Aran Islands. Duncan, Rose and Nigel left after breakfast and headed for the dock as Siobhán suggested.

"My friend John O'Shea will be waiting on his boat called *Saoirse*. He'll take you to the island. When the sun goes down, I'll meet you at Dún Aonghasa."

Rose was unusually quiet as they climbed into John O'Shea's boat. When the *Saoirse* pulled away from the wharf to head for the main island, Nigel walked up to the front of the boat to talk to John. Duncan approached Rose from behind and wrapped his arms around her. Briny sea spray flew up from the waves bouncing against the boat's sides.

He felt Rose tense when he pulled her close then finally relax against him. Duncan couldn't help the unease that washed over him. The sensation made him tighten his hold on her. He refused to let her push him away. He was her Anima.

Rose had tucked her long hair in the collar of her jacket for the trip over to the island. Duncan rubbed his nose in the thick mass near her neck, inhaling her sweet smell. The scent never failed to knock him in the gut.

*Why are you so tense?* he asked her as he took in all the boats sailing out on the ocean.

He heard her heart skip a beat and then felt her take a deep breath. *I've just got the impending meeting on my mind. Siobhán told me it would take place on Inis Mór tonight.*

She sounded so tired. Regret filled him that he'd been unable to resist taking her blood last night. Why didn't he seem to have any control when it came to her? His gaze locked on a lighthouse in the distance as he set his jaw in frustration.

*When we get back, we're going to have a serious talk about our mating, Rose. You're part Ruean. You need blood.*

*My taking your blood shouldn't come with such a permanent outcome,* Rose grumbled.

Duncan felt as if she'd kicked him in the groin. Before he thought better of it, he spoke what was in his heart. *You make it sound as if mating with me is a bad thing.*

Rose tensed, then sighed. "Duncan—" she began only to be interrupted when John called out, "Inis Mór!"

She turned in the direction the man pointed. "It's so beautiful," she gasped at the sight.

At the moment, Duncan didn't give a crap about the land. His grip tightened on Rose. "Finish what you were going to say."

But Nigel picked that moment to join them. "Ready to do some hiking?" he asked, a smile on his face.

John slowed his boat as it neared the dock and cut the engine to let them float closer. Nigel jumped on the dock while they pulled alongside. He took the rope John threw him and wrapped it around the hook to secure the boat.

Duncan helped Rose onto the dock, then joined them. John stepped down beside them, saying, "I'll help ye get transportation, then I'll meet ye back here in the evening."

Nigel began walking up the wooden pathway in brisk strides. "Come on, let's go visit the sites."

"There's so much rock," Rose commented, glancing around the island as she clasped Duncan's hand and tugged him along, following John's and Nigel's lead. The fact she willingly took his hand allowed Duncan to shake off the tension that had gripped him. They would talk when he got her alone, he vowed to himself.

John laughed at her comment. "Yep, even though Inis Mór is only eight miles long and two miles wide, it has several thousand miles of rock walls."

John whistled and a man drove up in a white van. The older man jumped out of the van and ran around to open the back passenger door. "Ready for a tour?" he asked.

John waited until Duncan, Nigel and Rose got in the van. He then tipped his cap to the older man in thanks before he met their gazes once more. "It's really steep in some areas of the island. Sam will take ye around. Keep yer eyes open for the seals. Have ye heard the Selkie legend?" When Sam chuckled, John glanced at him.

"These good people need to hear yer Selkie story, Sam."

* * * * *

When late afternoon turned to dusk and they headed for Dún Aonghasa as their last stop for the day, tension filled Duncan once more. He couldn't explain it, but the closer they came to the evening and their pending meeting with the Saoi, the more out of control he felt.

They paid their entrance fee and walked the twenty-seven hundred feet to the top of the hill to look around the old ruin.

"Wow, that was a hike," Rose said as they entered the fort and walked to the edge of the ruin the overlooked the ocean. Her hand tensed around Duncan's while they took in the breathtaking view over the side of the island. Dún Aonghasa was a semicircular prehistoric fort that had been built high upon a hill along the edge of the island.

As he stood overlooking the steep drop-off that went straight into the ocean, Duncan applauded his ancestors for picking a defendable location for their fort. One whole side dropped three hundred feet straight into the Atlantic Ocean. Since the fort was built at one of the highest points on the island, that meant it was a perfect strategic location for them to see their enemies coming from all directions, giving them time to react.

When the sun sank lower in the sky and the cooler wind picked up, the tourists made their way back down the hill to their tour vans waiting to take them back to the dock.

Siobhán waved to the last tourist leaving as she entered the fort. "How was yer day of touring?" she asked with a smile.

Nigel clasped her hand and pulled her to his side. "Very interesting, but not as much fun without you."

Siobhán laughed, then kissed him on the cheek. "There's a great restaurant on the dock. Come on, Nigel, I'll take ye to dinner."

"Aren't you kids coming?" Nigel asked, looking back at them as Siobhán tugged on his hand.

"They can meet us at the boat," Siobhán said, then spoke mentally to Rose and Duncan at the same time. *Yer meeting is here. Wait for the Saoi. He will arrive soon.*

Duncan felt Rose tense next to him. She hadn't spoken much in the last hour. He pulled her into the circle of his arms and was surprised at the sluggish beating of her heart. He nodded to Siobhán. "See you two later."

Once Nigel and Siobhán left, Duncan kept his arms around Rose as he turned her to face the ocean. Standing a few feet away from the steep drop-off, they stared out to sea. Duncan reveled in Rose's warmth as she leaned against him. The strong Atlantic wind blew against them, bringing with it the sounds and smells of the sea.

"I feel our ancestors' presence here," Rose finally spoke. "I sense the battles that took place, the anger, the defeats and triumphs." She sighed and wrapped her arms around his, hugging him close. "Ireland is truly a magical place. I've never felt a connection with a place as much as I do here."

"I feel it, too, *a ghrá*. Just like the pull between us." His arms tightened around her. "How can you deny our mating? Don't you see it was meant to be?"

Rose stiffened and stepped out of his embrace. "If it was meant to be, why didn't you feel this way before you converted me?" She glanced up at him, her gaze searching his.

"Because he is stubborn like all Atruan males," a man's booming voice said from behind them.

Rose and Duncan turned to see a tall man wearing a black robe that fell to his feet. His long, stark white hair, pulled back in a ponytail, blew in the wind.

Duncan took in the six male vampires that hovered an inch above the semicirclular rock wall behind the Saoi. Their arms were crossed over their chests, stoic expressions on their faces. Each of them had a silver stripe in their long, unbound hair that whipped in the wind around them. Atruan males.

The Saoi's pitch-black eyes narrowed on Duncan.

"Ye're Tressa's son. And half of another vampire race." His tone lowered as he stared out to sea. "All that we fought to prevent. We should've known we couldn't stop the inevitable."

"My father is an honorable man. He just recently learned of my mother's past, as did I," Duncan said in defense of his parents.

The Saoi's bottomless gaze landed on Duncan once more. "Ye possess powers ye haven't even begun to explore."

Surprised by the older man's comment, Duncan tried to probe his mind to find out more. Blinding pain swept through his head, knocking him to his knees. Duncan cradled his head in his hands, gritting his teeth at the excruciating pain. After a few seconds, it disappeared.

"Don't ye dare try that with me," the Saoi hissed in anger.

Rose stood by Duncan's side. A look of concern crossed her face as she touched his shoulder. She cast her gaze to the Saoi. "Leave Duncan out of this. I'm the one who called upon you."

The man's black gaze swept over her and he bowed his head in respect, though a haughty expression still glittered in his gaze. "State yer request, *a chailín*."

As Duncan stood, he sensed something more than vampire blood in the Saoi…something otherworldly. Not only did the man not have a heartbeat he could detect, but he smelled different, too.

"I've come to find out how to eliminate my Guardians," Rose called out over the wind.

"So much for not speaking of the past," he said with a deep sigh.

"Circumstances changed a vow given," she replied, defending her mother's decision to leave behind a description of her history for her.

The older man moved to a low rock wall and sat down. He beckoned her with his hand. "Come, Rose, daughter of Anna."

Duncan started to follow, but a cutting gaze from the Saoi made him slow his steps.

Rose walked over to the man and kneeled before him. The Saoi put his hand on her head and smiled down at her. "Ye look like yer mother, little one. I'm sorry to hear of her passing."

Duncan felt the sorrow well up in Rose at the man's mention of her mother, but she straightened her spine and said, "Thank you, Saoi."

*Go raibh maith agat,* he corrected, lifting his hand from her head.

"Pardon?" she asked, a confused look on her face.

"*Go raibh maith agat,*" he repeated. "It means 'thank you'." Glancing at Duncan, he asked, "Do ye have Irish?"

Duncan nodded.

"Ye'll teach her the language of her forefathers."

Duncan stiffened at the man's edict and replied in Irish. "If she chooses to learn, then I will teach her."

The Saoi looked at Rose once more, his gaze softening. "Why do ye want to eliminate the ones who are sworn to protect ye?"

"James Connor, known to you as Séamus Flannery, has tried to kidnap me and is still running free in the United States as we speak."

"So you want to eliminate James as a threat to you, but what about Rónán Keegan? Why eliminate the vampire who will protect you from those like James?"

"Rónán kidnapped my mother—" she started to say, when the Saoi cut her off.

"And he's been severely punished for his crimes."

Duncan crossed his arms over his chest. "The wrong man was punished while the guilty Guardian runs free."

Both Rose and the Saoi turned their gazes his way.

Duncan smirked at the look of surprise on the man's face. *Don't know everything, do you?* he thought.

"How is that possible? The Morrigan assured me—" the Saoi began.

"The Morrigan made a mistake," Duncan cut him off.

The man glared at Duncan. "What are ye saying? Who kidnapped Anna?"

Duncan relayed the information he'd learned of James' betrayal of Anna and Rónán.

Rose stared at him for a long, tense moment before sheer determination crossed her face and she turned back to the Saoi. "Rónán killed my father. He must be eliminated."

Fury swept through Duncan. He unfolded his arms and clenched his hands. "What! Why didn't you tell me?"

Rose glanced at him and replied in a calm tone, "Because I wanted to be the one to avenge my father's death."

Looking back at the Saoi, she implored, "Now that I'm converted, I can probably hold my own with James, but Rónán has The Morrigan's protection. Is there any way to defeat him?"

The Saoi sniffed in disdain. "The cursed Guardians might have been granted immortality, but they aren't invincible."

Leaning closer, he cupped her chin in his hand. "Distraction, misdirection and cunning are key when battling any enemy, Rose. The Guardians can be killed. When the time comes, you'll intuitively know what to do."

Duncan's temper boiled. That was it? "We came all this way to hear what we could've figured out ourselves?"

"Quiet!" the Saoi bit out, glaring at him. "I'll deal with you in a minute."

No matter how hard he tried to continue to voice his anger, Duncan found he was unable to speak. Fury filled him that the Saoi was using his power over him. The man was definitely not pure vampire.

The older man looked at Rose. "Siobhán told me of yer conversion. As a descendant of an Atruan priestess, I know ye use yer psychic powers to feed, but ye're also half of another vampire race that needs blood to survive."

Duncan reeled at the news Rose was a psychic vampire. All those times they'd made love and he'd felt so whipped afterwards…holy shit, she'd sucked the energy right out of him. He had been providing for her all this time. And last night…he realized what she'd done. She'd given back to him with no way to recoup her own energy reserve. He wanted to shake her for her stubbornness. The knowledge swept through him in waves—first shock, then anger, then firm resolution. She would take his blood. Enough was enough.

The Saoi continued as he pushed back his robe's sleeve. "I know ye haven't made your decision yet about this one." He glanced at Duncan then continued, "Ye must feed. I sense the weakness in ye."

"I know," she agreed. Rose didn't even spare Duncan a glance as she clasped the Saoi's wrist and lowered her mouth to his arm.

Fear ripped through Duncan. If she took the Saoi's blood, she'd be mated to the vampire! Blinding rage swept through him. Somehow the roar reverberating inside his head managed to escape, sounding like a battle cry in the dark night. He launched himself at the Saoi, claws extended, primal instincts to protect his own, unfurling within him.

The Saoi didn't even look his way. He lifted his hand and waved it in the air as if flicking away a fly. Duncan went hurling backward from the invisible impact…as if he'd been hit head on by a semi truck.

He tumbled through the air and landed on the balls of his feet, sucking air into his lungs from the impact. His heart raced and his muscles flexed as he tried to launch himself in the air once more. But his feet seemed to be rooted to the ground. His heart stuttered as the smell of blood carried on the wind.

When he heard Rose swallowing, Duncan's knees gave out. He sank to the rocky ground, his stomach clenching in knots. He'd never felt so disillusioned and hurt. Never once had he considered the possibility Rose wouldn't become his mate. Now she was lost to him. Forever.

Once Rose finished feeding, Duncan was surprised to see her falling over to her side. He tried to move and was thankful he'd been released. Duncan rushed to capture her before her body hit the rocks.

After he'd lifted her warm, limp frame in his arms, Duncan stood. His heart ached as he glared his hatred at the Saoi. "What have you done to her, you sonofabitch?"

The man narrowed his gaze on Duncan. "I could kill ye with a mere thought." His gaze softened when it landed on Rose. "I compelled her to sleep. She needs rest. Her body is adjusting to receiving blood again after going so long without it." He finished his last sentence in an accusing tone as he met Duncan's gaze once more. "I have given my heart and soul to serve my people. I am unable to mate. But my blood is rich and will sustain Rose for now."

Relief rushed through Duncan at the news. He still didn't like another man giving Rose sustenance or the fact she took it so willingly, but…she wasn't mated to another. He could deal with the rest.

The Saoi stood. His powerful presence made Duncan take a step back. The man had ties to the Celtic Gods, Duncan would swear it were true.

Standing eye to eye with Duncan, the older man said, "If ye want Rose to accept ye as her mate, ye must stop using yer head. Use yer heart to win her."

Duncan closed his eyes for a brief second, so glad to know he'd have another chance with Rose. When he opened them to speak to the Saoi, the man was gone. Duncan quickly turned to see all the Atruan vampires had disappeared from their posts above the rock wall.

He stared at Rose's face, her beautiful features calm in her sleep. The ocean breeze captured the words he whispered, carrying them out to sea.

* * * * *

Rose awoke feeling energized. Her gaze drifted to the moonlight filtering through the eyelet curtains. Someone had raised the shade for her. She blinked in confusion. How'd she get from Dún Aonghasa back to her room at the pub? How long had she been asleep? She frowned, trying her best to remember getting on the boat to come back. She drew nothing but a blank.

Duncan rolled her over on her back. His gaze was intense as he leaned over her.

"How do you feel?"

Rose stretched and smiled. "Better than I have in a long time."

Duncan grunted and turned. The bed jostled as he climbed out of it. While he shoved his leg into his pants, Rose asked, "What happened? I don't remember the trip back from the fort."

Duncan scowled and yanked his pants up his other leg, then buttoned them. "I hope you at least remember taking another vampire's blood, possibly mating yourself to him. It's not something I'll soon forget, I assure you."

Rose sat up, pulling the covers over her naked breasts. "I knew taking the Saoi's blood wouldn't mate me to him. I asked him."

Duncan narrowed his gaze on her. "I didn't hear you ask."

Rose rolled her eyes. "That's because I asked him mentally and he responded the same way." She shook her head and gave a small laugh. "To be honest I think he's more than an Atruan vampire."

Duncan paused as he started to pull on his shirt. "I agree. I think he's tied to the Celtic Gods somehow. There's a vibe about him…his powers were beyond anything I've ever seen."

Once he shrugged into his shirt, Duncan crossed his muscular arms over his chest, "It's bad enough I had to find out you were a psychic vampire from the Saoi. Then you shared the fact Rónán killed your father with him and not me. But to have to watch you take another man's blood, vampire or not…" His jaw ticced as he trailed off. He turned and walked toward her door, before facing her once more, his expression as hard as granite. "That's not something I care to repeat ever again."

"And what about you keeping the fact James was really the man who kidnapped my mother from me? Allowing me to believe Rónán was the guilty one?"

Duncan shrugged, his expression unapologetic as he opened the door. "I did it to protect you, Rose. Everything I have done has been for your protection."

Her stomach tensed and her heart sank at his comment. Looking away, Rose said with a sigh, "I know."

When she heard the door shut behind Duncan, she breathed out the rest in a whisper, "That's the problem."

Rose stared at the closed door, understanding some of Duncan's anger, but only part of it. She hadn't told him about Rónán. She'd kept that information to herself on purpose. And she'd just learned of her psychic vampire status herself. Okay, so technically she could've told him last night, but she wanted to give back to him what she'd inadvertently taken each time they'd made love. As for taking the Saoi's blood, once she learned she wouldn't be inadvertently mated to the Saoi, sheer hunger took over.

Rose threw the covers back and got out of bed. As she tugged on her clothes Duncan had discarded on a side chair, she glanced at her watch. Eleven in the evening. Sheesh, she'd been out for hours. She brushed her teeth and ran a brush through her windblown hair as she stared at her refection in the bathroom mirror.

The woman who stared back might look the same, but there was an awareness in her blue-green gaze that wasn't there before. The Saoi's blood tasted so smooth going down, like a three-hundred-dollar bottle of wine…aged to perfection. But even though his blood satiated her hunger, it was missing something…something she couldn't put her finger on. She furrowed her brow, trying to decipher exactly what had been missing.

Her gaze darkened when she thought of Duncan and how feeding from him would be an entirely different experience. He'd be hot and demanding, rough and sexy…he'd be…fire.

That's what was missing from the Saoi's blood…fire. Somehow she knew taking Duncan's blood would be an experience she wouldn't be able to put to words, but she had a feeling it would be an elixir she wouldn't get enough of.

She shook her head, turning away from the mirror. It didn't matter what she thought. Duncan held himself in constant check. Would he ever truly let her see his "real" self?

Rose opened her door and locked it behind her before she made her way to the pub. As she entered the main room, traditional Irish music was in full swing. She could feel the upbeat thump of the bodhrán drum in her chest while she walked across the room.

Duncan sat on a stool at the bar, drinking a Guinness. Nigel stood next to him talking to Siobhán who was behind the bar pouring a beer for a customer.

Rose waved to Siobhán and heard the woman's voice in her head. *Jeysus, child, I'm so glad to see ye up and about. I had to compel Nigel to keep him calm, but I was also worried when I saw Duncan carrying ye. I take it ye got what ye needed from the Saoi?*

Rose nodded as she approached her uncle at the bar. *Yes, but he was kind of cryptic with his advice.* She paused as Nigel enveloped her in a hug before she continued her mental comment to Siobhán. *The Saoi's not what he seems to be, is he?*

"I'm so glad to see you're up and about. Duncan and Siobhán said all that hiking on Inis Mór must've worn you out," her uncle said.

Rose kissed Nigel's cheek. "I'm fine now that I've had a good nap."

Siobhán handed the beer to the waiting customer and began pouring a Guinness. Her eyes twinkled when she met Rose's. *The*

*Saoi is very powerful. He's a hybrid in his own right, I guess ye could say. The Morrigan has bestowed some of her Goddess powers upon him so he could look after his people.*

"What did the Atruan leader tell you?" her uncle asked.

Rose took the pint of Guinness Siobhán handed to her and answered. "He told me to trust my instincts. That my powers would help me in the end."

Nigel eyed her, a worried look on his face. "Rosie, the whole situation scares me. According to what you all have told me, these vampires have years of experience and varied powers on you."

Rose glanced at Duncan, who'd been staring at her since she walked in the room. "Don't worry, Unc, I've got my very own bodyguard."

Now that her hunger for blood had been satiated, Rose found the Guinness she sipped went down pretty smoothly. She took another sip, then downed the entire pint. Handing the empty glass to Siobhán, she said, "I'm loving this Guinness. I'll take another."

After Siobhán gave her another pint, Rose said, "I think I'll check out the 'session' going on," before she headed across the room and crossed through a doorway that led to a small, dimly lit corner nook.

A gray-haired old man sat in a chair at small round table, playing a violin. A young dark-haired woman sat beside him playing a wonderful accompaniment with the bodhrán, and a middle-aged man with light-brown hair stood holding his Guinness in the air as if in salute as he sang a popular Irish song.

Rose sat down on a side bench and sipped her beer, tapping her foot to the Irish jig being played. She felt Duncan's presence behind her and immediately slid over on the bench to allow him room. For tonight, she didn't want to argue. She just wanted to enjoy their last night in Ireland in the most traditional way…sitting in a pub, enjoying the music and locals.

She felt a gentle brush against the nape of her neck, as if she'd been kissed. But when she glanced at Duncan, his hand was on his glass, his gaze riveted on the people entertaining them.

Her gaze dropped to the movement next to her leg and she couldn't help but smile as she watched Duncan tap his fingers on his thigh. She lifted her gaze to see his other hand tapped the glass too as if he were playing right along with them.

Rose ran a mental hand down the side of Duncan's face. When he glanced at her in surprise, she smiled and lifted her glass in salute. *Why don't you join in, Duncan? I'm sure they'd love someone to play the piano for them.*

A slow smile spread across his face. He handed her his beer and quickly kissed her on the lips before he took the few steps to slide onto the piano seat.

Without missing a beat, Duncan joined in on the song, his fingers flying across the keyboard as he added a musical layer that truly made the song come to life.

When the song came to an end, Rose jerked her gaze to the crowd that had gathered around the small intimate area they were in. It seemed the entire clientele of the pub had come over to listen in. "Sing us a song, Duncan," Nigel called out as he waved his beer in the air, a proud expression on his face. Siobhán stood beside him, her arm hooked with his. The sight made Rose smile.

Duncan started to shake his head when the crowd called out his name. "Duncan, go on, fella. Let us hear yer voice."

Duncan laughed and looked at Rose as he ran his fingers across the keys, warming up. He stopped playing and leaned back to whisper to the musicians behind him then faced the group once more. "Okay, just for ye."

Rose grinned at the sound of Duncan's Irish accent. She'd noticed it had become more pronounced with each new day in Ireland. When it Rome…

Duncan started playing the most beautiful ballad she'd ever heard. When he began to belt out the lyrics a shiver coursed up her spine. The music reached out and grabbed her in the belly, tightening her chest as she reacted to its heartfelt lyrics. Duncan closed his eyes and poured his heart into the words while his fingers moved in fluid motion across the keyboard.

The emotion filtering across his face as he sang tugged at her heart. She'd never seen anything so heartrendingly beautiful. This was the true Duncan. When he was playing his music, he didn't hide behind the controlled persona he projected to the world around him.

As the last notes died off, the crowd applauded and called for an encore.

Rose spent the next hour thrilled to see this "open" side to Duncan as he took requests, conferred with the musicians and basically had the crowd eating out of his hands. After he played one last song, Duncan turned to thank the musicians behind him and stood.

Nigel rushed forward and clapped him on the shoulder. "Your talent can't be denied. You brought tears to my eyes, son."

Duncan thanked Nigel and walked up to Rose. His amber gaze held hers as he took his glass back. Rose's heart skipped a beat when he reached down and threaded his fingers with hers. His hand tightened on hers and he tugged, silently telling her he wanted her to follow him out of the crowd.

Rose and Duncan set their glasses on the bar then made their way back to the hall off the main pub room. Rose's pulse raced as Duncan pulled her along until they reached her door. She turned and leaned against it. Her breathing grew shallow at the hungry look in Duncan's eyes as he stared down at her.

Grasping her chin, he lowered his mouth close. With the gentlest of brushes, he touched his lips to hers.

Rose's stomach clenched in response to the sexual tension emanating from him. She started to raise her hand to his face, but Duncan shook his head at the same time a warning growl escaped from his throat.

Rose lowered her hand to her side and took a deep breath. His lips barely brushed across hers once more and she opened her mouth, hoping he'd kiss her, needing their connection.

When she touched her tongue to his lips, Duncan's hand thrust through her hair and clasped the nape of her neck, his grip tight.

He touched his forehead to hers and took a deep, ragged breath.

Rose's heart rate jumped at the show of tightly coiled control he held at bay.

Raising his head, he pressed his lips to her temple and backed away. "We have to leave very early tomorrow to make our flight out of Shannon. It's best you get your rest tonight."

"Duncan—" she started to say.

"Don't, Rose," he cut her off, turning on his heel.

Disappointment welled within her, but this time she wasn't going to just let him walk away. "I heard your heartbeat kick up. I smell you. You want me."

Before she could say another word, Duncan had her slammed against the door.

He pressed his erection against her lower belly and hissed out next to her ear, "Hell, yes, I want. But I'm tired of fantasizing about your fangs sinking into my neck. I want the real deal, Rose. Nothing else will satisfy me."

He stepped away, the look on his face so dangerous, so on the edge, it scared her a little. Damn, she'd never been more turned on.

"You'll come around." She held her ground.

Duncan's hands landed hard on the door on either side of her head. He took a long inhaling breath all the way up the side of her neck. Her stomach tensed when he paused just over her pulse. She felt the tension vibrating within him.

"Don't count on it," he whispered in her ear before he turned and walked down the hall.

# Chapter Fourteen

"He'd make a great father," Nigel whispered in her ear.

Rose looked up from flipping through the magazine she'd picked up at the Philadelphia airport.

"Siobhán said you're not mated to Duncan." He paused and grinned at her raised eyebrow. "Her vampire term, not mine. So why haven't you mated with him? It's obvious you care for Duncan very much."

Rose shifted her gaze to Duncan who'd walked down the terminal to buy a newspaper in a side store.

She and Duncan seemed to be avoiding talking to one another. The entire first leg of the trip, Rose buried her nose in a book she'd purchased to keep herself occupied.

"He doesn't love me."

Her uncle snorted. "What are you waiting for, Rosie? The words? The man adores the ground you walk on. It's as plain as day." He spread his hands in frustration, then continued with a sigh, "Some people just can't say those three little words, sweetheart. It doesn't mean they don't feel them. If you wait to hear them, you might be waiting a very long time. Don't keep yourself from being happy."

Rose's stomach tensed and her heart skipped a beat at the hope her uncle gave her—that Duncan really did love her. But deep inside, she knew she needed more. She needed to hear the words. She wanted Duncan to open up, to trust her with his heart. He expected so much from her, but hadn't budged one inch in showing his true self to her, not when it really mattered.

The PA announcement system made a final boarding call. She stood to hug her uncle goodbye.

"I'm really disappointed we can't fly the rest of the way home together. I want to know how Duncan managed to be on your same flight," he complained.

"You just want more to time talk to me about Siobhán," she teased, kissing him on the cheek.

A sad expression crossed Nigel's face. "It upsets me to think she'll never be able to visit me here in the States."

Rose squeezed his hands. "Even if she could figure a way to hide from the sun all the way to the US, you know Siobhán's vow to act as a liaison for the priestesses holds her in Ireland." She shook her head. "Speaking of which, that just goes to show how off the deep end Rónán is to have risked being burned alive to come to the US."

"The Guardians were picked for a reason," Duncan reminded her as he walked up holding a paper. He reached out and shook Nigel's hand. "We'll see you back at home, Nigel."

Her uncle waved goodbye to them and walked through the doorway to board his plane.

Duncan snapped the paper open and sat down. "I'm not happy about the delay. It puts us arriving back later than I prefer."

"Did you call Mark to let him know our flight was delayed?"

"I left him a message," Duncan said, then lifted the paper.

Rose sat down and crossed her arms, staring at the black and white wall between them. First frustration, then outright anger began to simmer within her. How could he deny her? Deny them? The Saoi's blood still sustained her. She only felt a twinge or two of hunger. What she wanted—no, needed—from Duncan was the closeness, the physical connection. And he denied her, damn it.

*You know what I want.* She heard his adamant tone in her head. Duncan hadn't even bothered to lower the paper.

Her gaze narrowed. *You're reading my thoughts now?*

*No. I smell your arousal and I sense your anger. How does it feel,* a ghrá*?*

Rose stood, refusing to be baited. "I'm taking a walk."

"A little cooling off might do you some good," he said with a chuckle.

Grrrr! Rose stomped off, clenching her hands by her sides.

Duncan lowered the paper and narrowed his gaze after Rose's retreating back. Her jeans cupped her sweet ass to perfection. His body reacted instantly to the natural sway of her hips. She'd left her hair unbound and the movement down her back only made him ache for her.

He gritted his teeth and wondered how long he could keep up this farce. He wanted her so fucking bad, wanted to sink into her sweet body. But he spoke the truth to her last night. He wanted more. Correction. He needed more. When the hell did he go from wanting Rose to needing her? He shook his head at the irony that he *needed* her, yet she acted as though she could take or leave him. That, more than anything else, infuriated him.

Lifting the paper once more, he tried to focus on the news he'd missed while they were in Ireland.

Several minutes later, the smell of sweet vanilla filled his nostrils. Duncan lowered the paper to see Rose sitting next to him…licking an ice-cream cone.

"I see you've gotten over your aversion to human food," he said in a dry tone.

"Did you know that everyone eats an ice-cream cone differently?"

Duncan narrowed his gaze at her question as suspicion kicked in. Yet he couldn't stop himself from watching her pink tongue circle around the creamy mound of ice cream.

"I hadn't thought about it." He set his jaw at the first stirrings of arousal in his groin and folded the paper, laying it over his lap.

"It's true." Her aqua gaze lit up and she circled the ice cream once more.

He held back a groan as he watched her turn the cone.

"See, I prefer to lick all the way around," she began.

But this time when she circled the dessert again, Duncan felt her warm tongue flicking around his cock as if she licked him instead.

He locked his jaw at the sensations rocking through him. Tightening his lower stomach to fight off the arousing vibrations, he kept his tone light. "Interesting."

"And then there are people who like to nip straight from the top." She demonstrated by putting an openmouthed kiss over the top of the cone and pulling her lips together.

Duncan held back a groan at the erotic kiss over the top of his cock, especially when she mentally added the cool sensation of the ice cream to the mix.

"Rose," he warned.

Her eyebrow elevated. "You told me I needed to cool off. It was your suggestion," she reminded him. "Then there are the drillers."

He coughed, almost afraid to ask. "The drillers?"

She grinned. "Yeah, you know, those people who like to go right down the middle." She plunged her tongue straight in the heart of the ice cream.

Duncan's entire body jerked at the sensation of her sweet, warm tongue flicking over the opening on his cock. When she added pressure, delving inside, that was it. He'd had enough.

Rose gulped in surprise when Duncan grasped the back of her neck and yanked her forward, planting a hard kiss on her lips.

His tongue thrust inside her mouth, dominant and punishing as he tasted her flavor mixed with cool, sweet vanilla.

When she brushed her tongue against his, responding to his kiss, Duncan pulled back, his expression resolute.

"I prefer the 'all the way around' method, too." His gaze held hers at the same time she felt a feather light kiss on her sex. Swiping an invisible tongue from her slit to her swollen clitoris, he said, "Just remember, I give as good as I get."

Rose gripped the ice cream as Duncan continued his mental manipulation of her body.

It felt naughty to be so openly public, while getting so privately personal with Duncan. The fact no one knew what they were doing turned her on even more.

She held back a moan when he lowered his head and licked the ice cream that had dripped to her fingers.

*I love the stormy color of your eyes when you're in full arousal mode,* he said in a husky voice.

Before she could respond, Duncan stood. *I'm ready whenever you are, Róisín. You know the terms.*

He turned and walked off. Rose wanted to scream at his detached tone, to throw the ice cream at him, then lick it off him...slowly.

Gritting her teeth in frustration, she tossed the rest of the ice cream into a nearby trash can.

"Aw man, and I was just going to ask where you got that ice cream," a woman seated across from her said as she glanced after Duncan with a look of envy on her face.

Rose couldn't help but laugh at the lady's comment. So much for others not knowing what went on between them.

* * * * *

Duncan awoke to a sharp pain in his head as if someone had tugged hard on his hair.

He heard Rose snicker, her voice lowered to a whisper, "Hmmm, maybe let's not use his head as a track," as she untangled what had to be a toy car's wheel from his hair.

Duncan kept his eyes closed and held himself still while he waited to see what other parts of his body *could* be used for a "track". Once his temper had settled, Duncan had returned to the seating area and promptly stretched out on his back across three seats, falling asleep beside Rose. He hadn't slept much the night before since he'd tossed and turned all night long, dreaming of her.

He heard a little girl's high-pitched voice spoken in a loud whisper, "What about here?" at the same time he felt a car roll across his shoe and up his bent leg.

"Perfect!" Rose encouraged. "His knees can be the hills."

Duncan's feet were flat on the seat. His bent knees probably did make perfect hills for a tiny child to run a car up and down if the vroom, vroom sounds accompanied by wheels running up and down his legs were any indication.

Just for fun, he let one of his feet slowly slide forward, stretching his knee out flat. Not to be waylaid, the child's hands went around his knee and lifted his leg back up, then she began playing again.

Duncan let his leg slide forward once more. He repressed his laughter when he heard a huge sigh escape from the child before tiny hands lifted his leg for the second time.

His shoulders shook with silent amusement when he started to lower his leg yet again. But apparently the child was prepared this time. He felt a tiny hand lift the toe of his shoe and something was shoved underneath his foot. Other cars maybe?

He heard Rose's laughter in his head. *I know you're awake and teasing the heck out of her. Let her play. Her mother is exhausted. Her infant has just fallen asleep. I compelled the woman to sleep for a bit while the baby napped. I've been entertaining her older child.*

*She's a resourceful little tyke, isn't she?* Duncan mused to Rose, impressed with the fact the child figured out how to stop the huge "hill" from disappearing on her once more. Creating a wedge under his shoe was quite ingenious on her part.

*Indeed,* Rose agreed.

When he heard the little girl sigh, then yawn, he grinned. All that lifting had worn her out.

He tensed when he felt her little hands tugging on his shirt, then her body lying down on his chest.

Intuitively, his hands went around her slight form to keep her from rolling off as she snuggled her head under his chin.

The child smelled like baby powder. He couldn't resist inhaling as he opened his eyes and glanced at Rose.

She stared down at them, a look of longing on her face. When she saw him staring at her, she quietly cleared her throat and glanced at the sleeping mother, then whispered, "Her mother said she recently lost her husband to cancer. I'm sure this little two-and-a-half-year-old misses her 'daddy' time."

Rose touched the little girl's red curls, then lifted her and put her in a chair next to her mother.

Duncan sat up and looked down at the child dozing next to her mother. She had such an angelic face. A sprinkle of freckles across the bridge of her nose and her grubby shoes told him this little one loved the outdoors as well as the mud.

When Rose sat down next to him he glanced at her. "You could have it all if you wish, Rose. Just say the magic words."

Conflicting emotions stirred in her gaze from surprise to stubborn determination before she looked away, mumbling, "You first."

Duncan started to ask what she meant, when the little girl across from them said, "Hi, I'm Katie."

"Hi, Katie, I'm Duncan, your 'car track'," he replied with a grin.

"That was a fast nap," Rose said with a chuckle.

The little girl jumped down, smiling. "My mommy says I skipped the nap stage." Tilting her head to the side, a perplexed look flitted across on her face as she asked them as only a child would, "You look big like my mommy. Why don't you have kids?"

Duncan chuckled at the child's question. "Rose is much better at explaining things than me."

The little girl looked at Rose expectantly. Duncan heard Rose clear her throat. He waited, curious to see what she would say.

Rose stood and gathered Katie's toy cars. She handed them to the little girl with a smile. "Well, Katie, two people fall in love, then get married. Then they have children."

While Katie nodded as if what Rose said made perfect sense, Rose's words kept reverberating in his head. "Two people fall in love, then get married."

Duncan glanced at Rose as she sat back down, but even when he said her name, she refused to look his way.

The reason for Rose's resistance hit him. Did she not love him? She'd never told him she did. He knew she wanted him. That part she couldn't deny, but love? He'd never thought the idea she might not love him would strike him so hard.

His stomach clenched while he watched Rose continue to talk with the little girl, discussing one of her cars with her. Rose was so beautiful through and through. He'd find a way to make her love him, to want to be his mate.

*"Use your heart to win her,"* the Saoi's words came back to him.

Duncan clasped Rose's hand and lifted it to his lips. *Truce,* a ghrá*?*

Spreading her fingers to lace them with his, Rose smiled. *Truce.*

*I still want you.*

*I know.* She laid her head on his shoulder and sighed.

Duncan kissed her hair and inhaled her floral scent as he wrapped his arm around her shoulder and pulled her closer.

*****

Rose waved as Mark drove up to the terminal to pick them up in Duncan's black sports car.

"Hi, Mark," she said when he jumped out and took her suitcase.

"How was Ireland?" Mark's gaze darted back and forth between Rose and Duncan.

"Breathtaking and enlightening," Rose said at the same time Duncan said, "Educational."

She laughed at his one-word assessment of their trip, but Duncan seemed preoccupied. His gaze scanned the crowds around them several times, his entire demeanor tense.

"What's wrong?" Rose glanced around, trying to see what would cause his tension.

Duncan shrugged and put his suitcase in the trunk. "Nothing," he said, shutting the trunk. "I'll just feel better when we're back at Ian's house. We got back to Chicago later than I preferred with the hour delay added to our layover."

Rose glanced at her watch, then the blue sky with a laugh. "It's four in the afternoon and sunny. We'll be fine."

When Duncan insisted on driving, Rose just rolled her eyes. She climbed in the passenger seat and waited for Duncan to get in and Mark to slide in the backseat.

While Duncan punched the button to roll down all the car's windows as he turned onto the highway, she spoke in his mind, her tone teasing. *So when am I going to get to see your place?*

Duncan cast his gaze her way. *As soon as James and Rónán are no longer a threat to you. I can protect you better with Ian and Jax's help.*

"Anything happen while we were gone?" Duncan asked, looking at Mark in the rearview mirror.

Rose glanced back at Mark to see him nod. "Yep, with your mother's help we caught Rónán for a brief time. James got away."

"Where'd you find Rónán?" Rose asked.

"Fighting James at your house."

"What!" Rose's voice elevated along with her anger. "They were in my home?"

"Uh…yes."

"What happened?" Duncan interrupted, his hands on the wheel tightening.

"Your mother asked Rónán to join with us to fight James."

"Hell no!" Rose yelled, fury slicing through her.

"Huh?" Mark asked, glancing at her with a confused look on his face.

"Rónán killed Rose's father," Duncan said in a cold tone.

Mark ran his hand through his blond hair. "Man, Rose, I'm so sorry. Well, no worries on that one since Rónán refused to join us. He threatened to take your life, too, Duncan."

"Just what I need, a psycho Guardian on my tail," Duncan grumbled. He started to speak again when the sound of metal hitting metal caused the car to pitch forward. While Duncan jerked his gaze to the rearview mirror, Rose screamed and quickly turned to see an SUV had hit them from behind and was riding their bumper.

"Sonofabitch, he's got transers working for him!" Duncan yelled as he gripped the wheel. He had to swerve to the right to avoid another car that had come up on his left. "I hope to hell you came prepared," he gritted out to Mark.

"I'm a boy scout, remember?" Mark said pulling out a gun he had tucked in his boot.

"And that you have more than one of those," Rose yelled, gripping the dash as their car took another hit from behind.

Mark handed her his weapon, then leaned down to retrieve another one from behind the front seat.

"Shit!" Duncan hissed when the car beside them suddenly moved in front of them, then slammed on its brakes. Another car had moved to take its place to the left of Duncan's car, and a truck was now on their right. Duncan had no choice but to hit the brakes. It was too late. Wheels screeched as they rammed into the back of the black car in front of them.

Rose's airbag deployed, but Duncan's didn't. The impact sent him flying headfirst into the windshield.

"Duncan!" she screamed at the sight of his blood all over the broken windshield. He wasn't moving. *God, no!* she mentally screamed as she tried to pull him back, to see if he was still conscious. As she tried to shake Duncan's limp body leaning over the steering wheel, the smell of burned rubber and blood assailed her senses. She'd dropped the gun when they'd hit the car in front of them, but the sight of several men surrounding their car, guns pointing at them, made her dive for the gun to defend herself.

Rose glanced back to see Mark lying on his side, unconscious and bleeding from bullet holes in his chest. She bit her lip to keep herself focused when all she wanted to do was scream at the top of her lungs. Guilt overwhelmed her that she'd been so out of it seeing Duncan's still body and trying to check if he were okay, she didn't even hear the gunshots that Mark had taken to his chest.

The odor of burning flesh slammed into her as she gripped the gun tight in her hand. She started to aim her weapon at the men approaching her side of the car when the sound of James' voice outside Duncan's door sent an ice-cold chill down her spine.

He held a gun to the base of Duncan's skull.

"I'll put a bullet right through the back of his head if you don't leave with me right now."

James was wearing sunglasses, a hat, a long coat and gloves, but still she smelled his flesh burning. Even the slightest movement exposed his skin to the sun. The foul smell made her stomach turn.

She set her gun down on the dash. "I'll go, but if anything happens to Duncan, I'll kill you."

"Why would I kill him? He still has his uses."

One of the men pulled open the bent passenger car door so she could get out. Once she stood outside the car, Rose smelled James' scent on the men surrounding her. But they still smelled human, too. "Duncan called them transers. What are they?" she asked, narrowing her gaze on James who'd come around to her side of the car.

"My very own private army, bitten twice. Just one more bite and they'll be full vampri. A nice incentive, don't you think?" he smirked.

Sick at just how ruthless James turned out to be, she wanted to make sure he understood her terms in agreeing to go with him. "You know I have the power to inflict serious damage if you go back on your word."

James' laugh sounded off balance to her ears as he moved to stand in front of her. His burning flesh made her want to hurl. "I'm well aware Mordoor converted you." His lighthearted tone turned cold as he grabbed her by the throat and squeezed. "Why would you betray me like that, Rose?"

James' grip felt as if it were crushing her throat, that at any moment her neck would snap in two. Her fingernails turned into claws as she desperately ripped at his hand around her throat.

James roared at the wounds she inflicted. Lifting her bodily, he slammed her down on the hood of the crushed car. Pain splintered through her skull at the impact.

"You're going to give me what I've been waiting for," he hissed out between clenched teeth.

As he finished speaking, blessed darkness engulfed her.

# Chapter Fifteen

ꟙ

Sweet blood. The smell permeated her consciousness as she awoke. It was so close, she could almost taste it. Her head ached but she didn't care. The blood smelled so good as if it were on her lips. Reality kicked in and she realized blood coated her mouth. It smelled of Duncan, but different. She started to flick her tongue out to taste it when she heard Duncan's pained voice in her head. *No, Rose!*

Even though her heart thumped in happiness that Duncan still lived, the horror in his voice snapped her fully awake. She jerked her eyes open to see two of James' men holding Duncan by his arms a few feet in front of her. Two other transers trained their guns on his head. She quickly glanced around and realized she was in some type of abandoned warehouse.

Stacks of shipping crates surrounded them. Boat horns sounded off in the distance. Her heart jerked when her gaze landed on Mark's still body lying near a crate. Only a faint heartbeat remained. She held back a sob as her gaze shifted back to Duncan once more.

He was on his knees on the dirty concrete floor, his face pained, but his gaze full of intensity as it met hers. Two streams of blood made bright red streaks down his throat, staining his light blue shirt. From the pale color of his skin, the weakness she sensed from him, someone had taken his blood—a lot of it.

Her stomach knotted in fear.

James.

"I know you're hungry, Rose. Taste it," James demanded from somewhere to her left.

Rose sat up from her lying position on the cool, hard floor and narrowed her gaze on James. He'd removed his hat, coat and sunglasses. He stood there in black pants and a black T-shirt, his thick arms crossed over his chest. The blood he took from Duncan must've sped James' healing because his skin showed no signs of burns. Still, the smell of burned flesh clung to him. Her stomach lurched at the faint lingering scent.

She wiped her lips on her sleeve to remove the offending blood. "Nice try, but I'm not in the mood for tainted blood."

James clenched his hands by his side, roaring in fury. "You will take my blood. You will become my mate."

Stomping over to Duncan, he grasped his hair and jerked Duncan's head back.

James stumbled as if he'd been punched in the gut. The smirk on Duncan's pained face told her Duncan still had some kick left in him.

*Go Duncan*, Rose spoke to him mentally.

But James quickly recovered and slammed his fist into Duncan's solar plexus, knocking the wind out of him. While Duncan coughed, trying to bring air back into his lungs, James punched him in the jaw, then turned to Rose, his fangs extended. "Or do you want me to finish him off now?"

*He's mine to kill*, Duncan spoke in Rose's mind right before he lost consciousness. Rose's fear for Duncan's life skyrocketed. Unconscious, he'd be an easy target for the bastard.

"No!" Rose screamed. Without a thought, she launched herself at James, knocking him away from Duncan.

James slammed to the floor, deep red gashes striped across his torn shirt and chest. Rose landed on her hands and feet, panting as satisfaction rushed through her. The sight of the vicious wounds she'd inflicted surprised her. She glanced down at her hands to see she'd converted to a jaguar without conscious thought. The need to defend Duncan flared within her making her actions as primal and instinctive in nature as a jaguar protecting her mate. She'd protect him at all costs.

James ripped his shredded shirt off with angry, jerky movements and tossed it on the floor. As he ran his hand across his wounds, Rose watched in amazement to see his heated touch sear the wide, bleeding furrows closed. Once again the smell of burning flesh reached her sensitive nose.

She swallowed the bile that hit the back of her throat.

James narrowed his gaze on her. "I see Rónán has gotten to you. The jaguar always was his animal form of choice," he sneered.

*You've fucked with my family and loved ones for the last time,* she threatened as she pawed the dust on the floor and moved to place herself between Duncan and James.

The sound of guns being cocked didn't even faze Rose. She knew James wouldn't let his transers kill her. She was too valuable to him alive.

She'd barely gotten out her cat's *raaaaaagh* battle roar when James shifted to a lion and pounced on her.

The impact of his larger size and heavy body knocked her to the ground with a hard thud. Their claws dug into each other's hides as they rolled on the floor.

Rose gritted her teeth against the pain his claws inflicted. She smelled her own blood running free from her wounds, but couldn't concentrate on healing herself since she was protecting herself against new wounds.

Instead she took the offensive, swatting at James. Satisfaction rippled through her at his roar of pain and the sight of red welts surfacing across his lion's muzzle. Her head snapped sideways when he returned the favor. Searing pain sliced from her temple to her chin. Blood stung her left eye. Rose shook her jaguar head and blinked to clear her vision.

James took advantage of her weakness, locking his large, powerful jaws on her throat.

Her heart racing, fear paramount, Rose's jaguar instincts caused her to freeze at the sensation of his huge canines clamped on her neck. Panting, she blinked several more times, trying to clear the blood from her eyes.

James put a huge paw in the center of her chest, then released her neck. While his rough lion's tongue laved at her face, he spoke in her mind, his tone cold, bloodthirsty. *As much as it disgusts me to see you risk your life for Mordoor, you've given me what I needed. Leverage.*

He stopped licking her wounds and clamped his teeth on her neck again, this time piercing the skin.

Rose jerked at the pain but her heart sank at his next words. *If you don't take my blood, I'll rip Duncan's heart out of his chest as you watch.*

When James released her throat, Rose blinked once more, finally clearing her vision. She looked up to see his hazel lion's gaze staring down at her. She knew he spoke the truth. The vamp didn't have an honorable bone in his body. He'd attack Duncan while he was out cold and unable to defend himself.

Blood dripped from the wounds she'd inflicted on his face, landing with a warm splat on her neck.

The lion moved his head, letting his blood drip on her chin, close to her mouth.

Her stomach roiled in revulsion, but Rose knew she didn't have a choice. She closed her eyes and nodded her agreement.

The lion roared in victory over her, then James demanded in her mind, *Shift to your human form. I want to feel your fangs in my neck. To know you accept your fate.*

When he lowered his lion's body over hers and she felt his erection against her thigh, Rose's fear spiked. Her insides shuddered and her entire body began to quake.

Rage filled her. Never again would she be the victim. While she took his blood, he'd be vulnerable. He would die.

Duncan's voice in her head made her heart rate kick up. *Rose, fight him.*

*He'll kill you,* she said.

*A life without you won't be worth living. Fight him, damn you.*

The lion jerked his head to stare at Duncan, then roared when he realized Duncan was awake. James narrowed his gaze on Rose once more and growled in her head, *Shift and take my blood or he dies.*

Rose knew James would kill Duncan the first chance he had once she was mated to him. She had to do everything she could to help Duncan survive. She closed her eyes and focused on Duncan.

Gathering her energy, she let it build upon itself, like a tornado spinning around inside her. Her gaze locked with Duncan's as she spoke in his mind, *No,* a ghrá, *you fight for us.* At the same time she mentally directed every bit of strength she had left within her straight toward him.

The force knocked Duncan right out of the men's hold. Extreme weakness overtook her and the room began to spin around her. Rose met James' lion's gaze. *Kiss my ass,* she hissed in his mind before she lost consciousness.

*****

Ian's voice had shaken Duncan awake. *Good, you're back. Losing our connection freaked me out.*

*I'm so fucking weak,* Duncan had replied mentally. *I can't lose her, Ian.*

*I know. I'm tracking your scent. Just hold on.*

The impact of Rose's life force had slammed into Duncan like a freight train. He'd never felt so bulldozed and energized at the same time. He immediately rolled behind some freight boxes as bullets whizzed past him.

A split second later the crates in front of him shuddered as if they'd been hit. He heard the lion's roar at the same time the boxes jolted once more. Duncan saw them toppling and vaulted on top of another stack.

Staring down at the lion, he taunted, "You'd better shift to human form, James. You might have half a chance against me then."

James roared and jumped on his hind legs to rock the stack of crates underneath him.

Duncan leapt off the boxes and landed on the balls of his feet in front of James.

*How did you recover so quickly?* James asked.

*Because she's my Anima,* Duncan said in a smug tone, enjoying James' annoyance.

*I didn't smell any of your blood mixed with hers,* James roared in his head as he leapt for Duncan, his claws ready to dig into his skin.

Duncan concentrated on a cougar's form and felt his body instantly shift. At the same time James slammed into him, shots rang out once more.

While Duncan swiped his claw at James' heart, out of the corner of his eye he saw Ian and Jax shooting at the transers who'd taken cover behind several crates.

James landed a hard blow to his face, causing the room to spin around Duncan. He shook off the dizziness and bit down on the lion's front leg.

The lion let out a roar and dipped his head, ripping at Duncan's shoulder with his teeth.

A black jaguar appeared behind James, inflicting a powerful blow to his back. James growled at the pain and immediately let go of his grip on Duncan's shoulder to defend himself.

Rónán's appearance surprised Duncan. He'd worry about Rónán later. Right now the bastard had saved his life.

The two large cats rolled on the floor, delivering severe wounds to each other. Blood spurted amid roars of outrage. Duncan watched the battle, tension flowing through him. The Guardians were evenly matched in both size and strength. Each used his mental powers to knock the other back, but it seemed both vamps wanted the outlet of a physical fight more than anything else.

The gunshots had finally ceased and Duncan glanced over to see all the transers were dead. Both Jax and Ian were squatting next to Rose.

Duncan heard her heartbeat but it was weak. He knew she'd depleted much of own life force to help him, but she'd also lost a lot of blood in her battle with James. She needed to replace the blood she lost or he would lose her.

*Take her. Make sure she feeds,* he spoke mentally to Jax.

Jax lifted Rose in her arms, nodding to him.

*Mark's very weak,* Duncan spoke to his twin. *I think James also took his blood. Get him out of here.*

Ian walked over to Mark's limp body and lifted his bulk over his shoulder, then he turned to look at Duncan. *Rónán did come to us to help find you, but just the other day, he threatened your life. I don't think leaving you to battle him alone is such a good idea.*

Duncan paced in his cougar form, watching the two larger cats rip each other to shreds. *This is my battle to fight,* he growled.

Ian withdrew the knife he had strapped to his hip. *At one time Rónán was an honorable man. Mother maintains her faith in him.* Setting the blade on the floor, he kicked it across the room. When it skidded to a stop next to Duncan's paws, Ian continued, *To even the battlefield.*

Duncan glanced down at the knife. When he lifted his gaze back to his brother, Ian had already disappeared behind the crates, following in Jax's footsteps. His twin's voice entered his head one last time. *When you're battling against the odds, forging an alliance may be the best course of action.*

Duncan's gaze locked on James and Rónán. The two animals had reared up on their back paws. They were using their front claws to hold on while they bit at each other's upper bodies.

Duncan nudged the knife with his paw, considering the best course of action. Standing on the flat side of the knife's blade, his weight lifted the handle so he could grasp it in his jaws.

As he stared at the two Guardians who'd foregone weapons in lieu of face-to-face combat, Duncan's honorable conscience reared its ugly head. Even though he knew he would be at a disadvantage in size compared to the two larger animals, Duncan lowered his head and opened his mouth, dropping the knife to the ground. He'd respect their chosen method of fighting, but he'd do it his way.

Could he shift to a larger form? He was half Atruan with a priestess's blood running through his veins. He hadn't really tried beyond that first effort in the woods. Today, his cougar form might work to his advantage. Recalling the lesson he'd learned from the smaller cougar he'd seen in the woods, an idea came to Duncan. It was risky but he'd learned to depend on his instincts. He hoped he could trust Rónán to work with him.

Duncan took off running toward the fighting cats, gaining speed. When he was within a few feet of them, he stopped and let the combination of momentum and his paws on the slick, dirty floor carry him underneath the battling cats.

He had to sidestep to keep from getting crushed while he waited for the right moment to strike. But when James finally started to lower his front paws to the ground, Duncan reached up on his back legs and clamped his jaws around the soft skin covering James' heart. Duncan dug his teeth deep, twisting and turning his head as fury at James and protection for his Anima rushed through him.

The lion let out a yelping roar at the pain he inflicted. At first James stumbled in surprise but the desire to survive kicked in. He tried to shake Duncan off at the same time he dug his long lion's claws down the cougar's sides.

Duncan gritted his teeth at the horrific, ripping sensation that tore into his sides, but he held on out of sheer instinct. When James stumbled once more, Rónán knocked the lion over onto his side. Duncan went down with him. He released his locked jaw hold from the lion's chest right before the jaguar jumped on James, grabbed his throat with his powerful jaws and yanked, ripping it open. The lion's roar sounded more like a drowning gurgle as blood spewed from the gaping hole in his neck.

Duncan watched James convert back into his human form. His naked body was covered in fresh, bright red claw and bite wounds. The smell of blood and impending death permeated the room.

When James took his last breath, Duncan lifted his gaze to Rónán. *You must pay for killing Rose's father.*

Rónán had also suffered in the battle. Blood oozed from his wounds as he narrowed his metallic jaguar gaze on Duncan. *Another day*, he said and slowly turned around.

Duncan watched the powerful display of muscles rippling through the cat's broad shoulders as he walked away. He recognized the Guardian's action for what it was. Rónán was intentionally exposing his unguarded back to him. Daring him to attack or allowing him the advantage, Duncan wasn't sure. Maybe both.

Duncan reminded himself that before he'd been betrayed, Rónán had acted honorably by trying to save Rose's mother from James.

*Another day*, Duncan agreed.

The cat paused mid-stride at his comment. He didn't look back, but instead continued walking. Duncan stood there taking deep breaths as he surveyed the carnage. He was the only living being left in the building.

* * * * *

Once he'd burned all the dead bodies in a cleared field behind the warehouse, Duncan shifted to a raven and flew to the shore of Lake Michigan. He fed on a man out for an evening stroll. He needed the blood to regain all that James had taken as well as the additional loss of blood from the battle. His body on the mend, Duncan shifted back to a raven and swiftly flew to Ian's home. Only the deep wounds the lion had inflicted down his sides remained tender to the touch.

Ian met Duncan in the wide foyer as he closed the front door behind him. "Rose is upstairs resting."

Duncan exhaled the breath of relief he didn't know he'd been holding. "How's Mark?" he asked, his shoulders tense.

Ian grinned. "Mark's a fighter. He'll be fine by morning."

Duncan gave Ian a thankful nod then took the stairs two at a time. Ian followed by his side, his expression expectant. "Well?"

"James is dead," Duncan said in a cold tone.

"And Rónán?"

"Still lives. For now."

Ian stopped Duncan from proceeding into the bedroom with a hand on his arm. "And what of Rónán's status?"

"He must pay for killing Rose's father."

Surprise flickered across Ian's face, followed by anger. "That bastard has crossed the line one time too many."

"Agreed," Duncan said, then shook his head. "The vamp's a true conundrum. He could've battled me tonight, but he walked away."

Ian frowned. "Why did you let him go?"

"We worked together to kill James."

Nodding his understanding, Ian asked, "So what are you going to do?"

"I know what must be done with Rónán, but right now all I want to do is see Rose."

Jax was sitting on the bed beside Rose when the brothers entered the bedroom. She stood and walked toward them, her green eyes sparkling.

Clasping Ian's hand, she pulled her Anima out of the room, calling behind them, "She's a resilient one. By tomorrow she'll be as good as new."

"Thanks for the vote of confidence," Rose called after Jax in a tired voice.

Duncan's heart leapt at the smile she gave him. She was sitting up in bed, wearing one of his T-shirts.

"I could use one of those," he softly joked, glancing at his naked body.

"I like your naked self. Did you know that even though you're projecting clothes, I can see right through them?"

He winked at her as he took the hand she held out to him and sat down on the bed beside her.

While he laid a gentle kiss on her palm, she said in a quiet voice, "Ian told me what happened once I passed out." She paused. "Rónán still lives. I see the truth in your eyes."

Duncan's chest contracted at the anger reflected in her gaze. "He will be punished for murdering your father, Rose. I promise."

She nodded her understanding, then gave him a half smile. "So, how'd you like the mojo I sent your way?"

How he adored this woman! Duncan leaned forward and pressed a kiss to her lips. *I've always thought you packed a helluva punch. Now I know for sure.*

Rose grinned against his mouth, then pressed her lips to his. Desire stirred in his groin when she opened her mouth and her arms went around his neck, but Duncan pulled back. Regret clenched his stomach.

"I washed off in the lake but I need a bath and you need your rest."

"I need you," she insisted.

"Rose," he started to argue when a bright light flashed in their room.

Duncan and Rose turned their surprised gazes to stare at a woman with long, dark wavy hair who stood a few feet away. She wore a brown leather vest and a matching short skirt. A cream-colored cape fell to her ankles, swirling around her knee-high, lace-up leather boots. An ethereal white glow surrounded her like a ball of coiled energy.

"Ye are two of the most stubborn humans I've ever seen," she said in a lilting Irish accent.

"The Morrigan?" Rose asked, her eyes wide with wonder.

"In the flesh," she replied in a cocky tone.

The Goddess's dark gaze drifted over Duncan's form before she met his gaze. "As much as I can appreciate a well-built body such as yers, I suggest ye get cleaned and dressed."

Duncan frowned. "Why are you here?"

The Morrigan sighed as if to give herself patience with these humans' inferior questions. "Rose has a duty to fulfill. I assume ye would want to go along."

Rose sat up on her knees, her expression confused. "What duty are you—"

"I don't have time for all these silly questions," she cut Rose off, then waved her hand toward them both.

Duncan looked down to see The Morrigan had bathed and clothed him in jeans and a sweater. He glanced at Rose to see she was dressed in a similar fashion.

Protection for Rose's current weakened state weighed heavy on his mind. "Rose can't go anywhere. She's still recovering."

The Morrigan narrowed her gaze. "Rose has a duty to fulfill," she repeated.

Duncan gritted his teeth in anger. "Can't this wait until she's fully recovered?"

"Ye dare argue with me?" the Goddess' voice rose. "Enough," she said, then snapped her fingers.

*****

Rose took in her surroundings. She was in a forest and she heard water rushing. A creek must be near, she thought. The spring wind whistled through the new leaves on the trees above her. When she caught Rónán's scent, anger flared within her and she searched the woods for his presence. Her gaze narrowed when it landed on Rónán ten feet away. Wearing a black sweater and black cargo pants, Rónán slowly stood from his crouched position in front of a huge oak tree. He'd tied his long black hair back by wrapping the streak of white hair around it. His boots crunched the dead leaves under his feet as he turned to face them, anger in his gaze.

"You! I'm not going back," he gritted out, his fists by his side. But he wasn't staring at her. He was looking at The Morrigan who stood to Rose's right.

Rose didn't give The Morrigan a chance to speak. "Murdering bastard," she yelled as she launched across the distance between them. The impact took Rónán off balance, slamming him against the tree behind him.

She heard Duncan's voice behind her, calling her name, but Rose ignored him as she wrapped her fingers around the Guardian's thick neck. God, the man was massive.

His mercurial eyes narrowed on her as he clasped her wrists and yanked her hands away from his throat.

"I have no quarrel with ye, Rose," he bit out.

"Rose is here to set you free, Rónán," The Morrigan said in a calm voice.

Rose, Duncan and Rónán all turned to The Morrigan in surprise.

"The hell I will!" Rose yelled, yanking her hands from Rónán's grasp. She swung her fist, hitting his jaw. Rónán's head jerked sideways from the impact.

He grabbed her fist and squeezed, holding her in place. "Cease yer attack."

"He murdered Rose's father," Duncan explained to The Morrigan.

"Yer Saoi told me that James was the Guardian who betrayed Anna," the Goddess addressed Rónán.

Rónán released Rose's hand and crossed his arms over his chest. A belligerent look settled on his face. "Translated—ye fecked up the wrong man's life, Morrie."

The wind around them stirred and the white glow surrounding The Morrigan grew with her temper. "Watch yer insolent tongue, Rónán Keegan, or I won't set things straight."

She turned to Rose. "As the priestess's descendant ye must be the one to ask for Rónán to be released from his curse."

Fury swept through Rose that The Morrigan would ask this of her. Rónán deserved his curse. Maybe not for his past sins, but for his current ones.

"I won't." Rose clenched her fists by her side. Glancing at Rónán's stiff expression, she said in a determined voice, "It's a fitting punishment for killing my father."

The Morrigan walked up to Rose and put her hand on her shoulder. A sudden calmness swept through Rose. She felt The Morrigan's strong sense of self—a confidence that could only come with being a Goddess. The Morrigan looked at Rónán.

"I now know ye were an honorable man. All these years couldn't have changed ye. Basic good resides deep in the soul. Ye did what ye did for a reason. Rose's gifts allow her to see what ye refuse to speak of. She deserves to know."

Confused by The Morrigan's words, Rose turned her gaze to Rónán. "What is she talking about?"

Rónán stared after The Morrigan as she walked away to stand beside Duncan. Then he returned his steady gaze to Rose's.

Rose tensed when Rónán reached for her hand, but Duncan's softly spoken *Tóg go bog é* in her head calmed her.

Rónán uncurled her hand from its tight fist and placed it on his naked chest. Sheesh, did the man ever wear real clothes? Rose felt his heart's heavy thump beneath the thick pectoral as his steel gaze narrowed on her.

"If I allow ye into my mind, ye must promise to see only what happened between yer father and me."

*I don't want to see my father's murder all over again,* Rose whispered in Duncan's mind.

*I've seen the honorable side to Rónán The Morrigan speaks of. You must know for sure before you condemn him, Róisín. Seek the truth,* a ghrá.

Rose bit her lip and nodded her agreement.

Rónán laid his much larger hand over hers and spoke in her mind. *Remember yer promise.*

He closed his eyes and Rose closed hers. She let the physical connection between them help her move past his strong mental barrier. Then Rose saw her father through Rónán's eyes.

*So this is George Sinclair, Anna's mate,* Rónán thought as he approached her father sitting in his wheelchair next to the window.

"There's only a faint remnant smell of Anna on ye. Where is yer mate?" he asked George.

Her father's wrinkled face lit up at the mention of his wife. "Have you seen Anna? I miss her so now that she's gone."

Rónán frowned and repeated, "Where is yer mate?"

The old man looked away, staring out the window into the dark. "She passed away the day I came out of my coma. It's been too many years to count."

*How has the man survived their separation? He must suffer constantly without her psychic connection. In the end, everyone lost,* Rónán thought with a bitter twist of his lips.

George beckoned him close. When Rónán drew near, the old man whispered, "I sometimes blame myself. That if I hadn't woken up, Anna wouldn't have died. My daughter is the only reason I live at all."

"Ye no longer have to worry. It's me duty to watch over Rose."

George gave him a small smile. "You know my Rosie, then?"

Rónán nodded. "I'll teach her what she needs to know to survive."

When Rónán started to pull away, the old man grasped his shoulders. "I can't wait to see Anna again."

Rónán heard the slow, tired thump of the old man's heart. He sensed the man wouldn't last much longer…maybe a week at the most.

"Would you like to see her today?"

The man's grip on his shoulders tightened. "Please…"

The human had suffered far too long. At least he could help Anna once last time, by sending her mate home to her. He compelled the old man to fall into a peaceful sleep…a sleep his human body would never awake from.

Rose's heart constricted as she opened her eyes. She tried to remove her hand from Rónán's chest, but he held her still, his gaze locking with hers.

"I never got to say goodbye to him," she whispered, her tone more regretful than vengeful.

"Would you have wanted him to suffer even one more day?"

She closed her eyes and shook her head, holding back a sob.

Rónán released her hand and she turned her watery gaze to The Morrigan. "I ask you to release Rónán from his curse."

"That leaves you without a Guardian," The Morrigan reminded her.

"Rose is mine to protect," Duncan cut in.

Rónán glared at Duncan, then returned his gaze to The Morrigan. "Until Rose takes a mate, I'm still her Guardian, curse or no."

The Morrigan nodded. "My work here is almost done. How does it feel to give up your immortality, Rónán?" she smirked.

"I feel centuries old already," came his sarcastic response.

The Morrigan turned to Duncan. "I've spoken with yer mother. She told me Eamon's wishes. Ye will take his place as leader of the Sythens with Rónán by yer side as second-in-command."

"No!" Rónán said, his face livid. Without another word he shifted to a black hawk and flew away.

"I never agreed to become the Sythen leader," Duncan countered.

Rose could feel the anger flaring through him. She walked up and clasped his hand, giving him her support, no matter what he decided.

"Yer clan needs a leader, Duncan. Now more than ever," The Morrigan said.

"They aren't my clan."

The Morrigan looked at Rose. "Talk to him. As for Rónán, he may be free of his curse, but he now has a special connection to the Guardians." An amused smile crossed her face. "Even if he doesn't know it yet."

The Goddess started to walk away then she turned back to them. She met Rose and Duncan's gazes with a steady one. "I'm well aware that yer mothers broke their vows never to speak of their past as well as the reasons behind their decisions. Nature has a way of balancing itself regardless of the forces working around it. I got involved once. I won't make the same mistake again."

When Rose turned her gaze to Duncan, they were both standing back in their bedroom at Ian's house.

The Morrigan was gone.

Rose put her hands on Duncan's waist and looked up at him. "The Morrigan is right. We're both part Atruan, Duncan. You can't deny our ancestry."

Duncan gave her a grim look, then pulled her close and kissed her on the forehead. "I know you're right, *a ghrá*, but I'm not leader material. I've been a loner too long."

Rose laughed while she wrapped her arms around his waist and laid her head on his chest. "I've never met a more authoritative, commanding man. You'll make a wonderful leader. And don't forget I've seen you work a crowd. The word 'commanding' does come to mind."

"Do you really think so?" He rubbed his chin against her temple, sounding in deep thought.

She nodded. "I know so. You don't want the Sythen clan to fall apart yet again, do you?"

"No, I don't." Duncan gave a heavy sigh. "I hope they accept me and that I can smooth the way for the Sythens with the other clan leaders."

Rose smiled against his chest and squeezed his waist. "I'm sure helping smooth ruffled feathers between the clans will go a long way in establishing you as a great leader, Duncan."

He pulled back to meet her gaze once more. "What happened between Rónán and your father?"

Once she'd relayed what she'd seen through Rónán's eyes, Duncan shook his head. "Rónán's a puzzle I've yet to figure out. I know he's honorable, but I've seen his Machiavellian ruthlessness, too."

Rose nodded. "While I was in his mind, I kept my word and didn't probe deeper, but I felt the darkness within him, Duncan. Are you sure having him as second-in-command is such a good idea?"

Duncan slid his hands down to her hips, locking her body to his. "If he decides to join us, it's the easiest way to keep tabs on him."

"Good point." She kissed his jaw and smiled up at him.

Duncan lifted her in his arms and carried her to the bed. "You need to rest."

Rose pulled back the covers and after Duncan set her on the bed, he crawled in beside her.

Gathering her close, he kissed her neck and whispered in her ear, "No one means as much to me as you do."

Rose snuggled closer, reveling in Duncan's declaration. It was the closest he'd come to telling her he loved her.

Kissing her jaw, he continued, "I know you had to feed to regain your strength. I regret that my stubborn pride put you in jeopardy. It'll never happen again. If you're hungry, go feed."

Now why did it bother her that Duncan wasn't insisting she mate with him any longer? That he wasn't demanding his blood be her only sustenance? He'd said he cared for her above all others, so why was he backing away now?

Duncan's even breathing told her he'd fallen asleep, but her stomach tightened as she tried to understand the reasoning for his apparent change of heart about their mating. After several frustrating minutes of trying to come up with a reason, exhaustion overtook her and Rose's eyelids fluttered closed.

# Chapter Sixteen

ഗ

The next morning Rose awoke to the sound of the shower being turned on. She rolled over and the covers caught around her jeans legs. Ugh, she remembered she'd fallen asleep in her clothes. She thought she was only going to take a nap but she probably needed the sleep. Already she felt better, even if she was a little hungry.

She rolled over and punched her pillow, thinking about Duncan. Though she was glad she didn't have to look over her shoulder waiting for James to attack, the thought that Duncan wouldn't feel the need to stick around twenty-four/seven depressed her.

Thinking about Duncan made her stomach growl. The idea of feeding from his sexy body made her heart hammer, but *could* she bind herself to a man who held so much of himself back yet expected so much from her?

She pulled the covers back and walked toward the bathroom. One thing she knew for certain, Duncan fulfilled her in ways no other man had. She didn't know if that was enough to mate with him, but that wasn't going to stop her from enjoying their time together. At the moment, time together in the shower sounded pretty good to her.

Right when she opened the door, the shower shut off. Disappointment washed over her when Duncan stepped out and wrapped the towel around his wet body.

"Hi," he said as he ran his fingers through his wet hair. "I'm done if you need to hop in."

Rose gave a half smile at his tousled hair. It made him look even sexier. Something was different though…his smooth jaw drew her attention.

"You shaved," she said, working hard not to let her disappointment show.

Duncan rubbed his jaw and gave her a sheepish look. "I figured the day I meet with the Vité to tell him I'll accept my role as the Sythens' new leader, I should look somewhat presentable."

"Ah." She nodded. Unsure what to say next, she said, "Well, I guess I'll head back to my house and take a shower there."

Duncan stared at her for a long second and Rose waited with bated breath for him to ask her to hang with him. Instead, he pulled the towel off his waist and faced the mirror to dry his hair with the towel. Despite the letdown that he didn't ask her to stay, Rose couldn't help but glance at his cut body and impressive package. The man just made her mouth water.

"That's probably a good idea since there's a crew of men at your house as we speak repairing the damage Rónán and James caused."

Rose's heart jerked. "My house! They tore apart my house?" Turning on her heel, she rushed to grab her car keys from the nightstand drawer.

Rose was about to leave the room when Duncan poked his head out the bathroom door. "Hey, I'll call you later, okay?"

"Okay," she called out, anxious to get home and see for herself just what was left of her house.

* * * * *

Rose hung up her phone after speaking with Michelle and her uncle. Michelle thanked her for the earrings she'd sent via Nigel and had wanted to hear all about Ireland. Nigel, true to his word, hadn't told anyone about her vampire status. *Like anyone would believe him anyway,* she thought. One day she would tell Michelle, but not yet.

"We're done, Ms. Sinclair," an older gentleman called from the doorway of her home, drawing her attention.

Rose approached him with a smile. "Thank you so much for all your help. How much do I owe you?"

The man shook his head. "Mr. Mordoor's already taken care of the bill. Have a great evening."

Rose said goodbye and watched him close the door behind him.

Without all the hammering and drilling going on, her house was achingly quiet. It was five o'clock and she still hadn't heard from Duncan. Even though she was disappointed, she had something she needed to do any way. Rose picked up her cell phone from the coffee table and dialed Our Home's nurses' station's phone number.

"Our Home," Helen answered.

"Hi Helen. It's Rose. I'm back from my trip."

"How'd it go, sweetie?" Helen asked, concern in her voice.

"I learned a lot about myself over the last few days," Rose answered truthfully. "Do you have my father's remains ready for me to pick up?"

"I sure do. Come get the urn whenever you're ready."

Rose took a deep breath. "I'll be by in fifteen minutes."

She hung up the phone, picked up her keys and purse and headed over to the retirement home.

*****

As she walked up to her mother's grave, Rose's steps slowed. Rónán stood staring down at her mother's tombstone, his hands clasped behind his back. His long black ponytail blew in the wind as he turned his silver gaze her way.

She expected anger to rush through her at seeing Rónán again. Instead, she felt deep regret. Regret for the curse he had to endure and how that had changed the man he was. She sensed the inner battle within Rónán. He had nothing to ground him.

He glanced down at the urn in her arms, then met her gaze.

"I don't know that I can ever forgive you for taking my father away from me, but I'll be honest and say I'm glad he no longer suffers."

Rónán approached her. He looked a little more casual in jeans and a black T-shirt. Yet, the dark material didn't hide his muscular upper body. If anything, it accentuated it.

He stopped a foot away and Rose had to elevate her head to look him in the eyes.

"We still have a connection. I'm yer Guardian. If Duncan steps out of line, hurts you in any way—"

Rose cut him off. "Duncan is the only man I've ever trusted."

"Yet you aren't mated to him. Why?" Rónán demanded, crossing his arms over his chest.

Rose stiffened at his drilling question. "It's none of your concern."

"I'm yer Guardian."

He said that as if it explained everything. Rose sighed. "In all the ways that matter, Duncan is my mate." Then an idea struck her that just might work to get Rónán involved, to give him the grounding he needed. "But if you want to keep tabs on Duncan, the best way would be to join him in leading the Sythens. After all, they are your people, too."

Rónán snorted at her suggestion, then vaulted straight up into the air, shifting to a raven. The raven cawed and circled a couple of times. Rónán's voice entered her head as he flew away.

*I'll always watch over you.*

Staring down at her mother's tombstone, Rose reminded herself to have someone come engrave her father's name underneath her mother's as her father had asked her to do upon his death. She lifted the top off the urn and carefully poured her father's remains across her mother's grave.

Her spirits lifted to know her father no longer felt sadness. He didn't want a funeral or people crying over his grave. He just wanted to be with his Anna. "Now you're with Mom, Dad. I love you both," she whispered into the warm night air.

Rose drove home thinking about the comment she made to Rónán. "In all the ways that matter, Duncan is my mate." If she could say that to Rónán, then why did she hold back from Duncan?

She pulled into her driveway and cut the engine. The truth hit her as she stared up into the clear night sky and the stars sparkling like diamonds.

She didn't need to hold back any longer. She knew Duncan cared for her. Over time she was certain he'd open up. He'd already done so little by little. Maybe he just needed to know how much she cared about him before he could give back a part of himself.

Determination set in as she climbed out of her car. She'd show Duncan just how much she loved him tonight if it was the last thing she did.

* * * * *

Rose's heart rate elevated when Duncan drove up her driveway on his motorcycle. Standing by her window, she tugged at her leather miniskirt and gave a wry smile. *Oh well, I'll make this sexy outfit work, even on a bike. Good thing it's really warm tonight.*

After she'd pulled her hair back in a low ponytail to keep it out of the way while they rode, she opened the door to greet Duncan. He didn't say a word or even smile. Her spirits plummeted. What was wrong?

His amber gaze swept down her body, then back to her face before he grabbed her hand and tugged her behind him.

Rose stopped him long enough to lock the door behind herself, then allowed Duncan to pull her to his bike.

When he put his hands on her waist, she asked, "What's wrong, Duncan? Did the meeting with the Vité not go well?"

*No talking for now,* Duncan spoke to her mentally as he lifted her and put her on his bike.

His tone was gruff as if he had a lot on his mind. Rose took the helmet he handed her and put it on her head, then she scooted back for him to get on the bike in front of her.

Once Duncan put his helmet on, he surprised Rose by moving her to the front of the bike and hopping on behind her.

"I'm driving?" She glanced back at him in surprise.

Duncan flipped his visor shut and nodded.

Shaking her head in confusion, Rose started his bike and backed out of the driveway.

*Where to?* she asked him as she took off down the road.

Duncan wrapped his arms around her waist and molded his body to hers. *Drive like you're going to Ian's place. I'll tell you where to turn when we get close.*

As they sped across the open highway, Rose chuckled that she'd been thankful it was a warm night. Duncan's body heat seemed to surround her, blocking the cooler wind, even though it was an unusually warm spring evening.

At Duncan's direction, Rose turned onto a wooded path not far from Ian's home, then made her way deeper into the woods and up a hill.

* * * * *

When they'd neared Ian's house, Duncan spoke to his twin mentally.

*Ian, I need your help with something.*

*What's up, Dunc?*

*Remember the connection you felt when you and I were both touching Rose at the same time? How you knew I called her Róisín?*

*Yeah?*

*Do you think Jax would be willing to help Rose understand what it means to have an Anima?*

*What are you getting at?* Ian asked sounding intrigued.

*We're almost to a high point in the woods behind your house. I'd like Rose to experience a full vampire mating. I want her to feel what you and Jax have…to know what she's missing.*

*Uh, you know what you're asking, right?*

*I know exactly what I'm asking. I want my Anima, Ian.*

*Let me see if Jax would be willing.*

*We're at the top of the hill. I see you walking outside toward Jax.*

* * * * *

Ian approached Jax from behind. She stood on their brick patio, her hands on her hips. She never looked sexier than when she was in shorts and a tank top, her body glistening. He could tell she'd been working out after she'd practiced with her crossbow.

"I believe that tree is deader than dead, *a ghrá,*" he teased, staring at the fifteen or so bolts that scattered the target pinned to the tree twenty feet away. Ian wrapped his arms around her waist and kissed her bare shoulder.

"Lucian's sister lied. Vampires do sweat," she said.

"Only when they push themselves as hard as you do," Ian teased, turning her around in his arms.

*Duncan's here somewhere,* she spoke in his mind, wrapping her arms around his neck.

*Actually, that's what I wanted to talk to you about.* Ian cupped her rear through her shorts. *How far would you be willing to go to help my brother find happiness?* he asked, planting a kiss on her neck.

Jax's breathing increased when his incisors scraped her skin. She met his gaze with a raised eyebrow, then gave him a sexy smile. *I'm open to suggestions.*

*****

*Hey, there's Ian and Jax,* Rose said mentally, cutting the bike's engine. Once she removed her helmet and hung it on the bike's handle, she glanced back at Duncan and asked, "Why are we up here?"

Duncan removed his helmet and put it next to his foot on the ground. When he reached for her waist and pulled her back against his chest, Rose put her hands on his rock-hard thighs. She was glad he used his vampire powers to hold the heavy bike up in the upright position so she could be wrapped all over in his warmth from his hard chest to his muscular thighs.

"Look," he whispered as he set his chin on her shoulder.

Rose turned to see Ian kissing Jax, his hands wrapped around her upper back. Then his hand moved to her hair and pulled out the chopsticks holding the dark mass up. Rose's heart rate ramped up when Ian dropped the sticks on the patio then raised the hem on Jax's top as if her were going to pull it off.

Rose coughed, then spoke in a whisper, "Um, surely they don't know they're being watched. Why *are* we watching them?"

In response, Duncan's hands covered her breasts. Rose's heart hammered. She breathed out, "What are you doing?" at the same time she glanced down to see Duncan's hands were still on her waist, yet she felt someone tugging on her nipples.

"I'm seducing your body," Duncan said in a low tone.

Rose jerked her gaze back to Ian and Jax to see Ian touching Jax's bared breasts. He'd removed his shirt and hers. Jax kissed Ian as her hands moved to unbutton his pants.

Rose's sex throbbed at the sight before her. Even though she felt like a voyeur, for some reason she felt very involved, as if Ian had actually touched her breasts. The timing was just too coincidental. Her breathing turned erratic and her excitement elevated. She gripped Duncan's rock-hard, leather-covered thighs, crushing the soft material under her fingers.

Rose's nipples tweaked as if someone pinched them. The sensation went straight to her core.

"Dun-Duncan, I just felt what Jax felt."

"Are you excited, Róisín?" he asked in a husky voice.

"I…" She paused and swallowed hard when she felt fangs scrap against her neck at the same time Ian kissed Jax on the throat.

Rose gasped as her own fangs extended to their full length. Her body was in full arousal and hunger clenched her belly.

"Yes," she hissed out. Her skin pebbled in goose bumps and her body quaked at the scene before her.

Ian lifted Jax and laid her down on the wooden bench beside the patio, then he slowly spread her thighs with his hands.

Rose moaned when she felt invisible hands on her thighs, applying pressure. Instinctively her own thigh muscles relaxed and her sex began to throb in anticipation. When she felt fingers brush her entrance at the same time Ian touched Jax, she whispered in a shaky voice, "Duncan?"

"I'm experiencing everything you're feeling," Duncan responded. "Ian's not touching you. He's touching Jax. What you're feeling is what Jax is feeling, not your own response."

"But I *am* responding," she wailed.

"So am I," he breathed out in a husky voice next to her ear.

When she felt a finger slide across her clit, Rose tensed. "I can't…" she began.

Suddenly the sensation of Ian touching Jax stopped. The only thing left was her own throbbing arousal.

Duncan's hands cupped her breasts before he lifted her tank top over her head. Cool air teased her nipples, making them pucker and ache to be touched.

Duncan rolled her nipples between his fingers as he said in a dark, seductive tone, "Do you know what I'm looking forward to experiencing? What Ian feels when Jax feeds. I want that from you, Rose. I want you to want my blood, to revel in it. Just like Jax does with Ian."

Rose stared at Ian and Jax, watched him thrust deep inside his Anima, his hips rocking against Jax. Then she saw him kiss Jax's neck, but she knew he wasn't just kissing her. Rose's stomach tightened in sexual response. Ian had plunged his fangs into Jax's neck.

Even from their distance, she heard Jax's moan of pleasure. The sound jarred Rose all the way to her toes. She'd never seen or heard anything more arousing in her life.

Taking a deep breath, she nodded. "Okay, I'm ready now."

"Are you sure?" Duncan asked.

She squeezed his thighs once more to let him know she could handle it.

Rose gasped at the onslaught of emotions that began flowing through her. She felt Ian's fangs in her neck, the intense pleasure Jax experienced from his bite. Rose's hips rocked and her lower stomach muscles bunched as she experienced a slight fluttering within her own walls as Jax began to climax.

Rose gritted her teeth at the sensations rocking through her, but she maintained control. Barely.

Then Jax bit Ian's neck and Rose felt Duncan tense behind her. She heard his deep groan, felt his desire spike. Rose used her own powers to intervene, cutting off the flow of emotions between the brothers. Duncan would only experience that kind of pleasure with her.

She turned halfway in his arms, her voice trembling. "All I ever wanted was to hear you say you loved me. Just once."

Surprise lit Duncan's amber gaze. He cupped her face. "How could you question it, Rose? I love you more than life itself. You are everything I want in a mate, my match in all ways."

Rose gave him a sheepish smile. "Sometimes it's nice hear it…to be certain."

Duncan's gaze searched her face, his golden eyes turning tender. "I thought that constant control meant I was strong. That if I didn't show my emotions, no one could ever hurt me. What I've learned is the strongest men don't fear letting their emotions show." He gave her a devastating smile. "In case you're wondering…now I'm seducing your heart. *Tá grá agam duit, Róisín.* That means, 'I love you'. Your Irish lessons will start tomorrow," he finished with a wink.

Rose wrapped her arms around his neck and kissed him, speaking in his mind, *I love you too, with all my heart. You are my one true mate.*

Duncan kissed her hard on the mouth, then handed her the tank top he'd pulled off earlier. "Let's go."

Rose grinned at his serious expression. Excitement shot through her as she faced forward, shrugged into her top and grabbed her helmet. Placing the helmet on her head, she asked, *Where to now?*

Duncan put his helmet on and clasped her waist. *To my place in town.*

A chill shot down her spine at the knowledge he wanted to take her home. Excitement made her hands shake and her heart rate elevate as she started the bike.

* * * * *

Rose didn't know what to expect when she entered Duncan's home. While Duncan shut the front door, she took in the contemporary décor. The black furniture and chrome accents made his place appear cool to her, untouchable, at a distance—like the image Duncan showed the world.

He wrapped his arms around her waist from behind. Nuzzling her neck, he whispered, "You bring life to my place."

She glanced up at him. "I admit I like your other home better. It has a cozier feel."

"That's my getaway house. That house no one sees but Ian and me."

Rose smiled at the pride in his voice. "You picked out all the furniture at that house, didn't you?"

Duncan moved his hands to her thighs and laid a kiss on her neck, mumbling, "Mmmm-hmmm."

Shivers shot down her body when he laid his hand on her lower belly and pushed her backward at the same time he nudged his erection against her rear end.

While he nipped at her shoulder, Duncan waved his hand and the fireplace in front of the leather sofa and chair came on.

When the flames roared to life, Rose teased, "It's a bit warm outside for a fire."

She watched in amusement as Duncan flicked his wrist near the wall beside him and she saw the digital readout on the thermostat go all the way down. When the air conditioning kicked on, his husky voice entered her head.

*I want that night by the fire, Rose. The one we should've had together.*

Rose remembered how that night ended, how sexually frustrated she'd been. She'd been so desperate to maintain control.

She turned in his arms and wrapped her arms around his neck, pressing her hips against his. "You think you can handle the flood of emotions that'll be coming your way, *a ghrá*?"

Duncan's amber gaze burned, turning darker. He gave her a cocky smile and grabbed her rear, yanking her close. Rocking his hips against hers, he said, "I'm looking forward to the onslaught."

Rose's heart beat harder when Duncan pressed his lips against her neck, his voice a husky purr against her skin. "I smell your blood under your sweet skin. I hear it rushing through your veins." He nipped at her neck. "How much do you want it?"

Rose lowered her lips to his cheek, then ran her tongue along the five o'clock shadow that had formed on his jaw, enjoying the rough texture. She clasped his hard erection through his leather pants at the same time she nipped at his neck. "How bad do *you* want it?" she responded in her sexiest voice.

Duncan growled low in his throat and walked her back against the side wall. As his mouth descended to hers, Duncan's fingers dug into her hips, his hold tight, possessive. Rose reveled in the controlled urgency that emanated from him when his lips covered hers in a hungry kiss.

He pushed her miniskirt up her hips then slowly rocked his erection against her sex. Rose felt his heat through their clothes and her pulse skipped to a faster beat. Blood rushed to her sex, making it throb.

When he thrust his tongue against hers, she wrapped her arms tighter around his neck, returning his intemperate kiss. With deliberate movements, his hands slid past her underwear to cup her bare cheeks. The sensation of his fingers massaging her ass made Rose moan in anticipation.

Duncan's fingers flexed on her soft skin, then he swiftly lifted her in his arms. He ground his cock against her entrance through their clothes, then groaned into her mouth as he spoke in her mind, *I'm so damned horny. You make me ache, I want you so much.*

Their heated breathing mingled as she nipped at his lower lip, replying, *I've never wanted to be taken so bad in my life.*

Duncan turned and carried her over to the rug by the fireplace. Setting her down on her feet, he lifted his shirt over his head and tossed it on the floor. Rose began to pant as she kicked off her shoes and unzipped her skirt, pushing it and her underwear down to the floor.

As Duncan lifted her shirt over her head, she stepped out of the pool of clothes at her feet and moved them out of the way with her foot.

Duncan slipped his boots, pants and underwear off, then straightened to face her, an intense expression on his face.

The fire's flickering light highlighted the dips and hollows of his muscular chest, but the flames' reflection off the silver necklace on his neck drew her attention.

"This is new." She lifted the coin-like medallion that hung on the necklace in her hand. She ran her finger along the flat circle of silver. It was a couple of inches in diameter with black tick-marks along the edges. They were similar to the ones on the outer edge of her mother's locket.

Duncan stepped close and reached around her neck to remove her mother's necklace. Rose stared at him in confusion as he laid her mother's locket down on the coffee table.

"Duncan, I don't under—" But she gasped, cutting herself off when Duncan dangled another silver necklace in between them.

Rose lifted the charm hanging from it to see it was a Celtic trinity knot. It had similar tick marks along the smooth circular edge surrounding the knot.

Duncan hooked the necklace around her neck, then lifted her chin so she met his serious gaze. "I had these made while we were in Ireland."

Sliding his fingers along the cool chain that dangled in the hollow between her breasts, he lifted her charm and placed the trinity knot from her necklace on top of his medallion.

Rose's heart hammered as he turned the knot until the markings along the edges perfectly lined up with the markings on hers. She jerked her gaze to his as he continued, "I want to be the only man in your life, the only Guardian you'll ever need."

Tears filled her eyes as she clasped the two charms together in a tight fist. Her heart thudding against her chest, she said, "I know you said the markings were Ogham. What do they say?"

Duncan turned her tight fist over and placed a kiss on her wrist, his amber gaze full of love. "It says, 'I love you'."

Deep emotion rushed forth, stopping in her throat. Rose couldn't speak. *I love you, too,* she replied as she wrapped her hand around his erection and ran her thumb across the plum tip.

Duncan groaned and let go of her hand to kiss her neck.

Rose released the necklaces and bent her knees as she trailed kisses down Duncan's sculpted chest and hard stomach.

Then she licked his cock all the way around, her method slow and thorough. Duncan slid the rubber band out of her hair. He fisted his hands in the mass and rocked his hips as she took his erection deep inside her mouth.

"The next time we do this, I'm buying some ice cream," he breathed out, his fingers digging into her scalp.

Rose swirled her tongue around the ridge under the tip of his cock and Duncan growled, his hips moving faster.

Putting his hands on her shoulders, he pulled her away from his cock then tugged her to the floor with him. Rose sat down facing Duncan.

The firelight reflected off his burnt amber gaze as he traced his fingers down the chain around her neck. His hungry gaze followed the seductive trail his fingers took.

Duncan lifted her hands, kissed one palm and then the other and set them on the carpet beside her hips.

"Don't move them."

Rose chuckled, remembering the last time he did this to her. Her eyebrow elevated. "Do I have a choice this time?"

*You had a choice that night, too.* He smiled, displaying his fangs. The sight made her heart pump faster.

Rose sat with her hands by her sides waiting with bated breath to see Duncan's plan.

The air conditioning was doing its job. The room felt cool around them, but the fire's warmth penetrated her skin as well as the flame of pent-up desire burning within her.

Duncan bent her knees and put her feet flat on the floor, then crawled on hands and knees between her legs and over her body. The hungry look on his face was intense and so full of desire her body ached for his touch.

He put his hands flat on the floor beside hers, his mouth a breath away from her lips. Placing a kiss on her jaw, he spoke in her mind. *Tilt your head back. I want to see that gorgeous long hair touching the floor.*

Rose's breathing turned shallow at his request. She closed her eyes and obeyed.

"More," he said, his voice gentle, yet demanding. Her stomach clenched in anticipation as she moved her hips forward slightly and arched her back, leaning her head back farther.

Rose gasped when she felt his stubble graze the insides of her breasts. He planted a kiss on her charm as he spoke in her mind. *Mine to protect.*

Then his lips moved to her nipple, sucking hard. *Mine to take.*

The ache between her legs turned to a burning throb when she felt an openmouthed kiss on her sex. *Mine to love.*

Rose whimpered.

Then she felt Duncan move along her body until his teeth clamped on her throat and his cock pressed against her wet entrance. *And mine to mate,* he finished in a determined tone in her head. She felt his strong, yet loving presence in her consciousness, waiting outside her mind for her to let him in.

Rose's arms began to tremble. She felt so much love for this man, she couldn't contain it any longer.

She wrapped her arms around his neck and clasped him to her, lowering them to the floor at the same time she let down her mental barriers, allowing him free rein inside her mind.

She felt Duncan tense at the emotional onslaught that flooded his way. His hips jerked forward and he spoke in her mind, his tone barely in control.

*I-I can't hold back…wanted to take it slow.*

*I don't want you to,* she replied. *I want you out of control, Duncan.* Rose lifted her hips, relishing his forceful thrust. She keened her pleasure when Duncan's fangs sank deep into her neck. He groaned and began to suck hard on her throat as he withdrew and pistoned inside her once more.

Rose moved her hands to his rear, clasping the hard flesh to pull him deeper.

Her heart pounded at the sensations running through her, the white-hot energy that seemed to flow between them, zinging back and forth as her impending orgasm built. As she came, she forced heat to her center and below, groaning at the molten sensations vibrating in her core. Wave after wave of pleasurable sensations rippled through her, making her gasp at the intensity.

"Holyfuckingshit!" Duncan hissed out as he withdrew his fangs. He rammed his cock deeper inside her again and again as if he wanted to brand her his very own.

When her climax stopped, Rose rolled them over and pulled herself off Duncan's erection. His eyes darkened and his breathing came out in harsh bellows as she sat on his stomach and shoved his shoulders down on the floor.

Rose gave him the sexiest "fuck me" look he'd ever seen as she lifted up on her knees and rubbed her sex against the head of his cock, teasing him with her heat.

Duncan dug his fingers into her hips. *Take me as deep as you can,* he whispered.

Rose leaned down and kissed his mouth, rocking her hips. The tip of his cock entered her and Duncan thought he was going to explode. Then she grasped his shoulders and shoved all the way down on his cock, surrounding him in her slick, warm channel.

Duncan's hips jerked and he gritted his teeth to hold back his orgasm. Rose pulled off him once more, cock-teasing him with her wet lips as she rubbed against his erection.

*Rose,* he warned, clenching his jaw at the same time he moved his fingers to her rear and palmed the soft flesh. His fingers inched closer between her cheeks as he applied pressure to that sensitive spot between her entrance and her anus. Duncan relished her moan of passion and the sound of her heart rate stuttering. She wanted him.

Rose pulled him to a seated position and ran her tongue up his neck. Duncan stared into her aqua gaze as he cupped her sexy ass and guided her sweet body right over his cock. Then Rose sank down on him again, groaning in ecstasy. His shoulders tensed as he felt her muscles clenching around him in the throes of her second climax.

A deep growl vibrated within his chest. He expelled the breath he'd been holding in a long, low groan as Rose slowed her rocking movements to whisper in his ear.

"Is this what you want, *a ghrá*?" she panted out right before she sank her fangs into his neck.

Duncan had never felt anything more erotic than Rose clamping her teeth on his throat.

He rolled them over and began to shaft his Anima to the rhythm of her long, hard sucking draws as she fed from him. With each swallow she took, his heart swelled and his groin tightened. Gritting his teeth, he purposefully slowed his thrusts, wanting his arousal to build to an even higher pitch, to make it an explosive union.

When Rose grabbed the back of his neck and pulled him closer as she sank her fangs even deeper, he almost lost control. But he held on until he felt her walls clenching his cock once more. Feeling her orgasm was all it took to send him over the edge. Duncan roared through his own soul-deep climax. He relished all the sensory sensations hammering through him as he rammed his cock into Rose harder, faster, deeper than he ever had.

As much as he'd fantasized about Rose and him together, nothing could have prepared him for the reality of a full vampire mating with a woman he loved. He'd never get enough of this…of Rose taking his blood.

When he was finally spent, he realized she still had her fangs embedded deep in his neck. *Róisín?* he asked.

*Shhhh,* she spoke in his mind, her heart hammering beneath his. *Let me enjoy the sensation a little longer. It feels so primal.*

Duncan chuckled, then jerked his hips against her, thrusting deep once more. *And this doesn't?*

Rose withdrew her fangs and laved his wound closed. She laughed. "Is that 'male satisfaction' I hear in your voice?"

Duncan kissed her long and hard, tangling his tongue with hers. *Damn right, baby.*

Rose smiled up at him, then ran her tongue along her lower lip. "I hope you liked being bitten because I'm going to want to bite you all the time now."

Duncan's nostrils flared at the desire in her beautiful blue-green gaze. Nuzzling her neck, he said, "You're the only one who could make me this out of control."

She kissed him on the jaw, then smiled. "I seem to have very little control when I'm around you, too."

Duncan withdrew from Rose and planted kisses down her abdomen until he reached her thighs.

He heard her heart begin to beat faster when he pushed her legs far apart. Rose lifted her head to stare down at him. "What are you doing?"

He gave her a cocky grin right before he laved at her clit. "You really didn't think I was done with my Anima, did you?" He rubbed his thumb over her swollen nub, enjoying the smell of her scent mixed with his. He couldn't wait until she was ovulating again. If she thought he was all over her now… "Say *Sonuachar*," he said.

"*Sonuachar*," Rose breathed out, then moaned and arched her back, her pink nipples jutting in the air.

"It's the Irish equivalent of Anima," he said with a smile before he lowered his head to suck on her clit, nipping and teasing the sensitive skin.

Her keening cry of pleasure made his cock rev back to attention. Damn, she did it for him like no other.

"*Sonuachar*. I like the sound of that," she purred.

*Me too,* a ghrá. *Me too.*

## Chapter Seventeen

ꟙ

Rose picked up Duncan's phone on the first ring, her heart racing. Intuitively she knew it was her *Sonuachar* calling. "Hey, how'd your first meeting go?"

Duncan laughed. "Two days as my *Sonuachar* and already you know it's me before I say a word?"

"Yeah, I'm special that way," Rose replied with a grin. "So, how'd it go?"

"It was tense to say the least. I told the clan members it was their choice if they wanted to remain bald, but they no longer had to hide who they really were. Then Rónán showed up and all hell broke loose," he chuckled.

"That good, huh?" She was glad to see Duncan had a sense of humor about it.

"Actually, once the Vité and I got everyone calmed down, I think the Sythen clan members liked the idea that Rónán was going take James' place. I guess they saw it as his 'right'. Lucian and I agreed Rónán should take James' property as his own. Who the hell knows if he'll actually occupy the place. Now, if I could just get Rónán to call the clan members Sythens instead of Atruans."

Rose couldn't help but laugh. "I'm sure that went over well."

"Don't get me started." He sighed but she could hear the amused smile in his tone. "But the meeting isn't why I'm calling. I'm in the mood to celebrate. Why don't you meet me at the Five Star Pavilion at seven? There's a show I want to check out."

"You aren't coming home first?"

"No, I've got to debrief with Ian."

"Speaking of shows, how's all this Sythen politics stuff going to affect your gigs?" she asked, her stomach tensing. She knew how much Duncan's music meant to him.

"It'll all work out," came his positive response. "See you in an hour and a half."

Rose hung up the phone with a smile on her face, ready to spend an evening with Duncan. As soon as her fingers lifted from the receiver, a tingling sensation rippled up her spine. But she refused to let the fact that Rónán was near get to her. She turned to walk up the chrome spiral staircase and saw the Guardian standing halfway up the stairs.

He wore a black leather vest and black jeans and today he'd left his hair unbound. The wavy black hair surrounding his face made his sharp, handsome features even more distinctive and his persona appear even darker.

Rose took a deep, calming breath. "What are you doing here, Rónán?"

As he walked toward her, his feet made no sound on the stairs. How did he do that? she wondered. He moved like a cat!

When he was a step away, towering over her, he stopped and folded his muscular arms across his chest. A scowl formed on his face.

"Ye should've felt me coming, Rose. Expect the unexpected."

Rose raised her chin a notch and narrowed her gaze. "I did feel you coming. I just chose not to respond. You can see yourself out."

She moved to go around Rónán's large frame, but he blocked her path. "Ye need to expand and sharpen yer powers."

She raised her eyebrow at his arrogance. "My *Sonuachar* and his mother can teach me what I need to know."

Rónán snorted. "Tressa can't teach you battle skills and Duncan hasn't even tapped into the extent of his own powers yet."

Rose vividly remembered her first introduction to Rónán and his version of what she now realized was "teaching her". "Your methods are—"

"Effective," he cut her off in a harsh tone.

As extreme as Rónán could be, Rose had to agree he had a point. In battle mode, she'd reacted swiftly and without conscious thought, shifting in sheer defense. Yet she knew there was no way in hell Duncan would let Rónán train her. But if Duncan wanted to keep an eye on Rónán, to know the man's head and heart…what better way than to know how the man fought?

"Then teach us both," she countered, hiding a smile. She knew the idea of teaching Duncan would rub Rónán the wrong way.

"No."

"Suit yourself." Rose gave a nonchalant shrug, then bent her knees and took a flying leap over him to land at the top of the stairs.

She turned to walk down the hall, but Rónán blocked her path once more. Damn, he was unbelievably fast. Like a blur.

"So be it. Ye both will learn."

Before she could respond, Rónán shifted into mist. He spoke in her mind as he slid through a windowsill on the main floor. *I'll be in touch.*

*Don't be so sure you won't learn a thing or two from us,* she thought as she headed down the hall and entered her bedroom to change clothes.

* * * * *

As soon as Rose walked in the main entrance of the Five Star Pavilion, Michelle called out, "Rose! Come on. We're waiting on you."

Rose's brows drew together in confusion when she saw Ian, Jax and Mark standing next to her uncle and Michelle. What were the other vampires doing there?

Her chest tensed as she approached them. *Please, don't tell me you've told Michelle about me being a vampire,* she spoke in her uncle's mind.

Nigel hugged her and whispered in her ear, "No, sweetie, Michelle doesn't know the whole lot of you are vampires."

Rose hugged him back, replying in a low tone, "Thanks, Nigel. One day I'll tell her."

When Rose pulled away from her uncle, Michelle clasped her hand and tugged her close, hissing in her ear, "Why didn't you tell me Duncan had a twin?"

Rose smiled and whispered back, "Because he's already taken. Why torture you?"

Rose's gaze landed on the handsome couple standing next to Ian and Jax. They appeared to be in their mid-forties. The woman projected a comforting vibe—like her mother always did. Rose smiled and put out her hand to the woman with strawberry-blonde hair. "I'm Rose. You must be Duncan's parents." Rose glanced at the dark-haired man and continued, "I see a bit of both of you in Ian and Duncan. It's nice to meet you."

Tressa ignored her hand and pulled her close in a tight hug. "I'm Tressa and my *Sonuachar* is Marcus. You're a part of our family now, Rose. Welcome."

Rose hugged her back, loving Duncan's family already. "Thank you, Tressa."

*We'll talk later, dear,* the older woman spoke in her mind.

Rose smiled and nodded, thankful for Duncan's mother. Tressa understood what Rose's mother had gone through. She hoped Tressa would be willing to help her explore the powers she inherited from her mother.

Tressa kissed her on her cheek and spoke in her mind, amusement in her tone. *Of course I will.*

*You read my mind…without me knowing you were there?* Rose looked at the woman in surprise.

Tressa gave her a knowing smile. *As I said, we'll talk later.*

Nigel rubbed his hands together. "Well, now that we're all here. Why don't we head down to the show?"

Rose glanced around, looking for Duncan as she addressed her uncle. "I was supposed to meet Duncan here. What's going on?"

"Duncan just said for us to meet him here, too," Jax said.

"Yeah, we were wondering the same thing," Mark chimed in.

"My guess is Duncan's a bit busy at the moment, since Nigel was able to get Strainséir to play another night…well, at least a few songs, then a new artist will play for an hour," Michelle said.

"Come on, everyone," Nigel encouraged. "Duncan said he'd meet us inside."

So, Duncan was playing tonight. Rose's heart swelled as she followed the group. When she'd mated with Duncan the other night and finally shared her mind, he'd opened his to her as well. She was surprised to learn that none of his family, including his twin, knew of his band's success. They just thought he 'played around town'."

Tonight Duncan was sharing a part of himself with the ones who meant the most in his life. She smiled as they followed Nigel to their front row seats. She couldn't be more proud of her *Sonuachar* than she was at this moment.

The fans screamed and rushed forward when the lights dimmed and the band took the stage, but Rose was too busy watching Duncan's family's faces, waiting for the lights to illuminate the stage. When the lights came on, Duncan sang and played his guitar with all his heart. His excited energy projected outward as he walked the stage, interacting and working the crowd with his amazing charisma.

Rose smiled at the sight of tears streaming down Tressa's cheeks and the proud look on Marcus' face as he wrapped his arm around his mate. Mark looked pleasantly shocked, but Ian's expression tugged at her heart.

At first, he went pale and deep hurt crossed his face. When Rose saw Jax kiss her Anima on the cheek and wrap her arm around his waist in a tight hug, Rose moved close to Ian and grabbed his hand.

She spoke in his mind among the loud music and cheering fans. *I've been inside Duncan's mind, Ian. Your acceptance and approval means everything to him.*

Ian turned his amber gaze to her as the bright lights flashed up on stage.

*Next to Jax, my brother means everything to me.* He squeezed her hand. *Take good care of him for me.*

*I promise.* Rose squeezed his hand back and was relieved to see Ian smile—a smile so much like her mate's.

When she started to move back to her seat, Rose heard Jax's voice in her head. *Thank you, Rose. Tonight was a real shocker to Ian. He was truly thrown.*

Rose met Jax's steady gaze. *Thank you for helping us.*

*It was my pleasure,* Jax replied with a wink and a smile.

Rose grinned at Jax, then moved back to stand in front of her seat next to the stage. The lights had gone down and only a spotlight lit up the stage.

Duncan set down his electric guitar in the guitar rack and picked up an acoustic one before he sat down on the stool a roadie had pulled to the center of the stage. Hooking his boot heel on the lowest rung, he moved the mike to the right height.

"You all having a good time tonight?" he asked.

The crowd roared their approval. Catcalls and whistles followed.

Duncan grinned, then began strumming his guitar at a slow, ballad's pace. "I wrote this song entitled 'You are My Music' for a special person in my life." He glanced in Rose's direction as if he could see her beyond the bright spotlight, then finished, "I hope she likes it."

*I thought I had my life figured out, knew it backward and forward without a doubt.*

*But the day we met that all changed. In an instant, my life rearranged.*

*What had always seemed wrong, suddenly became very right. All I wanted was to hold you tight.*

*You are the flower in my life. The one who helped me grow into the man you see tonight.*

*These words come straight from the soul, 'cause baby I want you to know…*

*You've changed my life, my heart, my peace, made me whole and set me free.*

*You are the beat within my soul and I'll never let you go*

*You are the song, I can't refuse it…*

*Baby… you are my music.*

*I might not always know what's on your mind, but that's all right, 'cause we'll be fine.*

*You were the one who taught me to share, what it meant to care.*

*Now I know keeping things bottled up inside only lets the truth slide by.*

*Baby, no matter what life deals us, we'll get through it…*

*You've changed my life, my heart, my peace, made me whole and set me free.*

*You've given me what I need, you fill me up so completely.*

*You're my everything and I don't wanna lose it.*

*Mmmmm, hummmm, baby…you are my music.*

*From day one you saw right through to the rhythm within me. It took me a while to see what you see.*

*You've shown me life is about taking risks. When the day is done I'll have no regrets.*

*In return, I've given you my heart, my soul, my blood…'cause there's no question you're the only one.*

*You've changed my life, my heart, my peace, made me whole and set me free.*

*You've opened my eyes, made me feel. Oh, I've never felt so real.*

*You're the color missing in my life… that's all there is to it.*

*Mmmmm hmmmmm, you are my music. Yeah, baby, you are my music.*

As the music faded away and the stage lights came back on, Duncan looked right at her and said, "I love you, Rose. You are and will always be…the music in my soul."

The female fans in the room gave a collective sigh as the romantic song ended, then deafening screams and cheers for an encore ensued as they begged for more.

Choking back tears, her heart full of love, Rose put a shaky hand over her mouth. Duncan finally sang a song he wrote and composed. Just for her. Never in her wildest dreams did she think she'd meet a man who would take hold of her heart like this one did.

He stood and while a stagehand removed the stool, Duncan handed his guitar to another roadie. Then Duncan removed the mike from the stand and spoke to the crowd.

"I'd like to introduce you to Jake Harris. Come on out here, Jake."

A young, dark-haired man in his mid-twenties walked on stage, carrying his electric guitar. He had an engaging smile as he waved to the audience greeting him. Duncan turned back to the crowd. "Jake's an up-and-comer who has a voice unlike any I've ever heard. The band's going to back him up as he sings." He gave the fans a devastating smile. "I'll let you all decide for yourselves."

Duncan set the mike back in the stand and clapped the younger man on the shoulder. "They're all yours, Jake."

* * * * *

After the concert, Rose took Duncan's family over to Rosco's to wait for Duncan to join them. As they filed into a circular booth in the corner of the bar, Michelle made sure to sit next to Rose…or more specifically next to Mark. Rose chuckled at Michelle. The girl was incorrigible when it came to men. Mark didn't seem to mind at all, if the heated looks he kept giving Michelle were any indication.

*She doesn't know any of us are vampires, Mark. I'd like to keep it that way for now,* Rose warned him mentally.

When Mark glanced her way and nodded his understanding, she frowned at the pink gash on his cheek. It was a wound he had to have received recently.

*Where'd that come from?* she asked.

*Your Anima,* he replied in a dry tone. *He had me up at the crack of dawn this morning, working on battle techniques. Said my training was long overdue.*

Rose chuckled. *Be careful what you wish for.*

*I'll drink to that.* Mark gave her a wry smile as he picked up his longneck and took a swig.

When Tressa asked Mark a question, drawing his attention, Michelle elbowed Rose and whispered, "What do you know about Duncan's friend, Mark? That blond hair and sexy smile makes my stomach flutter."

"He's a cop and a good man."

"A cop?" An excited expression lit Michelle's eyes and she dug her hand in her jeans front pocket. "I almost forgot. I cut this out of the paper today. Didn't you say the boy's name who took advantage of you in high school was Jeff Greer?"

Her gut clenched at Michelle's mention of Jeff's name, but Rose couldn't keep herself from looking at the newspaper clipping.

*Jeff Greer turned himself into the authorities yesterday. After he was treated for a broken arm and cracked ribs, Mr. Greer confessed to being the serial rapist the police have tried to capture the last eight years. Mr. Greer said he started out date raping, but quickly learned the rush wasn't enough. Then he moved on to rape in his need to escalate the fear in his victims. Since his confession, several of his victims have come forward. Mr. Greer is being held without bond as he awaits his trial date.*

Rose's gaze jerked to Duncan's as he walked up to their table. The look on her face must've clued him in something was up. He glanced down at the clipping in her hand then met her gaze with an unapologetic one. His amber eyes narrowed as he slid in the booth next to her.

*I'll always protect what's mine, Róisín.*

*All I want to know is one answer. Was he guilty of those other crimes?* Her stomach tensed at the answer she might receive.

Duncan raised his eyebrow at her question. "Yes."

Relief flooded through her and Rose reached over and kissed him on the cheek, whispering in his mind, *Thank you for looking out for me.*

"By the way, your client, Mr. Reed—his phone number has been disconnected. I wasn't able to find him."

"Duncan!" She didn't like the fact he'd taken the information from her mind, even if she understood his motivation.

"As I said, I look out for my own," he replied as he kissed her on the temple.

While Duncan spoke to his parents, Rose was too happy to be angry with him. She crumpled the newspaper in her hand and put in on the table before she tapped Michelle on the shoulder. When Michelle turned to her, she hugged her best friend. "Thank you for telling me about the article. I've been kind of out of the loop with the news lately."

Michelle pulled back from her hug and spoke over the loud music playing in the bar. "You never did tell me…did you learn any more about your mother while you were in Ireland?"

Rose smiled. "I learned that my mother had wonderful friends."

"You *are* going to take me with you when you go to Ireland again, right?" Michelle asked, an expectant look on her face.

"You bet, Mish."

"Good." Michelle grinned. "Now, I've got a pressing matter to attend to…and that's how to entice a certain sexy blond cop onto the dance floor."

Rose glanced at Mark as he said to Duncan, "That was a helluva show, Duncan." She noted that was the first time Mark had taken his gaze off Michelle.

"Somehow, I don't think that'll be a problem." She winked at Mish.

Mark turned his gaze Michelle's way. "Would you like to dance?"

"I thought you'd never ask." Michelle laughed as she clasped his hand.

Rose and Duncan moved to let Mark and Michelle out of the booth, then settled back in their seats beside Ian and Jax.

"Nice show, Dunc," Ian said.

Duncan gave his brother a broad smile. "Thanks."

"I'm just so proud of you," Tressa said. "Thank you for inviting us, son," Marcus agreed.

Duncan grinned. "I'm glad you enjoyed it, especially since I'll be mostly behind the scenes from now on."

Rose glanced at Duncan in surprise. "What?"

He lifted her hand and kissed her palm. "I meant what I said. You are my music, Rose. That's why I was late. Nigel and I were talking in his office."

"And?" She waited, resisting the urge to jump in his head and extract the answer herself.

"Your uncle wants to go back to Ireland for a while. He plans to spend half his time here and half his time there. So he's going to need someone to help him run the Five Star."

"You can't give up your music, Duncan. It means too much to you." She felt her chest begin to tighten.

"I'm not giving it up. I'm going to be doing what I love most—creating and producing songs. I've held the band back long enough. Being what I am…you know I can't put myself out there on a national level. But with Jake, the band can see their full potential. You saw yourself how Jake had the crowd eating out of his hand tonight."

Rose tilted her head to the side, realization dawning. "Several of the songs he sang tonight…those were yours, weren't they?"

Duncan gave her a sheepish smile. "Yeah, they were mine. And this time around, you'll hear them on the radio, too. Jake just signed a recording contract and wants me to collaborate on this album."

Duncan clasped her hand. "I can't do this without you, Rose. You know this casino better than anyone. Nigel hoped I could convince you to join the family business."

"I'll do everything in my power to help Nigel find happiness," she vowed.

"Even giving up your PI business?" he asked.

Rose laughed. "My PI business paid the bills. I'll be a bit busy helping run the Five Star to continue it."

Duncan grinned, then kissed her hand. "I love you."

Rose's heart jumped at the look of desire in his gaze.

Tressa and Marcus moved to slide out of the booth. "Well, boys, we're going home," Tressa announced.

Duncan slid out of the booth, saying, "I'll walk you out."

Once they walked outside and the door closed behind them, muffling the loud music in the bar, Tressa hugged Duncan. "You put on a wonderful show. I'm thrilled to see you so happy."

Before his mother pulled away, Duncan met her gaze. "I've been meaning to ask you. Why didn't you tell me Rose was a psychic vampire when you told me the history of the Atruan priestesses?"

Tressa smiled up at her son as she stepped into her mate's arms. "I was inside your head, Duncan, remember? I learned what method you planned to employ to get Rose to mate with you." She raised her eyebrow. "I just wanted Rose to have her own ace up her sleeve."

Duncan laughed outright at her comment, then looked at his father. "Are we always going to be one-upped by our women?"

"Get used to it," Ian said from behind him.

Duncan turned to see his brother with his arm wrapped around Jax's waist.

"You leaving too?"

Ian nodded. "I'm impressed as hell at your talent. Call me tomorrow."

Duncan nodded his agreement. After his family left, Duncan walked back inside to get Rose.

When he slid in the booth, Rose was watching Michelle and Mark dance.

"Do you think he'll take her blood?" she asked in a tense voice.

"Only if she wishes it," Duncan replied. "But out of deference to you, he'll erase her memory of her blood being taken."

He clasped her hand in his. "Why are you so reluctant for your uncle to become a vampire and for your best friend to know what you are?"

Rose glanced up at him and squeezed his hand. "I'm happy for my uncle. It's not that I'm against him becoming a vampire. I just didn't want him to become a vampire while two rogue vampires threatened my life. I'd already lost my father. I didn't want to pull him into this and lose my uncle, too."

She glanced at Michelle and Mark, continuing with a sigh, "As for Michelle, she's very impetuous and has a mischievous streak a mile wide. Who knows what she'd do if she knew. I guess I'd like to wait until she matures a little more before I'll tell her."

Relief washed over him that it wasn't because she regretted being converted to a Ruean herself. The question had nagged at him ever since she'd first refused to tell her uncle about his and her vampire status.

She cut her gaze his way, a confused look on her face. "How did you know about Jeff Greer and Mr. Reed but not about my uncle and Michelle?"

Duncan gave her a wry smile. "Your mind has facets I've yet to break through. But don't think I'll give up trying." Tugging on her hand, he slid out of the booth. "Let's get out of here."

Rose squeezed his hand as she stood. Duncan smiled at the sound of her heart racing. "I've got to tell Michelle I'm leaving."

Duncan looked at Mark and spoke in his mind, then he glanced back at Rose, smiling. "It's done."

Rose smiled up at him, then followed him out of the bar.

* * * * *

Rose lay on the hammock, swinging slowly and enjoying the warm wind blowing in the trees. A thunderstorm threatened, the scent of rain hung heavy in the air.

Duncan had taken her back to his second home. She'd been unconscious when she'd arrived and when she left his home the first time around, so it was nice to know it was located not far from the North Shore between Lake Bluff and Waukegan.

On the way there, she told him about Rónán's visit. He grudgingly agreed with her assessment saying, "As long as the damn vamp puts on some real clothes during our training, I'll bet Rónán teaching us will be an education in and of itself." He'd been quiet the rest of the way, choosing just to hold her hand while he drove her car to the house.

She smiled when the first drops of rain hit the porch's roof above her head. The sudden smell of damp earth and wet leaves combined with the gentle rain lulled her. She really loved it here. Duncan told her she had free rein on his place downtown, so she planned to add more color and change out some of the furniture to give it a warmer, more welcoming feel. She knew they'd have to live closer to the Five Star to help out her uncle, but she was glad to know they had this getaway house, too. She had a feeling it would provide many wonderful memories for them.

When Duncan's footsteps sounded on the wood floor of the porch, Rose glanced up at him. The smell of vanilla permeated her senses. Her lips tilted in amusement.

"In the mood for some ice cream?" she teased, throwing her legs over the side of the hammock as she sat up. Her bare feet hit the wooden floorboards to stop the swing from moving.

Duncan set the plate he was carrying down on a side table. Without a word he squatted in front of her and wrapped his arms around her hips.

Rose's heart tugged at the serious look she'd seen on his face before he placed his head on her lap. She threaded her fingers in his hair, tensing at his suddenly somber mood.

"What is it?"

Duncan blew out a breath. "When I saw you with that little boy, blowing bubbles. You were so patient. I knew you'd make a wonderful mother."

Rose's fingers stilled in Duncan's hair. She held her breath waiting for him to continue.

Duncan lifted his head. "You haven't talked about having a baby since the day we fought about me impregnating you. I know being a mother means the world to you. Do you still want a child with me, Róisín?"

Rose's chest tightened at the expectant look on his face. She rubbed the stubble on his cheeks and searched his troubled amber gaze.

"My heart broke to think you didn't want children, but when I saw you with Katie, I knew you'd make a great father. I love you, Duncan. Of course I want to have your children."

Duncan's smile took her breath away. The man was so devastatingly sexy, he made her heart ache.

His grip on her hips tightened and he pulled her closer, sliding his body between her legs until his lips touched hers.

Rose reveled in Duncan's kiss. She threaded her fingers in his hair to pull him even closer as her lips opened against his.

Duncan's fingers moved to the tiny buttons on her shirt and he whispered in her mind, *I've thought of nothing else but watching you eat an ice-cream cone completely naked.*

"Think you can handle waiting until I finish the cone?" Rose teased between kisses as she raised his shirt, then lifted it over his head.

Duncan pulled her to a standing position. He quickly tugged her shirt, pants and underwear off. Picking up the ice-cream cone, he handed it to her.

"Think you'll be able to finish it?" A devilish look reflected in his gaze.

Rose smiled at Duncan as she sat down, then laid back on the hammock in a relaxed pose. Digging her toes in the hammock's mesh, she mentally popped open the buttons on his jeans. As she slowly slid the material down his hips, she licked the cone all the way around.

"Think you'll want me to?" she countered with a wicked gleam in her eyes at the same time she let her legs fall wide open in a sexy invitation.

Duncan's amber eyes darkened as he stepped out of his jeans and underwear. Bending down on one knee, he took the cone from her and touched the sweet cream to her nipples before sliding the cool treat across her belly and down between her legs.

Rose's body trembled all over when he handed her the cone.

His hungry gaze locked with hers as he lowered his mouth to her nipple and spoke in her mind. *Let's finish it together,* a ghrá.

## About the author:

ꟻ

Born and raised in the southeast, Patrice has been a fan of romance novels since she was thirteen years old. While she reads many types of books, romance novels will always be her mainstay, saying, "I guess it's the idea of a happy ever after that draws me in."

Patrice welcomes mail from readers. You can write to her c/o Ellora's Cave Publishing at 1056 Home Avenue, Akron OH 44310-3502.

## Why an electronic book?

We live in the Information Age—an exciting time in the history of human civilization in which technology rules supreme and continues to progress in leaps and bounds every minute of every hour of every day. For a multitude of reasons, more and more avid literary fans are opting to purchase e-books instead of paperbacks. The question to those not yet initiated to the world of electronic reading is simply: *why?*

1. *Price.* An electronic title at Ellora's Cave Publishing and Cerridwen Press runs anywhere from 40-75% less than the cover price of the exact same title in paperback format. Why? Cold mathematics. It is less expensive to publish an e-book than it is to publish a paperback, so the savings are passed along to the consumer.
2. *Space.* Running out of room to house your paperback books? That is one worry you will never have with electronic novels. For a low one-time cost, you can purchase a handheld computer designed specifically for e-reading purposes. Many e-readers are larger than the average handheld, giving you plenty of screen room. Better yet, hundreds of titles can be stored within your new library—a single microchip. (Please note that Ellora's Cave and Cerridwen Press does not endorse any specific brands. You can check our website at www.ellorascave.com or

www.cerridwenpress.com for customer recommendations we make available to new consumers.)

3. *Mobility.* Because your new library now consists of only a microchip, your entire cache of books can be taken with you wherever you go.
4. *Personal preferences are accounted for.* Are the words you are currently reading too small? Too large? Too...**ANNOYING**? Paperback books cannot be modified according to personal preferences, but e-books can.
5. *Instant gratification.* Is it the middle of the night and all the bookstores are closed? Are you tired of waiting days—sometimes weeks—for online and offline bookstores to ship the novels you bought? Ellora's Cave Publishing sells instantaneous downloads 24 hours a day, 7 days a week, 365 days a year. Our e-book delivery system is 100% automated, meaning your order is filled as soon as you pay for it.

Those are a few of the top reasons why electronic novels are displacing paperbacks for many an avid reader. As always, Ellora's Cave and Cerridwen Press welcomes your questions and comments. We invite you to email us at service@ellorascave.com, service@cerridwenpress.com or write to us directly at: 1056 Home Ave. Akron OH 44310-3502.